NEV

MW01601259

# NEW EDEN

## The Joining Trilogy
## Book 1

### J. A. Louvel

Copyright © 2017 by J. A. Louvel

All rights reserved

ISBN 13: 978-1-7752089-2-1

Three Moon
publishing


Cover by: Austin Legg
austinlegg.com

# Dedication

In loving memory of Donna, who was confident from the start.
And to my supportive, loving Brian, who believed in the finish.

# Acknowledgements

It's been a long journey to completion, and along the way I've encountered extraordinary generosity from friends and family who willingly gave their valuable time and energy to this book. I thank you all — current and past — for your encouragement and feedback, for slogging through poorly written drafts, and for patiently listening.

A particular note of thanks to Paloma Eguiagaray for her special skills, and to Sue Shank for her many layers of assistance in bringing this book to conclusion.

Also, I'm so very grateful to Hugh Podmore for his technical assistance, given wholeheartedly to a complete stranger.

And last but not least, a tremendous thank-you to my hardworking proofreader, Gillian Saunders, for helping me to become a better writer.

# PART ONE:

# *CRIMES & PUNISHMENTS*

# PROLOGUE

ROBERT WIPED his bloody nose on his sleeve and staggered to his feet, lifting the bookbag that had fallen to the ground.

"I tolds yuh tuh stays down!" bellowed the older boy. He let fly with a kick to Robert's backside that sent him sprawling face-first onto the rocky ground. A hoot of laughter erupted from the group of youths surrounding them. Benji squatted beside his victim, a malicious grin twisting his mouth. Taking painful hold of Robert's ears, he ground the younger boy's face into the gravel. With a final cuff to his head, Benji strode off; the others following close behind, their laughter ringing wildly.

Robert watched them cross the school courtyard and enter the dormitory. Then he was on his feet, running for the church. Once at the door, he moved inside with caution, listening for the sounds of priests. Voices could be heard coming from one of the anterooms behind the altar. He stopped, ready to bolt, but the voices continued to drone on, mixing with the sound of metal on plates. They were having lunch.

Robert crept through the gloomy interior until he was against the east wall. With increased stealth he advanced past the worn pews to the front of the church. He paused for only a moment before climbing onto the dais and crossing the few feet to the ancient wooden altar. There stood a silver cross with metallic flames twisted to encircle its top half, the golden flames affixed to each end of the horizontal bar. Grabbing the weighty firecross, he stuffed it into the bookbag before making his silent escape.

Once outside, he checked for signs of his tormentors, but they were not in sight. With quick steps, he crossed the courtyard, as though heading towards the dorm entrance, veering to the right at the last moment to hide behind the tall prickle bush at the side of the building. Hunkering down, he peered through the thick branches, waiting.

It started to rain, hard and cold, but he was not distracted from his purpose. A short time later, the bullies charged out of the building, heading towards the gaming field. He waited until they were engrossed in their sword practice before dashing up the steps and into the dormitory.

Despite the weight of the firecross, Robert ran lightly up the interior staircase, but not so fast as to draw attention to himself. An art he'd perfected during his eight years of life. When he reached Benji's dorm room, he slowed to a casual walk, entering with an air of innocence, ready to act confused, as if he'd accidentally entered the wrong room. But no one was there.

He'd been in this dorm room before, forced inside and tortured by those same boys. Benji, the eldest and the biggest, always in the lead.

Robert made straight for Benji's bed, pulling back a corner of the thin mattress to reveal the wooden planks beneath. He laid the firecross on the hard surface, snug against the wall, and replaced the mattress, making certain the bed was not perfectly tidy. With one last check of his handiwork, he quickly exited the dormitory. Mingling with the other students, he crossed the quad, arriving at the education facility as the lunch break ended.

Father Carmichael had barely started the history lesson when the church bell began to ring excitedly, announcing a general alarm. The boys leapt to their feet, grabbing their bookbags as they headed for the door. Already the hallway was crammed with students rushing for the stairway. Robert let himself be carried along by the press of bodies, down two flights of stairs and into the puddle-filled courtyard, the staff of clerics hurrying after them. When the entire school was assembled, the bell fell silent and Bishop Chang charged out of the administration building.

His bowl-cut hair flapping untidily in the breeze, the bishop crossed the fifteen feet to the stone statue of Pope Honorius Vecker II, the school's founder. With some difficulty, the middle-aged principal maneuvered his unwieldy bulk onto its base, which was wet and slippery from weeks of winter weather.

There was absolute silence, broken only by the patter of light rain.

Pensive and wary, every face turned towards the bishop, fear the one commonality, for there were no distinctive racial types but a blending of many. Skin color varied from deep brown to copper to dark olive. Hair was walnut brown to obsidian black, from straight to kinky, though this was not much in evidence as it was cropped close to the scalp, as befitted a gaming male.

"A heinous crime has been committed!" Bishop Chang announced sternly. "A holy firecross has been stolen from the church, and I want it returned *immediately*," he barked out, and every boy jumped in fright.

The bishop stood poised, waiting for a confession. When no one stepped forward, he continued in a voice that shook with rage, "You will stand here until

2

that firecross has been found and the guilty party punished!" He glared at the assembly for several moments before stepping carefully off the slippery surface.

Quickly he organized the younger clerics into a search party, and they hurried off to do his bidding. His expression darkening further, he strode into the administration building, slamming the door.

Dressed in rough spun tunics and short pants, the students stood shivering in the drizzle while the priests carelessly rummaged through their bags, dropping books and class work onto the muddy gravel. The boys retrieved them hastily, knowing they'd be punished for any damage done to school property. The search was halfway completed when a very young priest rushed from the dormitory, hurrying across the courtyard to the administration building. Moments later the bishop emerged once more; his face was stern, but the rage had now subsided.

"Benjamin Hardcastle, come forward!"

Heads swiveled in Benji's direction.

"It weren't me!" he shouted.

"Come forward!" the bishop roared, and every boy quaked in fear.

Reluctantly, Benji pushed his way through the students to stand before the bishop.

"What do you have to say for yourself?" the bishop demanded.

"I never done it!"

A shocked gasp broke from the student body at this audacity. It would go harder for him now. The bishop said nothing but motioned sharply to the two discipline priests standing off to the side. The priests turned a stern gaze on the boy, their black hoods folded back to partially reveal eye sockets indelibly darkened, making their cold stare all the more terrifying. With calculated steps, they strode towards Benji, his chestnut complexion draining to a sickly green.

Grabbing the boy, they dragged him to the discipline post, with Benji loudly claiming his innocence.

Rough hands removed his shirt from resistant limbs before tying him to the post, his bare back facing the assembly. The priests stepped away, one of them drawing out a whip from the deep recesses of his cloak.

With a solemn nod, the bishop gave the signal to begin. A moment later, the whip was raised, its tongue hissing through the air in a long arch before landing with a hard snap across Benji's back.

A howl of pain erupted out of the boy, but it was abruptly cut off by the next swipe of the lash. His howl grew louder, freezing the onlookers rigid. They were not accustomed to the sight of a whipping, caning being the usual punishment. The lash was used only for the most serious of crimes, and stealing from the Church was a serious crime indeed. Now Benji would live under a heavy threat. Any further offence would find him spending the balance of his school years inside an adult prison. Few boys would risk that fate.

Two more strokes crossed the boy's back before the bishop raised an arm.

"Do you repent?" Bishop Chang demanded.

"I never done it," Benji stubbornly repeated, his voice shaking with fear and anger.

"Do you accuse another?"

There was a long hesitation before he shook his head, "No."

Again, the bishop nodded to the discipline priest, and the whip hissed out two more times. Blood trickled in rivulets down Benji's back; his screams hung in the air.

"Do you repent?" the bishop asked once more.

The entire school held its breath, waiting for the answer.

In a small voice that all strained to hear, Benji finally repented his crime.

There was a sigh of relief from every student in the yard, but nowhere was it expressed with such feeling as it was in Robert Bountiful.

"Willie!"

The young prince started guiltily, expecting to see a soldier guardian, but it was his two older brothers who stood looming over him. They were grinning widely. William smiled back, nervous but hopeful.

He'd dared to sneak from the palace kinderhall to play in his father's study — a brave act for such a timid soul. He'd not considered running into his brothers, oblivious of their scrutiny as he made his careful way to the blessed isolation of the bookroom, which is how he always thought of it.

"Come on, there's something we gotta show you," Thomas said, lifting William to his feet by the scruff of his tunic.

"Let's go," Henry urged.

The older boys bolted from the room, dragging their little brother with them. Thomas was twelve, Henry ten, William just six. There was little in their faces to reveal their shared paternity. Thomas had high cheekbones and a small, flat nose, his skin a russet red. Henry's complexion was sepia brown, with a strong chin, broad nose and full lips. William's dark olive face bore signs of growing into an aquiline profile with thin lips and a receding chin. He was also slight of build in comparison to his brothers' burly strength.

Together, the boys raced up the stairs to the top floor where they stood panting over the banister, gazing down into the stairwell at the three floors

4

below. William drew back quickly; heights made him nervous. But coupled with this fear was what lay beyond the door behind them.

Looking at the illicit entrance, only a few yards away, William stammered out fearfully, "We, we, we aren't supposed to be up here — it's forbidden."

"Scared you'll be stoned for your sins?" Thomas asked in a mocking tone as he moved beside William, looking over his head to nod at Henry. Instantly, the boys pounced on their younger brother, pinning him to the floor. Thomas pulled a rope from under his shirt, binding William's arms to his sides, tossing the other end to Henry, who tied it to the banister.

"No!" William begged.

"Say: please no, Your Lordship," Thomas directed in almost a friendly tone.

"Please no, Your Lordship," William parroted desperately.

"Say: I am a piece of shit."

William repeated the words, close to shaming tears.

"What the hell's this piece of shit doing in the palace!" Thomas exclaimed in mock shock. "Henry, dispose of it!"

"No!" William shrieked as Henry lifted him onto the banister.

"Say: the Holy Fathers are pig swill," Thomas ordered.

William gasped in shock, "I can't say that!"

"Push him over."

"No! Wait!" William squawked.

"Say it," Thomas hissed.

"The Holy Fathers are pig swill," William whispered.

"Louder!"

William bleated the foul words out a little louder.

"Have you ever heard such talk, Henry? This calls for severe punishment."

"NO...!" William screamed as Henry pushed him over the banister. His cry filled the stairwell before it was cut off by the painful jerking of the rope as it brought his fall to an abrupt end, punching the air from his lungs. There was a short pause while William caught his breath, then he opened his mouth to let loose a high-pitched scream. He didn't notice his brothers running from the scene, doubled over with laughter.

Guards came rushing to the stairwell on the floors below. They looked up at the screaming, struggling prince, and each face split into a wide grin.

Like all who lived on New Eden, their multiracial ancestry was clearly apparent.

"They got him uh good one this time," the youngest amongst them remarked, and there were several snickers of agreement.

"Better brings him up," their sergeant ordered. "That screechin's enough tuh drives uh desert demon back tuh hell." He pointed at two guards, "Fetch 'im."

They bounded up the wide stairway, once a two-way escalator, now enclosed with wooden planks to hide the ancient tech. Their thickset bodies rippling with muscle, they easily scaled the two floors. A few moments later they reached the rope and began hauling up the prince.

The boy did not relent in his cries of terror.

The soldiers in the stairwell watched the operation with amusement. Sensing movement, their heads turned and all humor left them as a priest stormed past, climbing towards young William. The soldiers glowered after him.

"It's his doin' the prince be such uh weaklin'," the sergeant muttered.

There was a chorus of grunts supporting this view. They turned their attention back to the dangling prince, who was by now close to the banister. One more pull brought him over the side, where he was plopped carelessly onto the floor. But still he continued to scream, his eyes clenched shut. One of the guards bent to cut away the ropes binding the boy, and then stood back, at a loss.

"Should we gets uh guardian?" he asked his companion over the din.

"That won't be necessary," Father Gideon's cold voice interrupted as he pushed past him to bend over the prince. Frowning, the soldiers moved away from the crouching priest. "William, it's me, Father Gideon," the young priest stated firmly. "You're safe now." He had to repeat this three times before the words reached the terrified boy.

William stopped screaming and opened his eyes. "Father," he gasped, his body shaking violently in reaction.

The priest picked up the boy and quickly descended the stairway. The soldiers followed after, their faces scowling disapproval. On the second floor, Father Gideon strode down a wide corridor to the kinderhall. He did not glance at the soldier guardians inside but went directly to William's bedchamber. He laid the boy on the bed, covering his shivering body with roughly spun blankets.

"Father, I was so sc-sc-scared," he hiccupped.

"Yes, my son," the priest said. "You are safe now, I am here."

"Thank you, Father," he said, and the relief caused tears to spring to the boy's eyes, which he struggled to keep inside without success.

The priest leaned forward to pat William's back; his words sympathetic but the eyes were cold. When the boy finally cried himself to sleep, Father Gideon sat back with a satisfied smile. Once again William's brothers had pushed their sensitive young sibling into the waiting arms of the Church.

The priest nodded approvingly at William: he would grow to be the Church's tool, completely and utterly.

6

# Chapter 1

THEY WERE next in line.

Eric tried not to let his fear show as he followed his father up to the registration booth. The wrinkled face of the old priest scowled as he extended a hand for the documents his father placed there. He studied the papers, demanding, "You are Andre Wong?"

His father answered quickly, subdued. The tone deepened Eric's fear, for his father always spoke with harsh authority.

The priest continued, "This is your son, Eric Wong?"

Again, that quick reply from his father.

The old cleric entered the information from the birth and marriage certificates into the great ledger before him. Then, dunking the pen inside an inkwell, he turned the book to Andre. "Sign here."

Laboriously, Andre scratched his name onto the page. The priest handed back the documents and gestured to the exit on their left. "He goes through there," he said, his attention already turned upon the next applicant.

Andre pushed his son towards the door and shoved it open, letting Eric pass inside. A ragged leather duffel bag was dropped at the boy's feet. "Mind duh Fawders," Andre growled before shutting the door between them. Eric blinked at the sudden barrier; he was on his own.

Nervously, he looked around. It was not reassuring.

The school was an old one. Scarred and weathered buildings frowned down upon a wide courtyard of monotonous, graveled flatness devoid of all greenery but for a single prickle bush tucked against the dormitory.

At one end of the quad was a small gaming field where a group of students were practicing their sword skills while others wrestled on the muddy ground. At the other end was a Church, the most preserved building in the school, but still in need of repair. "The Holy Church of New Eden" was etched high across its wooden face, the once shiny paint, peeled away to nothing, making the words barely noticeable. In contrast, the discipline post loomed before the church doors, tall and threatening and very much in evidence.

Not far from Eric, clustered around the base of a large stone statue, was a group of newbies. Their long hair hung in tangled knots about their faces, their few possessions stuffed into worn leather bags. Struggling with his own shabby duffel bag, Eric made his way towards them.

Without warning, his feet were kicked out from under him and the bag wrenched from his hands. There was laughter as he landed hard, skinning his tawny brown face and knees on the gravel. He looked up to see his satchel being tossed between four older boys.

"Gimme it!" he demanded, leaping to his feet.

The biggest of the boys caught the bag. "Yuh wannit? Takes it," Benji said, ramming it hard into Eric's chest, knocking him down again.

Eric jumped up, grabbing for the bag, though the boy held it high, laughing at his puny efforts.

"Give it to him," a voice ordered. Eric turned, expecting to see a priest, but it was only another student, older than Eric, yet still no match against these bullies.

"He yurr bro or what," Benji snarled, tossing the bag into the dirt.

Robert's terracotta skin had flushed a livid red, and he stared fiercely at the bigger boy. Without looking from Benji, Robert ordered Eric to join the other newbies.

Eric rushed to obey, dragging the duffel bag after him. Panting, he waited expectantly for the fight to break out. But he was disappointed. His defender turned away, striding off towards the gaming area.

One of the bullies yelled after him, "Fawder Tyler be sharpnin' duh cutters!"

The others laughed jeeringly and jogged into the dormitory. Yet the taunt seemed to go unnoticed by Robert, who didn't pause or turn around.

What's he saying with such talk? Eric wondered. The words made no sense to him. He watched after the lone boy.

Who is he? Why'd those older boys obey him?

His thoughts were interrupted by the arrival of a priest, a man no longer in his prime. He looked over the group critically. "Pick up your things and come with me," he ordered sternly.

Eric stole a last glance towards the sword players before hoisting his bag once more to follow the priest into the dormitory.

From her position at a third floor window, Theresa secretly watched the exchange. This was not the first time she'd witnessed that boy's interference in the tormenting of a younger student. She stared after him as he crossed the

10

courtyard to the gaming area. He fascinated her: the only male to inspire something other than fear. Until this boy, she'd not known it was possible for a male to be anything but cold or cruel.

Someone was coming.

Quickly Theresa returned to cleaning the classroom but relaxed slightly when she recognized the rapid, shuffling steps. It was only another eve.

A girl of twelve entered and began speaking swiftly in sign language: "Be quick! Father Tommy's grouchy as a blue boar!"

"Nearly done," Theresa answered silently in return.

Conversation between eves was narrowly limited to passing information about duties. Any further discussion brought punishment. Most found it safer to use the subtle hand language learned at their mother's knee. Every quick grasp or pinch of cloth was rich with meaning: the bend of a finger, the amount of material, and even the speed blended to articulate their silent language. But still it needed to be used with care; discovery would bring repercussions beyond considering.

Theresa shuffled through the room, finishing her chores. Only nine years old, yet already her shoulders were stooped and rounded. Her head hung low in a cowed, beaten attitude, her face hidden by a heavy black veil that began above the eyebrows and ended well below the collarbone. The black scarf covering her shaved scalp was tied securely at the back of the head, its long ends brought forward and knotted in the front.

A high collar and long sleeves highlighted the loose-fitting gray tunic that covered much of her bulky gray skirt. Below the hem, baggy trousers made of heavy black material were briefly revealed before disappearing inside ankle-high leather boots. A large black overvest completed the outfit, disguising the outlines of her body, creating a boxy, unshapely appearance. Only her hands, a slash of forehead and part of her eyes were exposed.

She hurried from the classroom. There was still much to do, though little would involve study. Reading, writing, math and history were for boys alone. Religious instruction was the only commonality, for every child must learn what God demanded of them: strict obedience to the Laws of the Church.

As a female, this meant complete Obedience and Submission to Man. Only then could she achieve forgiveness for being born an eve, instrument of Satan, condemned to eternal hellfire but for the intervention of the Holy Church.

The Church was relentless and thorough. There was not a female in all of New Eden who didn't believe in her own wickedness. Every aspect of her life was designed to contain the evil she embodied, and to atone for it.

To prevent contamination of male students, eves were completely segregated. They were even allotted their own stairwells and corridors, which ran like a maze throughout each building within the boys' schools, making females almost invisible as a functioning part of these institutes. Yet it was the labor of young eves that kept the schools in operation. They were the cooks, cleaners, gardeners and seamstresses, crossing over from the girls' schools every sunrise to perform their vital duties. Returning at night to be locked within their high stone walls, walls that were heavily embedded on both sides with shards of glass and razor sharp metal. The boys grew up seeing eves as distant drudges, to be detested, contained — and feared.

Theresa made her way quickly to the ground floor, though it was difficult to see inside the narrow stairwell. Within this dark and isolated space, there was always an element of risk, for it was here that the girls were most often assaulted by the priests.

It was not only the act itself that was terrifying to consider, but also its harsher consequences. If the crime was discovered or the priest confessed, she would be accused of enticement and a lengthy punishment carried out upon her person.

So far, Theresa had avoided being compromised. She hoped to be quick enough to remain so.

Reaching the ground floor, she moved through the stone corridor that connected the two schools. Strong doors stood open, one at each end. At night the doors were locked and bolted with a priest on guard before each one. The Church was well aware of a boy's curiosity with the forbidden.

Theresa passed through the second doorway and entered the eve school. She made straight for a latrine. Once inside, she immediately lifted the heavy veil from her face, revealing the beauty of her oval shaped eyes and copper complexion.

The veil was comprised of two layers of coarse material. The bottom layer was punctuated with two small openings for the nostrils and a larger opening for the mouth to allow food and drink to be consumed without baring the face. Veil removal was allowed only in the darkness of the dorm room or while bathing, or sometimes during a discipline session. But the thing was hot and stifling, making breathing and seeing difficult. She detested it with a depth of feeling that would not be shaken by years of use. She removed it at every opportunity.

With sudden urgency, she covered her face and hurried to the garden, afraid her tardiness would attract Father Tommy's attention. But he was not outside when she picked up her hoe to join the other girls. They took no notice of her arrival but weeded in silence, heads down, faces carefully averted from their neighbors.

A noise at the barn door made them all turn. It was little Ruth, one of the new arrivals, scared and wanting her mother. The girls returned to their weeding; there was nothing they could do.

12

But Ruth was not to be ignored.

Pushing her way through the goats in the yard, Ruth bolted over the garden fence. She paused to rip off her newly acquired scarf and veil, exposing her freshly shaved scalp, before flinging herself at Sarah, the most senior girl in the school. Fearfully, Sarah motioned her to be silent and tried to push the little girl away. But Ruth pushed back, her cries becoming louder, her golden brown face streaked with tears.

The disturbance brought Father Tommy into the yard.

Tears were forbidden. In males it was a sign of weakness; in females, manipulation. That the child was new to both the school and the veil would not be a consideration.

Furious, he ordered the two girls apart, but Ruth only tightened her grip. The priest lifted the short whip hanging from his belt and struck her solidly across the back. She clung on harder. He began to whip the child, commanding her to let go with every stroke. At last she weakened and dropped to the ground.

Her back torn and bloody, Ruth was dragged from the garden. She would be taken before the school principal for judgment and further discipline.

The eves quickly bent back to their work. It would be unwise to show any reaction to the ugly scene.

Theresa attacked the ground with violent jabs of her hoe, sickened and angry.

I hate them! God forgive me, but I hate them! she silently raged.

Although Theresa understood that she was evil and that it was only through the intervention of the Church that she was saved from an eternity of damnation, she could not feel grateful. She had many bad thoughts about priests — thoughts she did not confess.

Theresa sighed deeply: I shall never find my way to Salvation.

It was cold and damp inside the dormitory, the rain falling in a solid sheet outside the shuttered window. Far past curfew, the room was dark and silent, no sound but the even breathing of children. Eric shivered and wrapped the blanket more tightly around himself, easing it over his recently shaved head. Plagued by homesickness, he couldn't sleep. He hated it here. You had to ask permission for everything and were ordered about all day long.

He was not used to this constant presence of priests. At home he saw them at Sunday service and Wednesday catechism only. But here, they seemed to hover over every moment. To think of being stuck in this place until his fifteenth year made his chest tight and swollen. He bit his lip, trying hard to keep in the forbidden tears.

Eric's reaction was typical of boys who came from the poorer families. With no house priest to report on their every infraction, they lived free of the Church's close scrutiny. The Church believed rebellion came only from the privileged and the wealthy; while the business of staying alive occupied the attention of the lower classes — and Eric's family was certainly low. His father was a miner and, like all miners, was descended from criminal stock.

Eight hundred years after establishing itself as the sole receiver of wisdom and Divine Law on the planet, the Holy Church of New Eden decreed that only those eves unfit for breeding could be used inside the mines.

In one quick stroke, the labor pool was cut to half its previous size, leaving the rich mine owners frantic to fill the gap.

Responding to their demands, the Church made a radical but necessary decision. It legitimized the use of prison labor — *male* labor — inside the mines. To any prisoner facing a life sentence, the Church approved the offer of a small wage, a company house, and the return of one wife, in exchange for a lifetime contract to work the mines.

Some did not sign, cruel as prison life was, for to do so would mean signing away the status of their sons and all the generations to follow.

On New Eden, boys inherited the occupation of their father, be it high or low, with few avenues of escape. Mining was eve work, the lowest of the low, putting the family forever in a position of poverty and ignominy. But there were many who gratefully signed away their future generations, eager to escape the hellish cells. One of these men was Eric's ancestor.

Like all mining families, each generation of males grew up, married and raised their children in the same house they were born in, creating overcrowded and oppressive conditions in the small company dwellings.

As was usual in New Eden families, girls left for school at age five and were never thought of again. Boys followed a year later for their own type of education, though ultimately the objective was the same: blind obedience to the Church.

In the more affluent families, boys spent their first six years in the highly controlled environment of a male operated nursery under a cleric's watchful eye. For these privileged boys their entry into a Church residential school, while indeed wrenching, was somewhat familiar.

But the poorer boys, having only brief and distant contact with the Holy Ones, were ill prepared to be thrust so completely into the strict care of the Church. This severely regimented program was met with varying degrees of shock after the undisciplined freedom of their first six years. They would all suffer a painful period of adjustment, but for Eric that adjustment would have added difficulties.

Eric's grandfather and his two brothers had died young, leaving only three

14

sons between them, two of which were killed in a mining accident before they'd had time to save the bride price.

The cost of a wife had risen steadily over the centuries, severely curbing the number of wives a man could own. In the poorer classes, it now took a combined family effort to buy a young man a wife. Eric's father, without family to help with the bride-price, was forced to wait many years before acquiring a wife of advanced age with few breeding years remaining. It was a great disappointment to him that she delivered only one son before drying up altogether. The four daughters she bore did not count for anything.

Andre Wong worked hard in the mines, spending most of his evenings in the pub showing off his strong head for alcohol or in the gaming arena trying to win the respect denied him elsewhere. There was little time or interest for his son.

Eric was left in the care of females — common practice amongst the poor, usually until the baby reached toddler age. But with no grandfather or other available males in the household, his dame and eve siblings were forced to continue as his caretakers. He also spent these years playing and even talking with them.

His older eve siblings had already learned their lessons and would not be engaged by his baby demands, but the young twins, still babies themselves, naturally responded to his overtures for play. The three became close.

As Eric grew out of toddler age, they were separated.

When his dame caught them at play, she would silently remove his young siblings. And though Eric never heard her speak or strike the little eves, they would cry for a long time afterwards, when already they knew tears were forbidden.

His father never spoke to his daughters and rarely to his wife, except to give orders, though there was little to make commands over in their small house. For the most part she tried to remove herself from his presence, as a good wife should, remaining with her daughters inside the eve sleeping room whenever her husband was at home.

The only time Eric saw his dame and his father deliberately share the same space was when his father pulled sharply on the bell above the door of the "spare-room," as Andre called it. From wherever she was in the house, his wife would come shuffling quickly to enter the room. His father would follow, closing the door and sliding the bolt hard into place. A few moments later, animal-like sounds would be heard and the squeaking of the bench. Eric knew it was a bench, although a strange one, because he once snuck a peek inside. For that, his father had boxed his ears and thrashed his backside til it bled. The same punishment he'd received after climbing onto a chair to ring the bell, and when he'd removed the red cord that sometimes hung there.

When Eric moved past toddler age, he began spending time away from the house to play with other boys in the camptown or to watch the men in the gaming arena. He also began his catechism and learned the evils of eves. But he did not equate these wicked creatures with the siblings he played with daily.

Eric was developing two parts to himself.

There was his at-home self, which was often content to remain silent and let the games become sedate and domestic. While his outside-self grew as the other boys grew: loud and aggressive, proud, determined to win at any cost. When he tried to bring this part of himself into the house, it left a hollow, disturbing feeling.

Eric also learned that males were master over any eve. Regardless of age or family status, she could not disobey.

He no longer allowed his dame to remove the little eves when she caught them at play. Only once did she ignore his command. With muttered words that begged forgiveness, she grabbed up the twins from the back courtyard and shuffled quickly into the house. Eric followed after, determined to have his way, but when he entered the main room of the house that childish command stuck in his throat — a priest was standing inside the front doorway.

Instinctively Eric shrank back into the kitchen, but a moment later he peered around the doorjamb to watch in dumb dismay as his dame placed the little eves before the priest. Taking them by the hand, he turned and, without a word, left the house. The sisters looked back at their mother in silent alarm, but she only clutched at her clothing convulsively. Their fear deepened, and they looked at the feet of the man with eyes round and staring. They turned for one last look at their mother before passing through the courtyard gates to the world outside.

Stunned, Eric stood behind his dame, gazing unblinking into the empty yard.

The two remained frozen in a long moment of shared grief.

Then Eric ran to the back of the house. Flinging the door open, he dashed to the coal shed to bury his head amongst the black cubes as tears spilled out uncontrollably.

The loss of his sisters was traumatic, though he'd known it was coming — someday, as it had to his other siblings. But he was barely five, with little thought for tomorrow.

For a time, he no longer found pleasure in playing with the boys of the camp. Yet he hated how the house felt so empty, and he was often seen roaming the camptown long after the other boys had been ordered inside for the night. His own father was seldom home to notice.

Soon, however, he recovered his interest in games and stopped his late night roaming. Though now he began ordering his mother around in the same manner as his father, taking out his anger on her for the loss of his sisters.

16

Without other males to challenge or interfere with his position in the household, he grew accustomed to wielding power, answering to no one but his father, whose presence in the house, though loud and gruff and sometimes violent, was also brief. For most of the day, the house was Eric's to command.

But all that was changed now. Here, he had no voice.

Eric held his breath suddenly, listening. What was that? Crooking a finger, he moved the blanket from his eyes. Nothing stirred. He was about to relax when a shadow blocked the light from the corridor. Tensing, he waited. The door opened only narrowly, but it was enough to reveal the culprit.

There was a second's hesitation before Eric drew on his short pants and imitated the other's silent movements. He slipped from the room in time to see the figure descending the staircase at the end of the dimly lit hallway. He tiptoed after him.

The boys' dormitory was on three levels. Each level contained two large rooms which slept thirty boys of varying ages and four smaller rooms for senior students. There was also a sleeping room for the dorm priests. This stood between him and the staircase.

Cautiously, he approached the open door and peeked inside. Two beds stood empty, while a third held old Father Michael, snoring heavily. Eric made a dash for the stairs, praying the two missing priests would stay that way.

His bare feet were silent on the stone steps. At the bottom he paused, afraid he'd lost his quarry, but there he was, heading down the corridor towards the dining hall. Eric remained at a safe distance as he trotted after him, entering the hall to crouch between the long tables, watching as the boy exited into the kitchen beyond. Eric dashed forward to peer through the swinging doors before entering warily, but there was no one inside. He noticed a small door standing open beside the cook stove and tiptoed through the narrow opening.

Eric found himself inside a storage room used for dried goods and fuel. Bewildered, he looked about: it was empty. Then he spied the fuel chute flapping open. Without hesitation, he ducked through to the outside.

Wood and coal surrounded him, though he could barely make them out in the darkness. A low overhang jutted out from the building, making a crude shelter against the elements. Eric took a step and tripped over a shovel that crashed noisily against the coal bin. Lying rigid where he'd fallen, he waited, afraid he'd given himself away, but the roar of the rain had muffled the sound.

Shivering in the cold, Eric got to his feet and hugged his bare chest, waiting for his eyes to adjust to the dark. It was difficult to see through the deluge.

A tool shed stood a few feet away. Beyond that was the gaming field. There was no sign of the boy, but a moment later he saw a hint of movement near the equipment room before it disappeared altogether.

Leaving the relative protection of the overhang, Eric felt his way cautiously through the dark, the force of the rain stinging his naked torso. At last he made it safely to the door of the equipment room, pushing it open with care. A dim light glowed from deep in the back. He crept towards it.

His defender from the other day was doing push-ups, hard and fast, his breath gasping out with each effort. They'd not spoken since the incident in the courtyard, but Eric had learned his name.

Hiding behind a rack of gaming equipment, Eric watched in amazement: Why sneak out to do what they were forced to do every day?

Robert jumped to his feet and grabbed a blunted broad sword, the type used by students. He jabbed at the air a few times before abruptly leaping forward, kicking over the tool rack and sending Eric flying backwards onto the floor. Before he could move, the tip of the sword was at his throat.

"What are you doing here?" Robert growled.

"I-I follows yuh," Eric managed to stutter out.

"I can see that. Why?"

"Tuh sees where's yuh goin'."

Robert studied him a moment, then removed the sword, hauling Eric to his feet. "It's not smart to follow people — you could get hurt." He turned away and began to clean up the mess of equipment, but abruptly paused. "No one saw you? No, of course not, or we'd both be at the whipping post." Eric's eyes grew big with fear. Robert smiled thinly. "Don't worry; you're not caught — this time. Just don't do it again." He returned to tidying up the mess of swords and knives, their edges rounded and dulled to prevent accidental injury.

Eric looked on, knowing any other older student would have forced *him* to pick up the mess. It gave Eric the confidence to ask, "How comes yuh doin' extra gamin'?"

Without pausing in his labors, Robert said, "Cadet Trials are in three months. This is my last chance to qualify." He was twelve.

"Yuh really wants tuh be uh soldier, huh."

"Yeah, I guess so," he shrugged. And by way of explanation, he added, "I'm illegit."

Eric digested this silently. That would mean Robert had lived at the school all his life. It also meant that if he didn't become a soldier, he must become either a priest or an overseer. "Ain't yuh gonna be uh priest? Yuh talks like 'em." His speech pattern was usual in boys raised from babyhood amongst the clergy.

Robert just snorted with disgust. Eric stared, surprised by this response: the priesthood was revered — and feared. But he found Robert's attitude reassuring. "Don't yuh wanna be uh overseer?"

Robert snorted again, "They're not making me into any eunuch."

18

Eric frowned in thought. He'd heard the word eunuch many times. Boys often insulted each other with it. He knew it meant something bad, but he didn't know what. He plucked up his courage and asked, "What's uh ewnik?"

Robert stated bluntly, "A guy with no penis and no balls — they've been cut off."

A look of horror crossed Eric's face, and his hands moved protectively to his crotch. He remembered the jeering call of the bully. Is that what Father Tyler did? he thought in shocked amazement. He managed to croak out, "Why they does that?"

"So he's protected from the wives he's overseeing."

"How come duh overseers needs tuh be protected?"

"So the eves can't corrupt him and lure him into sin."

"What yuh means?" he asked in confusion.

"If he gets corrupted, he'll want to go mating with the wives he's overseeing. You do know what mating is?"

"It's how we gets babes born." Robert nodded. "Why duh overseers wanna do that tuh duh wives?"

"They just do, that's all." Robert put the last of the equipment away and retrieved his sword from the floor. "What's your name?" he asked, returning to his imaginary opponent.

"Eric Wong."

"Mine's Robert. I don't have a real last name. The Bishop named me Bountiful cuzz they found me at harvest time — it was a good year."

Eric watched Robert practice for several minutes before getting the courage to ask, "Why'd that boy listens tuh yuh when he's so big?"

"Old Benj?" Robert shrugged, "Cuzz he knows he'd pay if he didn't."

"Would yuh tells duh Holy Fawders?"

"A lot they'd care."

"How yuh does it then?"

"Oh . . . different ways." A grim look appeared on Robert's face as he remembered Benji's whipping. Nobody ever guessed who really took that firecross. Only Benji guessed the truth, but he'd dared not seek revenge by his usual blunt methods. He couldn't risk being framed again. Prison was to be avoided at all costs. Instead, he'd sought to retaliate in kind. But he was never quick enough or smart enough, and neither were his cronies. Tiring of the game, Robert had written out a prison number and had left it on Benji's bed. That had stopped him — permanently.

But all Robert said to Eric was, "I know this school better than anyone. I can get in and out of any place without getting caught." The younger boy gazed at him with shining eyes.

19

Robert returned to his practice while Eric curled up on some sacks, watching. He woke to Robert shaking his shoulder, "Come on, we gotta get back."

Outside, they peered through the relentless rain, scouting for danger. Eric looked nervously up at the windows.

"Do yuh thinks we'll catch it?"

"We'll be okay."

"Fawder Sal and Fawder Don weren't in their bunks. What if they sees us?"

"Don't worry about them," Robert mumbled, "they're off buggering some place."

"What?"

Robert looked at him, reconsidering. "They always go off when Father Michael's on duty. They'll be back by now, don't worry."

"Yuh does this lots?"

"All my life. Now stay quiet."

"Can I comes with yuh again sometimes?"

Robert hesitated, but after a moment nodded shortly.

Safely back in bed, Eric was feeling much better.

Maybe it wouldn't be so bad here after all.

# CHAPTER 2

ROBERT COULD assume only two facts about his parentage: his father was likely a soldier, and his mother certainly a whore. The property of her husband, she would have been forced with his other designated wives into a life of prostitution. This would be the family business, passed down through the generations from father to sons, growing and expanding into a long chain of Houses.

Officially, prostitution was forbidden by Holy Order, but the Church was forced to turn a blind eye to this necessary evil. The Army, sworn to remain unwed, was in dire need of a heterosexual outlet. It was prudent not to oppose them on this small matter.

Out of this decision a tradition was born. The Houses kept a low profile and high prices, the soldiers kept their visits discreet, and the Church kept its eyes averted while receiving generous donations. But tradition was not the only birth. Babies were also born: illegitimate babies whose paternity was impossible to determine, babies who might grow to be mated with a close relative, who were perhaps even sired by one. The Church could not allow such abominations to threaten the purity of the breeding pool. Illegitimates must be denied the mating rite.

From the pulpit, the Church railed against the evils of debauchery. Profane couplings desecrating the Sacred Seed of Adam, their progeny growing to make unholy alliance. Such abominations would bring God's Wrath upon Humanity once again.

The Pope proclaimed every illegitimate baby a ward of the Church. Let the unconsecrated fruit come to God, for He shall save them from profanity. Obey the Commands of thy Lord God, for His Judgment can be Swift and Terrible.

Heeding the threat, the House owners laid their illegitimate children at the Church's door, always anonymously, always at night, a special bell now installed to alert the priests. And then later, when all young children were removed from their families to be educated by the Church, the illegit babes were placed at the door of the local residential school.

From the time of weaning at six months of age, the illegit babe became Church property. Female illegits would grow to labor in the vast farmlands of the Church or married off as non-breeders to work in the fields or industries of their husband, a tattoo on the forehead declaring their non-breeding status. Male illegits would be brought up to enter the clergy, if the Church had a use for them, or, if they'd skill and guts enough, trained to join the Army.

The remainder would be used for another purpose.

During the early part of New Eden's history, any man owning more than twelve wives was required to have a priest in residence to oversee the women, to ensure that wives were not infecting the household with any rebellious influences and to monitor the frequency of sexual relations.

But the confessions of these overseer priests were becoming more and more alarming. If steps weren't taken, it would only be a matter of time before a priest was caught in an indecent act with a wife in his care — and the Church would lose credibility forever.

There seemed only one solution. But to castrate priests would be a sign of weakness, leading to questions and doubts, for they were supposedly beyond such temptations.

The Church looked upon the bastards housed within its gates and came to a decision.

No, it can't happen! Robert thought frantically. He let the arrow fly, but it went wide of the mark. Swearing, he stalked past the target to collect the wayward weapon, suddenly fearful that, despite all his efforts, he wouldn't be chosen today — that he was doomed to become a eunuch.

"Damn them all to hell," he cursed again.

Dropping to one knee, he stabbed the arrowhead viciously into the ground.

Why did I have to be me? he demanded of himself. It was an often asked question.

With all his heart he wished he was like other boys. But he never enjoyed rough play or found pleasure in the tormenting of others. Self-contained and independent, he preferred the calm of solitude; intelligence and curiosity had pushed him to wander. Such a reserved child was easily overlooked by the harried nursery and dorm priests. It was this lack of attention that gave him the opportunity to explore — and to make discoveries.

Why did I have to find out? he railed inwardly.

He hadn't always been opposed to becoming an overseer or even a priest. In fact, he believed for a long time that he would grow to become either of these.

22

He'd given no thought to the military, hating brutality of any kind. The passive life of an overseer seemed ideal to him, even at the cost of castration. He accepted the necessity of it, for the safety of his own soul and the protection of all Mankind.

But gradually this unquestioned acceptance was chipped away as his explorations within the school became more daring, the discoveries more shocking, until the reasoned explanations for the mutilation of his flesh no longer satisfied.

Why should I be butchered while priests violate the young eves? he demanded silently, appalled by what he'd witnessed. They forbid touching between males, yet how many times have I seen them make abomination upon each other?

And there were other discoveries.

A shaved head was a symbol of masculinity: it proclaimed a secular male's virility and strength, his endurance and courage. It declared his right to enter the gaming ring and his worthiness to be part of the community.

To see the eves with their shaved heads was outrageous.

But the most shocking discovery had come later. And Robert paused to let the memory overtake him . . . .

He was ten years old and on a late night adventure inside the school church.

A sudden noise sent him flying into the confessional where he stood in rigid silence. Footsteps were approaching from the side entrance.

Robert cautiously peeked through the narrow slats of the door.

It was Bishop Chang, the school principal, with one of the nursery priests, young Father Hal, whose curly hair had sprung up in unruly tufts around his head, in resistance to the straight, bowl-cut style worn by the clergy. It often took time for a newly frocked priest to master the techniques used for controlling his hair's natural inclinations.

The priest held a small bundle that wriggled and gurgled. Robert tried to get a look at the new arrival.

"We can't keep him," the bishop stated without emotion.

"Should I send him over to Saint Donald's?"

The bishop shook his head. "No, the decree came down last week. Until further notice, we are to give illegal males into the care of the Vatican."

"For what purpose?"

The bishop hesitated before saying curtly, "I did not question the Pontiff's order." The priest dropped his eyes at the tone but raised them again as the older man continued in a slightly milder voice, "I only know I am to give the Blessing immediately and then deliver him to the Vatican."

Surprised, Father Hal opened his mouth to question these instructions but wisely thought better of it, keeping his silence with difficulty. The bishop took the baby from his arms, ordering, "Prepare the wagon, you will drive me." Bowing shortly, the priest departed.

Robert watched the blessing of the baby, as puzzled as the young priest.

The Blessing Ceremony was a highly celebrated event, with every schoolboy and staff member in attendance to witness the child's initiation into the Church. This lonely evening ritual was unheard of.

Robert smelled a secret.

The brief ceremony over, the bishop departed. Robert waited a few moments before he dashed outside, creeping through the shadows towards the tool shed. With practiced ease, he scaled up the side of the shed and ran surefooted across the roof, hoisting himself up onto the neighboring outbuilding, and then over the school wall, finding the little handholds and toeholds that time had carved out of the brick, making it an easy climb to the ground. Staying close to its concealing bulk, he sprinted towards the entranceway, stopping a few feet from the gates to wait in the shadows.

Several minutes passed. Finally, the gates opened to release an ancient pair of oxen pulling an equally ancient cart. Father Hal held the reins while Bishop Chang sat beside him with the baby.

Creaking and moaning with effort, the vehicle maneuvered slowly onto the road. Neither man noticed Robert slipping over the side of the cart and under the cloth sacks piled in the back.

Robert had made many forays outside the school grounds, but never before had he dared to ride upon a moving vehicle. Ordinary citizens of New Eden were not permitted to ride; only royalty, the clergy and military officers held this privilege. All others walked or were carried in litters, but this was considered weak, and only the very old or very sick succumbed.

They drove slowly through the deserted streets, Robert certain he could have walked faster. Still, they'd come farther up the mountain than he had ever ventured before, and he was sorry his view of the city was hampered by the high sides of the cart. He craned his neck painfully, trying to see without emerging from his hiding place. The cart turned a corner and Robert caught his breath in wonder as the night seemed to suddenly disappear.

Driven by curiosity, Robert strained forward dangerously to stare open mouthed at the largest building he had ever seen. Torches and lanterns burned along its battlements and walls, pushing back the darkness.

The Palace! Robert gasped.

The elaborate scrollwork and carvings that had once covered the building's outer face had long been removed or covered over, leaving it plain and unadorned, this stark grandeur far more imposing than the ornamented style of

24

New Eden's ancient Ancestors.

Soldiers stood at attention on the parapets and on either side of the massive gates that marked the main entranceway.

Robert shrank back in fear, suddenly conscious of his unlawful position. Hiding amongst the cloth sackings, he remained motionless as the cart slowly creaked past the palace. Finally, it moved out of the torchlight, returning to the cover of night.

The land grew steeper, making it difficult to keep from sliding to the end of the cart, his arms aching from the effort. And then once again the night was lit up with torches.

Very carefully he peeked out from under the sacking, and the blood drained from his limbs.

The Vatican!

In the thrill of the chase he'd not stopped to consider the bishop's final destination. Barely breathing, he lay frozen as the cart came to a halt at the entrance to the Holy District. There was a short discussion with the Vatican guards before the gates were opened and they were allowed inside. The oxen, winded from the climb, had slowed their sluggish pace even further. It seemed to take forever to plod through the length of the brightly lit buildings of the Holy District. As the wagon wound its way across the mountain face, the light gradually grew dimmer, fading to almost nothing, giving Robert a greater sense of safety.

Abruptly they came to a stop.

With the baby in his arms, Bishop Chang climbed awkwardly from the wagon. His feet crossed the gravel briefly before raising a hand to give a solid thump on the door of a tall, narrow house. Moments later it was answered by a sleepy-eyed priest.

"I have one of God's children to deliver," the bishop announced coldly.

"Please enter, Your Grace. I will wake Bishop Shaffley."

The Principal crossed the threshold, and the door closed behind him.

Father Hal and Robert waited.

Feeling a little braver, Robert surveyed his surroundings. They were now far from the great residence that he assumed housed the Pontiff. The many smaller buildings that encircled its base fanned outward or upward in neat rows, gradually becoming sparse out here near the private farmlands of the Vatican.

In the distance, he could make out the shape of a barn and a few other outbuildings. It dawned on him that if he'd been born an eve, his life might have been spent working this land. A sudden fleeting regret left him shocked and shaken. He'd just wished himself Satan's instrument! He stifled the impulse to spit the thought into the dirt and grind it under his heel, a custom amongst the populace to ward off evil.

His disturbing thoughts were broken by movement from above as the priest jumped from the cart and headed for the dimmer light of the fields.

Bet he's taking a piss, Robert thought.

An overwhelming urge took hold and before he could think, Robert was out of the wagon, peering through the window at Bishop Chang, who was still holding the baby. Another bishop also stood inside the room. Robert assumed this was Shaffley, who was saying sternly, "It can't be helped. We are over quota."

His face grave, Bishop Chang handed the baby to an old priest.

"It will be merciful," Bishop Shaffley stated in a milder voice, but the principal had already turned and, without any warning, marched out the door — leaving no time for Robert to get back to the cart.

Light flooded from the doorway, forcing Robert to move quickly across the front of the building and into the shadows.

Feet struck the ground, crunching a quick pace towards the cart. Abruptly they stopped, and the bishop swore violently before yelling for the young priest.

There were more sounds of rapid footsteps.

"Forgive me, Your Grace," Father Hal panted, jumping onto the vehicle. The older man followed more slowly. Looking towards the doorway, he gave a sharp nod in farewell.

Robert realized with horror that whoever stood at the entrance was going to watch the bishop drive away.

I can't get back to the cart!

Helplessly, he watched it move farther and farther into the distance. At last the door closed, but it was much too late. The cart was surrounded by the revealing light.

Stunned by this turn of events, Robert hurried around the corner of the building and down its side, moving deeper into the shadows where he could think in safety.

There was no chance of leaving by the main entrance. Instead, he must cut through the dark fields to the western border of the Holy District. There, he would find a way over or under the wall. He refused to think how heavily guarded and fortified it might be. He tried to cheer himself with the thought that he always found a way into — or out of — anywhere.

But, his mind harshly reminded him, this isn't the school where you know every nook and cranny and creak; this is the Vatican. Again he refused to consider any doubts. He had until morning. It would be enough.

About to start off, he arrested the motion. A cart was approaching.

The Bishop has returned! Robert thought in elation.

But with a bitter pang, he realized the sound was coming from the opposite direction. The vehicle stopped at the back of Bishop Shaffley's residence, and a doorway was opened.

Robert recognized Shaffley's voice. "Take them to the forest," he ordered dispassionately.

"Yes, Your Grace," a younger, but no less impassive, voice replied.

When the bishop spoke again, the tone had become curt, the words clipped. Robert knew he was speaking to an eve. "Take the illegit north, as always."

At the mention of the baby, Robert was once more compelled to move into danger. He tiptoed forward in time to see Shaffley hand the baby to an eve sitting in the back of an enclosed wagon. Robert could hardly believe his eyes. No eve was permitted to ride. It was completely forbidden, a far greater offense than his own infraction.

Robert stared at her. The weathered skin exposed above the veil was wrinkled heavily, the red tattoo faded with time.

The bishop closed the door to the wagon, snapping Robert out of his distraction. He backed away carefully. At a safe distance he broke into a run, speeding around the building to its opposite side. Squatting low, he waited for the wagon to take the corner. There was plenty of time to crawl underneath and wedge above the axle housing.

The wagon turned onto a less-traveled road, bumpy and dimly lit by the lights of the few buildings nearby, until gradually their faint glow disappeared altogether. Only the pale light of New Eden's three moons remained to illuminate their way through the Church farmland, the oxen taking careful steps on the indistinct track that wound its way across the mountain to the western face.

As the side gates to the Holy District closed behind them, Robert breathed a heavy sigh of relief. The cart had entered one of the poorer agricultural areas of District One, and the dim lighting from the distant farmhouses was barely discernible.

He could safely get back to the school from here. If he cut across the dark fields to the royal hunting grounds, he could make his way through the trees to the southern slope and down the mountain to enter his neighborhood unnoticed — he might even make it back before the bishop's slow moving cart.

But all thought of returning to school had fled from his mind.

He had to know where they were taking the baby.

Dark forested mountains loomed above them as the cart made its cautious way to the western valley floor. And even with his limited view from beneath the cart, he could see that the area was uninhabited, the night deeper.

They were getting close to the protective mountain barrier.

The priest turned the oxen northward to follow a narrow track that eventually led into a small meadow. Here they stopped, and the priest ordered the old eve

27

out of the enclosure. She took a long time. When she picked up the baby, he started to cry.

"Get into the woods. Tend to it there."

Robert heard her shuffle off. When the wagon began to move again, he slid from the axle housing to lie flat on the ground as the vehicle rolled over him. He waited until the priest's shadowy form had disappeared from view before putting his attention onto the old woman, trying to locate her in the increased darkness against the trees. The baby cried once more, giving their position away. He crept into the forest.

Inside the thick canopy, he could see almost nothing. As he waited for his eyes to adjust to the sudden blackness, he followed by sound alone, which was not difficult, for her movements were loud and clumsy. Robert too found the going demanding, tripping and stumbling over bared tree roots while low hanging branches slapped at his head, scratching his face and nearly blinding him.

He expected the eve to react to the sounds of his presence, but she could hear nothing beyond her own noisy passage.

After a few minutes it became quiet, and Robert stopped to listen. There was still movement, but now much less distinct. Cautiously, he crept towards the sound, stepping onto a narrow footpath. He stopped in surprise to stare down at the well-worn track, unaware how few people knew of this path, even within the clergy. Wondering at this discovery, he continued his stealthy progress.

The eve stopped frequently to rest her ancient bones or tend to the baby while Robert sat motionless, trying not to nod off. He was very tired, and his arms ached from holding himself in position inside the cart. Sometimes he would hear her loud snores, and he would have to force himself into quiet activity before he too began to snore.

Hours dragged by with little ground covered to show for them. Dawn slowly encroached, blazing a deep red before giving way to the blue sky of day, clearly exposing the mountain pass through which they travelled. Robert stared up at the imposing, tree-covered edifice on either side of him. Vanguards against evil these mountains were believed to be, and looking every bit the part to his young eyes.

The old woman continued to rest her exhausted body for long intervals while Robert fought against sleep. He had lost all sense of time and the distance they had covered, only that it must be less than ten miles, for ten miles would mark the end of the protective barrier. She must certainly reach her destination before then.

It was early afternoon when the trees began to thin out, becoming increasingly sparse the farther north they walked, and when they emerged from the pass the forest disappeared altogether.

They both stopped dead, the old woman and the boy.

There was nothing but scrub grass and brush before them, the land running flat for thirty feet before angling downwards sharply for another forty, to lay itself at the border of an immense expanse of flat rock.

They shrank back into the cover of trees.

Robert could hardly breathe, he was in such terror. On the other side of that bit of scrub grass were the Unholy Lands, a wasteland of rock and dust and demons. The place he'd been warned about and threatened with his entire life. A demon-filled desert waiting to ensnare the unwary — the body tortured and defiled, the soul ripped out to suffer endless torment in the bowels of Hell.

What demons were lurking there even now?

Shuddering, he huddled further into the protective forest.

Why would a path lead to this terrible place?

There was movement from the eve.

Robert watched in horrified disbelief as she scuttled across the plateau for several feet to lay the baby within the limited protection of a small clump of brush. Then she shuffled back into the trees as fast as her old legs could carry her. Groaning in pain, she lowered her weary body to the forest floor. Soon he heard loud snores.

For a while Robert's fear kept him alert, but the long night finally took its toll: he slept.

He woke with a start.

Dismayed, he saw red streaks beginning to steal across the sky. In a few hours, darkness would be upon them. He looked around quickly, alarmed, but the old woman was still there. Rising, he moved forward slightly to stare at the baby. Something was wrong. Automatically he crept over to the bundle. The blankets lay messed in a pile, but the baby was gone.

Robert backed away fast, his head swiveling in every direction, arms outstretched behind him, feeling for the trees. His hand brushed bark and he sped up, still too frightened to turn his back on the desert. A moment later he stumbled over something, falling backwards onto the ground. He screamed, thrashing about in terror before realizing he'd tripped over the old eve. She lay very still. Robert poked her lightly on the hand. She was ice cold: dead.

He ran.

He ran as if the hounds of hell were snapping at his heels — tearing his way through the ten miles of woods until he was safely back inside the city.

Robert returned to school a changed boy, the depth of the Church's duplicity galling him to illness. But this is what saved him. His presence at school had eventually been missed. When he was discovered in the tool shed in a fevered delirium, it was assumed he'd been there the whole time. Instead of a beating, he was put inside the infirmary and treated with reasonable care.

For days he could only stare unresponsively at the priests who tended him.

Each time he saw their robed figures, he heard the bishop ordering that baby into damnation. An innocent baby! he'd thought, appalled. Not an eve or a contaminated one, but a pure male. One of God's Chosen given over to Satan because of quotas!

It went against everything Robert was brought up to believe, everything the Church had taught him. How could they? And why? he'd demanded silently. They could have just killed the babe instead. But no, killing was forbidden — only those possessed by Satan killed.

He'd gone very still at that thought, an idea plucking around the edges of his mind, but he was still too young, too unready, to face that truth.

Yet he did understand that he was in real danger. No one must ever know the evil deed he'd witnessed, or guess his changed feelings towards the Church.

Survival instinct took over, and before long he was able to assume his old inconspicuous shell. His brief abnormality done with, he once more faded from the notice of priests. They did not look, so could not see that he was lost to them.

Robert soon realized that he needed to get as far from the Church as possible — as far as it was possible for anyone in New Eden to get — and that meant the Army. But he was already ten and did not excel at the games, doing just enough not to draw attention to himself. He could do this no longer. He must overcome his dislike and work hard at perfecting his skills if he had any hope of becoming a cadet.

He'd not been accepted last year. There was only one chance left.

He must not fail.

Determination calmed him. He walked purposefully back to the line and sighted the arrow once more, his aim steady.

Bulls-eye. Without a pause, he let go two more.

"Hey, Rob," the boy from the next pit called out, pointing towards the administration building. "They're here."

Two men, hard as granite, marched crisply towards the gaming field, their dull green uniforms almost indistinguishable from the muddy dirt and gravel of the courtyard.

Well, it had come. Now he would know if there was any chance of escape. Noting his calm without surprise, he joined the other boys gathering to meet the soldiers.

The system of recruitment that was established by the Independent Space Agency's security force on Earth, almost two millennia ago, had not been altered much over the ages. Complete loyalty was still demanded and found in those with nowhere else to turn, those from the poorest families or, preferably, no family at all. But, unlike their ancestors' time, training began as early as nine years of age and no later than twelve. This was to undermine the effects of such close confinement within the Church.

Once entered into cadets, education took place in an Army training camp, but students were still required to spend their nights inside a Church school until coming of age at fifteen. Cadets were then placed in a military installation for intensive training and initiation into the Army proper before being posted to a permanent station.

Robert and the other thirty-four young hopefuls began the test. They wrestled in the muddy gravel — five matches each — before facing four different opponents with a sword and five more with a knife, using the dulled weapons designed for students. They shot thirty arrows to display their bow skills, and ran the obstacle course five times in succession.

The Army was looking for speed, strength and stamina, and of course, weapons skill. Later, dedication and loyalty would have to be confirmed. What was offered out of this day was probationary entrance into the cadet corps. In a year's time they would be re-evaluated, and every year after until facing their final test, as young adults.

When the trial was finally over, the exhausted boys formed a straggly line to await the outcome. Six names were cited.

Robert felt his body move forward on its own, for he was beyond all command, his calm completely dissolved. Shaking with reaction, he stood before the Recruitment Officer with the other chosen boys, barely comprehending the man's harsh announcement:

"The Lord Chairman's youngest son will begin training next week with the Cadet Corps. You recruits, and others in the district, will be his training partners." The boys snuck excited glances at each other. "If any of you manage to make it to enlistment," he continued, his tone doubtful, "you could be assigned to the prince's personal guard."

He stepped back and handed them over to the sergeant.

"OK, yuh-sorry-assed-excuses-furr-humans, listen up! Tomorrow yuh reports tuh duh Duty Officer at O-seven-undrid 'ours. If yurr late, I'll kick yurr worthless asses tuh hell an' back. Dis'smissed!"

The soldiers did an about-face and marched crisply off the field. Robert watched them go, his emotions threatening to display themselves in tears of relief. He sucked in deep drafts of air, blowing them out in noisy bursts. Sucking and blowing, his mind chanted:

I'm going to be a soldier!

I'm going to be a soldier!

# CHAPTER 3

"COME, SIRE, It's time."

Trying to keep the disappointment from his face, William looked up at the priest. "Yes, Father, I'll just finish this passage."

Father Gideon nodded and prepared himself to wait. He watched the young prince's determined expression as his eyes moved across the page of scripture, not at all displeased with William's obvious dislike of gaming, for it would prevent him from forming close bonds with the Army. But, as he always had to remind himself, the child must overcome his aversion if he's ever to ascend the throne. Without adequate arena skills, he would not be considered for a moment.

It was the ruling Lord Chairman who chose an heir from amongst his sons, guided in that decision by the Church — wittingly or otherwise. The Church must ensure a satisfactory outcome to the ascendency to protect itself from any rebellious or radical ruler who might try to disturb the power balance and loosen the Church's grip on the planet.

In its roles as religious instructor, nursery attendant and educator, the Church had years of intimate contact with the Royals. Candidates for the throne were identified well before their coming of age. The two eldest sons of the present Lord Chairman had proven completely unacceptable. Strong-willed and irreverent, they held the Church in neither fear nor awe, and deeply resented the power it held over their lives and their rule. Not an uncommon reaction within the Royal Family, and one the Church was continually alert to.

As the princes grew older and more devious, they tried to hide their feelings behind a mask of obedience. But the Church knew these adolescents better than they knew themselves. It was not fooled.

Their father, however, was another matter.

Chairman Alexander was completely unaware that his eldest sons despised him, though their displays of devotion and respect reeked of pretense. They considered him weak, the Church's tool, and only slightly less loathsome than their cowering younger sibling.

But the Chairman's blindness was not without cause. The princes were blessed with great physical prowess; they were skilled gamers, expert horsemen, and daring hunters. They walked tall and spoke proudly. Already, Thomas, only sixteen, had bagged a blue boar single handedly. They were a credit to any man, even a king. The choice of heir was obvious, and the Church seemed powerless to alter that decision, for not even the Pope could veto a Royal Heir without evidence of just cause.

Their only hope lay in William, the youngest. He was all the Church could hope for: devout, respectful, and obedient. He was also possessed of a sensitive nature that suffered badly in this brutal world of New Eden.

The Church was quick to capitalize on such weakness.

Refined mannerisms and speech had always distinguished the Clergy from the rest of the populace, as did the small luxuries they permitted themselves — and denied to others, such as wearing soft robes of spider silk, playing musical instruments, and indulging in artistic pursuits or other useless activities. They were also not required to prove their worth in displays of physical strength and courage, being beyond such testing, as they were beyond temptations of the flesh.

To the sheltered William, these outward appearances suggested a softness that was completely false. The Church encouraged this belief and handled him with the utmost care.

Unwittingly, the Church was aided in its efforts by William's brothers. Teased, tricked, and tortured, the already susceptible William was driven further into the only comfort available.

Having assured itself of a co-operative ruler, the Church now had to put him on the throne. But for that, much time and patience would be required. Their usual methods of obliterating opposition with a fatal "accident" or "illness" could not be used against the Royal Family. In fact, it was critical that the Church make every effort to ensure the safety of all royals — no matter who they grew into. To do otherwise could bring catastrophe upon the Church.

Instead, the priests tried to encourage William in his riding lessons and hunting skills, but horses terrified him and killing made him violently ill.

Anxiously, they watched over William's lack of progress and over the continued health of the Chairman, ever conscious of Alexander's deepening attachment to his elder sons. The Church remained alert, ready to capitalize on any opportunity to declare the princes unfit to rule. They also prayed.

Their prayers were about to be answered.

The young prince trudged unhappily into his dressing room, yanking off the heavy woolen tunic and knee-length trousers; a short gaming tunic already laid out for him.

33

A soldier, who was not much older than William, waited silently as he stuffed his body into the unwelcome garment. The aide was new, only assigned since the prince's move from the kinderhall a few weeks ago. William never spoke to him except to give an order. He resented his presence.

Royal sons were raised by both Church and Army. The Clergy had possession during the early years, closely watched by the Military. Later, the roles were reversed.

At the age of six, William was removed from the priest-run nursery and placed in the army kinderhall. The move was traumatic. He was completely unnerved by these loud, rough men who found humor in cruelty and pleasure in pain, and encouraged him to be likewise. For four hateful years he'd endured their care. His only interaction with his friends, the priests, was during lessons and catechism, or after some terrible trauma.

Now he had his own apartments, yet the Army was still forced upon him and would continue to be until the age of fifteen. Then he would finally have the right to choose his own servants from the civilian labor pool inside the palace, descendants of the original domestics transported from Earth.

Shivering in the brief attire, William rejoined Father Gideon. Together, they walked through the ancient corridors of the palace. A legacy from their Ancestors, and as strong and impressive as the day it was built: Colonial Headquarters for the Independent Space Agency — before the End of the Earth, before The Cleansing.

They hurried downstairs and out to the area reserved for the prince's training. The cadets, already practicing since early morning, were sweating heavily in their brief tunic and undershorts, standard dress code for a military student. Now they waited at attention for the prince's arrival. But William took no notice. He saw only his father and two brothers as they emerged from the stables at the other end of the courtyard, having returned from a morning in the royal hunting grounds.

It was William's first glimpse of his father in weeks. The Chairman had no time for a son who couldn't act like a man. By William's age, Thomas and Henry were already joining in the hunt.

William knew that he could never take part.

The three Royals moved across the courtyard, deep in conversation. Probably talking about the Tour of the Realm, William thought wistfully, longing to be included in the event.

It was customary for the Chairman to visit a number of Districts within North and South Regions before the commencement of the Triennial Championship Games being held in six months time.

In honor of their royal guest, each District would put on a grand display of local talent as a preview to the Championship Games. The custom, older even than the Games themselves, was created to help the sprawling populace feel connected to their king.

But when the population began to spread farther across New Eden, eventually creating West Region, the Tour of the Realm continued its route through the two original Regions, ignoring the third completely: the western landscape considered too mountainous and time consuming for the Chairman to cross.

Father Gideon cleared his throat noisily, reminding William of his duties. Reluctantly, the prince tore his eyes from his family and moved towards the instructor. The cadets bowed shortly at his approach.

"Sergeant Pallard," William commanded, pointing a finger at one of the boys, "he shall be my partner today."

"Right-yuh-be, young Sire." Surprised, the sergeant beckoned Robert forward.

The prince was never known to challenge himself, Pallard thought, and now he picks an older boy much bigger than himself. He's a strange one alright.

The company fell back into practice drills while the Prince and Robert received careful instruction from Sergeant Pallard. But William was not paying attention; he was studying Robert.

This boy had grabbed William's interest soon after he began training with the cadets, though he didn't understand why. Physically, the boy was unremarkable: average height, average build, medium skin color, facial features without distinction. Even his priest-like speech was not unusual; several of the cadets spoke that way. And though he was well skilled in the combat exercises, William's brothers were more impressive.

Sensing himself watched, Robert dared a glance towards William, who pulled a face and rolled his eyes at the sergeant. Surprised, Robert grinned, and quickly returned to the lesson. The instructor, sensing he'd lost his pupil, admonished William roughly, "Yurr royal backside be booted round this field if yuh don'ts concentrates 'arder, Sire."

William nodded and tried to pretend interest, but he wished the whole business over with, frustrated at being forced into something he hated and knew he could never learn.

Royals were automatically given the honor of cadet training without the need for enlistment. It would be unwise to have a prince working his way up the ranks with an Army at his disposal — far too much temptation. The chairmanship possibly plucked from the rightful ruler's grasp and the world thrown into civil war. Instead, the boys he trained with would become his personal guard. Growing up together would create a tight bond of loyalty.

At last the lesson ended.

Robert bowed and made to leave with the others, but William forestalled him. "You talk like a priest."

"Yes, Sire — as do you."

They grinned at each other.

"You're an illegal, aren't you?"

"Right, Sire."

"That means you don't have a father."

"I've got one, Your Highness, I just don't know who."

William thought on that for a moment, then said unexpectedly, "I never see my father either. He . . . he doesn't like me."

"Your Highness, how can you say that?"

"Because it's true."

"But why would you believe such a thing of your own father?" Robert asked, stunned.

The Prince hesitated. "Cuzz I'm a sissy." He lowered his voice, "I can't—" he stopped, unable to go on.

Now it was Robert's turn to hesitate, reluctant to speak up. But the cadets were already getting edgy, and the prince's secret would not be hidden for long. So far, only Robert had guessed the truth. When the others figured it out, respect for the prince would be gone forever. He steeled himself and said, "I don't like gaming either, Sire."

William looked at him in disbelief.

This boy was someone the prince envied, he seemed so at ease in the arena, yet here he was confessing to the same weakness.

"You swear?"

"I swear, Sire."

"Then why are you here? You could be a priest." He added wistfully, "I wish I could be a priest. The Holy Fathers say no, because I'm a prince. Why aren't you?" William demanded.

Robert answered cautiously, "I guess . . . I don't have the calling, Sire."

William nodded; he knew this expression, even if he didn't truly understand it. "You could be an overseer."

"I wouldn't like that. This is better."

William now understood why this boy stood out from the rest. He could speak to him without getting strange looks or nervous shifting. "Yes," he agreed, "I'm glad you're here."

Encouraged by this intimacy, Robert said earnestly, "Sire, forgive me, but it's my duty to speak." William nodded, worried by his solemn expression. "Your Highness, if you're to keep the respect of your guard, you must pretend to like the gaming."

"I'm not you — I don't know how."

"I can show you."

36

William was suddenly hopeful. "You mean, you would teach me?"
Robert bowed low. "Willingly, Sire."

# CHAPTER 4

"ROBERT BOUNTIFUL . . ." Bishop Chang considered thoughtfully, but could not recall the child he'd named fourteen years ago. He called for his assistant, "Bring the file on Robert Bountiful, and send for his dorm supervisor."

When the file was placed before him, he studied it closely. "Ah, yes, of course, Robert. Always an obedient lad, never any trouble, almost forgot he was here."

The smile he gave the visiting Cardinal melted in the coldness. Arrogant Vatican snobs, the bishop thought resentfully. They always meant trouble. He was already annoyed at having his dinner plans canceled by this unexpected visit. A meal at the Chandlers' was always a feast and not to be missed. But Lambert was Cardinal Vecker's lackey; he dared not ignore the demand for an interview.

There was a soft knock, and Father Don entered. The bishop motioned him forward. "Robert Bountiful is under your supervision?"

"Yes, Your Grace."

"Describe to His Eminence something about the lad," said the bishop.

"I don't want to know something," the visitor broke in sternly. "I want to know *everything*."

"Of course, Your Eminence," the priest quickly assured him. "But there's not much to report. He was left here at approximately six months of age, a healthy baby who grew into a healthy boy — only had the sickness once, if I remember correctly." He paused, considering. "Always been a quiet one, rather a loner . . . never in any serious trouble — actually, never in any trouble at all." He paused again, obviously struggling to remember something more. "Oh, yes, he seems to have some kind of knack: the older boys tease him but rarely interfere with him physically — which is actually quite remarkable." A sudden thought struck Father Don: "It's a shame we didn't snare him ourselves."

"You didn't snare him because you damn well didn't know he even existed!" the cardinal accused sternly. There was a short, defensive silence. "Continue,"

Lambert ordered wearily.

"Two years ago he was chosen for cadet training and placed in the young prince's unit. Has Robert got himself into trouble at the palace?"

He's got himself into trouble alright, the cardinal thought, only wheedled his way into the favor of the next Lord Chairman. But aloud he growled, "That does not concern you."

The priest bowed his head at the rebuke.

"What of his piety?" Lambert demanded. "Is he devout?"

Chang and the priest exchanged a quick glance before Father Don answered, "Yes — yes, I believe so."

"You do not sound convinced. I suggest you pay closer attention in future, and when you have come to a decision, inform me immediately." He rose to his feet, adding, "But I don't want you questioning the boy. Not about his piety, nor anything else. Treat him as you've always done: with utter indifference." With that, he strode imperiously from the principal's office.

The Bishop glared at Father Don. "Arrogant bastard! What does he know about running a school? Indifference, indeed!"

But the priest was not listening. He said musingly, "What do you suppose our young Robert's been up to?"

Chang's forehead wrinkled fiercely. "I don't know and I don't care. I could give him a good thrashing for bringing the Vatican down on us. Making me miss the first decent meal I've had in months! I'll tan his hide for sure!" At Father Don's look, he said impatiently, "I know, I know, nothing different. But if I—" he was cut off by a sudden crash overhead. "What in the name-of-all-saints!" he exclaimed as the pounding racket of running feet could be heard on the floorboards above them.

The two men focused on the air vent directly over the Bishop's chair.

"Those little devils!" the priest swore. He tore out of the room, hoping to catch the culprits at the base of the stairway. But when he emerged from the corridor he saw the outside door was already wide open, announcing a hasty retreat. Dimly, through the night and the driving rain, he could make out the dormitory door in the same condition. He set off in pursuit.

Robert and Eric were flying through the dorm in a wild panic.

Robert had recognized the cardinal as he passed through the schoolyard on his way to the Bishop's office. It was the same man he'd seen at the palace. The cardinal's eyes boring into Robert every time he thought himself unnoticed. And now he was here. Robert had to find out why, so he'd dared this little venture. Eric, as usual, tagging along.

The fugitives slid past the staircase, their wet boots slippery on the wooden floor as they sped down the deserted corridor. It was time for evening prayers, and there was not another soul around. They dashed inside the dining hall, cutting through with speed to burst into the kitchen where Robert finally pulled the younger boy to a stop.

"Does yuh think he's followin'?" Eric gasped.

Robert answered by pushing him inside a low cupboard. "Stay there."

Eric watched the older boy disappear into the fuel room, reappearing a few moments later to crawl in beside him.

"What yuh done?" Eric asked.

"Unlocked the fuel chute — now quiet," he hissed.

He was about to close the cupboard door when he saw two figures cowering in a corner. At the first sign of Robert sighting them, the girls dropped their eyes to the floor. Without a word, he pulled the door closed. Footsteps were approaching fast.

Through a wide gap across the top of the cupboard door, they saw the priest dash into the kitchen, his sodden shoes squelching noisily. He stopped abruptly at the sight of the young eves. The taller one carried a large bowl and was walking towards the boys' hiding place.

"Did anyone come in here?" Father Don snapped.

She placed the bowl on the countertop, her bulky clothing blocking most of the gap in the cabinet door. Without looking at the priest, she pointed towards the fuel room.

He rushed inside, and they heard him swear, "Those little buggers!" before returning to the kitchen. "Did you see who it was?" he demanded of the older eve. She shook her head. "You?" he asked the younger.

"No," she said, looking at the floor.

He sped from the kitchen and back into the dining hall, commanding as he went, "Lock up that fuel chute!"

The four waited, listening as his footsteps disappeared into the distance.

Eric felt Robert give him a shove, "Quick, vespers are nearly over — we can mingle with the others."

The eve moved away from the cupboard to stand beside the younger girl as the boys emerged from hiding. Catching sight of the two eves, they stopped and stared. Neither had been this close to a female in a long time.

Except for the old woman in the forest, Robert had never experienced an unobstructed encounter. Always there was a door or a priest, or some other barrier between him and the eves.

Now he didn't know what to do. They were not to be trusted, yet both had shielded them from the priest. Being a secret witness to the punishment of eves, Robert knew the danger they'd put themselves in.

And eves were always cringing and plucking frantically at their clothes, even when no males were around; he'd seen that during his spying. It gave him a creepy feeling. But these two eves were not cowering, as if expecting to be struck at any moment. They stood motionless with bowed heads, eyes below knee level, as was proper.

Confused, his training reasserted itself; he sought to put distance between them.

But to Eric, their nearness stirred old memories of happier days. He found his voice, "Yuh dids yurr work." The only phrase of approval permitted to an eve.

Appropriately, the girls did not respond in any way.

"Come on, we've got to go," Robert said, tugging at him.

Eric continued to stare at the little eve as Robert dragged him from the kitchen.

Once they were gone, Theresa locked the chute and closed the fuel room door. The two girls looked at each other. "We are both stupid, evil eves," Theresa signed.

Not quite believing what they'd just done, they returned to preparing the bread dough for the morning.

"They were so quiet, they almost caught us barefaced," Ruth whispered in awe. "How do they move with such silent speed?"

Theresa only shrugged indifferently. She was furious with herself.

We shouldn't have hidden those boys. They could turn us in, make us to blame for whatever they did. But no, she thought, that boy would never put another child in danger.

Over the years, Theresa had watched him grow bigger and, with it, bolder in his defense of the weaker children. Gradually, whenever she witnessed this, an odd but pleasant feeling would come over her. But she'd no frame of reference, no conception or understanding of how to identify this sensation: it was the feeling of hope.

Again she reminded herself: We have nothing to fear — not from him.

Theresa ceased her labors to stare down at fingers heavy with dough Lying to a priest! she thought with dread. What have I done?

But Theresa knew, if given the opportunity, she would do the same again. She could not give that boy up to them — even if it meant lying to the Pope Himself.

As for Ruth, the scars on her back were still too fresh.

She would give no one up to them.

41

# CHAPTER 5

ROBERT WAS not disliked, but neither was he sought after. How much this had to do with his position as William's confidant and friend, Robert didn't know. He was simply grateful to be left to himself, uncaring that he remained isolated from the camaraderie of his cadet unit.

It was Robert who encouraged William to take advantage of his princely right to dismiss those cadets he found unsuitable for his personal guard, and it was Robert who guided the young royal in these decisions.

Gradually, slowly, William was collecting around himself a group of cadets whose natural dispositions were less brutal and callous than the average New Eden male, boys who were more like Robert, boys he could feel comfortable with.

Robert was determined to deliver to the prince a Personal Guard that could feel true loyalty to his friend.

Of course he now realized that his friendship with William had been a mistake. He could feel the Church breathing down his neck, watching, waiting for him to put a foot wrong. But he pretended ignorance of their interest, and continued in his usual habits, altering only two things: he no longer allowed himself to appear distracted or bored during Mass, and he ceased his nocturnal excursions through the school.

He watched Eric sneak off alone, sorry to see him go.

Robert was worried about his friend. The younger boy had been acting strangely since coming across those eves in the kitchen. At first Robert would catch him staring up at the classroom windows when it was time for the eves to be cleaning. Soon he realized that Eric was sneaking inside while they were still working there. Then one evening Robert tracked him down inside the kitchen to find him actually *speaking* with the little eve — at least he guessed it was the same one, but how could you know with all that covering?

He'd dragged Eric outside and boxed his ears, hoping to snap some sense into him, and it seemed to have an effect, for the boy ceased his illicit activities.

When Eric gained entry into the cadet corps, Robert hoped his interest in the eve would fade completely, but instead it seemed to recharge his confidence, as if being a cadet put him beyond the power of the priests. He began skipping vespers a couple of times a week to sneak inside the kitchen, in the hope, Robert assumed, of finding the little eve.

All the teachings of the Church rushed at Robert: she was corrupting him, leading him into sin and the loss of his immortal soul. Despite knowledge of the abuse eves suffered at the hands of the priests, Robert could not shake his beliefs. The danger to his friend would not let him. Eric could lose everything.

Robert tried to warn him, remind him of his catechism, but Eric only laughed at his fears. Nothing was going to happen; he was just having some fun.


"Want to go look at the ancestor junk?" Robert suggested.

"Nah," Eric answered in a bored tone. "I sees it enough." He threw a rock into the river, emphasizing his discontent.

It was Sunday afternoon and both boys were free until suppertime.

Robert was fifteen and would be taking his Rite of Manhood in six months' time, at the end of the semester with the other fifteen-year-olds in his school. As a senior, Robert was allowed the privilege of leaving the school unchaperoned for a few hours, every Sunday. He was also permitted to sign out a younger student.

Until their senior year, most students had little contact with the outside world, unless they were cadets or dared to scale the school walls. Robert's nighttime forays often brought him to the river during the dry season, to explore the ruins of the Ancients, or to play in the sparse forest that followed the river's path. After he met Eric, the younger boy would usually tag along.

Growing into a senior, Robert continued his visits to the river, even if it was now permitted — or almost permitted. They were much too close to the ruins of the power plant to be strictly proper. The power plant was technology, and technology was forbidden to everyone, which made it very quiet here, away from prying eyes.

Eric continued in the same bored manner, "There be nothin' new tuh sees."

"Guess not," Robert answered distractedly, focused on luring a big fish into taking the bait. He could just make out the pointy blue nose in the churning waters.

"There just be one place we ain't never beens — leasts I ain't."

Robert tensed, knowing what was coming.

"Duh eve school, that be somethin'."

Robert stood up, winding in his fishing line before he turned and began striding quickly away.

43

"Where's yuh goin'?" Eric chased after him, "What's duh matter?"

But Robert kept walking, ignoring the younger boy.

"Just cuzz yuh done turns chicken shits don't means I have tuh," Eric yelled after him.

There was no response.

"I be doin' it anyways."

Robert stopped, and Eric was beside him before he could draw breath. "Yuh beens there, ain't yuh?"

"They'll yank you out of cadets," Robert stated. "You won't get another chance. You'll be a miner forever."

"I won't gets caught, I never does. Yuh knows that."

"This time it's different — you're under some kind of spell!"

"I ain't! Yuh don't knows nothin' about it. All yuh knows about is priests!"

Robert stopped short, for that was too true. Sighing in resignation, he said, "It's a long time since I've been there."

"Yuh *was* there!"

He gave one last try. "Don't go."

"Yuh does it," Eric said pointedly.

Robert gave up and sat on his haunches. Eric followed, waiting expectantly.

"Inside the church, behind the vestry," Robert explained shortly, "there's a small room with a closet. The back of the closet slides open like a door. Behind it, is a way into the eve's church."

"How'd yuh finds it?" Eric asked in amazement.

"One time I almost got caught — I had to hide in the closet. The bishop came inside and opened the panel."

"Wow!" Eric said in awe. "And yous standin' right there."

Robert shrugged, "I was hidden in some robes."

Eric looked at Robert. "I didn't means tuh calls yuh chicken shits. I knows duh Fawders watchin' yuh. I knows yuh hates them same as me."

Robert shrugged again. "It doesn't matter." Suddenly he wanted to get away. He felt ashamed of Eric — and of himself. "I gotta go practice," he said, standing upright. "See yuh." And off he ran.

Eric watched after his friend. He was sorry Robert was mad, but he had to do this, though his nine–year-old mind couldn't have said why. The girl stirred up memories of home, and the sensation was pleasant. And he always got a thrill from outsmarting the priests — the bigger the risk, the better. And he missed Robert's company. Being with the eve would satisfy several needs at once.

Eric was very different from his friend.

Robert disliked cadet training, but was conscientious and loyal. Eric excelled in the art of combat, enjoying the rigorous training and the thrill of a hard win,

44

and these days he won often. His body had grown tremendously this past year, and so had his strength. No boy his age could best him, and more than a few older students had suffered defeat by his hand. But he lacked the selfless devotion to duty the Army demanded. It was only the power in winning he sought, the thrill of defeating his opponent, not the honing of his soldiering skills to serve the Chairman with complete and utter dedication.

Three days later, he ordered Ruth to meet him outside the eve dorms; he would be there at midnight. She had no choice but to obey.

"Don't go," Theresa signed, her fingers adamant. "Yes, he could report you for disobedience and you'd be punished. But if you're caught outside with a male, the punishment would be extreme. Stay in bed."

She glanced around to see if anyone in the dorm had read her signing. There were thirty-four eves in the room, all making preparations for bed; no one was looking in her direction. Theresa removed her overvest and tunic, looking to Ruth for an answer.

"I can't," Ruth's hands flashed back before she bent to pull off her leather boots.

Theresa waited until she lifted her head again. "I know it goes against the teachings to disobey a male, but you must be strong," she signed.

Ruth only shook her head. She couldn't explain. Theresa would think her possessed, and she'd be right.

When that boy first came to the classroom to speak with her, she was frightened, but she was also excited, knowing a priest might arrive at any moment — and hoping one would. Then she could hide the boy and pretend innocence, like that night they'd lied to save him and the other one. How often she relived that scene, playing it over and over, the first big thrill of her young life. She yearned to feel that sensation again. Going out with the boy tonight would be another trick on the priests, and the thought filled her with elation. But all she could sign was, "I must go."

Theresa pulled the rough spun nightgown over her head and leaned close to Ruth's ear. "We never should have lied to the priest," she pronounced in a low whisper. "This is your punishment." Silently, Theresa wondered what her own would be. "We must never repeat such wickedness."

But Ruth knew her wickedness had only just begun. She would not think of her ultimate punishment. Involuntarily, she shuddered.

Theresa's fingers flashed again, "God be with you."

The words reminded Ruth how far she truly was from Him.

45

Cramming herself into the nightgown, she picked up her boots and clothes to scurry with Theresa over to the wooden cubbyholes lining the wall at the end of the room. A few quick movements and they'd laid their worn belongings neatly inside the cubicles before dashing back to stand at the foot of their narrow beds. It was almost time for evening inspection.

The last few girls made it into position, just as the door opened and Father Tommy stepped inside. He looked them over critically, all in thin nightgowns and bare feet, scarf and veil in place, heads bowed and bodies rigid. No movement of any sort was permitted during inspection.

Most eves failed at this exercise when they first entered the school, and Ruth had been particularly slow to develop her self control. Every night for an entire month, she was sent to the discipline priests before she could train her body into stillness. Ruth hated these inspections with all the passion of her young heart, though she knew it was wicked to do so.

Father Tommy began his walk down the aisle between two rows of closely spaced beds, though several of them were no longer in use. He stopped at each girl, inspecting her carefully from head to toe before moving on to the next.

Except for the priest's slow steps down the line, there was absolute silence in the room. Abruptly the stillness was shattered by the long tooting squeal of escaping gas. Father Tommy turned around sharply, and every girl in the room sucked in a silent breath of fear.

"Who did that!" he demanded, his voice shaking with rage.

There was a moment's pause before Theresa took a step forward. The priest covered the space between them, snatching the short whip from his belt and raising it high overhead, smashing it viciously across her shoulders. "You disgusting cow! If that's what you do with your supper, you don't deserve any!" he spat at her. "Get out of my sight!"

As Theresa moved towards the door, he followed behind, slapping at her with the short whip until she was out of the room.

Her back smarting painfully, Theresa turned her steps towards the discipline room. She knew her supper would be withheld for the next week, and her stomach gurgled quietly, as if in regret for its earlier loss of control. But her mind was not on food.

What punishment waits for me tonight? she thought fearfully.

She had travelled this nighttime path many times before, as had all the eves in the school. An inspection never passed that someone wasn't found worthy of punishment. The punishment always changing so they could never know what horror lay in wait for them.

Farther along the corridor she was joined by three more girls as they were ejected from their dorm rooms by an irate priest. They travelled down the stairwell together in silence. It was too dark for signing and no one dared risk speech. There was nothing to say in any case; they'd all been here before. Each focused on containing her own terror.

On the lower landing they were joined by four more eves before proceeding to the main floor. There they waited for several minutes to be certain no other girls had been chosen. Once they were confident, they walked to the back of the building, reaching a narrow, dimly lit passage.

The girls slowed their pace, feeling cautiously in the near dark for three small steps, and when these were safely negotiated they held out their hands, waiting for the feel of wood. On making contact, one of the girls tapped lightly on the door — it was flung open instantly.

Two cowled figures, large and looming, blocked the entranceway. After a moment's pause they moved aside, and the young eves could see the inside of the room, dark but for the huge glowing fire in the hearth. The ceiling was low and seemed to hover menacingly, covered in instruments of torture: finger screws, branding irons, eyelid clamps, flesh pinchers, head screws, and many other devices the girls couldn't yet identify. They glinted dully in the light of the fire, sending shivers through the children. Tables, benches and stools were scattered about the room, and each had the look of a threat to the terrified girls standing in the doorway.

"Enter," one of the figures commanded, and the girls scuttled inside as if stung. With quaking hearts they stood waiting while the two faceless men silently surveyed them. Several moments passed before a finger extended outwards and pointed directly at Theresa.

"Come," the voice ordered. A small whimper of fear escaped as she moved forward to follow the figure deeper into the room. She was led towards the hearth where a large tub filled with water stood a short distance away. Her arms were pulled behind her back and the wrists tied together.

"Kneel," the voice said coldly, removed from all feeling.

Visibly shaking, Theresa knelt before the tub. Without looking up, she knew the other children were standing directly in front of her across the room. It was always this way, so they could watch and know what was coming; it increased their terror.

The two robed figures stood behind the kneeling child. Abruptly, one of them ripped back her veil and grabbed her neck, shoving her head under the water. Instinctively she tried to struggle, but the hand was a vice, and her bonds prevented all but the most futile efforts.

She could not even kick her legs, for her bare toes were pinned painfully to the floor by the booted feet of the second priest.

Theresa tried not to inhale, but her body could not resist the need for oxygen.

47

It overrode every consideration: she breathed in. A moment later she was jerked from the water and forced back to her knees.

Coughing and sputtering, she gulped in great draughts of air. The moment her coughing ceased, the priest repeated the process, grabbing her head and burying it under the water. Once more, she struggled uselessly against the hands that held her, before succumbing to the demands of the flesh. And once more she was yanked out and allowed to recover only briefly before being dunked back inside the tub.

Again and again, they replayed her torture until she was rendered half senseless. Finally, hands still tied, she was pushed back towards the other children and forced to watch while each young eve received the same cruel treatment. And with every child, her anger grew.

I hate them, she chanted over and over again, uncaring how wrong and evil this was, or even that it might lead to further punishment. The hatred helped: she could ignore the pain in her arms and her frigid exhaustion.

When the bonds were cut from her wrists at last, she could not move her arms; they were numb and useless. Shivering in their wet nightgowns, the traumatized girls made their way up the stairs, some still coughing from the water in their lungs. As the feeling returned to Theresa's arms, she had to bite her lip to keep from crying aloud.

Gradually, the girls slipped away to their own rooms without a word or a sign, leaving Theresa to finish the last part of the journey alone.

Murderous rage was competing with deep fatigue, causing her to stumble inside the darkened sleeping room. Theresa felt her way to her bed, removing the soggy head covering and damp nightgown, though it was forbidden to be without clothing. She laid the gown on the floor and crawled gratefully onto the hard little plank she called her bed.

Pulling the thin blanket over her bare shoulders, she thought miserably, I will certainly live a very long life for my sins, and then I will burn in Hell forever.

But at that moment the thought was almost appealing, because in Hell there would be no priests.

Sighing heavily, she began sliding into sleep, but a moment later her eyes flew open and she sat upright. Cautiously, she leaned over to put a hand onto the bed beside her. It was empty.

Ruth!


The two children began to meet secretly twice a week. It was only a matter of time before they were caught.

At first their adventures were confined to the outbuildings in the girls' school, but they soon grew bored with this. Eric began leading Ruth into the boys' yard, and eventually over the wall and out to freedom, Ruth eager to follow.

Gender lines became blurred.

Ruth began the practice of removing her veil the moment she entered the shelter of night. Eric didn't comment, and after some initial surprise hardly noticed. He'd spent too much time with the bared faces of his treasured siblings. During their treks over the wall, they had to rely heavily on each other to keep ears and eyes sharp for danger, to help pull a hand or push a leg, or to touch in silent warning.

He even insisted on knowing her name, and she'd mumbled it low. When he demanded her last name, she bent her head beyond its customary hunch and pointed to her arm.

"What yuh means?" he asked, confused.

"No name," she said, stooping even further, making it difficult to hear. "Only a number."

"Uh number?" he repeated, perplexed. He pointed to her arm, "Yuh gots uh number there?" She nodded. "Let's sees."

She hesitated, then bravely undid her sleeve button and pushed the material up to her shoulder. It was a brazen act, exposing her arm, and even more so her number to a male who wasn't a priest.

"Uh tattoo!" he said, studying the ink in the moonlight. He'd never heard of such eve markings — very few males outside of the clergy had. "R775," he recited. "That's yurr last name?"

"Since school," she whispered to the floor.

"They takes yurr name and gives yuh uh number?" Eric said in awe. It gave him an uncomfortable feeling in his tummy to think about it, and he pushed it away. "Let's go sees stuff!"

Once over the wall they sought out the safest areas to explore. Sometimes they'd investigate one of the deserted houses that were springing up across New Eden, but more often they went to the river, the dry season still upon them. Here, in the sparse forest, they could run and climb and jump, as children should.

One night, as Ruth leapt down from a tree, her scarf became entangled in the branches, the material tightening around her neck while her feet kicked frantically inches above the ground. Eric rushed to pull the scarf from her head, revealing her shaved scalp. As she lay in the sparse grass recovering, he stared in amazement at her lack of hair.

"Yuh gots uh shaved head — as if yuh was male!" he hissed at her, confused and even shocked but not angry. He crouched down to study her scalp, giving it a little poke. She looked up at him, startled. "Why'd they shaves yurr head, and yous uh eve?" he insisted without rancor.

49

Ruth's eyes instantly shifted to the ground.

Although speaking to Eric was becoming easier, she still couldn't look at him as she did so. "So it doesn't lure Man into sin," she whispered.

"With yurr hairs?" he asked, disbelieving. How'd anybody be tempted into sin by hair? he wondered.

He laughed, and Ruth looked up at him in confusion.

"Can yuh sees Chang's hairs bein' uh lure tuh anybody?" He laughed again, and though she knew it was wrong, she couldn't keep the smile from her face.

Ruth had no memory of feeling happy — she didn't even possess the words to describe such feelings. Her mother had raised her as custom demanded, curbing her every natural impulse and reminding her daily that she was evil and a danger to all life in the Garden of Eden.

But now, twice a week, the fun of their adventures made her body shake with silent laughter — laughter shared with a male.

Eric had easily fallen back into the role he played with his little siblings, though he knew that everything they did together, the touching, the talking and the fun, was supposed to be wrong and a sin. But he could not believe it. Instead, he wanted her to be more like a real friend. He tried to teach her gaming.

In the small barn at the eve school, Ruth listened with wide-eyed attention to Eric's wrestling instructions, completely engrossed by this view into the sacred world of gaming. But she was too well trained. She could not fight back or even protect herself. Eric grew frustrated by this passivity. Trying to get a reaction, he tripped her onto her back, but she only lay there, eyes closed, waiting.

Disappointed, Eric ordered, "OK then, forgets it!"

Suddenly he was grabbed from behind and flung across the barn.

"What in the Name of the Holy Father is going on here!" a priest roared down at them. He pointed a finger at Ruth's exposed face, "Devil's whore! Detention room! Now!"

She disappeared from the barn.

He turned and grabbed Eric's ear, dragging him outside. "You little son of a whore!" the priest swore, shaking Eric violently. He boxed both ears painfully before marching him to the Principal's office.


It took until mid-morning for the news to circulate through the school, the biggest scandal to happen at that institute in some years. The boys all waited expectantly to see what would happen.

Eric was given ten lashes at the whipping post and made to perform eve duties at the busiest times of the day, so all could witness his humiliation and learn. When not cleaning, he was on his knees in prayer and penance.

Temporarily banned from the gaming exercises, his hair was left to grow, marking him as unfit to game or to be part of the school community. He was not permitted to talk or interact with the other boys, and could only speak to an adult when addressed. But the worst of the punishments was his removal from cadets. He would not be given a second chance.

The eve's punishment was not publicized.

# CHAPTER 6

WILLIAM NOW had skill enough to join the family hunt, though he made no move to do so. He believed his presence an annoyance to his father, an embarrassing reminder of the weakling he had sired. Robert argued fiercely, but could not budge William out of his certainty.

Knowing that the brothers had planted and encouraged this belief in William, Robert swore vengeance on them both. He only feared the Chairman would die before he succeeded, for then a higher oath would interfere, forcing him to protect Thomas as the new Chairman.

Robert kept his plans to himself, for William had no grudge against his siblings, even while he feared them, but instead, looked upon them with reverence. The young prince thought himself completely inferior, and believed his weakness deserved whatever punishment his brothers inflicted upon him.

Each year the distance between William and his family grew wider. Often Chairman Alexander allowed his youngest son's existence to slip from his mind entirely, though occasionally the obligations of a father and a king would momentarily resurface. Only to be smothered under the snickering tide of derision Thomas and Henry directed towards their younger brother, causing the weak Chairman to further ignore his responsibility to William.

The Church could have forced the Chairman to fulfill this duty; it was well within their mandate. As a prince, William was entitled to the opportunity to prove his worthiness for the throne. As a son, he was owed the modeling of Manhood by his father. But the Vatican did not interfere. It continued to watch and wait, now with a lessening of tension brought on by William's new-found skills — although the source of that improvement was another matter.

For two years Bishop Stehr, the Pope's ambassador to the palace, delivered enthusiastic reports to the Vatican filled with William's ever increasing abilities and growing confidence. The bishop, however, was unaware of the developing friendship between the prince and Robert.

Even William's confessor, Father Gideon, was kept in the dark. The priest's open disdain for the cadets and anything military had frightened William into silence, too afraid Father Gideon would order an end to the relationship. Robert was his first friend without robe and collar, and his first child friend. William was not about to lose him.

When the relationship was eventually discovered, it sent a small buzz of activity throughout the Vatican.

An immediate investigation was conducted into Robert's character. The examiners produced nothing — nothing to indicate what form his influence on the prince would take. All they knew for certain was that he was Army, or soon would be, and the Army had no love for Church Law but obeyed with grudging compliance.

The uneasy alliance formed during New Eden's early history was still in existence. The Chairman, through God's Decree, held sole ownership of New Eden. The Army defended that right of ownership. The Church sanctified it.

It was vital that the soldier standing next to the Chairman understood this.

Robert was an unknown, and was therefore suspect.

They prayed he would fail at the cadet trials or at the Rite of Manhood, and briefly considered rigging the games against him — perhaps drugging the boy to make him too aggressive, thus causing a deadly mistake within the ring. But young Bishop Gervais had interceded.

"Without this boy, will the weak prince be capable of completing his own coming of age? Are you willing to take that risk?"

The Pontiff was forced to concede that he was not.

Perhaps William will lose interest, was the faint hope.

Months later, all such hope was gone.

Robert graduated easily into Manhood, and soon after into the Army. He departed the school to reside inside the grounds of the palace, where he was immediately assigned private rooms within the Royal Household, a privilege given only to the most trusted, and only at the request of a Royal. He was there to stay.

His move within the palace prompted the Church to re-examine his files, to once more cross-examine teachers and students, and even to question William himself. No one remained inscrutable to the Church.

After a lengthy investigation, they were finally forced to change tactics and use a frontal approach.


I'm getting old, thought Bishop Stehr. I care less and less for the business of politics.

53

The bishop had been in residence as the Vatican's ambassador for nearly twenty years. It was a hard job pleasing both masters.

Stehr eyed his visitor with unease and shifted his thickening body more comfortably in the chair. "Do you think this course of action wise?"

"Due to your negligence, it is the only course left to us," Cardinal Lambert snapped disdainfully.

The bishop let the insult pass; they both knew the Vatican had also failed.

Cardinal Lambert straightened his red robe into severe lines before folding his hands into its deep sleeves. "Bring in the boy."

Stehr rang the bell on his desk, and a moment later Robert was ushered inside the office by the bishop's assistant. The door closed behind the adolescent as he bent on one knee to kiss the cardinal's ring. Then he rose to stand composed before them.

Bishop Stehr sat back, leaving the cardinal to conduct the interview.

"Do you know why you are here?"

"Yes, Your Eminence."

"And why might that be?" the cardinal asked with interest. He had planned to insinuate knowledge of some offense to see where it led, but instead he was going to have a confession laid effortlessly before him.

"You have concerns about my friendship with the prince."

The cardinal's face twitched slightly with surprise. "And what makes you think we would concern ourselves with any passing interest the prince might have for one such as you?" he demanded with a hard note of contempt.

But Robert didn't flinch. "Excuse me, Your Eminence, but you want to know if I am a loyal friend to the prince, and if I respect the Divine Laws of God."

Cardinal Lambert stared in disbelief.

Amused by his colleague's loss of composure, Bishop Stehr shifted forward and spoke for the first time: "And if we did want to know of such things, what would you reply?

"Your Grace, I have no ambitions regarding the prince, except to serve him as a loyal soldier and a true friend. I have great faith in the Lord God and obey His Laws, as I do the Laws of the Lord Chairman."

"Why you? Why befriend *you*?" the cardinal demanded.

"He dislikes the gaming, as do I. I taught him how to overcome it."

"*You* don't enjoy gaming?" the bishop asked in surprise. "Then why did you join the Army?"

"I didn't want to be a priest."

The answer brought a smile to Stehr's lips.

The cardinal was studying Robert with sharpened interest.

So the lad didn't like gaming . . . not only William, but now his closest

54

confidant . . . which meant Robert wasn't true Army, Lambert thought with satisfaction. And if the lad was after power, what of it? It could only work to our advantage. He will do nothing to inhibit William's chances to the throne. And if he proves too ambitious, that could be dealt with — later.

"You're a very bright young man."

Robert bent his head only slightly at the praise.

"You do understand our concern? The prince cannot be guarded too closely."

"I heartily agree, Your Eminence."

The cardinal studied him intently, but Robert's eyes did not waver. Damn those incompetent teachers. How could they let such a prize slip from our grasp? But all he said was, "You may go."

Robert bowed respectfully and departed.

The bishop slumped back in his chair. "Well, that was certainly a surprise."

The cardinal studied his ring. "He's an interesting lad." He looked at the other man sharply. "Keep a close eye on him."


Robert returned to his rooms, surprised by the Church's directness. Why did they care so much? It wasn't as if William was going to be Chair—

He stopped short in sudden realization, Of course! William was solidly theirs. Thomas and Henry paid lip service only.

It was now clear that the Church had plans for William. He wondered how they would make such a thing happen. It would take a lot to move Thomas out in favor of William. But Robert was certain the Church would have its way.

Mulling over this discovery, Robert changed out of the formal uniform he'd worn for the interview. There were still a few hours before going on duty, time enough to walk down to the school for a visit with Eric. Robert tried to do so whenever possible. He blamed himself completely for Eric's corruption.

I didn't stop him; instead I *helped* him onto the path to damnation. Why did I do that? he kept asking himself.

Eric's punishment had been painful to watch, knowing that he was trapped in the hateful mine pits forever, all chance of escape gone.

Guilt weighed heavily on Robert.

Arriving at the school, he found Eric alone in the dorm room — as usual — though his ostracism had been lifted almost a year ago now.

The younger boy was changed since his punishment. So quiet and subdued, all enthusiasm gone from him. Even teasing couldn't make him explode into temper, and this worried Robert more than anything. Eric had always been so proud. It was as if all the fire had been shamed out of him.

Eric greeted his friend without interest, listening to Robert's halting conversation with only the barest response. He declined the offer of gaming, and was obviously relieved when his visitor had to go.

It was always the same, but Robert couldn't keep away; he felt too responsible. And he missed his friend and the time they'd spent together.

It's funny, Robert thought. Until this happened, I'd always thought of him as just tagging along. I wonder when it changed . . . .

# CHAPTER 7

ALL SONS of the Royal Family were trained for the position of Magistrate. The closer they stood to the throne, the higher the court they prevailed over. With the Chairman at its head, the Royal Family spread out and downward, blanketing every class and district of the populace.

Tutoring in Law began at the age of fifteen, usually by an aging relative. The exception to this was the heir to the throne, whose duties and responsibilities were unique to the position he would hold. His teacher would be the Supreme Magistrate, the Chairman himself, who declared his chosen successor by personally escorting him through the doors to the Supreme Court.

Having been selected for this honor, Thomas spent his days watching Chairman Alexander pass judgment in the highest secular court in New Eden, or studying the dusty law books in his father's private study. Or, more precisely, appearing to study the dusty law books, for this prince had no intention of being encumbered with such restrictions. On the day he became Chairman, Thomas would break free of the Church forever. And though some part of him shuddered at this risk to his immortal soul, a larger part shivered with anticipation of civil war.

The Church was quite aware of the prince's intent, and kept close watch over the health and safety of the Chairman while waiting for William to come into his own. It was decided he would be ready by the Rite of Manhood. And at last the time drew near. Preparations for the sacred ritual were well underway when William's confessor made an alarming discovery.

"But you *must* invite the Lord Chairman," Father Gideon said, keeping his voice calm with effort.

"No, I've asked enough people," the prince stated with quiet firmness. But it was a lie, for the prince had no friends outside of the clergy and Robert. The few hangers-on that clustered around him were there only at the express orders of the Church.

"But he's your father! All boys want their fathers to witness their Transformation."

"*Their* fathers *want* to be there."

"You believe your father does not want to come?" the priest asked in amazement.

"I know he will not."

"My boy, of course he will come." He *must*, the priest thought in fear.

"No, Father," William said miserably, thinking of the taunts his brothers had subjected him to only the night before. "The Lord Chairman will not come."

"To exclude your father would be the highest insult. To exclude the Lord Chairman would be an act of treason," Father Gideon said sternly. "You must follow protocol."

Reluctantly, William wrote out the invitation.

As the priest had predicted, the Chairman did attend the ceremony, the two older princes and a large entourage in tow to witness the Transformation of the King's youngest son.

Informed of his father's presence in the stands, William was overcome with fear. His hands began to shake, his legs went weak, and the blood slowly drained from his face.

Robert gave the prince a calculating look, and then jabbed him painfully between the shoulder blades.

William turned on him. "What the hell was that for?"

Robert replied by ramming his thumb into William's solar plexus.

"You son-of-a-whore," William swore, jumping at him and knocking them both to the ground. They struggled in the dirt, William desperately trying to land a solid punch while Robert applied steady jabs to William's ribcage.

Father Gideon broke up the fight. "This is no time to be fooling around! Get up! The ceremony is about to begin!"

The prince jumped to his feet, grabbing the ceremonial sword from the priest's hand. Still seething, he took his place at the head of the procession. Robert moved directly behind him: the First Guard of Honor.

As a royal, William was attended by his personal guards clad in the dark brown uniform of the Ritual Honor Guard. But even a prince must take his first challenge dressed in the everyday clothes of childhood, a subtle reminder that the Church alone sanctioned every transformation into manhood, not the Army or the Chairman.

There was the sound of a horn, and the procession entered the arena. Marching to a brisk drumbeat, they crossed to the podium at the far end. The drums fell silent and all in attendance knelt in preparation for the Ritual Prayer.

Bishop Stehr stood on the platform before an altar, with two priests in attendance on either side of him. Several feet in front of them, standing on its end, was a large metal ring supported by metal struts. The ring was covered in rags soaked in seed oil from the common tree.

The Bishop raised his hands to heaven, imploring in a loud voice:

"Oh, Lord, in the name of Your servant,

William Simon Cartwright, we beseech You:

Imbue him with the courage to face the challenges before him.

Bless him with the strength and agility to meet muscle and blade.

Find him, oh, Lord, worthy to enter the Company of Men.

Amen."

The "Amen" was echoed by the spectators.

Bishop Stehr moved in front of the metal ring to sprinkle it with holy water before descending the short flight of stairs leading into the arena. He drew the sign of the cross over William, and after a short pause announced dramatically, "Let the Rite begin!"

The bishop retreated onto the podium as the honor guard rose to its feet. It moved quickly to form a large circle, and within its center stood William and his opponent for the trial.

There was a murmur of surprise through the audience, for the prince was matched against a young man unmistakably his senior, with the strength and height of those extra years obvious to all.

Placing the flat of his sword against his brow, William gave his opponent the traditional salute, and Robert saluted in return. He could see that William was still angry, but only enough to put an edge to his fight.

The prince lunged and the game began.

There was an added tension to the games during the Rite of Manhood, for it was the first time a youth would use or face a proper sword, a sword with a highly sharpened edge that glinted in the sunlight. The challenge was to overcome the fear of that blade and give an aggressive, skillful fight — without getting killed. It was also considered a failure to kill or maim your opponent. Expulsion was the consequence.

The prince was putting on a good display, with the crowd well entertained. He seemed at ease facing the sharpened sword, as if he'd done this many times before — which in truth he had, sneaking into the night with Robert to practice amongst the trees of the royal hunting grounds, their thick foliage absorbing the clash of metal. Robert was no longer concerned if the Church was watching, he knew they'd not interfere.

When the sword was finally flung from William's hand, the crowd cheered appreciatively. There was no disgrace in losing to an overmatched opponent, not when he'd shown such skill and confidence.

Having survived the first test, they were now permitted to strip down to loincloths.

A loincloth was worn only by soldiers for training exercises or when they entered the gaming ring. The exception to this rule was during the Rite of Manhood.

If a boy was trained in cadet skills he had earned the right to take his second challenge draped in only one small piece of cloth. This increased his chance of injury, but, more importantly, it garnered him a greater degree of respect.

The two youths faced one another, each holding a knife in his right hand. Once again, William had to prove his skill and courage against a naked blade, and once again he did so with an unusual flair of self-confidence. When he was finally pinned to the ground, the blade at his throat, the crowd rose to its feet with a roar of approval.

William stood and shook Robert's hand, saying breathlessly, "I know what you did back there."

"Back where?" Robert asked innocently.

William just grinned and collected his discarded clothing. Sobering, he turned to face the bishop once more.

Robert returned to his position as head of the honor guard that was reforming behind the prince. When they were all assembled, the procession marched forward to stand several feet from the podium. Two priests moved down the steps carrying a large earthen urn. A third priest followed to lower a torch inside the container. Fire spewed from its wide mouth.

Piece by piece, the prince lowered the garments of his childhood into the blaze: short pants, a woolen tunic, a cloth belt and an ankle-high pair of leather boots. When the last article was deposited, William walked towards the podium.

The moment his foot touched the bottom step, flames erupted upon the platform, the great metal ring now a circle of fire. William, like any youth of New Eden, had been expecting this. He could just make out the form of a priest moving away from the flames, torch in hand.

Solemnly, but without hesitation, William approached the ring of fire, his naked skin growing hotter with every step. "Keep going," he heard Robert's instructions in his mind. "Don't pause, don't slow down, it'll only get hotter. Just walk up the stairs and through the circle."

Feeling as if his body must burst into flames, William passed through the fire and into Manhood, the heat rapidly receding as he moved closer to the solemn face of Bishop Stehr, waiting at the altar.

There was nothing in the older man's expression to indicate the pleasure he felt at William's surprising display inside the arena.

And we owe it all to Robert, he thought. A debt we will never acknowledge.

William came to a stop a few feet in front of the bishop, and as he did so a priest moved forward to offer a new set of clothing: long pants, a rough cotton shirt, a leather belt, and a pair of shin-high leather boots. With great dignity, William donned the uniform of Manhood.

The bishop commanded the assembly: "Let us pray."

Again, every man and boy sank to his knees before the bishop proclaimed,

"We thank Thee, Oh Lord, for this gift of Manhood.

May he live out his life in strict accordance to Thy Laws,

That he may share with his brothers in the Kingdom of Heaven.

And through obedience and piety, keep Your Garden free from evil,

That Your Wrath may never again be visited upon Mankind.

Amen."

"Amen," the crowd echoed.

Bishop Stehr removed a large golden goblet from the altar and offered it to the prince. William gulped down the wine, draining the container. He raised the cup over his head, announcing loudly, "May I meet you all over a keg of beer!"

The spectators cheered noisily and the ceremony was over. The crowd would now retire to the reception area where beer would be handed round in plenty and William would be required to drink himself into a stupor.

Bishop Stehr sought out the proud Chairman.

"I didn't think he had it in him," Alexander confided to the bishop.

"You do not know your son, my Lord. You have neglected your duty as a father." Alexander could only nod in agreement. "Perhaps this can now be rectified," the bishop stated, his tone neutral.

But the Chairman knew it was not a request.

"Of course, Your Grace," Alexander agreed hurriedly.

"A private hunt, perhaps, just you and William."

"A hunt, yes, excellent." And the Chairman left immediately to give the command to his youngest son.

The bishop watched him disappear into the crowd before noticing Thomas and Henry standing together in close discussion. Becoming aware of the bishop's attention, the princes turned and acknowledged him respectfully.

Stehr returned the gesture, bowing low, hiding his thoughts: Now we've got you, you nasty vipers.

The two youths stood motionless within the undergrowth of the hunting grounds: William's bow at the ready, Robert's sword drawn.

They'd been hunting together for years, working in secret to overcome

William's severe aversion to the bloody violence of the hunt, finding ways to keep the blood flow controlled and the animal's death quick. But to ensure this, the young prince had to develop the skill of a master.

Long before he knew of the Church's intent to set William on the throne, Robert had encouraged the prince in this endeavor as the means of bringing the youngest royal into the family fold.

For the chance to gain his father's approval, William had committed his time and effort, though he'd never truly believed he could ever surmount his revulsion. But with Robert's constant faith and guidance, he persevered, succeeding at last. Yet even this triumph could not overcome his brothers' barrage of belittling insults, and he remained convinced of his unworthiness as a son.

Now William drew back the bowstring, blocking out all other considerations — as he'd been trained to do. He saw nothing but the stag standing in the limited space within the trees. He ignored Robert positioned by his side and the King with his guards watching from a distance.

The creature stopped eating and raised its majestic head to stare directly at the youths — then the arrow flew straight and true towards the eye, and the stag dropped to the ground instantly. Robert dashed forward, sword ready to open its jugular, but the arrow was buried deep inside the brain, causing the body to spasm a few times before lying motionless.

Turning his head, Robert could see that the prince had paled but was holding steady, while behind him the Chairman had let out a shout of surprise and praise.

Never had he seen such skill!

Again, Alexander felt a great pride in William, and once more acknowledged that he knew nothing of his youngest son — only what Thomas and Henry had poured into his ear.

Informed of a successful hunt, the Church waited for developments.

With a long history of such machinations, and a thorough knowledge of its Chairman, the Vatican was confident it would have its way, given time.

They did not have long to wait.

Deprived of his father's presence for most of his life, William was now in complete awe of the man. He hung on his every word, instantly and willingly obeyed his commands, and followed his every suggestion.

At first Alexander was unsettled by such open idolization, and confessed as much to the bishop. But what ruler can resist the lure of genuine devotion? He grew accustomed to it. Alexander no longer needed a sense of duty to seek out

William, but looked forward to the sight of his son's adoring face. The Chairman's time with William stretched out past the hunting grounds and into the castle proper.

Now the Church made an overt move. It endorsed William as a fit ruler for New Eden. The Chairman listened with interest.

On the day William accompanied his father through the doors of the Supreme Court, the Church breathed a collective sigh.

It had won.

# CHAPTER 8

BY CHURCH Decree, the Chairman was God's chosen ruler on New Eden, and, as such, owned all the habitable land within the planet. Entrusted to his care, it could not be sold or given away, but it could be borrowed through the purchase of a lease.

The Chairman alone issued these leases, but it was the Church who chose those fortunate men worthy of consideration. Only those who bore the signs of God's favor could be entrusted with the responsibility of lease holding. And though wealth was a certain indicator, it was not enough in itself. A candidate must also be endowed with the Qualities of Manliness: an aggressive nature, correct control of emotions and adequate abilities in the gaming arena were all essential. To be born with a large frame or great strength were further indications of favor. He must also be a productive citizen, show piety and obedience to the Law (both civil and canon), display loyalty to the Chairman and devotion to duty. However, the greatest of all the virtues was virility. To father many pure sons was the highest achievement for any civilian, though few men were endowed with this sacred blessing.

Every year, almost fifteen percent of Eden's adult males applied for the privilege of buying a lease. Many did so to obtain a home for a growing son, others to expand the family business, or increase their already rich holdings. Hundreds of clergy were employed in the task of screening applicants, but still they were heavily backlogged. It often took years to receive the letter of recommendation necessary to approach the Royal Department of Leases, where another lengthy wait was usual before being granted an interview with one of the Chairman's representatives — who could deny the application.

The only way to circumvent this queue was to win a lease, and there were just two ways of doing that. The first, and most common, was to emerge as a victor at the Triennial Championship Games, where the three champions were each awarded a small cash prize and an even smaller lease. The second option was to win the title of Great Father Bull, awarded for siring a record number of pure sons. It was the highest honor available to an ordinary citizen, and as lucrative as it was rare. The current record had stood for over one hundred years.

"Damn it, I said I'd have that prize, and I won't stop 'til I do!" Patrick Marchelie raged as he kicked open his front door, smashing it into the wall behind.

He charged into the entrance hall and down the corridor to the den, where he walked directly to the keg of beer sitting on a high table. Turning the wooden peg, he let the warm brew spill into a metal decanter.

"You'll do it, Father," his eldest son reassured him, following the older man inside and placing himself behind a large wooden chair at the opposite wall. He was thirty-six years old, but when his father was in a rage, he felt like a small child again.

"I was so close!" Patrick railed in frustration, and took a long pull of the liquid; it spilled down his chin with every noisy gulp. Turning to his son, he continued his rant: "But only three of those cows dropped humans last year, Goddamn them to hell! Even that prize heifer I bought was a waste of sperm! Cost me an arm and leg for her too, damn her soul!"

"You have three years to prepare for the next Games. You'll do it then."

Traditionally, the title was presented at the Championship Games, to allow the maximum number of citizens to pay homage to this most blessed of men.

"I wanted it now!" the older man roared, smashing the decanter onto the table, spraying the dark ale halfway across the room.

"What's three more years?" Peter spoke quickly, trying to keep his voice level. "You're still strong and healthy," he continued, putting heavy emphasis on the words. "The record has stood for over a hundred years; no one else is in competition with you." He studied his father, trying to gauge his reaction. "Great Father Bull," he said musingly. "You'll wear the title well."

Puffing out his chest, Patrick strutted across the room in the fashion of the wealthy class. "And I'll wear those leases very well too, damn it all! Just think of the riches they'll generate. We'll crush our competition into dust!" But far more important to Patrick Marchelie was the prestige. The most honored civilian in all of New Eden. He'd pay anything — do anything — to gain that title.

Peter relaxed slightly. It was alright now; his father's mood had swung out of the danger zone where his rage could so easily turn to violence. Like most of Patrick's sons, Peter carried the scars of earlier eruptions. Though with the passing years, these were occurring less frequently, or had been until this fixation with the Great Father Bull award.

Now the old man seemed more volatile and dangerous than ever, the pressure to attain that most coveted title mounting daily, for to come close and fail would mean financial disaster for Patrick Marchelie — and his sons.

"Better get to business," Patrick leered, swaggering with exaggerated steps toward the door.

Peter watched him go, praying for a successful outcome to this night's mating. Winning that title was now the only way his inheritance could possibly be saved, for every year his father sired more sons to share in his legacy — a legacy that was being significantly dwindled by extravagant bidding for the best breeder wives, bought in his father's frantic attempt to sire an even greater number of sons.

Peter had the uncomfortable suspicion that his father was borrowing money to do so, but he could not verify this, for no one but his father and the head bookkeeper saw the accounts. "Time enough when I'm gone," his father would say. But Peter knew that if he wasn't successful soon, there'd be no time.

With a leaden feeling, he realized that another bride auction would soon be upon them. How fast six months could go.

In the chilly predawn darkness, Father Tommy escorted six, fifteen-year-old girls through the streets to the District One auction hall. Eligible eves of every age would be herded there: young virgins to ancient crones, all to be put upon the marriage block and sold to the highest bidder.

The enormous auction hall was connected by a breezeway to an unimpressive barn-like structure. It was to this building that the girls were led. The dimly lit barn was bare except for a large pile of straw in one of the dark corners and two long tables positioned against opposite walls near the entrance. At each of these tables sat three priests with various books, boxes and binders laid out before them. High on the wall behind them was a flag: a black flag on the right for widows, a white flag on the left for schoolgirls and unmarried illegits.

Father Tommy led the girls to this table.

There was no lineup as yet, the hour being too early for most, which was precisely why Father Tommy was standing there at that moment. He had no intention of being trapped inside this barn a moment longer than necessary. He had far too many rivals at seminary school, and the chance of bumping into one at the auction was very high indeed. He squirmed at the thought of being discovered representing a school that serviced illegals and miners and others of low stature, when he'd expected greater things for himself — and unwisely let it show, sealing his fate.

His superiors knew that such an ambitious priest would resent every moment spent inside an inferior institute that held no chance for advancement, and that he would take his frustrations out on the eves in his care.

"Which school?" the sleepy auction priest asked, not bothering to look up.

"Pope Honorius Vecker II," Father Tommy answered loftily, trying to maintain his dignity. He eyed the priest's bent head with a sneer while the man searched through one of the wooden file boxes that sat before him. The auction priest removed a thick leather case, passing it along the table to his colleague.

"Name?" the second priest demanded, opening the clasp on the case.

"E764: Esther," Tommy said, jerking the girl to stand before the priest. The man withdrew a slim leather-covered binder and passed this to the third priest at their table. Father Tommy pushed the girl towards him, immediately jolting Ruth forward to take her place.

"R775: Ruth," he clipped.

Another binder was removed and passed on. Father Tommy shoved Ruth after it. She stood quaking before the third priest while he rummaged through a box and removed a worn wooden plaque, which he placed on the table. There was a hole drilled at each end, with a thick cord knotted through them. Etched into the middle of the wood was her number: 775.

"Put it around your neck," the auction priest ordered. She did so. "Stand over there, in the white circle," he instructed, pointing deeper into the barn where Esther was hunched fearfully within a large circle painted on the floor.

There were several such circles on the rough wood: red ones and black ones, even some that were red and black, but there was only one white circle. Ruth scurried towards it before Father Tommy could give her any more encouragement.

She stood close to Esther, and soon the other maidens from her school joined them. Covertly, they watched the increased flow of eves entering the barn, and stared in fascination at the young illegits: each with a firecross tattoo on her forehead. Only a few days old, the red ink stood out starkly in the gloom. Ruth followed their progress across the barn to one of the red circles nearby.

The white flag priests continued to process the young eves from the four schools in the District and the illegits raised on the Church farmlands, but there were not nearly enough fifteen-year-olds to fill the large white and red circles.

There were far more widows, who, upon the deaths of their husbands, reverted back to Church property to work the farmlands until the next bride auction. Each widow was categorized by age and breeding status, then ordered to wait in her appropriate circle: brood widows stood in the black circles, non-breeders in the red and black circles.

The processing went on, the various circles swelling in size until hundreds of females stood at the bottom end of the barn, but still there was room for hundreds more.

Daylight was nearly upon them and sounds of street activity could be heard when the last eve was shuffled past the registration table. The six priests quickly gathered up their paraphernalia and disappeared from the building. They were immediately replaced by others, who laid food and drink on the tables. Then the eves were permitted to approach, group by group, to take their small share. When all were fed, they were allowed to use the primitive toilets at the rear of the barn and some water for washing, after which they were ordered to sit.

They waited.

It was fully daylight now, and outside the streets seemed to resound with the bark of male voices, made all the louder by the silence within.

"Are we to marry?" a girl from another school asked Ruth with her fingers.

"I think so," she signed back.

"I'm scared."

"I too," Ruth answered, and noticed an old woman signaling her from a group in a black and red circle a few feet away. There was no tattoo on her forehead, indicating that she was once a breeder wife. In the dimness of the barn, it was difficult to make out her words. "Repeat," she signed.

Her gnarled fingers moved stiffly: "Today is the auction. It's bad, but no pain."

"What happens—?"

But her question was interrupted by the movement of a priest coming towards them. He pointed to the twenty young maids within her circle and ordered them to follow. They were led through the covered breezeway and into the massive auction hall.

Ruth flinched as the noise and smell of the place hit her senses. The hall was filled to capacity, reeking with the stench of stale beer and unwashed bodies. Ruth felt as if she was suffocating under her veil. The noise was deafening, as these men swaggered and bragged and tried to intimidate each other with their show of money or muscle, or both. Ruth had never been near a man other than priests. To be thrust amongst so many like this was almost unbearable.

The eves climbed the steps to a long, raised platform. Each girl was made to stand at the front of the stage beside a priest seated at a small table. A book lay open in front of him. This contained her personal history and her bloodline.

When the eves were stationed satisfactorily, the Auction Bishop moved to the center of the platform. He raised his hand, and immediately the hall fell silent. Every eye was on the cleric. Not a glance was dared towards the eves until permission was granted. To do so could mean the loss of bidding privileges and eviction from the hall. No man would risk that.

The bishop waited until the room had attained perfect stillness before announcing quietly, "Viewing may now begin."

68

Though her head was bent towards the floor, Ruth knew the moment those six thousand pairs of eyes swung from the bishop to bore into the twenty young maidens exposed on the platform. The impact was staggering. The fear, anger and sexual tension of six thousand psyches struck with vicious force. The girls had no defense against it — nor even understood what it was — but had the priests not kept a painful grip on every girl's arm, they would have lost control completely and bolted from the platform.

It was the usual reaction.

The men began to move. Some approached the platform, forming straggly queues to speak with a priest seated at the table, but most held back, watching only: the price of a virgin beyond their reach.

A man approached Ruth's table. He gave his name and that of his father's, their occupation and address. The priest ran his finger over the pages of the book before he decreed, "The bloodlines are too close." Ruth watched the feet move away, knowing this was her kin and not caring. Another man stepped forward.

"Eric Wong," his voice announced loudly.

Ruth silently gasped and glanced toward the young man's face before she recovered and forced her eyes downward.

The priest passed a scornful look over Eric's clothes and the coal dust ground deep into his skin. "Don't waste my time, boy, move on."

The men waiting in line behind him laughed mockingly as Eric stalked away, but he turned his head back in time to catch Ruth covertly staring after him. For one intense moment they locked eyes, recognition and pleasure surfacing briefly before painful memories caught them up, reminding them of danger. They broke contact.

Ruth sagged slightly at the sudden feeling of loss — as if she'd been offered something, only to have it ripped away.

"You are permitted to bid," the priest was saying to another man as he rose from his seat and motioned Ruth forward. "The eve is very healthy. She has survived two winter contagions." There was an appreciative grunt from the man while Ruth sucked in her breath at this bold-faced lie.

The priest flipped up the first layer of veil and forced her jaws open to display teeth and gums, pulling her head downward so the man could look up into her mouth, but always careful not to disturb the veil still covering her face. Then she was released and motioned back.

Ruth was shaking with reaction. They'd treated her like one of the barn animals!

She hung her head as low as possible, rounding her shoulders even further, trying to hide herself away. To add to her shame was the thought that Eric may have witnessed her treatment, and somehow that was worst of all.

She did not raise her eyes again.

Ruth went through the rest of the proceedings in a numbing daze. Men came and went, but she did not really hear them or feel the wrenching of her jaws. And at last she was led off the platform and back to the barn.

Ruth passed the waiting women sitting in their circles, without offering a glance or a sign. She strode to the back of the barn and flung herself into a corner to hide amongst the straw. She remained there while one group after another was led out for the viewing.

The old woman she'd spoken with that morning had to tap her shoulder several times before Ruth would look at her. "It's over, the priests have gone. Come eat," her stiff fingers signaled.

Ruth shook her head, hiding once more in the straw. But the woman would not leave; she bent her lips close to the youthful ear. "It was bad, yes?" she asked in a raspy whisper. Ruth nodded. "I remember my first time on the block," the crone continued. "All maidens feel this way. It's over now, and school days are over too."

Ruth lifted her head slightly, her eyes wide in realization. "No more priests?" she whispered.

The old woman nodded at her, saying, "For confession and Mass only. A good thought, yes?" She laid a hand on Ruth's shoulder a brief moment. "I am Mara," she said, before shuffling away.

Suddenly Ruth was very hungry. She stood up and joined the other women standing beside tables laden with food. Ruth stared in awe at the size and variety of dishes laid out for them. Never had she seen so much food allotted to eves. Her stomach growled and she obeyed, heaping her plate as high as she dared.

As was the custom during mealtimes, she lifted the top veil out of the way and tucked it under the rim of her scarf.

Like many others, she remained by one of the tables, adding more of the best dishes as she ate. A woman of thirty years and more, by the look of her hands, motioned towards the auction hall, fingers flying with information, "The bidding goes on now. Tomorrow you'll be taken to your intended's house and married there."

Another woman's fingers spoke, "This night is the Best Night, the time between widowhood and marriage. It's worth the auction for." She motioned to the old crone, "Mara, she's had four Best Nights."

The first woman added, "Maybe she'll have more, she's too old: no one will buy her. She'll be back in six months."

"All this food, it's like a miracle," Ruth signed back.

"It's more than food," the woman motioned.

"What else—?" Ruth started to ask, but realized they were completely

70

unsupervised, not one priest in attendance, and no duties had been assigned, although it was still afternoon. "You mean that for the rest of today and all the night, no work and no priests?"

The two women nodded. Ruth set her plate carefully onto the table and then reached up to remove her veil entirely. There were gasps of shock at her action — and at the sight of her face, for each cheek bore the deep brand of a firecross.

"No priests, no veil," she said simply with words.

There was a flurry of frightened fingers as others around the table began to notice her exposed face.

Mara frowned, motioning to the deep burn holes. "Didn't you learn anything?"

Ruth touched her scared face. "It was worth the penalty, as it is now."

One young woman spoke in a nervous whisper, "I have heard that long, long ago, during the Best Nights, eves always removed their veils and used only words to share."

"And God punished them for their indulgence, you can be certain," an older woman hissed at her. "The Law is clear on such things."

The younger eve bowed her head at the rebuke.

Someone approached Ruth from behind and spoke quietly in her ear, "Still disobedient, I see."

Ruth whirled around, recognizing the voice. "Theresa!" she whispered in excitement, grabbing her hands and squeezing tight, "You're here!"

Theresa's eyes shone with pleasure.

"I thought I'd never see you again," Ruth continued in a low voice that shook with feeling.

"And I, you. Four years it's been."

Recovering from her initial surprise, Ruth took back her hands, realizing: "You are widowed."

"Yes," she said, a cloud coming over her face.

"What happened?" Ruth asked with a certain dread.

"In the gaming, his opponent died."

Ruth caught in her breath. Death was not permitted in the games.

In the early part of New Eden's history, two generations after Earth's destruction, young men — youths barely past boyhood — began moving the games outside the arena and into the backstreets, where they took on a more sinister aspect. It was no longer enough to simply best an opponent; one had to literally beat him until he begged for mercy. Many of these young men were flogged unconscious rather than show such weakness. Violence seeped into everyday life. Fights erupted without warning and knifings were common, many ending in death.

The Church, the Chairman, and the Army, in a rare moment of agreement, saw the beginnings of anarchy in this unrestrained behavior. Feeling control slipping through their fingers, they began a concerted effort against all violence outside the gaming arena. But the knifings only increased.

The Church had created gaming as a vent for the anger and frustration that was growing amongst its flock. The tight restrictions and controls instituted by the Church may have been acceptable to the refugees from Earth, when all energy was spent on survival. But their Eden-born sons had energy in excess, and they chafed at the limitations placed upon them. The gaming ring allowed them freedom to express their pent-up feelings in the violence of the games.

The Church also realized that by honoring physical strength and aggression, and even brutality, dishonor would automatically fall on that which was not. It would help make the chasm between female ways and male ways unbridgeable. Machismo would become the way of men, skill in the arena further proof of Manhood. And if some should die in the games, what of it? It would only assist in keeping the female population in high ratio to males.

But a generation later their creation had a will of its own and would not be easily tamed.

The Church was forced to decree all violent death punishable by Expulsion. Destroying Man was Satan's business. To murder meant a man was possessed beyond all hope of salvation. Already lost to God, the murderer would be driven from the Garden and into the barren wasteland.

The Church invited the mob to help in the cleansing of their Garden through the ancient tradition of stoning, ensuring guilty silence from some, and from others, eagerness to lead the assault.

Women soon came to bear responsibility for this too. The crowd's anger must be focused away from the authorities who ordered the Expulsion, and back onto the cultural scapegoat.

The eve had allowed Satan to enter her body and take possession of her husband while he lay exposed and unprotected inside her. Public punishment was decreed for her as well, although nothing that would result in death. And if there was no wife to blame, the dame carried the responsibility.

"And did he mate before the game?" Ruth asked. Theresa nodded, her face grieved. Ruth took her hand, squeezing it hard. They were still a moment, each in silent prayer for the eve who had succumbed to the evil lurking inside her.

Theresa freed her fingers to sign, "How is it for you these past four years?"

"I've tried hard to obey the Law," she spoke, pointing to her discarded veil. "But I do not always succeed."

"You've not had possession again?"

Until today, she could have answered no, but one look at Eric and she knew it was no longer true. Ruth lowered her eyes, unable to lie to Theresa's face. "No," she said, touching her cheeks. "The Cleansing drove the demon from me forever."

Theresa gave thanks to God; her prayers had been answered.

"And you?" Ruth asked, staring deeply into Theresa's eyes. "There is a new pain on you."

"God has punished me for my disobedience." She paused, her hands motionless for several moments before she continued: "I have birthed three sons."

"They were not pure?" Ruth guessed.

Theresa nodded, her pain shining vividly. "I pray I will not be bought today."

Before Ruth could answer, old Mara interrupted, "Few eves birth three sons in four years. They will bid high for such a breeder."

"But they were all born corrupt," Ruth whispered near the ancient eve's ear.

"The priests will not disclose that information," The old woman whispered back. She shook her head sadly, signing, "Thank God, my breeding days are over. Maybe married days are over too. Could be God has finally forgiven me and will let me die soon."

"What will happen tomorrow?" Ruth asked.

"Priests come at first light: a house priest if husband's rich, an auction priest if poor. For you," she nodded to the young eves, "rich ones. But rich or poor, it makes no difference, you will suffer."

A shadow came over Ruth; there had been a small hope.

Without the veil, her expression was easy to read.

"Child, that is life. It will end soon enough," the crone's fingers admonished.

The girl nodded and lowered her eyes away from the old woman.

Mara snapped her fingers under Ruth's nose to get her attention. Reluctantly Ruth looked up, and Mara continued to sign, "I'll tell you this. The marriage bench is painful. But after a time it does not happen often and your body gets used to it. It's the inside you," she motioned to Ruth's chest, "that always bleeds a little — or a lot. Pray for God's mercy."

Ruth made no sign she'd heard.

The old woman moved closer to whisper in her ear, "I tell you a secret, an ancient one told many years past by an old crone like me." She had Ruth's full attention now. "When you know the time for mating, prepare yourself, rub down there." She pointed to Ruth's groin. "Rub it nice, so it feels good, so it makes you wet. It won't hurt so much." Ruth looked at her, puzzled and disbelieving. But the woman nodded. "Maybe do it when the husband doesn't come, then it feels *very* good." Laughing silently she moved off to join the older women.

Ruth watched her go, confused and frightened once more. Theresa whispered in her ear, "The old ones often say strange things. Do not listen to her."

"Why do you think she lives so long?"

73

"She must have sinned greatly."

Turning her back on the old woman, Ruth grabbed hold of Theresa's hands. "Let's not waste this day worrying of tomorrow. I want to share with you until they come for us, and I will use only speech to do so."

Two eves who'd been watching Ruth from across the barn now approached with hesitation. "Your crime was great to merit such punishment," the taller one signed, indicating her scarred cheeks.

"It was," Ruth replied shortly.

The two eves exchanged a look before she continued, "But still you are brought to the marriage block."

"Yes," Ruth acknowledged, wondering at her meaning.

"I too was guilty of a great crime," she said, speaking with words. "My punishment should have been Expulsion, yet I am here."

The smaller woman spoke, "I's from the South Region, brought north for the Expulsion inside a wagon. I's put in the Vatican fields, and now to the auction."

It was Ruth and Theresa's turn to exchange a look. How could this be?

"I's too come from the South Region, riding in a covered wagon," whispered a maiden, stepping out of the cluster of eves still standing near the food table. "The priest brings me here for the Expulsion, but instead I's sent to the marriage block."

"What does it mean?" Ruth asked.

"It means you should fall on your knees and thank God for his mercy," an agitated young woman announced in a loud whisper. "You are questioning the Church — the first sign of degeneration! Now speak no more of this before you spread corruption throughout the room!"

The small group of eves stared after her as she turned a bent back and shuffled off fearfully.

"She is right," Theresa acknowledged with a sign. "We should not endanger others." The four women nodded in agreement, and the little gathering dispersed. Ruth and Theresa moved off together.

"We must collect hay for our bedding," Theresa's fingers explained. "The later we wait, the skimpier will be the bed." Ruth nodded, noticing several others were already doing so.

Together they gathered enough hay to make a comfortable resting place before they returned to the food table and collected their heavily loaded plates. Easing themselves onto the makeshift bed, they leaned back against the wall to look out across the barn.

"This truly is the Best Night," Ruth sighed, relaxing into the straw. "To sleep all night in a soft bed . . . heaven on earth."

Theresa looked at the scarred, rebellious face of her friend, and raised a hand

74

to touch the discarded veil. "I haven't done that since my first child was born."

"It's been some time for me as well," Ruth admitted. She noticed frantic signing taking place amongst the eves, and looked about for the cause. Five young women had dared to expose their faces, and even three of the older eves, Mara among them. Ruth smiled. "Things look different this way. I'd forgotten."

Theresa spoke with sudden determination: "I too will use only speech until morning."

Ruth turned towards Theresa, and her smile deepened.

It was a night without sleep, not a wasted moment of freedom. But too soon dawn came creeping and relaxed attitudes disappeared. Veils were replaced and solemnity settled in. The eves sat motionless, waiting for whatever fate this day would bring them. Priests came throughout the morning to collect the newly purchased eves. And, as predicted, Ruth and Theresa were taken by a house priest, each to a home of great wealth.

Eric was still moving in a daze.

The moment he saw that number hanging from Ruth's neck, he'd given no thought to anything but her, even daring to approach the priest, to see if she'd react, to see if she remembered — a reckless act, for had the priest checked her file, Eric's name was certain to be found there and that would have led to serious trouble. But it was worth the risk for that small moment of connection, to perceive the person behind the veil before sanity returned to move him deep into the crowd. But still he kept her clearly in sight.

This was not Eric's first auction. Like others who lacked the bride price, he came for the thrill of the forbidden and the dangerous. Unlike others, however, he understood that the danger came not from the eves but from his own needs and desires.

He'd seen number 775 hanging from an eve's neck at his first auction, but he knew instantly she wasn't Ruth, even through the heavy veils. Yet seeing that familiar number made him realize that one day it *would* be Ruth on that platform — and he would know it when she was.

And so he had.

Eric had witnessed the bride-viewing before without any compunction. But to see Ruth being treated so callously had suddenly sickened him to the whole process. He had to leave.

Yet when the bidding started later that day he was back to witness the sale of number 775.

Eric noted the buyer, and when the man left the auction, he followed after, trailing him to his home. Even after the man passed through the massive gates that led into the fenced courtyard, Eric remained standing outside the property.

To keep their eves contained, all households in New Eden had enclosed courtyards, but few were so tall or made with such perfect craftsmanship; it was an important family.

She be another man's wife for the rest of his life, he thought in sudden despair. And there ain't nothin' I can do.

Still, he waited through the night, and when the house priest emerged in the early dusk of morning, Eric followed him through the deserted streets to the auction hall. The priest disappeared inside, and Eric hurriedly backtracked, hiding within the shadows of an alleyway.

A little later, the priest returned with Ruth shuffling six paces behind, covered head to toe in a black, tent-like sheath worn by adult eves on the rare occasions they appeared in public. Circular metal bands at the top, middle and bottom of the tent held the rigid material away from any accidental contact with her body.

As the priest approached his hiding place, Eric sunk deeper into the gloom. But once the cleric passed, he quickly returned to the entrance, crouching low so he could claim the attention of her downcast eyes through the narrow gap in the sheath.

There she was.

He whispered her name so very softly, but still she heard. Ruth eyes lifted; catching sight of Eric's face they widened in surprise and pleasure. Her step faltered and she glanced towards the priest, confusion darkening her gaze before her feet continued their quick, shuffling walk. The priest hadn't noticed.

Eric followed after, dogging their trail all the way to her husband's property.

When the gates swallowed her up, he finally turned his steps towards home, confused by his actions and by the pain in his chest.

Ruth was led to the eve-cloister and put inside a small room that contained only a wide wooden bench bolted to the floor. Standing alone, Ruth could hear the low droning of the priest from the room next door, but it meant nothing to her. She was still recovering from the shock of seeing Eric on the street. For one brief moment she'd thought he was to be her husband, and all the fear had fled from her, only to come rushing back more vividly than ever, and with it the pain of disappointment — and some other pain she couldn't identify.

The voice next door stopped abruptly, and a moment later the priest entered to stand before her. "Kneel," he commanded. She did so, lowering her hands and

76

face to the floor in the traditional pose of subservience, while the priest intoned:

"You will honor and obey your husband.

You will not entice him into sin or corruption,

You will forsake all evil thoughts and lures of the Devil.

You will bear him many pure sons,

Free of corruption in spirit and flesh.

Until death parts you from him,

You are now pronounced the wife and property of,

John Andrew Kininski."

There was a short, profound pause. "Rise," he ordered. And once she had done so he stated in a cold voice, "In this household you will be known as Number-Five, that is your room number. Is that clear?" Ruth nodded obediently. "Remove your trousers. When your master arrives, kneel upon the mating bench with your face to the wall." Abruptly, he left the room.

Ruth remained frozen to the spot. She'd never been so afraid. Then the door opened, and she caught only a brief glance of booted feet before removing her trousers and positioning herself upon the bench, her body shaking with terror.

The man approached quickly, pushing her forward until her head rested on the planks and her backside was poised towards him. Hard fingers grabbed her thighs as the other hand pushed up her long skirt. Something was shoved between her legs. She tensed. The next moment a stabbing pain shot through her. She reared upwards, crying out in agony before a strong hand forced her roughly back to the bench. She thought she was being beaten to death from the inside. It took every bit of training not to cry out for mercy.

He gave a final hard thrust before shuddering spastically and sagging over her. A moment later he had moved away from the bench. She heard him rearrange his clothing and leave the room.

Ruth curled into a ball, clutching her stomach, her body cramping painfully. She felt a deep sickness way down inside. There was blood smeared on her legs, and Ruth thought she was dying. She welcomed the thought.

77

# CHAPTER 9

IT WAS a large household, this new home of hers, and Ruth and the other eleven brood wives were responsible for its smooth functioning. This was what Ruth was trained for, and she fit easily into the routine.

After the harsh supervision of school priests, these domestic-overseers seemed mild in comparison. It was easy to stay out of trouble, as long as the work was done and one kept her indiscretions confined to the eve-cloister.

The house priest had little contact with the eves, appearing only for Saturday Mass and confession, Sunday Mass being for males.

Life here might have been bearable, except for that fifteen minutes every day when she was mated by her husband, the unknown assailant, for Ruth saw nothing beyond his booted foot. Not even a brief glance during the cleaning of the household, as all was regulated to ensure that no eve ever crossed paths with her husband, nor any male that was not a cleric or a eunuch.

As she'd done during her sessions with the discipline priests, Ruth managed to find a haven in her mind, a small corner to hide in while her body endured the agony of the Mating Rite. And just as the old crone had predicted, there grew a terrible aching deep within that consumed her. Nothing the priests had done could equal this daily punishment.

In her classification as a new bride, her husband was expected to mate her every day for three months. Only her bleeding time brought temporary release, as would a pregnancy. Sexual relations were not permitted during gestation: mating was for procreation only. Yet, every day, Ruth prayed she would not conceive. It was her only hope of a permanent end to this torture.

Brood wives who did not conceive within a two-year period were declared barren and removed from the breeding inventory and the household. Reclassified as worker wives, they were sent to labor in the fields or industries of their husband. But this practice was only for the wealthy and the middle class. In families too poor to replace a barren wife, she would remain to continue her vital role inside the household: to grow and cook the family's food, sew and clean their clothes, and keep the home free of dirt and vermin. Inside a royal household, however, where a wife had no other function but to produce an heir, she was given only a single year to conceive before the marriage was annulled and a new wife presented in her stead.

Three months after her marriage to John Kininski, Ruth was put on the Standard Mating Roster, taking up her position as wife number-five in the mating rotation; a replacement for the former number-five wife, whose sudden death had brought about Ruth's arrival into the household.

Mating would now be in numerical order, and with a dozen wives married to a middle-aged husband, Ruth would not be mated more than once a week — usually less. Yet still she prayed to be released. For whether it was once a day or once a year, she could not bear the pain the mating act brought to her entire being.

And there was another compelling reason for craving release.

In all but the poorest homes, male children were taken from their dame at the moment of birth. She was not permitted to see him or touch him. The only connection was the milk she expressed for his feedings every day and night for six months. When it ended, she was once more available for the mating bench. If no milk was required, she knew the child had been declared corrupt and sent back to Satan.

The eve would have to live with the agonizing knowledge that it was she who wavered and allowed evil to enter her womb, that she alone was responsible for the corruption of her child. And male infants were found corrupt with dependable regularity, especially within the more affluent families.

Female infants were rarely sent back to Satan, as all females were born corrupt. Only newborns who displayed their corruption outwardly were pronounced unfit to reside in Eden, those who were physically deformed or sickly. But if whole and healthy, the eve babes were left in the care of their dame until school age — then they were taken, never to be seen again.

Ruth remembered the separation from her own mother — short and shockingly painful — and the unforgettable look in her mother's eyes as the priest took her away with barely a moment's warning. Suddenly he was there, and her mother was gone.

Now Ruth prayed every day for forgiveness and tried determinedly to follow the teachings of the Church in a way she'd never done before. Like Theresa, she no longer removed her veil or practiced unauthorized speech. She would give up anything to gain release from the mating bench.

And at last it happened.

Her prayers were answered.

Though it would mean hard labor in her husband's fields, working dawn to dusk in heat or cold or pouring rain, under the constant threat of the foreman's lash, to Ruth this was a liberation: the Mating Rite was over.

# CHAPTER 10

ONCE MORE declared fit for the Mating Rite, Theresa waited for her husband. She did not feel fit.

Unconsciously, a hand strayed to her abdomen, where so short a time ago it had bulged heavily with child. Even now her stomach remained distended, not quite returned to its natural shape.

Realizing where her hand had strayed, Theresa removed it. I won't go there again, she thought bitterly.

There was a hard edge to her now, acquired since her arrival to this household.

As was customary with new brides, her husband had mated her every day, cold and silent, without regard or tenderness. But when months passed with still no conception, her husband broke silence, ordering her to exchange places with the other wives at their time for mating.

It had not been difficult. The two harem overseers were heavily addicted to the demon-drug, or neuter madness, as it was nicknamed, because it often caused sterility and eventually drove the user insane.

Covered as they were in bulky clothes and a heavy veil, it was a simple matter for Theresa to exchange rooms with another and wait to be brought out to the mating chamber by a distracted overseer.

To her great grief, Theresa finally did conceive, and for all the months she awaited the birth, she prayed the child would be born human. But it was not to be. The baby was pronounced corrupt, a Spawn of Satan.

She did not know how to bear this fresh pain. Silently she raged at herself, at the priests — at God.

Within six weeks she was back on the mating roster, and within another five, she was pregnant again. But this time she held out no hope. As her belly grew larger, her heart grew colder, and when the child was declared impure, her heart solidified completely. Now only her rage remained.

Theresa heard her husband's heavy tread coming down the corridor. Quickly, she peeled off her trousers and climbed onto the mating bench, assuming the position as Patrick Marchelie reached the mating room door.

She knew in an instant that things had altered since their last coupling.

The door was kicked open with tremendous force, smashing against the wall, and making her rigid with fright. It was closed with the same violence, and a moment later she was grabbed by the neck and wrenched off the bench, her face slammed onto the floor.

"You drop another demon between those legs," he hissed fiercely, snapping her head savagely from side to side, "and I'll cut you in such tiny pieces, even Satan won't recognize you."

He flung her against the wall, and ordered her back to the bench. She pushed herself up, legs weak with terror, and scrambled onto the mating bench. She was never so terrified in her life.

Again she was grabbed, cruel fingers digging into the tender flesh of her thighs as her legs were wrenched apart with brutal force. Then he mated her.

It was the most savage beating she'd ever experienced.


Patrick Marchelie was in a state of near panic. Not one son had been declared human in almost four years. He could feel the Great Prize slipping from his grasp, and he was powerless to stop it.

More powerless than he knew.

For he was trapped in an elaborate and long awaited plan to bring down the entire House of Marchelie, an act of revenge conceived from a feud so ancient it was no longer part of his family's history.

During those first two decades on New Eden when the refugees from Earth struggled for survival and then for positioning, Toni Marchelie went into business with a man named Pascal Lambert. At a time when Lambert was short on cash from a second and unwise venture, Marchelie began pressuring his partner to expand their holdings. He then offered Lambert a loan at zero interest, assuring him that he needn't make payments until his second business was stabilized. The written contract was just a formality. Lambert took him at his word. But when the loan came due, Marchelie went directly to one of the Magistrates — commoners, happy to receive large cash donations — and in less than an hour, Marchelie became sole owner of the business.

A short time later, Lambert's second enterprise folded completely.

To feed his many wives and children, Lambert was forced to take on whatever jobs he could find: usually at the tannery or slaughterhouse during the day, and at night, in the beer houses or other less savory establishments.

Lambert tried hard to put the past behind him and focus on a brighter future for his sons. But by the time his sons were grown, any opportunity to become something greater than their father was forever closed to them — as it was to all New Eden's young men. It was this that turned the hurt and anger he felt at Marchelie's betrayal into bitterness and vengeance.

And so began a legacy of hatred, passed down from one generation to the next, for over nineteen hundred years, until, at last, one descendant stood in position to extract payment.

It was Cardinal Lambert who secretly ordered the birthing priests to declare every Marchelie son human — until Patrick became certain he would win the Father Bull title. Then, gradually and inexorably, the pure births began to fade away, leaving him just four births short of the prize.

Lambert had also taken measures to ensure that Marchelie was given every loan he applied for, at a high rate of interest, with no pressure to make payments.

The cost of a proven brood wife had become exorbitant as the eve mortality rate increased, yet Marchelie kept bidding on the best breeders, even using money from the family business to do so, desperate for those last four sons. And, as expected, he eventually took out several large loans.

With so few births standing between him and the title, Marchelie knew he was certain to win it. He *must* win it.

At the next bride auction, Patrick spent heavily, increasing his already burgeoning debt.

He began neglecting the family business, spending his days trying to utilize the maximum number of mating rites permitted in a twenty-four hour period — even using illegal substances in the attempt. And when he could no longer perform properly, he refused to stop trying. Taking his frustrations out on his wives, beating them unconscious, and sometimes this would excite him to an erection. But he was over fifty and feeling his age. He could not continue this way. He began forcing his eldest son to take his place at the late night matings.

At first the younger man had refused, appalled his father could even suggest such iniquity. But after several beatings with a horsewhip, and a reminder that his inheritance would be nothing without that title, Peter finally complied.

During the dark hours after midnight, disguised in a long cloak and hood, he would ring the bell outside the door to the eve-cloister belonging to his father. The drug-fogged overseer would notice nothing amiss as he escorted Peter to the anteroom beside the mating chamber to wait while he retrieved a wife.

But once she was delivered to the chamber, Peter could not bring himself to do such a disgusting act. It went against all that the Church had raised him to believe. Instead, he waited quietly, letting the time pass until the mating should

83

have been completed.

The eve remained positioned on the bench, suspended in terror while she waited for whatever this new torture would be, and when it didn't come, she wondered . . . .

Did they even know it wasn't my father, with their faces to the wall and not a word spoken? Peter would speculate. Not that it would put him in any danger. Eves would never speak out against a man, not unless directly questioned. Still, he was curious.

The eves, of course, did realize it was not their husband during these late night non-matings, for he never missed an opportunity to inflict some form of abuse on them.

With four sons still between him and victory, Patrick continued to drive himself too hard, forcing his body into feats of virility a younger man would find a challenge. He could feel his dream crumbling, and with it his entire family's future.

Without that title, he could never hope to repay all the monies he'd borrowed. Already he'd been given several extensions. Soon they'd demand payment in full, and if he couldn't deliver, the business would be forfeited to the loan companies. He and his large family would be sentenced to debtors' prison, the younger sons made wards of the Church, no better than bastards.

The stress was taking its toll. He couldn't eat or sleep, and the slightest provocation would send him into an uncontrollable rage, lashing out at the nearest person to hand.

The whole household seemed to be holding its breath, waiting for something to give. And, at last, it did.

Theresa was married to Patrick Marchelie for almost three years when he suddenly collapsed and died during his fourth mating of the day. The unfortunate female was held responsible for his death and sentenced to a public whipping.

Marchelie's entire extended family was arrested shortly afterwards: his forty-one adult sons, along with his brothers, uncles, cousins, second cousins, and all sons who'd reached their fifteenth year. Each would be sentenced to life in debtor's prison, their marriages annulled. His twenty-two younger sons, grandsons, and all other underage Marchelies, were made wards of the Church, their fates sealed.

Patrick's widows, and the now former-Marchelie wives, reverted back to Church property. There, Theresa waited in dread for her new marriage contract.

But the time for the bride auction came and went. The whole world was in mourning.

The Chairman was dead.

# CHAPTER 11

ERIC CROUCHED before the fire, a cup of strong tea and a piece of thick bread smeared with bacon fat his morning meal. It was a solitary one: his dame dead years ago, his father these seven months. He was left to live alone in the small, company house.

Eric heard the sound of hooves approaching, but he remained by the fire, listening as the rider dismounted and entered the miniscule courtyard. A moment later, an impatient knocking rattled his door. There was a long pause before a piece of paper was slipped beneath it. The visitor retreated, and soon the horse cantered noisily into the distance.

Eric picked up the note, crumpling it roughly before throwing it into the fire. "Damn yuh, Robert. Lets me be."

He'd been avoiding Robert since his return to his birthplace deep in the forest. But Robert had staunchly refused to forsake his old friend.

I don't needs his pity or his charity, Eric thought with spite. Both were dirty words in New Eden. He was coming to hate the sight of Robert, whose rapid rise through the ranks made Eric sick with jealousy.

Captain of the Chairman's Personal Guard! Just brown nose uh prince an' things gets easy.

He almost wished he'd told the Vatican priests all about Robert when they first came snooping round the school.

Won't have changed nothin', he thought bitterly. He gots a horseshoe up his ass. Well, he sure be untouchable now with the old Chairman dead and William sittin' on the throne, Robert snug at his side. And me stuck in these stinkin' mine pits forever. No! Not forever — I won't lets it happen!

Breakfast soured in his stomach as he remembered the ruination of his plans. Those events which promoted Robert's rise to power were the very ones that had stopped his own ambitions cold, and that knowledge twisted his insides into an ugly knot of hate.

All the years of plannin' and trainin' for nothin'! he thought with bile.

After his disgraceful discharge from the cadet corps, Eric had spent two years drowning in self-pity before rousing his determination to find another way out of the mines. Only one way lay open to him now: winning a title at the Triennial Championship Games and the cash prize and small land lease that went with it.

But which event? Strength, speed, or weapons skill?

By the age of thirteen, he knew his only chance lay in his great strength. I'll win the Samson Trophy, Eric decided, and immediately began training towards that end.

After passing into manhood, he returned to Mining Camp-6 and his childhood home. He quickly realized this community contained none of the equipment needed for a serious trainer. But he was not deterred. Instead, he developed new ways to hone his skills, spending most evenings — after a hard day in the mines — lifting great sacks of rocks over his head, ripping young trees from the ground, and running hard up the mountainside through the dense forest undergrowth.

Some nights, he would show up at the camp's gaming arena to challenge the men there to a wrestling match, three at a time. He always lost, but it took a little longer each time to defeat him.

Sunday afternoons found Eric in the city at one of the large public arenas, where he could match his skill against the strength of others in his field and use the official weights for the Pull & Lift category.

At nineteen, he was still too young for the Senior Arena, but he'd gained a strong reputation at the Intermediate level. And during the preliminary trials for the Championship Games, he'd moved easily into first place. He knew the competition would be much tougher at the Games themselves, when competitors from South and West Regions arrived, but he was still confident in his ability to win the Intermediate Title. And that laurel would gain him automatic entry into the Senior Arena at the next Championship Games in three years' time. And then he would win the Samson Trophy and the lease.

But now that wasn't going to happen.

Out of respect for his father's passing, the newly crowned Chairman had ordered the Championship Games canceled.

The cancellation brought disappointment to all in New Eden. It was an event the entire male citizenry looked forward to with great anticipation. For two weeks the Number One District of North Region would bulge and rock with the revelry and excitement of visitors from all over New Eden, some travelling hundreds or even thousands of miles to participate, or to watch and bet on the Games. It could take years to save the cost of the journey and months to travel on foot over challenging mountain terrain.

The cancellation of the Games had disrupted the plans of many, but nowhere was it felt with such misery as it was within Eric Wong.

When the Games resumed in three years' time, he'd be too old for the Intermediate Arena. And without that intermediate title, his lack of years would put him at the bottom of the standings in the Senior Division. He'd have to fight his way through the long ranks of well-seasoned competitors just to gain entry into the qualifying trials. He was not so very confident of doing that.

Realistically, he knew it would take him years to earn a top placement in the standings, where he need only beat a dozen men or so. Too many years trapped in the mines without family — or wife.

Wife . . . .

Eric let out a long sigh and tossed the last of his tea into the fire. Grabbing his lunch, he headed for work. It wasn't far, less than a quarter mile from the camptown. He walked it alone.

Upon his return to the mining camp, Eric made a critical mistake. Encountering his old nemesis, Benji, now a man of 23, it suddenly galled Eric to remember that he'd been under Robert's protection the last time they'd met, unable to defend himself against the big bully.

A small boy no longer, but a great, strapping youth with a bitter edge to him, Eric laid Benji out flat without a pause then leaned over him threateningly: "Yuh ever jerks me around, I'll kills yuh."

Benj could see he meant it and that he'd the strength and the crazies to do it. He got to his feet and left without a word.

Eric had no way of knowing that Benj had become a citizen of high standing in this tiny community, and that he now used his bullying aggression to stop arguments that might threaten production, or to keep men from seriously wounding or even killing each other in drunken brawls — a highly dangerous thing to do. During cave-ins at the mines, it was Benj who took charge: shouting orders and getting everyone mobilized into action, but he'd be the first one in to rescue the trapped men. And when it was Benj caught underground, he'd refused to crawl to safety until he'd dug out every man in his crew. Once he finally reached the surface, his hands were shredded and bloodied from clawing through the rocks in search of his crewmen.

He'd earned the respect of the whole community.

To be ostracized by Benj was to be ostracized by all. He declared Eric crazy, not to be trusted, and the camp listened. Benj's opinion was strengthened by Eric's obsession with training and the forms that it took.

The sight of Eric ripping small trees out of the ground, or disappearing for runs into the thick underbrush with a sack of rocks on his back, was cause for head shaking and knowing looks.

But they could not avoid all contact with Eric in this small community, and they were too afraid of his crazy strength to deny him access to the arena or the pub.

Only Eric's father and the camp priest understood his driving purpose.

Father Jim watched the shunning and did not intervene, though one word could have put an end to it. But the Church saw misery and pain as the lot of every man; the more he had to bear, the better for his soul.

Eric passed through the entrance to mineshaft No. 4 and stood on the lift with the rest of the crew. They were lowered jerkily into the darkness by pulley ropes attached to oxen on the surface.

When they reached the bottom of the deep shaft, they could see the eve laborers waiting as usual with their overseer-foreman. His long hair, pulled back in a tight bun, was dyed a bold yellow that proclaimed his status as a foreman eunuch and distinguished him from a domestic eunuch.

The foreman informed the crew boss that the eve gang was a new one: a common occurrence. Eves did not survive if they worked the mines too long. They were rotated often. But today their overseer-foreman had also been replaced, a less common situation. Where the other had gone, no one knew, and it was wise not to ask, though rumor had it that he was heavily into the Satan drug, as so many eunuchs were, despite the high price they paid. The drug drove them all mad eventually, some much sooner than others.

Whatever the reason, his dismissal meant Eric's morning would be spent training the new eves and their foreman. This task was usually passed around a work crew, but here it had become Eric's permanent assignment, part of the camp's punishment. He was also assigned the unlucky task of rescuing eves trapped inside the cave-ins, because touching eves outside the mating chamber was extremely dangerous.

But Eric didn't care. It made him laugh to think how frightened they were of eves, and of him. He knew they thought him crazy. What did he care? He despised them all. Filthy miners with no hope of being anything else. He wasn't like them. He *wouldn't* be like them.

The rest of the crew hammered at the rock face while Eric instructed the foreman in his duties and showed the eves how to load the coal onto carts and pull them into the lift to be taken to the surface.

At the beginning of New Eden's history, it was the eves that dug out the coal and carried it to the surface on their backs. And then, later, after the lifts were installed to increase production, they continued to mine the ore, while women remained plentiful and cheap and didn't die so easily.

Eric grabbed a shovel from one of the eves to give instructions on how to use it correctly. When he handed it back, she snatched it from his hands and bent quickly to work, but not quick enough. He recognized her, or thought he did.

Eric started work on the rock face, disturbed and disbelieving. Could it really be her? And what if it was? Nothing had changed: she was still married to another.

He shook his head, as if to drive out the tempting thoughts that began rising up.

He'd spent the last three years trying to forget her — even believed that he had. But no, Ruth's image flooded his mind at the first hint of her presence.

Forget it, he cautioned himself. The gang will change in a few months, and that'll be the end of it.

But he could not restrain his curiosity. He pointed a finger at the eve and growled, "Gets some water." She brought the bucket and ladle, setting it down close to his feet. Eric crouched as he drank, looking up into her veiled face. Abruptly, he tossed the ladle back into the water bucket and motioned her away, attacking the rock face with renewed energy.

It be her!

Crazy thoughts flew into his head. He tried to banish them, but they were just too appealing. For two weeks he fought against himself, twisting and turning through sleepless nights. And then he began to plan.

During his evening run through the forest, he diverged from his usual route, creeping close to the eve barracks situated on the other side of the mines, well away from the camptown. No one but the overseer-foremen and the domestic-overseers came near here. It was forbidden and dangerous.

Hidden amongst the bushes, he studied the layout of the area.

He'd expected the foremen to be bunked nearby; they were neuters after all, but their barracks were a safe distance from Eric's hiding place and well hidden by the surrounding trees.

It was clear his objective wasn't going to be difficult: security was lax out here away from the city. The courtyard gates stood wide open, although several eves were outside washing clothes while two others stirred a great pot over an open fire. From the smell, Eric guessed they were making soap.

He saw only one domestic overseer with his distinctive dyed red hair, coming and going from the building. Eric could hear him clearly fussing and complaining at the eves. He said enough for Eric to glean that he was stationed there alone.

He watched their routine as they prepared for the night. The doors and shutters closed, and the gate-bolt pushed firmly into place, locking the compound securely.

The place was all in darkness, but still he lingered, not yet decided on a plan.

Finally giving up, he readied himself to leave when the squeak of a door hinge reached his ear. Straining, he peered through the night and could just make out the shape of the overseer slipping through a small side gate. Eric watched the man steal onto the path and disappear into the trees.

He was tempted to follow, but realized it didn't matter where he went, only what time he returned.

Eric waited through the night, dozing off and then jerking awake at the slightest sound, but the overseer did not return until close to dawn. Once he was back inside the gate, Eric turned his footsteps homeward, arriving at the camptown as if he'd been out for an early run before breakfast — crazy people did that.

For seven nights he hid within the bushes, watching the overseer slink away and then waiting the long hours for his return, certain now that this was his usual habit. While he plotted, Eric didn't go near Ruth or even look in her direction.

On the tenth day, he once again ordered her to bring some water. As he ladled up the liquid, he whispered low, "Waits outside t'night, I be there."

She picked up the bucket with hands that shook.

Now that Eric considered himself committed, the old excitement took hold. His appetite was wetted for adventure, and it had been too long a drought. Impatiently, he waited for night to settle the camptown before slipping silently from his house and into the woods.

At the eve barracks, all was still. Then he heard the familiar squeak of the gate and the shadow of the overseer dissolved into the blackness of the forest.

Quiet returned. Time passed.

With sudden certainty, he knew she wasn't coming.

He hesitated, almost ready to let it go, but he couldn't.

Eric crept through the gate and into the sleeping quarters. "Ruth," he called softly. A fully clothed figure sat up in bed but made no move towards him. Anxious to be gone, he strode over and scooped her up, leaving the other eves staring after them in shock. He wasn't concerned; they wouldn't speak against him unless asked directly.

Once outside the gates, he set her down, commanding, "Come." But she remained immobile. He had to pull her unwillingly onward through the darkened trail. He released his hold on her hand at the outskirts of the camptown while he made a careful examination of the buildings and streets. All was deserted.

When he returned for her, Ruth was gone. Swearing softly, he set off in pursuit, but she hadn't put much distance between them. Without a word he took her arm, leading her back toward the camp. Within minutes they were safely through the back courtyard and into his house.

Eric bolted the door, making certain the shutters were securely closed before stoking the hearth fire. Flames lit the room softly. Adrenaline pounded his heart, making him pant with excitement.

90

I done it! he crowed inwardly.

He looked at Ruth standing frozen where he'd left her.

"I feels like uh kid again."

But she made no sign he'd spoken.

Her reaction disappointed him. He had expected some resistance, but figured that once they were together she'd be glad of it, like when they were kids.

But we're kids no more, came the unbidden thought.

"Takes duh seat," he offered, pointing to a chair. "It be warm by duh fire."

Still she did not respond.

This was not how he imagined their reunion. At a loss, he ordered her, "Makes some tea," and was relieved when she did so.

Eric sat before the fire, watching the preparations. It was good to have company again, especially her. She offered the tea, eyes to the floor, her behavior completely circumspect.

"Gets some bread."

She went off to hunt for it inside the tiny pantry, returning with a chunk of dark seed bread. He took it, looking at her with irritation. "Yuh gots yurr face cover on. Yuh never does before, off it comes, first thin'."

But once again she was as still as a statue.

"Okays then, I be tellin' yuh tuh takes it off. Do it now," he snarled, his disappointment turning to anger.

No response.

"Damn it Ruth, do *somethin'*," he complained in frustration, reaching out to tug sharply at the veil, the action revealing part of her face. "Freakin' Gawd," Eric swore, jumping to his feet, shocked by the deep, scarring cross on her cheek. He had a sudden, sickening thought: "That be yurr pun'shment furr that other time?"

She nodded, eyes still properly downcast.

Hesitantly he pulled the veil away so he could see the rest of her face. "Gawd damn," he swore again, his guts turning over. "What else they does tuh yuh?" And when she only shook her head, he was gripped with a terrible fear. "Gawd almighty, they cuts out yurr tongue!"

Vigorously she shook her head, but he needed to see, sighing in relief at the small tip she exposed to him. Eric studied her mutilated flesh. He had caused this, and now he'd put her in danger again.

Remorse assailed him as he reached out to gently touch the scar tissue. "I never knows they be doin' such uh thin'."

Startled by his words and soft touch, her eyes flew up to his face before she could stop herself. What she saw in that brief glance shook her deeply. His face was full of pain — pain for her.

Ruth had prepared herself for tonight, determined to keep to the Law as much

91

as it was in her power to do so. She was resolute that the demon inside her would not possess her will — not this time.

After a year of laboring in her husband's fields, Ruth was chosen for a rotation in the mines. And from that first day, she'd been wrestling for control of herself: since the moment she saw Eric standing on the lift and something in her chest had leapt with pleasure. But immediately she'd dropped her eyes to the ground so none could see the emotions shining there, her good feelings turning to fear.

It was going to happen again: she would tempt him into sin, and they would both be punished — this time far more severely.

She prayed he wouldn't recognize her, though she understood that some knowing was beyond sight. And as the weeks passed, inner chaos consumed her. At times she was certain he didn't recognize her, and the momentary relief she felt was quickly overridden by grief and disappointment. How could he not know me? And this thought would shock her back to sanity, and her prayers would begin again.

She lived in dread of the moment he succumbed to temptation, and when it finally came, her hands shook — not from fear, but with excitement. She had to fight hard against the forces within her to regain her strength of will. She refused to be responsible for Eric's damnation or her own.

Now all the resolutions were eroding away.

Her slight head movement had caused his fingers to graze the unblemished skin on her face. It was the softest thing in the world. His hand strayed across her cheek, reveling in the velvety texture.

Ruth held her breath as the tentative fingers explored her face. She'd never been touched with such tenderness, and it sent warm shivers through her.

They both went very still, intensely aware of each other. Her scent curled its way into Eric's nostrils. She breathed his musky odor. Her pulse quickened.

A burning curiosity seized Eric, pushing all other considerations aside.


Ruth lay motionless as Eric slept, his arm tossed casually over her. How is it possible to mate with such pleasure? she wondered in awe.

Ruth remembered the mating with her husband with deep revulsion. She shivered and pressed closer to the young man beside her. Eric stirred, tightening his arm about her before drifting back to sleep. The feel of his hard muscles, so gentle against her skin, brought a smile of glee, and she wished he would explore her body once more with those wonderfully inquisitive hands.

Kneeling before the fire, he'd slowly removed her clothing, running his fingers tenderly over her skin. When he touched the old welts on her back, he swore softly. "My doin'?" he asked.

"Some," she said, and when he'd hesitated, she was afraid he was going to stop, but a moment later he continued his explorations.

Naked, she felt no shame before him, only an aching need. He removed his own clothing, and took her hands, placing them on his chest. She caressed the hard muscle covering his torso. Slowly, he drew her hands down to his groin. Ruth caught her breath as she felt the stiff organ. Was it this that had caused her such pain?

He guided her hands, stroking the organ gently. She was amazed at its silky surface. When he eased her onto the bed to cover her body with his own, she welcomed it. And when he entered her, she felt a deep sense of relief.

When they were done and lay together recovering, tears suddenly brimmed in her eyes. A lifetime of harsh training had not prepared her for sudden tenderness and passion. A single drop broke free and rolled down her cheek.

"Yurr cryin'," Eric said in awe. He could not remember ever seeing the tears of another. Fascinated, he reached out to touch it with the tip of his finger.

A wave of sadness abruptly dried the wetness from her eyes. "I have led you into sin again," she said, turning her face from his.

"I thinks I done duh leadin'," his tone was light. He put the tear up to his tongue, tasting it gingerly.

But she continued, "I've tempted you, as the catechism warns. You could be damned forever."

"I don't believes it," he stated simply, and bent forward to lick the salt off her cheek.

The sensation was delicious, exciting her beyond anything she'd yet experienced. And his face, so close to her own, brought uncontrollable urges. She stroked his cheek and the short stubble of hair growing on his head. Moving her face against his, she rubbed them lightly together, and this had led to further discoveries and deeper sins.

They had committed many sins this night. Not merely adultery, but fornication: mating face to face, she touching *him*, wrapping her arms and legs around him while they mated — not once, but three times.

They had touched tongues together and explored each other with their mouths. He'd covered her entire body, licking and sucking and tasting. She was sweeter than honey, he'd said.

And their greatest sin of all: the words they'd spoken while his penis moved inside her.

"Yurr my wife now," he whispered. And the thrill this gave her charged her almost unbearably. "Calls me 'usband," he urged. But she could not.

He withdrew his penis, and when she tried to pull him back, he resisted, "Say 'usband," he repeated huskily, using his tongue to make a hot trail between her breasts and up to her lips. Staring deeply into her eyes, he asked again, "Say 'usband."

"Husband," she whispered, almost inaudible. But when he entered her again, she chanted the word over and over, her excitement growing into an explosive spasm of exquisite pleasure.

When they were both finally spent, he promised never to bring her out again, "I won't be causin' yuh no more sufferings." He would not listen to her reminders of Law, that she was responsible for their crimes. "I never be hurtin' yuh agains," he repeated. "It's my oath — and don't say oaths ain't made tuh eves, cuzz I be makin' it."

She'd said nothing more because he could not know that staying away would be the cruelest pain of all. Why did everything pleasurable have to be evil?

The thought reminded her that she must soon return — dawn was not far off. She did not want to leave. It was heaven lying here next to Eric, his body warming hers. She closed her eyes to enjoy one last breath of sensual comfort.

She slept.


Eric woke to the sound of his front door crashing open. Two priests and several Vatican guards stormed inside the sleeping room, surrounding the bed.

"No!" he shouted, trying to shield Ruth from the blows of the priest's short whip. A club smashed down upon his back, knocking him to the floor. He lashed out with his foot, connecting hard. A guard staggered back, but six more were instantly on him, clubbing the fight out of him. Dazed, he watched two guards drag Ruth's naked body from the room while a priest chanted over her.

As he recovered his senses, he realized the danger he was in. This was no child's indiscretion. He'd committed adultery and fornication — and he'd fought men to protect an eve. The seriousness of his position overwhelmed him.

He threw himself at the feet of the priest, begging, "Fawder, forgives me, furr I have sinned!"

"Yes, my son, you let the child of Satan tempt you."

"Yes, Fawder, helps me, Fawder!"

The priest laid a hand upon the young man's head, "All may find forgiveness through the Church, my son."

# CHAPTER 12

RUTH WAS put on public display before the Vatican gates. For two days she was hung by the wrists on a raised platform for passersby to pelt her with garbage, mud and spit. On the third day she was to be flogged, branded on the forehead, and then have her tongue cut out. The flogging was to be administered by her victim, so that he might demonstrate his release from the spell she'd cast upon him.

During a public flogging, eves were presented with an exposed back. It was a tantalizing event and always drew a large crowd. Today was no exception.

A path had to be cleared through the tightly packed bodies to make space for the Cardinal of Discipline and his entourage, draped lavishly in ceremonial splendor, astride magnificent steeds of regal bearing.

The prisoner followed behind, surrounded by Vatican guards in black uniforms trimmed in cardinal red. The crowd hurled insults at Eric as the parade passed through the crowd to arrive theatrically upon the platform. The taunts continued as he was led to center stage and ordered to kneel and remove his shirt.

A discipline priest stepped forward, lash in hand.

Eric remained stoic throughout the punishment, the pain of the whip small in comparison to his humiliation, the crowd hooting and cheering with every stroke. After twenty lashes he was told to rise and put on his shirt, which clung to the pulpy, bloody mess of his back. He was led stumbling to the side of the platform, his powerful New Eden body allowing him to regain his footing, unlike his Earth ancestors, who would have been incapacitated by such a brutal whipping.

At the cardinal's signal, a priest approached Ruth. He was holding a sharp knife, and a sudden hush came over the throng.

Ruth's bladder had eventually given out, and the priest's nose twitched in disgust at the smell of dried urine. Mud and garbage clung thickly to her, and he had to be careful not to get the mess on himself. Taking hold of one corner of the baggy overvest, he cut it off her body with two efficient strokes of the knife, revealing the still clean tunic underneath. Then he slashed through the tunic's coarse material.

A collective sigh rippled the air.

He stuck the knife in the post above her head, and with dramatic flourish ripped the material wide open, exposing her naked back.

"Ah . . ." came the subdued moan of the crowd.

Eric looked upon her scarred back with shame and self-loathing.

How heavily she must pay for my mistakes.

As for Eric, his crimes had earned him a life sentence in the Vatican prison. But it seemed light punishment compared to the price they would exact from Ruth.

Vatican guards prodded Eric over to the cardinal, where he knelt to receive the benediction. As he rose to his feet, a priest stepped forward and presented Eric with a whip. After a moment's hesitation, he accepted. When he took up position behind Ruth, the crowd began to shout and whistle.

Eric stood flexing the whip between his hands. He could see the effects of two days of hanging by her wrists and was sickened anew. The cheering crowd was beginning to grow restless, but he didn't care. Through the noise of the spectators, he heard her urgent whisper, "I release you from your oath." But still he made no move. "They will Expel us both," she stated calmly, yet the words were enough.

Pausing only fractionally, Eric raised the whip and lashed at her naked back. A flood of cheering went up as it connected with her body. Doggedly, he continued the strokes. Blood splattered him, and Ruth cried out in anguish.

He stopped.

"Continue," the cardinal ordered. "You have twelve remaining."

"Please . . ." Ruth whispered weakly, terrified for him.

But he could not go on. Dropping the whip, Eric grabbed the dagger from the post and slashed at the ropes holding her upright. She collapsed against him, moaning in agony. Nobody moved, too stunned to react.

In one swift motion, he lifted Ruth over his shoulder and leapt off the platform, landing on the cardinal's horse and startling it into action. The animal lunged through the spectators, who scrambled back in fear as Eric hung on with desperate effort. Then the beast was free of the crowd and moving fast.

The cardinal shrieked out, "Stone them! Drive them from Eden!"

The spell was broken.

An animal sound rose up behind them. Something struck Eric's shoulder, and Ruth cried out once more as a rock hit her open wound. He shifted her awkwardly in front of him, laying her across the horse. She cried out again and fell unconscious.

The rocks and noise had frightened the beast to greater speed. Eric leaned across Ruth, holding onto the horse's neck, trying to point it towards the forest.

He could hear other horses in pursuit now as the beast lunged dangerously down the hillside while men leapt out of the way and shops and houses blurred past. Then they were clear of the city, the valley floor rushing up to meet them. If only he could make it to the trees. Just a little farther . . . .

Suddenly the forest was before them, and the horse stopped dead in its tracks. Eric flew over the animal's head, landing hard against a tree. Staggering to his feet, he looked for Ruth, and then he saw her: a limp pile on the ground. He scooped her up and ran for cover, grabbing the knife that had flown from his hand.

A blinding light exploded through his skull. Eric stumbled and almost fell, but forced his legs to keep moving. Shaking his head, he tried to clear it as the blood trickled down his scalp.

Diving into the forest, he scrambled low, pushing desperately through the underbrush. He could hear the horsemen leaving their mounts to follow on foot, but their missiles would be useless in here: the forest was too dense. And these were Vatican guards, not real soldiers. They didn't have the training of the Army.

He could hear the sound of the mob hurrying after the horsemen. Soon the woods would be filled with hunters, thirsty for vengeance. He needed to put distance between them.

His head was clearing now, his strength returning. He stuck the knife in his belt before once more draping Ruth over his shoulder. With a deep breath, he started to run, thankful for the hard years of training. And he knew these woods, how to move in them and how to use them.

The hunters did not.

They were used to the Expulsion Trail, a wide swath cut through the forest, once used as a road by the Ancients. It allowed the mob an easy target for their rocks and abuse; the recipients bloodied and often broken by the time they reached the edge of the forest. But rarely would anyone willingly cross into the demon wasteland; most preferred a savage beating by the mob over the unspeakable agony and defilement at the hands of Satan's evil fiends. Beaten unconscious and near death, the mob would catapult their limp bodies down the hill and onto the deserted flatlands, where ancient ruins lay buried under two millennia of rock dust. Those who regained consciousness would see these ominous shapes hovering around them and mistake the ruins for encroaching demons. It would send most insane, tearing the flesh from their bones in a desperate attempt to escape. There were few who retained enough sanity and mobility to find their way onto the vast and empty flatlands.

Hoping to slow the mob still further, Eric resisted the temptation to stay at the base of the mountainside; he ran up and across it instead. Eric kept a steady pace until his lungs were ready to burst and his leg muscles shook from the strain. He needed a hiding place.

And there it was: a tight knot of vines climbing the base of three trees that had grown together in a twisted loop. He pushed his way inside the foliage and fell to his knees.

Easing Ruth to the ground, he collapsed beside her, his breathing ragged and noisy. Through it, he strained to hear sounds of their pursuers, but the woods were quiet — he'd put much distance between them. He lay there listening, letting his breathing return to normal.

Suddenly he felt like howling in triumph.

They ain't never gonna forgets this day!

Eric felt his strength return as he viewed his rash act as a daring maneuver — only partially completed. They still had to reach the forest's edge, whole and able. He pushed aside what waited beyond the trees — that was wasted energy. There was no place left to go now for either of them, he'd seen to that.

Ruth moaned, and he covered her mouth to muffle the sound, but she didn't gain consciousness.

"Gawd in heaven, looks what I done tuh yuh," he whispered, appalled at himself.

With the priest's knife, he cut away the band of rope still constricting her wrists. Underneath, the flesh was raw and swollen. He was thankful she was unconscious while the blood returned to her numbed hands. Gently, he rubbed her limbs down to the fingers. She would hurt for days.

He removed the filthy scarf and veil, throwing them across the floor of the den with disgust. Next, he took off her urine-stained trousers, knowing how shamed she must feel to have done such a thing.

Reluctantly, he moved to her back, and with great care picked off the small bits of wood and dirt stuck to the wounds. He tried not to think how the blood came to be there.

When he was finished, he reversed her ripped tunic so that her back was protected. With the knife, he cut a strip off his shirt, wrapping it around her like a belt to keep the tunic tied shut. His own back was begging for notice, forgotten while he'd been on the move, but there was nothing to be done.

Eric cocked his ear: there were noises in the distance.

Painfully, he got to his feet. Lifting Ruth onto his shoulder, he abandoned their hiding place.

More confident now, he ran at an easier pace, sure that he could outstrip his pursuers. But after ninety feet, a voice yelled out, "He's over there!"

Ducking low, he forced more speed from his legs, making a zigzag course across the mountainside, running until his breath ached and his muscles were near jellied.

Again, he collapsed inside dense shrubbery, panting into the ground, listening for the approach of hunters.

They were getting close.

He put a hand over Ruth's mouth, and waited in complete stillness. Footsteps neared their hiding place but passed on again. Gradually he relaxed as the mob sounds grew fainter.

When he tried to move again, every muscle shrieked in protest. He bent to rub his strained calves and discovered Ruth watching him. Immediately, she shifted her eyes to the ground.

"Don't looks from me," Eric said tiredly, easing his leg muscles.

She brought her eyes up to rest on his face.

"I be messin' everythin' up real bad."

Ruth shook her head, amazed he could still hold himself responsible after what she'd driven him to. She made to sit up, but he stopped her.

"Yuh rests, gets back yurr strength," he said, stroking the stubble on her scalp. "I be gettin' us outta this." He said it with such conviction that she almost believed him. "I dunno what's gonna happen outside duh trees, but I be strong, we be OK."

With effort, she leaned forward and took his hand, moving it onto the hilt of the dagger. "Use the knife," she whispered. He stared at her in confusion. "It doesn't matter about me, I'm damned anyway. Save your soul. Go back with my blood on your hands. You'll be forgiven."

He pushed her hands away. "Stop it!"

But she forced herself to speak: "Better to kill me than live in eternal damnation."

He grabbed the knife and stabbed it hard into the ground.

He clasped her arms, thrusting his face close to hers and whispering passionately, "Don't yuh understands? I don't believes it! No Devil! No dam'ation! No Gawd! There be only yous and me and tryin' tuh stays alive!" His intensity dissolved and he said more calmly, "Yurr likes uh part of me self, how could I kills yuh? We be two halves of duh same blade. I be knowin' that since duh first day I saws yuh." Gently he helped her to lie down on her side. "Yuh rests now, wife," he said, close to her ear.

It brought a weak smile to her lips. She closed her eyes, and he thought her asleep when she whispered, "Husband."

He took her hand and they rested together in the shrubs.

But too soon it was time to move, before the mob realized they'd overshot their prey and started to backtrack. He had to force himself into action. Crawling stiffly from their hideout, he stretched his aching body in preparation for the next leg of the run.

A few moments later, Ruth emerged to join him. Pain etched her face but she made no sound.

"Does yuh thinks yuh can walks?"

"I'll try."

"Let's gets goin' if yuh cans." They started out, but she stumbled and had to balance against him, fighting off the dizziness. "Cans yuh do it?" She pushed herself away and nodded. Eric started off again, slowly this time. He was grateful that Ruth was keeping pace; he didn't know if he could carry her much farther.

Now they descended as they continued onward, gradually getting closer to the base of the mountain, but not too low — not yet. They came across a little stream and Ruth sucked up the liquid gratefully; it gave her the strength to carry on. After an hour, Eric stopped to whisper in her ear. "It can't be far, duh trees are startin' tuh thins. When I says run, yuh runs. Don't stops furr nothin', not even duh Pope 'imself. Yuh understands?" She nodded. "We goes then," he said, taking Ruth's hand and pulling her along.

Moving cautiously through the decreasing coverage, they crept down to the mountain pass. Ruth was panting hard now, her last reserves fading fast.

In the distance a shout went up, and a moment later Eric felt something whizz past his shoulder — an arrow! The bastards have changed the game! he thought in angry frustration.

Only stoning was permitted during an Expulsion, but these Vatican guards sought revenge by their own hand no matter the means. His insult was too great, too personal. But it was more than this, for they understood that Eric too had changed the game. That he was so profane, so truly corrupt, that he didn't need to be driven from the Garden but was seeking to escape it.

"Run!" he ordered.

They ran noisily, not caring now. But Ruth's legs gave out and she dropped like a dead thing. "Leave me," she cried out in her whispery eve way as Eric went to pull her up.

"No, damn it!"

Again he draped her over his shoulder, almost buckling under the weight. He steadied himself, pushing a wobbly trail through the trees. He was near giving up when the forest evaporated, the barren land suddenly in view. It gave him the strength to push on.

Howling a battle cry, he ran to the edge of the bank, feet closing in behind them. Then he was struck. Ruth gave a sharp gasp of pain and Eric stumbled. They fell to the ground, rolling crazily over each other to the bottom of the slope.

They were out of the Garden.

The hunters stood back from the bluff, not daring to come closer; quickly, they melted away.

Eric shouted after them, "I wins, yuh stinkin' assholes! I wins!" He laughed loudly, looking to Ruth — and the laughter fizzled out of him. An arrow protruded from her back.

Falling to his knees, he turned her over. Ruth's eyes stared into his, lifeless.

He leapt to his feet, screaming, "Cowards! Lousy, stinkin' cowards!!"

But only his voice echoed back at him. He was alone.

He returned to Ruth, cradling her in his arms, howling out his rage and loss. And when exhaustion forced him into quieter grief, his fingers stroked her scarred face as he spoke the forbidden words she would never hear.

Gradually it came to him where he was. Eric looked around, suddenly nervous. Nothing stirred but the wind out beyond the shelter of the mountains. It was so utterly barren.

And empty, he tried to remind himself, not a demon in sight.

Twirling columns of dust appeared from nowhere, making his hair stand on end. He'd been told about such things, that these were demon spirits. His gaze remained fixed on them as they skirted across the open plain, billowing wildly before gradually dissipating altogether. He shook himself, snapping out of his growing fear. Wind and dust! That's all they be! he told himself sternly, turning his attention back to Ruth. He would allow nothing to interfere with his last moments with her.

Eric gathered rocks and placed them over her body. And because he knew Ruth would have wanted it, above her head he formed a ring of stones with a cross in the center.

It would be dark in a few hours. He looked back at the forest with yearning but knew the hunters would be waiting to prevent his return. With no other choice, he faced the desert and began to walk.

# CHAPTER 13

ROBERT STAGGERED from bed, his head feeling like hell. He groped for the washstand, dousing himself in icy water, the shock of it making him gasp and sputter, but he felt fractionally better. Unsurprised, he saw he was still in uniform. It was heavily caked with mud and grime, the result of several drunken falls.

His personal aide entered with breakfast. "There's a clean uniform on the chair, Sir."

Robert grunted, the smell of food making him heave. "Take it away," he ordered, motioning at the tray. "Bring me a drink."

"Yes, sir."

The aide retreated hastily, returning with a shot of whiskey. Robert tossed it down his throat, shivering at the trail it blazed to his stomach.

My guts have soured, he thought, but considered it a fitting testament to his life. Through a booze-saturated brain, he reflected over the past six months — or was it seven? How long has it been since it all turned to vinegar?

Since the death of the Chairman. That's when it began.

William had cared nothing for his sudden position of power. Stricken by his father's death, he'd hidden himself away, seeing no one but his confessor, Father Gideon. The priest reminded the young Chairman of his responsibilities. He had a world to govern; life did not stop because he grieved. Then he'd offered William the assistance of the Church. The grateful Chairman had accepted, placing himself completely in their hands, so that he need not participate in the rule of his world. He signed what they placed before him and then retreated back into his consuming misery.

And so the Church teaches him to govern, Robert thought bitterly. They tell him when to rise, when to wed, when to bed, when to take a bloody piss. All without even the appearance of needing his opinion, or conceding that he might have one.

For Robert, this sudden influx of robed ones into the Palace was suffocating, as if he was back at school again. Only this was much worse. An inconspicuous child could escape their notice, but not the Chairman's personal protector and friend.

Some friend, he'd thought bitterly, and had raged inwardly at his feelings of helplessness.

Robert had always found ways to help the prince overcome his challenges. Now, for the first time, he could be of no service to William, not in his governing or in his grief. Even his role as William's protector had seemed redundant, with a phalanx of Vatican priests and bishops surrounding the young Chairman's every moment.

Then, months later, the news of Eric had arrived.

Robert had spent the past ten years trying to make amends for destroying Eric's life, for he held himself completely responsible for that tragedy.

If only I'd refused to tell him the way inside the eve school. Eric never would have tried it otherwise, despite his threat to do so. Why? he berated himself repeatedly. What made me send him to certain corruption?

Robert had visited the school as often as he could, anxious to shake Eric out of his lethargy. Finally, the boy seemed to regain some of his former interest in life, at least within the gaming arena. But he'd never regained his interest in people, shunning all attempts at friendship — not only mine, Robert thought.

Still, Robert had been amongst the spectators to witness Eric's Rite of Manhood, a typical coming-of-age ceremony for a boy of his class, shared with the other graduating students of that year. Eric's father, a big man like his son, had stood next to Robert and they'd cheered together as Eric passed his trials. But Eric had shown no pleasure in his achievement. And at the ceremonial beer-fest afterwards, he'd barely acknowledged Robert's presence.

After leaving school, Eric disappeared completely from Robert's life, as if going into the mines had removed all vestige of his past. But Robert had been unfailing in his attempts to stay connected with his childhood friend. He'd offered money, beer, food, or anything Eric needed, although none of these overtures were accepted.

It was Eric's father that Robert spoke with when he called. They would share a jug of beer while the older man boasted of his son's strength and explained Eric's plan to win the Championship Title, Robert being the only friendly ear on the subject.

Eric's ostracism had made Robert more determined not to abandon his friend, and the visits with his father had kept him connected. But after the old man died it became increasingly difficult to keep steady in his devotion. Robert had visited rarely, and was almost resigned to the fact that there was nothing he could do for his childhood friend.

And then Eric was arrested.

Robert had gone immediately to William, begging him to intercede, but the Chairman only stared at his captain uncomprehendingly, and that expression was painful to witness.

Until the Chairman's death, William had performed his duties as the future Supreme Magistrate with impressive dedication, for here was something the prince could excel at without fear. Unmolested by his brothers — whose deadly wrath was kept at bay by the king's own guard — William had spent six years engrossed in dusty law books or in close study of Supreme Court sessions.

Feeling secure amongst his books, and often able to engage his father in discussions on points of law, William became immersed in the whole legal process.

But that time had come to an end.

The young Chairman had shaken his head at Robert's request, a vacant look in his eye. He did not know this law. Robert should ask Bishop Stehr, he would know what the law permitted.

Without a word, Robert had turned away; there was no help here.

He'd gone to the Vatican prison to speak with Eric, but visitors were not allowed, not even Captain of the Chairman's Personal Guard. As he'd left the Vatican gates, he stopped to stare at the eve tied in the docks. Was it the same one?

He didn't know, but the old guilt came crashing down on him.

He had to help his friend.

Though it cost him dearly to do so, Robert had petitioned Bishop Stehr for an audience. His Grace had refused to see him. Desperate and frightened, Robert forced aside his own frustrated fury to hunt out some other avenue of escape. Only one option remained. Commander Belcher, Counselor to the Chairman and Supreme Commander of the Army, the third most powerful man in New Eden. Robert wondered where the Commander stood amongst all these priests and Bishops. But of course he stood, as always, behind the royal chair, advising when asked, keeping silent vigil when not. Certainly, Belcher held no sway in this court. William looked only to his friends in the Church. But Robert was desperate. He'd sent the Commander an urgent request for an interview.

It came too late. Eric was already driven from Eden, his body and soul lost forever.

Once more, Robert had gone to William, this time for leave of absence, saying only, "I've got my own grieving to do." Silently, his friend had signed the order.

Robert had handed command of the Chairman's personal guard over to his First Lieutenant, and then proceeded to drink himself into numbness. He'd spent his nights in the beer houses, his days in bleary solitude.

That was over a month ago.

Rousing himself with effort, Robert changed into a clean uniform and headed for the stables. As captain of William's personal guard, he was permitted unlimited riding privileges. It was the only thing about the service he truly enjoyed, and he seldom missed a morning ride, though these days it was closer to noon.

Leaving the palace, he rode hard through the trails of the royal hunting grounds, stopping at last to rest his winded horse. Head still aching, he collapsed under the thick shade of the common trees and immediately passed out. He woke much later to the sound of voices. Unbelieving, he peered cautiously through the foliage. William was riding with his two older brothers, all carried hunting gear — and they were alone.

A terrible urgency came over Robert.

Quietly he led his horse a good distance from the trio before he remounted and approached noisily, chanting a lewd limerick he'd heard the night before,

"There once was a miner named Mick,

Who went everywhere with a pick.

It was his fine friend,

Loyal to the end,

'Til it screwed him right in the—

My Lord!" he exclaimed, appearing surprised at coming upon the small party. He bowed deeply to the young Chairman.

"Robert!" William returned in surprise, genuinely pleased. "Have you returned?"

"Yes, Sire," Robert replied, bowing once again. Then he looked around as if noticing for the first time, "My Lord Chairman, where are your guards?"

William laughed. "They are here," he said, indicating his brothers.

Continuing the pretense, Robert dipped his head slightly at the princes, acknowledging their loyalty. "But who shall protect *them*?"

William looked uncertain at this reasoning, and announced, "You see, Robert, I need you. You have been gone much too long."

"Yes," he said. "I have." He looked to the brothers: "How goes the hunt?"

"Not well. We've seen no signs."

"What's your game?"

"Blue boar."

Robert's eyes narrowed. Blue boar was a nasty creature at best, but during rutting season, wisely avoided. "At this time of year?"

Thomas, the elder, smiled, "It spices the kill."

"Of course."

"They're going to show me the best way to bag one," William announced, trying to sound enthusiastic.

"Shall we proceed?" asked Thomas.

They rode through the fading afternoon but without success, finding only packs of doggers who growled fiercely at the riders before dashing deeper into the forest.

Attempts by New Eden's ancestors to domesticate these canine-like animals had failed utterly. Their dog-like appearance and behavior had convinced the Earth-born survivors that they could replace the loving and loyal companions they'd lost. But these beasts had no such tendencies, never losing their fear or their ferocity. All efforts at domestication were abandoned.

The light was dimming when the riders finally agreed to head for home. As they swung their horses about, the two princes exchanged a look.

"A race?" Henry suggested.

William's face tightened: he did not like speed.

Robert said quickly, "My Lord, I must decline. My horse is footsore. And as your personal guard, protocol demands that you remain with me."

William gave him a grateful look. "You go on," he told his brothers. "I'll stay with Robert or he'll have me in irons."

With the barest of bows, the brothers took off at a fierce gallop. William and Robert watched their distancing figures in silence. At last the Chairman spoke: "I was sorry to hear of your friend."

Robert waved it aside. "It's done now, time to get on with things."

William turned to smack him on the shoulder. "God, it's good to have you back."

"It's good to have *you* back, Sire."

A flicker of pain crossed his face. "Yes, we've both been too long with the dead." Then he cheered. "But due to my brothers, I too have returned."

"What has happened, my Lord? I was surprised to see them with you."

William nodded. "It surprises me also. To be reconciled with my brothers is the answer to my prayers."

"But how, Sire?"

"They came to grieve with me. Thomas said it was time to put old wounds to rest." William laughed suddenly. "They thought *I* hated *them*! I could hardly believe it!" Robert merely grunted. "We've been together ever since. They've taught me their gaming tricks and how to gamble and . . . and other things."

Full of foreboding, Robert returned with William to the palace.

As the Chairman climbed from his horse, he announced, "There's a supper at Thomas' apartments tonight. Would you join us?"

"Willingly, Lord," Robert said with a bow.

106

Grinning widely, William slapped him on the shoulder once again before striding into the palace.

Seething with anger, Robert gave the horses over to the wrangler and marched to his office. The door crashed against the wall as he threw it open, startling the young officers within.

"Fuckin' hell!" they swore, before realizing who it was and leaping to attention.

"Why in the name of blue hell was the Chairman left unguarded?!"

"But, sir," First Lieutenant Biter explained hurriedly, "the princes — and the Chairman himself, ordered us off. What could we do?"

"*Anything!* Anything, but leave him unprotected. When I think what might have happened—" he stopped short, brushing a hand over his stubble of hair. "It was my responsibility, I should have been here. Well, it won't happen again, you can be sure of that." He moved behind his desk, ordering tiredly, "Alright, dismissed."

The officers turned to leave but were stopped by a broad figure blocking the open doorway. The old Commander let the soldiers pass, his eyes burning into Robert.

Once they were alone, Belcher said coldly, "It's a damn good thing I heard yuh say that, Soldier." And with a crisp turn of the heel, he marched angrily from the office.

Robert watched the retreating back of the Commander, knowing he absolutely deserved his disgust.

How could I have left him so exposed? he wondered at himself.

Because I thought the Church was there to protect him — and why weren't they? They know William's still vulnerable. Thomas would never give up the throne so easily.

Although married at sixteen, the young Chairman had yet to sire a son, no matter how often the Church insisted he wed. And until he'd produced an heir or two, he would remain a target for his brothers' ambitions.

But Robert was not about to blame his mistakes on the Church or anyone else.

Another friend almost destroyed by my stupidity — so wrapped up in self-pity. Well, no more!

He sank heavily into the hard chair at his desk, rubbing bleary bloodshot eyes. His head hurt like hell and he wanted a bath — and a drink.

He forced himself to concentrate. Obviously things were slack. I'd better shake up the company: impose some harsh discipline — starting with myself.

There was a sharp knock on the open doorway. He looked up and just managed to stifle a groan. "Come in, Your Grace."

"I won't take much of your time," said Bishop Stehr, closing the door. Then he turned on him fiercely: "Just what in damnation do you mean by taking off on a drunken binge, leaving William wide open to his brothers!"

Robert was sick and tired, and he'd guilt enough to deal with. He said, sarcastically, "What's the matter, cutting into your territory?"

The bishop inhaled sharply. "Don't get lippy with me, young man, your position here is not immutable!" He gave Robert a look meant to shrivel before stating angrily, "They have the Chairman completely bound to their will, and you're responsible for it!"

It occurred to Robert that the bishop was not referring to the hunting incident. Something else was in the wind. He said neutrally, "There's nothing I could have done to interfere in that relationship. Even you must know how highly he reveres them."

Stehr was becoming less certain. "But surely, as his friend, he would listen to you?"

"Not when it comes to Thomas and Henry. Is that what this is about? Have you been maneuvering against them? Stupid of you, after all the time you took perfecting him," he said mockingly, all his normal caution dissolved by a month of steady drinking.

But the bishop didn't react, he merely sat down, shaking his head. "No, there was not one move made against the princes. We simply underestimated their cunning." His face became drawn as he confessed, "*They* are turning William against *us*."

For a moment Robert stared at the bishop, as if not understanding. Then he threw back his head and roared with laughter.

# CHAPTER 14

THE BISHOP approached the dais, his stomach tightening in a sudden knot; it was not going to be an easy interview.

Since his conversation with Robert, the princes' influence over their brother had gained even greater strength. The captain was right, he was powerless to interfere.

There were some within the Vatican who thought Robert had been swayed to the princes' side, but the bishop knew better. Robert was as dedicated to the Chairman as he was to that poor, lost miner. He would do all that he could to protect William from his brothers and from the king's own excesses.

But would it be enough?

The Chairman was slouched upon the throne, one leg swung carelessly over an arm, his head bent in concentration upon ragged fingernails. Bishop Stehr prayed for patience as he bowed low before him.

William continued to pick at his nails. Without looking up, he motioned Bishop Stehr to rise. The bishop straightened, extending his hand. A long moment passed before the Chairman beckoned him forward. Not bothering to lift his eyes from his work, William leaned over to kiss the bishop's ring, then slumped back onto the throne, waving the older man away.

Bishop Stehr stepped back and waited.

A full three minutes passed in silence while the Chairman struggled with a stubborn bit of hangnail.

Fighting to contain his annoyance at this unprecedented disrespect, the bishop noted the other occupants in the room. The Commander, who stood rigid behind the throne, trying not to look anxious, and four of the King's personal guard: two at the door and two near the throne. Not quite a private audience.

Still without raising his head, the Chairman finally broke the silence, "My Lord Bishop, your private audience has been granted at great inconvenience, so be quick, my time is valuable."

The bishop sucked in his breath at this further irreverence. Controlling himself with difficulty, he managed to say levelly, "Your Majesty honors me by granting my request so speedily—"

"Yes, yes," the Chairman interrupted impatiently, "get to your purpose."

Thrown off balance, the bishop plunged in, "You have no sons and—"

"I have no sons . . ." William echoed, interrupting once more.

"His Holiness is very concerned. He—"

"I thank his Holiness for his concern. Is that all?"

The bishop's face reddened with anger, and in a tight voice he replied, "No, your Majesty, that is not all. His Holiness wishes to know how you intend to rectify this situation."

William leaned back in his chair to ponder the ceiling. "Hmm, interesting question." And for the first time he looked directly at the older man. "How many ways are there? I know of only one way to produce a son — or has the Church received some further enlightenment?" There was muffled laughter from the guards, and even the Commander could not successfully hide his amusement.

Bishop Stehr's eyes bulged with rage. Didn't this young halfwit realize he was being warned? How long did he expect his addiction to be overlooked?

"Don't play the fool with me! You are the Chairman, you must have sons!" The bishop paled, aghast at his own loss of control.

But William seemed only amused at the cleric's outburst. He nodded in agreement. "Yes, how could I not know the need for sons. Didn't the Church present me with my first wife when I was sixteen, and how many times since then have I been pushed through the marriage door — even on my coronation day the Church insisted that I mate, though I mourned my father's death." He leaned forward, his voice harsh: "I need no reminders from you! Or do you seek to give instruction? Is that the purpose of this visit? Will the celibate priest give lessons in begetting sons?"

The bishop's mouth flapped wordlessly at this sudden attack.

The Chairman continued: "The Church has always had an overzealous interest in my personal life. I have to ask myself what motivates such attention?"

The bishop managed to whisper, "We are merely acting as loyal servants, my Lord."

"Loyalty!" William exclaimed, pouncing on the word. He appeared to consider the point. "And exactly how is this loyalty to be demonstrated?"

"We are sworn to guide you to Salvation, to protect you and obey you in all civil matters."

The King repeated softly, "Sworn to *obey* me. Remember those words." Once more he returned to his relaxed position upon the throne, "Now leave me. I will not hear another word on this matter — not now — not ever."

The doors to the audience chamber closed upon the bishop with a solid thud. This was followed by a brief silence that was broken by the Chairman's howling laughter. The guards smiled openly. Only the Commander looked unhappy.

"What a burr I set under his robes!" William crowed, slapping his knee in triumph. "That was worth a year's taxes to see!"

"It might cost you far more than that, my Lord."

"You worry too much, they will do nothing."

"No one can survive the enmity of the Church, my Lord," Commander Belcher warned, and then hesitated. "Also, Sire, their concern *is* justified."

The Chairman turned suddenly grim. "I thought I made it clear, I will hear no more on the matter — not from anyone."

"Yes, my Lord," Commander Belcher responded, bowing low.

But William's good humor quickly returned. With a grin, he rose from the throne, slapping the Commander on the back. "Don't worry, Belcher, they'll swallow my insults and learn the lesson within: I'm no longer their mindless puppet, but their king. That is all, you will see."

The old soldier tried to look reassured but failed. "As you say, my Lord."

"Enough of this, I must prepare a feast in celebration of my victory."

The Commander's face became wooden. "Is it wise to jeer at a bested opponent, Lord?"

William slapped him on the back once more. "Belchy, you worry too much."

Pope Validus Leonardo IV shook his head in silent contemplation: All the years of waiting, of planning and preparation, has it all been in vain?

We were overconfident, that was our mistake, too sure of William. And, of course, we completely underestimated the cunning of his brothers. Damn their souls for eternity!

But we did make it so very easy for them. Like boys in the honey jar, we didn't know when to stop.

And there was William, such a willing accomplice: so devoted, so obedient, so innocent. How else could we have acted?

Wisely, he admonished.

Well, William is innocent no longer. Pray his rebellion ends as quickly.

He roused himself from speculation to cast a stern expression on the bishop before him. "You incompetent dolt, you let that young goat goad you into losing complete control of yourself and the interview. What do you have to say in your defense?"

111

"I have no defense, Your Holiness. I betrayed your trust, there can be no forgiveness."

"It was not my trust you betrayed, but God's," he answered sternly. "And as for the matter of forgiveness, that is too soon to judge. I suggest you occupy yourself in deep prayer. Perhaps you will have the cause of your weakness revealed to you. Now remove yourself from my sight."

The bishop backed out hurriedly, in obvious relief at being let off so lightly. As the door closed upon Stehr, a voice behind the Pontiff declared coldly, "He's getting old."

Validus turned to study the sculpted face of Cardinal Adam Vecker, his administrative assistant: an intimidating presence with his piercing stare and stony personality. Even as a baby he was known for his long silences and sharp gaze, inspiring the nursery priests to endow the illegit with the name of Monk. But upon his ordination Adam Monk had taken the name of Vecker, it being common practice for an ordinand to change their first or last name to that of a saint or former pope.

"Not old, Vecker, complacent," Validus said. "He's been in the palace since Alexander mounted the throne; he's not had much to deal with since." He laughed shortly. "I'd have given six month's revenue to see his face when Willie made that crack about giving lessons."

Cardinal Vecker allowed the image to amuse him, his thin lips drawing back narrowly for a moment before returning to their stern position. "What action will you take against this latest outrage?"

"No action."

The cardinal strode toward the desk. "Your Holiness, I have remained silent while you ignored the Chairman's acts of rebellion, but now I must strongly recommend that we reply to this insult."

"But we will, Vecker, we will. Today we were delivered a message: Treat me as a man and your King. And that is what we shall do. He has been insulted, and has hit back. It's within his sovereign rights." He leaned onto his elbows and looked sternly at his assistant. "William must be appeased and brought back to the fold willingly. Coercion will only drive him further from us."

"And if he takes it as a sign of weakness and never returns?"

"Then we pray for the quick arrival of a son."

"And how will that happen while he persists in this disgusting addiction? Do we pray for a miracle?" He looked away from the humorous glint in the Pontiff's eyes. "Damn those brothers! Why can't he see what their purpose is?"

"Let us be thankful that we can see it plainly enough. At the first opportunity, they will be exposed."

"Pray it won't be too late," Vecker said dryly.

112

The Chairman was drinking heavily, flushed with a heady feeling of power. Pleased with himself, he bragged openly, "I thought the old bugger would croak on the spot!" He imitated the outraged expression of the bishop, and a roar of laughter went round the table.

He looked expectantly at his two brothers seated across the table from him. Their response was more subdued. Thomas smiled crookedly while Henry raised his beer mug in a short salute. But it was enough. He felt accepted, at last worthy of his brothers' company. Swelling with a newfound pride, he smiled widely, toasting them in return.

From the corner of his eye, William saw an officer enter the palace dining hall to join the guards standing watch against the walls. "Robert!" the Chairman called out, "You've come at last! Did you hear of my victory today?"

"Yes, Lord," Robert said neutrally. He did not offer congratulations.

"Would you not honor my success?"

Robert could feel the gloating expressions of Thomas and Henry fixed upon him. He forced enthusiasm into his voice: "I have already offered up prayers of thanks for a King wise enough to teach God's own servants a lesson."

The company went deathly silent.

"For are not humility and obedience virtues to be practiced by all men — particularly those in skirts?"

A loud guffaw broke out from one of the revelers. Others slowly joined in, and the tension went out of William. Relieved, he pushed himself up and staggered over to Robert, smashing him heartily on the back. "Damn, you've a wicked tongue in your head. I salute it!" he announced, whipping his hand a sharp cut to the brow in an exaggerated pose. "And I toast it! We all toast it!"

He leaned over to grab a drink from the table, almost losing his balance. Pushing himself upright, he raised the mug over his head, shouting, "To Robert's tongue!"

The toast was echoed roundly, and all drank to honor it — all but the princes, who merely put the mug to their lips.

"Come, sit!" William ordered, dragging Robert back to his seat. "Where's your drink? Give the man a brew!" Robert accepted the mug and pretended to drink, joining in the banter of insults to avoid notice.

Every evening since his return to court, it was the same: the two brothers, with the aid of their noxious friends, kept the Chairman entertained and drinking late

113

into the night — before moving him on to other things.

Most of the revelers were passed out, or busy settling old scores in noisy skirmishes around the hall when Thomas bent over the very drunk William: "Are you ready to leave, my Lord?"

William stared up at him, a glazed look coming over his face. Without a word, he rose to his feet and followed Thomas unsteadily from the room, Robert and his personal guard closely in tow.

Outside, they mounted waiting horses, riding from the palace grounds and into the empty streets beyond. After many twists and turns, they stopped at a walled-in courtyard of such unusual height that the building within was almost hidden from view; only the topmost peak could be glimpsed by a passerby. Another uncommon feature was the entrance into the yard: a single door, barely wide enough for a horse.

The place held every appearance of a residence for worker wives, but it was not.

The party dismounted, and Thomas tapped a signal on the solid door. A peephole was opened and then shut again quickly. Moments later, a bolt was drawn and the door swung inwards to reveal a large well-armed man.

He stood aside to let the company enter, locking up the entrance again as several soldiers took up defensive positions inside the courtyard, while the remainder swept through the household.

"I gets duh man'ger," he mumbled incoherently, before disappearing into the three storey building. It looked dark and sleepy, the windows closed and shuttered.

A few moments later, a short, portly man arrived, bowing low. "Majesty, yuh honors me house again, yuh does."

Robert and William followed the proprietor inside and up a narrow staircase.

"Yurr chamber be gettin' readied furr yuh," he spewed unctuously.

As they reached the second floor, a male servant scurried from one of the rooms.

"All be done now," the manager stated with relief and pride, leading them through the doorway. "Majesty, yuh makes yurrself comforted."

William stretched out on a low couch, propping his back against the thinly padded arm. On the squat table near his elbow stood a clay teapot, a small round mug waiting beside it. The little man poured the brew into the cup. "My Lord," he said, offering it to William.

Robert stood watching, careful to keep his face neutral. William's hands were not steady as he blew at the cup briefly before sucking down the scalding liquid. With a sigh, he settled back onto the couch, eyes closed.

"I be back soonish, Lord," the manager assured William with a bow. As he

114

turned to leave, he saw the look in the captain's eye and trembled.

Once he was gone, Robert sank to the floor and prepared to wait. He wondered, not for the first time, what Thomas did with himself on these excursions. Robert was certain he didn't similarly indulge. Well, it was a whorehouse. Perhaps he passed the time in that fashion? No, he thought, he's spinning webs.

The Chairman was deep into the drug now, and Robert allowed his fear to come fully to the surface. How much longer did William have before the drug made him permanently sterile, or, God forbid, insane? Robert didn't know exactly when William began using the demon drug, only that it started while he was gone from the Chairman's side — wallowing in self-pity, he thought again with disgust.

And now, William is surrounded on all sides and the trap will soon be closing.

As God's anointed Ruler, the Chairman was expected to uphold the Law, both civil and canon; he could not flout it. Not even the Army could protect him from the Excommunication and ultimate Expulsion his drug use laid him open to. Their sworn oath of loyalty to the Chairman would be neutralized without the divine blessing of the Church upon him.

And if the Church didn't destroy him, the drug certainly would. Then Thomas would mount the throne.

And that fact, thought Robert, is the only thing saving William at this moment.

But William's new rebellion would not be swallowed long. They will begin gathering evidence, and will certainly act upon it if he doesn't return to docility — which seemed unlikely. The brothers have completely seduced him away from the Church.

Robert grudgingly gave the princes credit.

They've been clever, claiming the Church despised their father, and that it was William's friendship with the priests that provoked their anger towards him. The princes even insinuated that it was *they* who were instrumental in bringing William and their father together.

William eagerly embraced their lies — far more comforting than the truth.

The brothers laughed at him for letting the Church control his life, calling him Little Puppet with a pretended humor that gnawed at the young Chairman, who strove to prove himself unworthy of the nickname by adopting the views extolled by his brothers and then putting them into practice.

During these past few weeks, William had repeatedly ignored the summons of the Pontiff, and then today treated his ambassador with utter contempt. But this was not to be the end of his inflammatory behavior. William had plans to order the removal of every cleric from the palace, even Bishop Stehr. They would be permitted to return only to perform the weekly Mass for the palace residents.

Father Gideon, the Chairman's confessor — once considered his friend and protector — was to be summoned to court at William's convenience.

The brothers were very close to winning.

Time passed. The manager returning at regular intervals to administer more of the noxious brew while William lay in a stupor, oblivious to anything but the cup pushed between his lips.

Dawn was approaching when Robert went to the couch. "My Lord, we must return now."

William looked around in confusion. He tried to focus on Robert's face, but failed. "My faithful friend," he slurred, offering an arm to Robert, who helped him to his feet.

In the courtyard they were joined by Thomas, who carefully avoided Robert's eye. Together, they put the Chairman on horseback and navigated him through the narrow gate. Keeping his mount between them, they made their way back to the palace.

# PART TWO:

## *ANCESTORS*

# CHAPTER 15

"MY LORD! Wake up!"

The persistent nagging of his privy servant finally roused William from a sleep thick with drugs and alcohol. He cast a bleary eye at the man and growled in annoyance.

"Forgive me, Majesty, but the Commander has sent word that your presence is needed at once!"

William allowed himself to be pulled from the warm covers. Cold water was splashed over his head and a steaming cup of liquid pushed into his grasp. Shivering, he tried to drink it down as the servant forced reluctant limbs into the ceremonial garb. The cloth was heavy and uncomfortable, making William moan in protest: "Baldwin, what are you doing to me?"

His only answer was the cinching of the sword belt. The well trained servant knew an emergency appearance required an imposing presentation. Urging the Chairman into leather boots, he panted, "Quickly, Sire, your guards are waiting!" Then he half pushed William into the hallway, where Sergeant Perez took hold of the Chairman's arm and propelled him forward, guards encircling him protectively.

"What in hell's going on!" William demanded, extracting his arm from the sergeant with a violent jerk.

"Commander's orders, Sire. Yurr Lordship needs tuh be on duh spot right quick."

"What *spot*? What in damnation's happened?"

"Ain't knowin', Sire, but it must be somethin' 'orrible."

William pushed ahead of the soldiers, increasing the pace. As they filed downstairs, he saw Commander Belcher and Robert waiting on the bottom landing. Belcher held up a hand to forestall the Chairman's questions, nodding towards the entrance hall below. A squad of nervous soldiers was marching past, and within their midst was a lone figure.

William and his guards stared in appalled disbelief. It was an eve, yet unlike any they'd seen before.

She did not shuffle, but walked like a man: her long legs striding with a strong, confident gait, her spine straight and erect. She was easily taller than everyone in the room. Her head was uncovered, allowing thick black hair to flow freely down her back. The young face was barely screened by a filmy piece of material, held there with one hand and revealing much of her dark amber skin. The robe she wore was as long as a priest's, but the lightweight fabric outlined every curve of her body.

She looked about her, studying the palace with open interest. Her gaze fell upon the men standing frozen on the stairs, who recoiled in horror. William averted his head sharply as her eyes settled briefly on his face, and when she shifted to Robert, he cringed but held his ground, though afterwards he could not have said what he'd seen.

As she passed out of sight, William looked to the Commander, who stated evenly: "A miner found that eve in the forest with a man as strange as herself. The miner immediately ran off to raise the alarm at the nearest guard station — but he heard the stranger ask for an executive."

Such an archaic word, William thought.

"When your soldiers located them, they were lying on the ground, so weak they had to be brought to the city by litter. Again, the stranger asked for an executive. Then a priest arrived." Belcher stopped to clear his throat. "In light of recent events, your men refused to release the prisoners over to him, as he demanded."

Still recovering, William only nodded, thinking, Is this how my soldiers interpreted last week's removal of the clergy from the palace? Thwart the Church's servants in every way. Not *only* the cleric removal, an inner voice reminded him. Yes, I've been rebelling in many ways. And now my guards carry out what they perceive is current royal policy.

"I've ordered the eve put in a cell," Belcher continued. "That priest is inside the audience chamber, screaming for their immediate Expulsion. I thought you'd want to examine the stranger for yourself, Sire."

William knew how difficult it was for Belcher to disregard the Church's spokesman. How many others were forcing themselves to do the same — for me? Such loyalty, he thought, I must be worthy of such loyalty. "

You and your men have done well, Commander," William said, straightening his shoulders. "What have you learned from the man?" he asked, moving down the staircase.

"Nothing, my Lord. The priest would not let him speak."

"I see."

William entered the audience chamber, surveying it quickly. News of the stranger had not yet spread. There were only the usual guards and administrative staff in attendance, their eyes riveted in one direction. Then William saw the object of their interest. Transfixed, he could only stare in amazement.

The stranger was barely recognizable as male: narrow shoulders, scrawny neck, slight of back — weak. Taller even than that frightening eve, his long frame towered above everyone, but seemed to stand without benefit of muscles, with legs like sticks and long, frail arms that supported hands that were refined and dainty. His skin was a pale tawny brown, the color of sun-bleached leather and just as smooth. The face was hairless, as were his arms and hands. Yet the head hair was plentiful and long. Golden brown strands were held neatly back with a colorful sash. Another sash was tied around his neck, and around one wrist was a wide black band made of a hard shiny material, with a smoky colored gemstone embedded across the flat top.

The outfit he wore was of the same light material as that terrifying eve's. It clung to his body indecently, outlining his generous genitalia and destroying any question of his sexual identity. A thin, feeble man, barely able to stand erect, whose bulging manhood was the envy of every eye in the room. He was a gross mockery of all New Eden held as masculine and proper.

Lying at his feet were two satchels made of a soft fabric. Both bore the look of having been thoroughly searched.

Four soldiers stood close by, trying unsuccessfully to hide their nervousness.

Becoming aware of the Chairman's presence, the attendants within the hall bowed hastily. The Stranger's gaze travelled over the bent figures, coming to rest on William. He smiled at the Chairman, giving a brief wave with his long, delicate fingers.

William averted his head and proceeded to the dais, with the Commander and Robert closely in tow. The Chairman sat upon the throne as Robert took his place at the side of the platform. Belcher, as usual, stood behind the royal chair.

Immediately, William fixed his gaze on the stranger, demanding, "Who are you? Where do you come from?"

The young man flinched at the tone and after a moment answered in a soft voice, with each word pronounced distinctly, every syllable clearly enunciated: "I am named Frayne. We are from a planet many parsecs from your world."

"Lies!" came a shriek from across the room. All heads turned towards the disturbance. A priest moved away from the wall and took a few steps towards the center of the room. Clutching the firecross hanging from his waist, he brandished it dramatically to ward off any evil emanating from the slight figure standing before him. "He's a demon taken on human form!"

The priest was unknown to William. Belcher whispered, "That's the one."

121

William was tempted to have the man removed. But the fact that he had wheedled his way inside the palace, when all priests were denied entry, made the young Chairman hesitate. And he could not ignore the warning. Did not the History state that only New Eden held the last of Humanity: the Chosen Ones.

He motioned to the guards. "Cut him."

With trepidation, two soldiers held the stranger while a third took hold of his arm, exposing the skin. The stranger did not struggle, appearing only perplexed by these actions. When the fourth guard unsheathed a small dagger to hold over the limb, he still did not react. The blade made a swift pass, and a moment later blood welled to the surface.

The stranger stared at the blood in stunned surprise. "Why have you done this?" his voice barely a whisper.

"To see if you are human."

"What else would I be?"

William ignored the question. "Bind his arm," he ordered.

The guard sheathed his knife, and, with a practiced hand, bandaged the wound securely. Once again the stranger stood alone, the four guards a short distance away.

The Chairman relaxed a little. "Explain where you come from, Stranger."

Forcing his eyes from his bandaged arm, the stranger answered in the same soft tones: "Our planet is now called Mirandus, but two millennia ago it was named Proximus."

"Impossible!" the priest broke out. "Proximus was destroyed by the virus!"

William eyed the stranger with renewed suspicion. "What the priest says is true. It is written in our History. Why do you lie?"

"I do not understand," the stranger answered in confusion. But after a moment his countenance cleared. "To lie: to tell an untruth, a fabrication." He became puzzled once again. "To what purpose?"

"Perhaps to avoid explaining where you really come from," William said dryly.

This caused a look of surprise on the stranger's face, and he repeated his question: "To what purpose?"

Unable to restrain himself any longer, the priest broke in excitedly: "My Lord, I must insist you hand this creature over to me immediately! This is a matter for the Church!"

With exaggerated patience, William replied: "Father, this . . . this person is obviously a man, and is therefore entitled to all the rights and privileges of a man. Though he be grossly strange, he has broken no law."

"He speaks blasphemy!"

The priest was correct. To contradict the History was sacrilege.

William could now give the stranger over without dishonoring his men. But at that same moment he came to the startling realization that he did not want to give the stranger over — at least not yet. He intrigues me, the Chairman thought. And there was so little that did.

William gave an expressive sigh, regretting the necessity of surrendering the man. He opened his mouth to give the order, but before he could speak, a thought occurred to him.

"The stranger's History is obviously different from our own. He can't be condemned for being taught a falsehood," the Chairman decreed.

The priest saw the obvious hole in this reasoning, and appeared ready to argue the matter when it occurred to him that the Church might be better served if he didn't put too fine a point on it, especially in such public surroundings. Instead, he shouted, "Then give me that demon creature you've hidden away! She is unnatural! You endanger your immortal soul!"

"I agree, Father, she is a danger, as are all eves," William said, staring hard at the priest. "And like any eve, *we render her harmless through knowledge of her guile*," he recited. "You insult me with your ravings, enough of this!"

The priest took a different tact, directing his attention to Frayne, whose pale face was shiny with perspiration. "Tell me, *cousin*, how did you come to be here? A stellar ship is enormous. We saw nothing in the sky."

"The ship is in orbit around your planet. We landed in a small shuttle craft."

"More lies! You are a—"

"Enough!" William shouted. With a sharp wave of his arm, he motioned for the priest to be brought before him. Lowering his voice, the Chairman stated harshly, "Out of respect for your office, I have tolerated your interruptions, but you are trying my patience. I am conducting this interrogation. Any further disruption and you will be ejected from the palace."

The priest fumed, but kept silent.

William looked to the stranger. "How many aboard your ship?"

"There is no one aboard the ship," he said quietly, yet clearly.

"I don't mean the small one. The big one in the sky."

"Yes, that is my meaning also. Althaia and I are here. Therefore the ship is empty."

"Are you saying you operated that ship alone?"

"Althaia and I did, yes."

"Hah!" the priest squawked triumphantly.

"Do you expect us to believe this?" William demanded. "We know our History. It took ten men to make such a ship fly."

"Yes, your history is correct. But our ships have not required a crew of that number for more than one thousand, six hundred and twenty years."

"Why didn't you come before this? Why does our History state that all died on your planet?"

The stranger spoke slowly: "It will take many words."

"Then use many words. We have words and time aplenty."

The stranger removed the colorful scarf from around his neck and mopped his brow delicately. "Your gravity is much stronger than on our world, it is fatiguing. Am I permitted to sit? "

"Of course," William said, motioning for a chair.

But before it could arrive, the stranger had collapsed to the floor, unconscious.


William slid back the wooden slat and peered cautiously into the cell through the small opening. The eve was standing with eyes closed, arms at her sides, hands curled with thumb and index finger touching.

Now that he could study her in safety, he saw how fragile she really was — far more delicate than the eves of New Eden. It was her height and bearing that spoke of un-eve-like power. Even the face was deceptive. All the strength suggested by the boldness of her stare was undermined by delicacy of bone structure.

William had never seen an eve's naked face before. As he studied it, an odd feeling of calm crept over him, and he didn't flinch away when two large orbs suddenly met his own. Dark and inviting, he stood glued to the warm life within. Then their focus changed — sharpened, as if seeing into his very soul. With a muffled cry of alarm, he slammed the window shut.

"My Lord! What be duh matter?" the guard on duty rushed to ask.

"Nothing! Nothing. You'll forget this incident, that's an order."

"Knee bent, Sire."

"The male's cell — take me."

"This be duh way, Yurr Lordship."

He followed after the guard, deep in thought:

Have I made a mistake? *Is* the stranger's eve too dangerous for ordinary men to handle — even a king? It might be wiser to hand her over to the Church.

His rebellion did not stretch so far as to endanger his immortal soul.


Frayne had never been in such filth. Had never known such filth could even exist. Though he was drained and longed to rest, he could not bring himself to sit upon the hard cot he'd woken on.

124

His return to consciousness was an assault on the olfactory senses. Nausea assailed him as he stumbled to his feet, desperately seeking a way out of the tiny room. But the door would not open, and his efforts to force it brought a harsh warning to "Keep away!"

"Why do you confine me in this room of filth?"

"No talkin'!" And the threat of violence in that voice stopped the protest in his throat.

He paced the small cell, a gloomy cubicle lit only by a slit of sunshine from a narrow window too high to reach. His body began to itch. It took all his self control to keep from beating at the door for release.

Closing his eyes, he prepared himself for meditation but was interrupted by the sudden opening of his cell door. The young man in the big chair stood warily in the doorway, studying him with a hard stare.

William motioned at the guard to move away, waiting until he was well out of earshot before he demanded, "What were you doing just now? Your eve was doing the same."

"My eve?"

"The one you came with."

Confused, he answered, "She is named Althaia, and she is neither mine nor anyone's. Is she too confined in a room of filth?"

"In a cell, yes," William answered impatiently. "Now tell me what you were doing."

With difficulty, Frayne put aside his own questions. "It is called meditation."

"What does it do?"

"I use it to center and calm myself. But for others on my planet, it is the way to induce a trance for healing, or to enter the Realming state."

"Your words make no sense. Explain again."

"We must enter the trance state to allow the healing of self."

"Your medicine will not work otherwise?"

"We have no need of medicine."

"No need for medicine?" William asked in disbelief.

The stranger nodded in understanding. "It can seem unlikely if one does not have the ability to heal one's own body, as I do not."

"Is that why you're so sickly?"

"My health is excellent, but your planet is very different from my own. It has taken all my strength."

"Doesn't look like you ever had much to lose," William commented dryly.

"I am considered abnormally strong on my planet."

William grunted in disbelief. "If you've no medicine on your planet, what happens when you're sick or wounded," the young Chairman asked, motioning to his bandaged arm.

"A healer would come, a person gifted with the power to heal others."

"I see," William said in a tone that announced he did not see at all.

"But few are in need of their services."

"There's not many like you?"

"No, I am an anomaly. My genetic coding is from another time in our planet's history. Althaia also possesses genetic coding that is not of this time period, although she is capable of healing self."

"Genetic coding?" was the irritated demand. "You talk gibberish! Explain!"

"Certainly," the stranger said agreeably. He tilted his head, considering. "Are you familiar with the science of heredity?"

"Science!" William hissed in alarm. "Science is forbidden!"

"Forbidden? For what reason?"

"Science destroyed the world of our Ancestors. It is a tool of the Devil, a lure to consume Mankind."

"On Mirandus we see science as a tool which can be used to build or to destroy. We choose to build. But I will speak no more of this if it is forbidden to you. I wish to respect your customs."

As he fell silent, Frayne came to the realization that he could no longer offer proof of their shared ancestry by inviting the young man to examine their starship or even their shuttlecraft, for such a suggestion would clearly terrify him.

William clasped the hilt of his sword for reassurance as he studied the serene and open expression of the stranger. It occurred to the young Chairman that they were likely close in age, yet the stranger seemed so much younger. William was struck by the young man's unmistakable innocence — a guilelessness impossible to manufacture, unlike the pretended artlessness of priests — or others, a small voice whispered, but he pushed the thought aside.

"You are saddened. What has caused this response in you?" the stranger inquired.

"I was thinking how much I've changed these past months."

"Change is growth."

"Not all change; some has the stench of death about it."

"What is death but the transition to a new life?"

"That priest already thinks you devil spawned. Such talk would make his case against you."

"I do not understand your words."

"It doesn't matter — yet," William said, studying the stranger. I must keep you close if you're to remain safe, William thought. But do I want you safe? "If what you say is true — that you are from Proximus — why come now, after all this time?"

126

"It will take many words."

"So you said. Are you recovered enough to continue?"

"Yes," Frayne answered, and paused to consider: *How can I illustrate to this ignorant person the complexities of our world? Althaia ought to be the one to explain our planet's circumstances. But their fear of her has made that impossible. Do they fear all women?*

The young man was becoming restless. Frayne forced himself to focus, deciding to begin at the most relevant point.

"On my world, the population is declining. We have become too . . . refined." Frayne paused, considering. "We are losing the instinct that enables a species to survive: the ability to reproduce. There is a high probability that within four generations, we will become extinct." William listened intently, never taking his eyes from the stranger's face. "Because of our genetic mutation, Althaia and I have the ability to recognize the instinctual deficiency of our peoples." William was beginning to feel lost, the words undecipherable. Frayne continued on: "Regrettably, it is impossible to reproduce our mutation sufficiently to stop the decline. Our only hope was to journey to your planet to ask for assistance." Frayne became silent and looked at the young man expectantly, but he appeared quite baffled.

"*Our* assistance? William asked. "How could we possibly help?"

"By adding to our genetic pool," Frayne explained simply. But William continued to look confused. "A number of your people would return with us to Mirandus."

William waited impatiently for the food to be served and then motioned the servants to leave them.

Robert studied the Chairman with interest. They were sharing a private meal together, a rarity these days, and William was sober. He could see his friend's barely contained excitement, an excitement that had nothing to do with receiving his drug. Yet Robert could not help a growing sense of apprehension.

He nodded to the guards who stood along two walls of the Chairman's private dining room; quietly they melted away.

Once they were alone, Robert said, "You spoke to the stranger again, Sire?"

"Yes," the word erupted out of him.

"He made an impression on you."

William nodded. "He's . . . fascinating." He lowered his voice, "He does frighten me, Robert — but not in the way I'm usually afraid. I don't want to run

127

away . . ." he trailed off, at a loss.

"What makes him fascinating, Sire?"

"Everything," William said, throwing up his hands in a sudden passion. "His very existence. His clothes, his puny body, his words . . . ." He relaxed slightly, dropping his arms. In a calmer voice, he said, "They have no medicines on his planet, only healers that come when there's injury or disease, or they heal themselves. I don't understand how they do this," he trailed off again, considering the idea. After a moment, he continued: "Yet his people are dying out — unable to breed as they once did." Abruptly, he leaned towards Robert. "That's why he's come," William's voice hissed with excitement. "To take some of our people back to Proximus — to replenish their breeding stock."

Robert's breath expelled noisily, "My God . . . ."

William continued, the words rushing out: "Might we soon suffer this same fate? Look how easily our eves die. Could this be the answer to New Eden's problem? Proximus would add to our broodstock, and we to theirs — a reciprocal solution."

"You speak blasphemy, my Lord," Robert said quickly, his tone a warning. His eyes flickered towards the door and back to William. "You know it is God's will that our eve numbers are diminishing — a sign that we are winning the battle against Satan."

"You speak the Truth," William said in a loud voice. Then he leaned closer to whisper, "Do you think it could be possible?"

Every fiber in Robert's being cried out in affirmation, but he forced his mind to ignore all considerations save for his sense of duty: seeing only what possible danger these new ideas could hold for the Chairman. Satan alone knew what further acts of disobedience would come from such thinking.

"Could the Holy Church be so wrong? God would not allow it."

"I suppose you're right," William reluctantly agreed, expelling a heavy sigh.

Robert saw the burning excitement in his friend begin to fade. "If he's not a demon himself, his world must be overrun with sin," Robert continued, pressing home his point. "You saw how weak he is. And his eve! She's completely out of control — like the tales of Earth. No wonder they're dying out."

"What you say is probably true, but I wish it were not," William whispered.

"Did the stranger say anything else?"

William hesitated. "No, he grew tired. I thought he might pass out again, but he refused to lie down, said it was too filthy." He smiled wryly. "I had to agree. I've ordered him taken to a suite in the east wing." Robert nodded, aware of the stranger's new location, down the corridor from the Chairman's apartment. "Make certain the stranger is secure, Robert. I commission you with his safety."

"As you order, my Lord," the young captain replied, bowing his head slightly

128

in compliance. "But His Holiness will not approve of the stranger's removal from the cell."

"He will not interfere."

"I pray your recent victories won't cause you to underestimate him."

"Don't worry, my friend, I'm learning how to deal with my old wardens."

"Sire, do you truly believe the stranger could be from Proximus?"

"Where else then? His humanity is certain." William looked at Robert quizzically. "You have some other idea?"

Robert shook his head. "No, Sire, though I sincerely wish I did."

William did not look as though he agreed.

"The stranger's very existence is a blasphemy," Robert stated quietly. "He must be kept hidden and all talk of him forbidden. It's unfortunate so many witnessed his arrival. Let's proceed as if he doesn't exist; that will hold back his Holiness. But," Robert warned, "the Church would take him in a moment if it knew of the stranger's mission. If you wish to keep him alive, this information should go no further."

He's right, William realized. "I'll hand him over shortly, but for now, they'll let him be."

Robert studied the young Chairman thoughtfully. What are you keeping from me? A great unease crept through Robert. We're in for a rough time.

# CHAPTER 16

"YOU'RE AWAKE, good," William said briskly. "I want to talk to you."

It was early morning, an unusual time for the Chairman to rise. He'd slept only a few hours before waking, eager for the day, though at first he could not think why. Then he remembered the stranger and sat up instantly, the sudden movement making his head spin. He was still suffering from the effects of the drug. His limbs were weak and shaky, his mind full of cotton wool. Still, he felt better than usual. No alcohol, he recalled, just a cup of wine with supper. When was the last time I did that?

He couldn't remember.

William called for his surprised privy servant, and a short time later he was ready to question the stranger. Frayne was sitting on the bed, propped up against the wooden backboard, his face looking drawn and pale. He forced himself to rise and stand before the window, his back turned to the Chairman. "I will not speak with you."

"What has happened? Did my men rough you up?"

"No one has harmed me. I am clean, fed and rested. But what of Althaia? How does she fare? Are her conditions improved?"

William hesitated. If he answered truthfully, the stranger might be angry; he seemed to have a concern for his eve. "Your eve fares as well as you."

Frayne paused, trying to understand the strange wobble in the young man's energy. Frayne had never experienced this situation before, but a moment later he had a disturbing insight. He said sadly, "I can hear the falseness in your voice."

A prickle of fear went down William's spine. Reflexively, he stepped back towards the door.

"Why are you suddenly afraid?" Frayne asked, his eyes still on the window. "Your world is so full of fear the weight of it burdens my soul."

William's hand remained on the doorknob but he didn't turn it. "Is there no fear on your world?"

"Yes, there is fear, but it is not all-pervasive. And we do not fear each other."

"What *do* you fear?"

"We fear repeating the mistakes of the Ancients."

"Yes!" said William in sudden relief at this commonality. Removing his hand from the door, he continued. "We too fear bringing God's wrath upon Mankind once more."

"Fear the Creative?" Frayne gasped, turning in shocked surprise. "We do not fear the Divine, we fear only our human excesses."

"You do not fear God?" William repeated, equally shocked. "But you must fear God! How else is one to honor and obey His Laws?"

"Through choice, certainly. We honor the Divine and all creation because we fear repeating the past. Our entire society is based upon this principle."

"Our world is based on the same principle," William insisted.

"Yet you live in fear of your God." How terrible, thought Frayne, to live in fear of the Creative and all It's gifts. An idea suggested itself. "Is this the reason your world fears women, because you honor them beside your God?"

"Honor *eves*," William gasped out, his face almost white. "Blasphemy!"

Frayne was alarmed for the young man's health. He spoke quickly, "My words were not intended to distress you. I concluded, incorrectly, that your fear of women was—"

He was cut off by a violent roar of protest: "We are NOT afraid of eves!" William was almost shouting the words. "Do not *ever* suggest this to me *again*!"

"My ignorance of your customs has angered you once more," Frayne said quickly, his voice quiet and gentle. "It is because I have witnessed your . . . reaction to Althaia, and have seen no sign of your own women, that I reasoned there must be some extraordinary explanation."

In a much calmer voice, William said, "The eves are kept separate to prevent contamination."

"In what way would you contaminate them?"

"Not *them*! *US*! They would contaminate *us* with their Godlessness. They are evil, working always towards the destruction of Man."

His words shocked Frayne deeply. He could only state, "They are the givers of life."

"Yes, she bears our sons, but it is God's test of faith that we must lie with her while escaping her poisonous seduction."

Frayne said almost to himself: "That explains the heavy miasma gripping this planet." Abruptly, he turned away. "I will talk no more until Althaia's conditions are improved."

William looked at the set of his back, and stormed from the room.

Frayne whispered to the window glass: "Althaia, I pray I did not bring an early death upon us both."

Althaia was deep within herself. The oppressive conditions on this planet had stimulated her spirit, inducing a trance state far beyond her previous capabilities. From the moment she'd stepped off the shuttle, her body had been working to adapt — and to evolve — pushing her self-healing skills into something much greater.

She could now observe the entire workings of her body, right down to cell formation, as one whole moving picture, no longer having to study each system or organ separately. She now saw all, understood all, and could make several adjustments in one fluid reflex of will.

But the changes had gone beyond even this. Something else had awakened within her, growing in strength with every breath.

I am a Healer, she acknowledged with some surprise.

On Mirandus, where all heal themselves and disease and accident are almost non-existent, the ability to heal others was a gift often unrecognized by those who possessed it. Her talent had lain dormant while on her own healthy world. This sickly planet brought fertilizer to the seed.

Her awareness angle shifted. There was someone in the room. Moving her attention outward, she opened her eyes. Three men stood in the doorway, staring at her in fear. The biggest one commanded harshly, "Cover your face."

She removed the scarf holding back her hair, and held it over the bridge of her nose.

"Come," he ordered, the hard tone in his voice increasing. When she moved forward, they all stepped back quickly, exiting her cell.

Out in the corridor, another set of anxious guards stood waiting. The first group took up position ten paces behind her, while the others placed themselves ten paces in front. "Move," the big soldier snarled, prodding her with a pikestaff.

They marched her rapidly down the corridor, but she had no trouble keeping up.

This alien gravity no longer drains my strength, she realized in astonishment. My body feels refreshed, as if having slept in my own bed. Such extraordinary healing this planet offers me.

At the end of the long passageway, they made a right turn and continued on for several more paces before coming to an abrupt halt at an open doorway. She was ordered inside, and with some apprehension she stepped over the sill. Immediately, the door was shut and locked behind her.

This room was much larger and considerably cleaner than the one she'd previously occupied, the air less damp and musty, though sunlight was still scarce. Relieved, she saw there was a low cot with a clean blanket, a primitive toilet and a tub filled for bathing. Quickly, she stripped off her clothes and immersed herself in the cold water, the filth of that room soon washed from her body.

Unable to bear dirty clothes against her clean skin, Althaia lifted the dress to feel along the back of the neckline, finding a small, flexible depression the size of her fingertip. She pressed it firmly and a sudden subtle vibration began to spread throughout the garment, radiating to the outer edge of the hemline and sleeves. She lifted her undergarments, seeking the same depression on the back seam of both items. Within a few minutes, the three sonic dry-cleaning systems automatically shut themselves off, her clothes now fresh and clean.

Feeling quite chilled, she dressed hurriedly and wrapped the rough-spun blanket around her shoulders for added warmth.

Am I to be detained permanently inside this room? she wondered.

As if in answer, the door to her cell was flung open and two men entered with their pikestaffs leveled at her.

"Move back and veil yourself," one of them ordered.

She stood close to the wall, using the edge of the blanket to hide her face as three more men entered the room, their clothes of a different style than the two who threatened her. Quickly, they replaced the toilet with a clean bucket and took away her bathing tub. The soldiers followed them into the corridor, making certain not to turn their backs on her. The door closed and the lock turned once more.

Why this vehement fear of me? she wondered again, deeply mystified.

She had learned not to speak during her first encounter with the soldiers — the lesson dramatic. Spears and swords suddenly aimed at her. Their fear so intense she was certain they meant to kill her.

There had never been a moment's harsh anger in her life. To be the object of so much hatred and violence had almost overwhelmed her. But now she was healed and strong, and it was time to look for answers to this world of fear.

She examined the room, considering her options, but there was little available here. The cot and blanket were much too new. Something of age would be more conducive. The foundation of the building was made of ancient plazcast, stronger and more durable than concrete. It melded well with the plasteelite structure it supported.

Althaia placed her hand upon a wall that bore traces of dust and grime from almost two millennia. Clearing her mind, she opened up to receive. There was a sudden rush of information, a whirr of sound and pictures as centuries blurred passed. Then sudden, stark clarity burst upon her as she was thrust into a single space of time:

"We need to shorten the shifts," said a middle-aged man, small and wiry. He was irritated, strained with fatigue.

"We've already cut them back another hour," answered a woman of lesser years. She too was fighting off irritation; it had taken considerable effort not to lash out at him.

"Then cut them back some more."

"We'll be way past deadline as it is."

"Well, it's too bloody bad about the bloody deadline! No one can work in this damned atmosphere." He mopped his face with a worn bandana. "Who's the bloody genius that said it'd be just like Earth?"

"Almost like Earth, they said. And it's not the atmosphere, it's the gravity. No one could know the affects of working on an alien planet without environmental suits. It's not as if it's ever been done before." Why the hell am I defending them? she thought with increased irritation.

"It doesn't take a bloody Einstein to figure out if something's pulling you down, you're gonna get mighty tired pulling back!" He mopped his face again. "I feel like I weigh an extra hundred pounds."

"I know, I know," she agreed tiredly, taking a handkerchief from her trouser pocket to pat her own face and neck. "We're all feeling the effects."

"We need more crews," the man said, his anger gone now.

"I've already put in a request. They should be here on the next available ship."

"Thank god for that," he said with feeling. After a pause, he continued sheepishly, "Sorry for snapping your head off. This place seems to bring out the worst in me."

She nodded in empathy. "I've never felt so bitchy in my life." Nonstop PMS, she thought, and turned to unroll a blueprint. "I've got something to show you." Laying the design on the partially finished foundation, she continued: "Only two other people, besides you and I, know these plans exist."

"Damn it, not another order for secret panels and hidden doorways. Those bloody things gum up the whole operation."

"It's worse. Look at it."

The man whistled. "That's gonna cost a bloody fortune."

"Yes, it will," she said, distracted and tired.

"Something this big is gonna be impossible to hide from the crews."

"We won't have to. This whole system of passageways is designed to look like

134

a servants' access. Simon Cartwright will bring his own crew up for the final finishing."

"Who's he?"

"ISA's head of Security."

"Who else knows?"

"Just the Chairman of the Board."

He studied the blueprint again. "Man, they don't fuck around, do they? Nothing by halves." She frowned at his language, but he was too tired to care. He mopped his brow again. "I'm never gonna make it back to bloody Earth at this rate."

The woman, who'd been leaning on the foundation, abruptly stood upright.


There was a sudden rush of sound and color as the man and woman disappeared.

Althaia was back in her own time.

# CHAPTER 17

"I HAVE done what you asked. I've improved your eve's conditions," William announced with annoyance. Why do I protect this obviously contaminated man? Even indulging his outrageous demands, simply because I want him to speak with me. And William realized one other thing: he wanted the stranger to think well of him.

"Thank you," Frayne said from where he was kneeling beside the far side of the bed. Slowly, using the wall for support, he raised himself to his full height and stared down at the young man across the room. "I now wish to meet with her."

"That will not be possible," William said firmly.

"I hear the truth in your words, though I do not understand the reasoning."

"It's much too dangerous. You must be kept hidden or the Church will remove you from my custody."

"In what way could this be dangerous? From the history of the Ancients, I know that a church gave spiritual guidance. Although I did not read in-depth — it was not a subject I enjoyed learning."

"You do not attend Church?" William demanded, shocked.

"There are no buildings on Mirandus designated for the worship of the Creative, nor are there any doctrines or practices one must follow apart from the most basic teachings on meditation and the Universal Laws."

"There is no Church on your entire world?" William asked in disbelief, his fear re-activating.

"That is correct," Frayne acknowledged. "Formal religion was replaced at the beginning of our history by the Joining."

"And what is this Joining?" William demanded.

"The power that unites our community in a common direction."

"What *kind* of power?"

"The Creative Energy that gives life and substance to our Universe," Frayne explained. "It was the presence of this energy that allowed rapid tech—" he stopped abruptly, remembering the young man's aversion to such subjects. "That allowed rapid social advancements," he amended. "We were then freed from the daily tasks of maintaining existence, to explore our creative potential."

Frayne was relaxing now, talking of his world: "There was a time in our history when every person was involved in projects highly creative. It was a glorious age: wonderful works of art, literature, dance and theater. Artistic projects in all genres. Eventually this age was followed by many healing advances, and later . . ." he paused, considering. "And later, other discoveries." Frayne stopped and looked at William. "Perhaps the reason why your world has so few gifts from the Creative is that your world despises those who could bring you peace and freedom from struggle."

"Whom do you speak of?" William demanded heatedly, knowing.

"The women of your world. The eves, as you call them."

"What could *they* have to do with peace and freedom?"

"Everything. They are the Joiners."

"Your eves control this power?"

"No, not control, but they are the ones who receive and transmute the energy. In all our history, no male has ever been summoned."

William sucked in his breath with fear, but still he was curious. "What do you mean, summoned?"

"I cannot say precisely; only those who are called know by what process."

"Summoned to Satan, you mean! Answering the call to destroy Mankind, and doing a damn good job of it from your account!" William sputtered excitedly. "And now you've come here — to my world — to spread your corruption!"

"I have frightened you once more," Frayne said with regret. "Is there nothing of me and my world that does not disturb you?"

"How can it not! You and your world should not even exist!" William was shouting now. "And where has it been all this time? Our History says it was destroyed. And still you haven't explained!"

"You are correct," Frayne admitted. "I will do so now." He lowered his exhausted body onto the bed, resting his back against the headboard. "Sit, please, you will hear better in comfort." Relenting, William perched upon the nearest chair, unpadded and without decoration.

"Our world is as ignorant of your existence as you are of ours. Only recently were you made known to me," Frayne began.

"But why? How—" William interrupted. Frayne held up his hand and the Chairman subsided, listening.

"I will begin at the beginning, or perhaps it is truer to say at the end, during the last twenty years of Earth's history. Perhaps you are familiar with this

137

chronicle?" But he didn't wait for William's nod of assent. "There was much trouble upon the Earth during those last years: acute overpopulation, severe polluting of the air and waterways, and even the land where food was grown. The Earth had been stripped of her natural resources to such a degree that the mineral ores used to manufacture tools and other products had to be mined on asteroids and moons. This was done at great risk to the lives of their workers, and at great expense. Their starships were slow and costly to operate, taking years to reach their destination and return home."

He paused for a moment: even speaking was a strain.

"These institutes of business exerted considerable effort and expense in an attempt to discover faster and more economical methods of harvesting off-world resources. This was finally accomplished by the Independent Space Agency."

William grunted in sudden recognition of the name.

"Using their newly proven and highly complex quantum formula, they were able to construct a drive system that could propel interstellar ships faster than the speed of light, and at small expense. The Quartermaine-quantum-drive it was named, in honor of the founder of the company, who believed uncompromisingly in the possibility of faster-than-light speed. However, it was commonly called the Q-drive, and the communication system developed from that same formula was named the quantum-wave." Frayne paused again, patting his damp forehead with a colorful scarf.

"Within eight years, this agency's deep probes discovered two habitable planets. The first was Primus, your world, where mining could be accomplished without the expensive equipment needed to support life in a hostile atmosphere, thereby reducing the cost of production tremendously. This, in addition to the exceptionally shortened travel time, allowed the Independent Space Agency to offer its products at a much lower price than its competitors. Eventually, these competitors could no longer sustain their off-world bases or their businesses. Only the Independent Space Agency remained to colonize new worlds." Frayne paused, organizing his thoughts. "It was on the second habitable planet — my world — that the Agency expanded its interests beyond mining to begin its first alien farming project. Much of the vegetation on Proximus was akin to certain Earth species, which allowed humans to digest them easily. Proximus' harvests were to be exported to Earth. But events decreed otherwise. The final war broke out over the Earth, and all life on that planet was extinguished."

Frayne stopped again, gathering his energy. Several moments passed before he returned to his tale. "After learning of Earth's destruction, the two thousand colonists living on Proximus — mostly agriculturists and miners — came to a radical decision: they would dismantle all those social and economic structures that had led to the annihilation of Earth. But they were not free to institute such

138

dramatic societal changes without permission from the Independent Space Agency, which held ownership of the planet."

Frayne paused. He was becoming very tired now.

"There was a high probability that a number of executives within the Agency had escaped the holocaust on Earth. It was feared that when these people arrived on Proximus, they would come with men carrying tools of violence, and Earth's ancient and destructive systems would be forced back upon the colony."

Frayne stopped to mop his brow once more. "The colonists believed their only recourse was to prevent the arrival of these executives, and this would not be difficult. Already the planet was under quarantine. A virus native to Proximus had severely impaired the health of many colonists, bringing several close to death. Until their healers could restore the health of these patients, no one would approach the planet."

Again he was forced to stop and recover his strength before continuing.

"The survivors of Earth had no choice but to seek refuge on the planet Primus. But eventually, these survivors would try to make contact. It was decided that when contact was initiated, Proximus would keep its communication equipment silent. If a ship approached, they would hide within the mineshafts, where their life signs would be undetectable. Primus would believe the virus had brought death to all. In fear for their lives, no one would approach the planet. And, they did not," Frayne concluded.

"No, they did not . . ." William echoed. He could see Frayne's increased weakness. "You may finish when you're rested."

"Thank you," it was barely a whisper. He stretched out on the bed, his wounded arm lying exposed at his side.

"Your arm is not healing properly," William noticed. "I will send the royal physician — my healer — to take care of it."

"That is kind of you," Frayne managed to say before sleep overwhelmed him.

William ordered his evening meal brought to the room, and while he ate he watched the stranger, thinking, I believe even our smallest eves have bones larger than this oddity. Certainly they are stronger. Yet he towers almost a foot above us all. How does one survive in such a body? To think we come from the same Ancestors. Unbelievable.

Yet, he did believe, despite his fear.

It was not so much what the stranger said. It was how his words *felt*.

They felt true.

But what did that truth mean for New Eden? he wondered. The Church says *we* are the only survivors: the Chosen Ones. Yet it would seem we were not chosen alone. How could the Church make such a fundamental error? The Church was beyond all human frailties.

Then why did Frayne exist?

His head spun from the questions this man's presence ignited.

It fascinated William that both Proximus and New Eden had resolved not to repeat the sins of their Ancestors. But Frayne's world has failed. It is dying out.

And so perhaps is ours, his inner voice reminded him.

*Is* he here to infect our world with corruption?

Frayne woke to William's intense scrutiny. "You study me without revulsion, not as others on your planet do."

"They don't see your allure."

Rising to a sitting position with effort, Frayne said, "I am rested now. I will continue." He folded his long limbs, and began: "The colonists on Proximus chose to keep their descendants ignorant of your planet's existence. They feared that, after a time, warnings against contact would not be heeded, that curiosity about the other surviving humans might overcome caution. To prevent this, all references to Primus were deleted from our records. Even the name of our planet was declared too suggestive. The translation of Proximus is 'nearest' or 'next'. It was feared that someone might ask, 'Nearer than what?' And, of course, the interstellar communication equipment was dismantled."

"But not the ships," William observed.

"No, not the ships," Frayne agreed. "The ships were needed. Each year a pilgrimage was made to Earth, to remind us and to warn us against our human excesses."

"Then how did you learn of our planet?" William demanded, unable to contain himself.

"Our colonial ancestors could not know that a small number of their descendants would develop a gift for seeing into the past. These gifted ones were wise; they did not reveal the secret."

"Until now."

"Now, it is necessary."

William drew a deep breath, releasing it slowly. "I like this story. It would have you Expelled in an instant should the Church hear of it — but then every word you utter would bring that fate." He felt suddenly less frightened of the Stranger and his world.

"I have forgotten your name."

"Frayne is my name."

"You need rest. I will leave you now."

"May I make another request?" Frayne asked hurriedly.

"What is it?"

"May I send clothes and grooming items to Althaia, the one you call eve?"

William paused fractionally. "Yes, that would be permitted."

140

"Thank you."

Frayne struggled to his feet and walked around to the other side of the bed where he'd been crouching earlier. Bending over, he was forced to sit down on the hard mattress, unable to keep his balance while he lifted a satchel from the floor. He placed the bag on the bed beside him, and mopped his brow before he said tiredly, "Today, I found grooming tools within the clothing cupboard. They appear quite ancient. I have put them inside her travel bag. Is this acceptable?"

William nodded abruptly. "The palace is filled with old things. You may do as you like with them." Opening the door, he ordered a guard inside to pick up the satchel. "I will speak with you tomorrow," William stated. As he turned to leave, he stopped abruptly, remembering, "You don't eat your food. Are you ill?"

"We do not eat animal flesh on Mirandus, and there was much in the food that was brought to me. I do not mean to insult your culinary practices, but I cannot tolerate the taste or even the smell of cooked flesh."

"No meat, eh?" William said, eyeing Frayne's exhausted body. That explained his weakness. "I'll give instructions that you're to have no meat."

"Thank you. Althaia, also?"

William grunted in confirmation, and he was gone.

Frayne allowed himself to fall back onto the hard bed and relax. He was content. Much had been accomplished this day for Althaia, and for their mission.

# CHAPTER 18

THE BOOTED foot connected hard against her buttocks. She cried out in protest and tried to get to her feet, but was hit solidly and sent sprawling to the floor, her ears ringing painfully.

There was a sudden rush of sound and color as Althaia snatched her hand from the floor, and the woman disappeared.

Back in her own time, Althaia's body shook with reaction. What brutality! Never had she conceived of such violence. Witnessing it had scarred her psyche deeply.

Drawing a long breath, she went into healing trance.

Althaia realized she must develop some form of protection from this planet's negative energies. A thick shield of healing around her heart and mind before journeying into the past should be sufficient.

Her healing completed, she shifted her focus outward in time to see her travel bag dropped to the floor and the door hurriedly slammed shut. Offering thanks to the Creative, she crossed to the satchel and pulled it open. With another burst of gratitude, she threw aside the blanket she was wearing and drew on one of her long outer robes, the material warming her instantly.

Althaia crouched beside the bag to sort through the rest of the items, feeling Frayne's presence clearly as she did so. He is alive and well, she saw with relief. He was frightened for her safety and exhausted by the gravity, but otherwise sound. She could also see that he was responsible for her improved living conditions and the return of her possessions, but, most importantly, that he was in dialogue with one of these Primus citizens.

Althaia was thankful that the task of communicating their mission had fallen to Frayne, for he was far more articulate than she and enjoyed the act of conversing in a way she could not fathom.

Perhaps our mission will be concluded successfully despite its uncertain beginning?

Then her eyes fell upon the grooming tools Frayne had placed inside the bag.

Plasteelite, from the time of the Ancients! Assuredly these were not constructed in this low-tech society, she thought with excitement.

Althaia lifted the hairbrush and prepared herself for trance, wrapping a protective shield of energy around her heart and mind. When it was completed, she allowed herself to be drawn back through time — Earth time.

"Son-of-a-bitch!" a woman shrieked, striking hard with the brush at a dark haired man as he entered the bedroom.

He put up a protective arm and tried to defend himself. "What the hell, Mallory? What are you doing?"

"You Son-Of-A-Bitch!" she shrieked with even greater feeling, the violent brush strokes increasing.

He managed to grab her wrists, but she didn't relent. She continued to struggle furiously, her auburn hair standing wildly around her head.

"Mallory, what is going on!" the bewildered man demanded.

"I just heard back from my doctor — I've been ingesting a fertility drug!" she spat at him.

"Dr. Hobson told you that?" he asked in disbelief.

"I said *my* doctor — not one of your Agency stooges," she said, kicking him in the shins. "I went to see her on my last business trip because I thought I might be pregnant."

Her words made his eyes light up with pleasure, and when Mallory saw this she screamed with rage, wrenching her hands free. She began hitting him with renewed ferocity, curses pouring from her mouth. They scuffled fiercely until the man managed to grab her from behind, pinning her arms to her sides.

"Lucky for you, you bastard, that I wasn't," Mallory panted, "because I would have had an abortion on the spot." He went rigid, as if she'd struck him a great blow. Stunned, he continued to hold her while the panting changed to shuddering breaths: she was crying now. "How could you, Simon? How could you feed me that shit without my consent? Do you have any idea how violated that makes me feel? Do you have any understanding of what you've done?"

Simon released her, and she turned to look at him, tears running down her face. "Why couldn't you leave it alone? You always have to win, no matter the cost." She moved away, tossing the brush towards the bed.

143

The scene shifted, blurring slightly. Althaia understood that the vision had moved forward in time.

Mallory stuffed the brush and several other items from her dressing table into the leather bag hanging from her shoulder. She hesitated, fingering the handwritten note lying on the dresser top, re-reading it quickly.

*Simon,*
*I won't be back. We're not healthy together.*
*Don't try to find me.*
*Mallory*

A sudden feeling of regret was easily squelched.

Turning to the bed, she closed her two suitcases, the locks snapping home with finality. Then she hurried into the hallway and down the stairs, pulling the hovering cases effortlessly along behind her. In the foyer, Mallory released her grip on the suitcase handles and the luggage lowered itself to the floor as she opened a hall closet, hunting for her coat.

Suddenly the quiet was shattered by the scream of a siren.

"Damn it to hell," she swore, "not another evac-drill! Now I'll never get out of here!" She wrenched the coat from its hanger, revealing a large suitcase standing at the back of the closet. Mallory stared at it with loathing.

"No way — not today!" she declared, and resolutely closed the closet door.

Tossing her coat onto a chair, she began to pace the tiled floor, glaring at the black and white checkerboard. Abruptly she stopped, overcome with frustration. "I have to at least *try* to get out of here." Grabbing her coat and suitcases, she flung open the front door, running smack into a solid wall of muscle.

"Cord!" she exclaimed in surprise, pulling away from the thickset man, his rigid body clad in a starched green and white uniform.

"Sorry, Ms. Cartwright, didn't mean to scare yuh. Simon sent me. He was worried you'd think it was just a drill and ignore the siren."

"It's not a drill?" she asked suspiciously. She wouldn't put it past Simon to send a lie.

"Sorry ma'am, but no, it's not. War broke out on the moon durin' the night. This morning, Earth-based missiles were spotted headin' toward Washington and New York. They were destroyed en route, but missiles were returned in kind to Argentina and India. Three hundred missiles are now headin' for North America, another twenty towards Japan, four hundred towards Europe and Russia. Six hundred retaliatory missiles have been directed to India, Africa and South America, and another six hundred to China. It's expected that the mass bombings will overwhelm the defense systems."

144

"Those stupid bastards," she said softly, stunned.

"Yes, ma'am."

"Okay," Mallory said, snapping out of her shock, "let's go—" She stopped short to look at the luggage in her hands. Mallory released both bags and turned back into the house to grab the suitcase from the closet. "I'm ready" she said, striding past him.

Cord eyed the two suitcases sitting on the porch before following her to the jeep. He climbed inside and started the engine. "You know this place is shut tighter than Fort Knox during evac-drills. What made yuh think you could get out?"

She looked at him in surprise, his face already turned away, concentrating on the road. I always forget how direct he is. "I had to try, Cord. I had to try." He nodded in understanding.

They drove through residential streets lined with large, elegant houses, all less than a decade old. There were dozens of vehicles on the road, all heading in the same direction. Only a few jeeps travelled in the opposite lane, driven by men in uniforms of green and white. They were picking up pedestrians caught away from their homes.

Cord continued driving onward, the houses becoming more numerous and considerably smaller, but no less new. Automated hover-trains, with cheerful patterns painted on their sides, were transporting women and young children waiting at the curbsides with their luggage. The children were jumping and skipping as the trains moved towards them, while the mothers chatted and kept a close eye on their little ones.

"The evacuation is proceeding smoothly," Mallory commented. "I wonder how calm they'd be if they knew it was for real."

"We'll know that when we reach spaceport."

Mallory looked over the changing scenery as the houses disappeared to be replaced by public buildings. She noted the shopping centers, movie theaters, and recreation complexes.

As Cord drove past the deserted hospital grounds, Mallory shivered involuntarily: the empty parking lot was like a dark premonition.

It's just an illusion, she reminded herself. The patients are being loaded into specialty hover-trains beneath the hospital.

But she couldn't shake the eerie feeling.

With relief, they passed schoolyards lively with lines of students goofing around noisily, happy to be let out from class. They were being shunted into the hover-trains with speed, but still it took time.

Sixty-four thousand people in this community. Would there be enough time? she wondered. Stop thinking like that, she reproached herself again. We aren't being targeted — not yet. No one would deliberately destroy the only source of the Q-drive.

Four limousines were approaching from a side street. The traffic lights changed immediately, allowing the chauffeur-driven vehicles to turn onto the main road. The lights became green again and the jeep followed after.

The long line of vehicles left the town, maintaining a steady 80 mph as they followed the paved road across the desert grasslands to the spaceport: a collection of massive towers and hangers three miles in the distance. Running parallel to the road, the hover-trains zipped past, their colorful exteriors belying the somber journey they represented.

Two miles to the west stood an enormous structure, one hundred stories high and a mile long. From this dull featureless building, another road ran directly to the spaceport, and it too was crowded with vehicles as hover-trains packed with passengers sped past.

Squinting from the morning sun reflected on its many windows, Mallory studied the great building. As she watched, the brightness was snuffed out, floor by floor.

"Central Control's dropping their lead shutters," Mallory said aloud, though she was really talking to herself. Cord nodded without comment.

Her gaze moved past the enormous structure and far into the distance, to the sixteen-foot-high electrified fence made of solid plasteelite and plazcast. It encircled the entire perimeter of the compound, enclosing the town, central control, the spaceport, and a vast array of weapons aimed at the sky and at every inch of that impenetrable fence.

The Agency's certainly well defended, she thought — not for the first time — but it was the first time she really appreciated this fact.

Mallory looked overhead at the dozens of sleek-looking planes waiting to land on the runway outside the spaceport. She recognized the Agency's logo on several of them.

The last of the Board of Directors, she assumed. The other planes would be carrying those in good standing with the Agency — receiving their reward for whatever favors they'd provided.

She returned her attention to ground level as the hover-trains diverged from the road to unload their passengers at the southern gates into the spaceport, while the line of motor vehicles sped towards the six parking lots located near the western entrances. In an orderly, well practiced manner, they lined up on the paved surface. Immediately, their human cargo leapt out to form tidy lines at the gates leading inside the port.

Mallory followed Cord to the Women and Children's VIP entrance.

"Thanks Cord, you can go now. I know you have a lot to do."

He shook his head. "I'm to see you safely aboard."

"You're a stubborn man, Cord."

"No ma'am, just followin' orders."

Simon's orders, she thought, studying his face. Was Simon right? Did he command this man's unshakeable loyalty because he offered him a job? No, not a job — a cause. Simon's cause: protecting the Agency.

Without Cord and his army of security guards, there would be no Agency. They were invaluable, and they knew it. Simon made sure they knew it: every single one of them. Thousands of young men rescued from a life of poverty and isolation — that was important, Mallory remembered. They had to be without family or other close ties, their loyalty must be to the Agency alone. But it wasn't; it was to Simon, the head of their very extended, very dysfunctional family.

They are all completely and utterly devoted to my husband.

She shivered again despite the increasing desert heat, and turned to study her surroundings. The lines of women and children were moving steadily towards the entrance. Above the gateway was a sign bearing the symbol of a starship eclipsing a planet, the words "Independent Space Agency" written around the outside edge.

We're moving much quicker than usual, she thought. Not surprising.

Soon she was standing close to the entrance and could watch the people being admitted inside. It should be obvious now that something's wrong, Mallory thought.

The guards barely looked at each color-coded identification pass offered for inspection before slapping a label below the left collarbone with unusual firmness and brusquely ordering the next person forward.

As Cord and Mallory approached the guard, he saluted them briefly and then quickly applied the label to her blouse: an orange sticker with BERTH-A printed in bold letters. They were immediately directed by another guard to their assigned queue, and joined the growing number of people filling the spaceport, moving in long tidy lines past massive docking bays. Yet even these were dwarfed by the starships berthed beside them.

Only a short time ago, the eighteen gigantic vessels were unloading their cargo, but now the long-necked pipes that extracted the ore hung limply above them. Ground crews scurried over the ships, readying them for their return to the stars while, far below the nose of each ship, heavy streams of pedestrians moved purposely towards the gaping mouth of a huge underground entrance.

Mallory noted that the usual bored expressions were missing today: they know now. Thank god there's no panic. Maybe it was all those practice drills, she thought. Or maybe the warning that was drilled into our heads: no running — runners will be left behind.

Although she did observe that everyone, including herself, was walking at a very brisk pace.

Closer to the underground entrance, she could see the three tunnels leading below the surface. Each displayed a large, brightly lit sign. The signs were in alphabetical order: Berths A-D, Berths E-H, and Berths I-L.

As they approached the passageway, Mallory sniffed distastefully: livestock — the aroma filtering up from D-Berth.

She'd always thought it cruel to raise animals in the belly of a ship, in artificial light and bottled air, but now she was grateful. They could mean our survival. No! she stopped herself again. We'll be back, they'll come to their senses — they had to.

Mallory and Cord entered the tunnel assigned to those wearing the orange badge: women and children only. Soon the tunnel divided into two, with Berths A & B on the left, Berths C & D on the right. With practiced ease, the passengers turned into their assigned channel. Mallory and Cord took the left channel.

A few feet from the entrance, they stepped onto a conveyor mechanism, grasping the handrail for balance as it moved them forward. The conveyor gradually increased speed as it lowered the passengers deep below the surface, and then gently slowed to allow them to disembark with ease, each person heading to their assigned berth.

Mallory and Cord walked the short distance to A-Berth. It was crowded here, but still there was no pushing or suggestion of panic. Six long neat lines had formed to the starship.

Even now it's business as usual, Mallory thought. Maybe they're like me: they don't believe it can really be happening.

Inside the berth, the ship was mostly hidden behind thick walls of plazcast and lead, with only the six passenger entryways visible.

Mallory stared at their surroundings, thinking: It's hard to imagine that behind that wall is a starship the length of three football fields and as tall as a thirty story building — or that it was once a freighter now redesigned. The cargo hold made smaller and the living quarters expanded to house and entertain six thousand souls on a journey that would take over a month.

"I've criticized the Agency often enough for all the money it spent planning our escape route: all the specialty ships and hidden bunkers. I guess I owe them an apology."

"You didn't want to think it could really happen."

"No, I didn't."

"None of us did. Not even the ones that planned all this," he nodded at the plazcast surrounding them.

The lines were moving steadily towards the ship. In another minute she'd be aboard. "You don't have to stay now, surely?" she couldn't resist asking.

"Mallory!"

She turned to see a dark-skinned man hurrying towards them as fast as the crowded conditions would allow. In one arm he carried a suitcase, and his other arm was thrown around the shoulders of a woman, her pale skin blotchy from crying.

"Daniel!" Mallory said in surprise.

"Mallory, can Erin stay with you, she's upset."

"I'm not upset, I'm furious!" Erin said, shrugging off his arm. "And I'm not leaving until you're safely off the ground."

"Erin, you know I can't leave, I'm needed."

"Then I'm coming on your ship."

"No! I won't be able to concentrate until you're safely out of here."

"Damn it, Daniel, don't make me leave without you!"

"Erin, please, you're scaring people."

She looked around, startled, as if unaware of the presence of those crowded around her. Mothers were holding their little ones close, glaring at Erin over the tops of their heads.

Women and children first, Erin thought bitterly, though she knew it was right — for others.

"Everything's going to be okay," Daniel said with conviction. "I'll be right behind you, I promise." Releasing the suitcase, he pulled her to him and whispered in her ear, "We're soulmates, remember? Nothing's going to keep us apart." Daniel felt her relax a little at that. He kissed her and she pressed herself hard against him. With a last reassuring squeeze, he hurried out of the hanger, his focus on the job ahead.

Erin watched him go, a knot in her chest. "Damn it, I love you," she whispered after him.

"It'll be alright," Mallory assured her.

"Damn it, anyway," she swore again, but under her breath. How could she explain? I'm not used to being loved; it's unlike any threat I've ever known.

She turned towards the ship and a flight attendant beckoned her inside, urging her towards a seat.

Mallory entered close behind, but she paused at the door to take one last look at Earth. Cord was already gone.


Again the image blurred with a sense of motion before settling into sharp focus.

149

"How far is the townsite?" Mallory asked, letting her suitcase settle onto the road before perching precariously on top of it, the handbag slung over her shoulder.

Behind Mallory, thousands of women and children followed her example.

It was a wide road, covered in durable plaztar, built for the enormous trucks that carried the raw ore from the mines to the processing plants nestled between the spaceport and the protective mountains.

The spaceport's terminal was not designed to handle thousands of people converging upon it at once. Most passengers had to disembark directly into the open and walk across the apron, exposed to the baking heat and the dust.

At least here, near the shelter of the mountains, the dust was minimal. Mallory strained her neck to look up at their summits. She found them imposing: so immediate, so there.

"It's ten-per, ma'am," a young man answered. He was dressed in coveralls with the ISA insignia on the chest.

"Pardon?"

"It's street slang, he means miles: ten miles," Erin said from behind her.

Mallory groaned inwardly. We're barely out of spaceport and I'm exhausted already. Simon said the gravity was a little draining — a little! Can that man make an understatement.

Should we go back to the ships? she wondered, but shuddered at the thought.

After weeks of being trapped inside, we were all desperate to escape.

It doesn't matter how big and luxurious a wobbly tin can may look, it's still a wobbly tin can. Even our present discomfort is preferable to returning to those horrid metal containers, which seemed to feel even worse once we landed.

The Agency should have spent their time acclimating us for space travel instead of doing all those bloody drills.

She looked at the long sloping hill they needed to climb, barren except for sparse clumps of scrub grass.

At least we'll be in the shelter of the trees, once we're at the top.

As she continued to stare at the hillside, she realized that everything had a pinkish quality to it, like looking through faintly tinted glasses. She turned to study the spaceport, and saw that it too had the same slight hue.

Then she remembered that this phenomenon was caused by the rock desert: something to do with light refraction on dust particles in the atmosphere. She didn't remember much, except that it made for beautiful sunrises and sunsets.

Glancing towards the runway, she could see more ships coming into berth.

They'll be unloading thousands more in minutes, Mallory thought, all of them eager to return to terra firma. We'd better move.

She wasn't quite certain how she'd been delegated the role of leader once their ship had landed.

I guess, like always, I just took charge. Simon isn't the only one who needs to be in control, Mallory conceded ruefully. But we were all at a loss for a bit, after weeks of not knowing what was happening back on Earth, and then to get here and still not have any word, she reflected in her defense. I just recovered quicker than the others.

"We'd better move," Mallory said to the young man who was crouched beside the road in the slim shade of a low ditch. He looked as tired as she felt.

Maybe I should have accepted the site manager's offer of a ride? Mallory thought with some regret. But she'd already taken on the leadership role, and the position came with responsibilities.

Mallory lifted the strap of the handbag over her head and let it lay at the base of her neck. She stood up and waved a hand to signal that the rest was over. When they were all moving again, she asked the young man, "How long have you been stationed here?"

He answered wearily, "Six months."

So one didn't acclimate quickly to this change in gravity, Mallory thought in sudden despair, and wondered at her strong reaction.

"Looks like I'll never make it home now," the young man added grimly.

"Don't say that!" she snapped. He looked at her, startled. "We can't give up hope."

There were mutters of agreement from the women nearby, and he nodded, but his face said otherwise. Moving closer to him, Mallory demanded in a low voice, "Do you know something?"

"What do you mean?"

"Has there been any news about Earth?" she asked in exasperation. What the hell did he think I meant? Did this goddamn planet affect intelligence as well?

He hesitated. "Well, no. No *news.*"

"But . . ." she led him.

"Well, we should have received *something,* but we didn't."

"You mean the connection is dead?"

He nodded.

"It's just the satellite relays, they were all knocked out."

"We stopped receiving before they went offline."

"There's only one Earth station with quantum-wave capability," she said optimistically. "Losing that doesn't signify too terribly much."

He nodded again, looking unconvinced.

But what it did signify hit her with a shock.

The Agency was gone — destroyed.

If the constant connection to their colonies was no longer operating, it could mean nothing less. She stopped in her tracks, digesting this startling news.

Someone bumped into her, bringing Mallory back to the needs of the moment. She continued onward, watching her feet move, one step after the other up the hill as her shock turned slowly to speculation.

Was it the Agency's own defense system? she wondered. Its self-destruct would automatically activate if Central Control was breached. And which enemy was it: political or industrial? What better time to risk a raid on your rival than now, with nobody home.

The Q-drive was a prize many would consider well worth the risk. But they could not succeed, she was certain of that; there were too many backup systems. The Agency's Earth site was gone.

Now the Agency will have to move its headquarters up here, to Primus, just as Simon has been demanding they do for the past seven years. She remembered how furious he'd been when the Board approved funding for only a small version of Central Control to be built on the colony. It would not handle the everyday workings of the Agency. That would remain on Earth. Instead, it was to be nothing more than a repository for their valuable secrets — a large repository by most people's standards.

But even that had not come to pass. The Board always found another reason to delay, unwilling to divide Central Control, as was Simon. But Simon believed moving the Agency's entire headquarters to Primus was the only way to keep it safe from espionage and terrorism — and war.

He always seems to get his way in the end, she thought spitefully, but was immediately contrite. Simon would be deeply disturbed by the destruction of the Agency. The loss would probably affect him more than anyone. It was, after all, his baby. He designed the plans, found the men and equipment to build it, and created a security force to protect it. And because of all that, the ISA was — no, *is* the most powerful company in the world.

Mallory was forced to stop once again, the gravity dragging at her like metal weights. She was only halfway up the hill.

Wiping the sweat from her brow, she thought tiredly, I feel like I gained ninety pounds and haven't exercised for a year.

She looked back at the others. Most had already stopped. Only Erin continued on ahead of her. Mallory watched her slow progress: step, pause, step.

Was this a climber's technique? Mallory wondered, as she remembered Erin was an amateur mountaineer.

She's wearing one of my designs, she realized. And in spite of everything, it still gave her a twinge of satisfaction. In the skintight suit, every ripple on Erin's slight frame was clearly defined. She's all muscle, Mallory realized in admiration.

Once more she looked towards the spaceport: more ships were docking.

"The men are arriving," she said to no one in particular. The statement produced a small burst of energy in those that heard. Several heads turned to watch the ships slide into berth. "Well, we'd better make room for them," Mallory said, forcing herself to stand. She grabbed the handle of her suitcase and continued upward.

After a moment, she heard the others following.

Erin had stopped to rest near the crest of the hill. With a crooked grin, she watched Mallory struggle up the slope. When Mallory collapsed in a panting heap just below her, Erin said in a flat tone, "I guess you only design sportswear, you don't actually use them."

"Up yours," Mallory gasped, laying back and closing her eyes.

Erin laughed appreciatively, a short barking sound. "Did they teach you that at finishing school?"

"No," she panted. "College: Obscenities 101. It was my major."

Once more that abrupt bark escaped Erin as she rose to look over the spaceport. From here, the long runway could be seen clearly. "More ships," she announced, and had meant her voice to be deadpan, but the excitement sung through.

"Which ship is he on?" Mallory asked.

"I'm not sure." Erin paused. "I should have found out."

"They'll all be here soon, in any case."

"Yes," she said, grasping her suitcase handle and preparing to continue onward. "We should keep moving. It's getting crowded at the bottom of the hill."

"In a minute," Mallory said, but pulled herself up anyway. Reluctantly, the women and children covering the road behind her rose to their feet.

Mallory followed Erin up the last of the hill, matching her strange walking style: a step, a pause, a step. It made the going slightly easier, allowing her to make it over the final hump at the top. Then relief: she was on flat ground, the cool of the forest beckoning her onwards, keeping her exhausted body moving forward. But she remembered her duty and made herself turn back to help the others over the top of the rise, encouraging those at the bottom to keep moving.

Erin stayed by her side, assisting.

"You should keep going," Erin suggested. "People like having someone to follow."

Mallory nodded, relieved at the excuse. She walked tiredly with the growing numbers of women and children, past stubby bushes and increased patches of scrub grass. She'd covered fifty feet and was almost to the trees when from over the hilltop came the long, high scream of ripping metal, immediately followed by human shrieks of terror.

For one flickering moment she froze before whirling around in fear: "Simon!"

Releasing the suitcase, she forced her legs into a run, flinging off her handbag.

Althaia felt a prickly sensation as the vision made a bigger leap forward.

Mallory entered the bedroom with only a brief knock, "Here's the brush you wanted, Jillian."

A young woman of Asian descent looked up from her writing in surprise. "I di—" she began, but was cut off by Mallory's fierce motion to silence.

Mystified, Jillian watched Mallory lock the bedroom door as she continued in an overly bright voice, "I've got some great ideas that could do wonders for your hair. Come into the bathroom and I'll show you what I mean."

Now completely confused, Jillian followed her inside.

Putting a finger to her lips, Mallory closed the door before quickly turning on the taps at the sink and bathtub. Then she waved the younger woman over, pulling her down onto the edge of the tub, saying in a hushed tone, "Speak quietly."

"Mallory, what are you doing?" Jillian whispered.

"In case your room's bugged," she said.

"What!"

"Whisper!" she hissed. "They've got bugs planted everywhere — Simon's fanatical."

"Here? Jeesus, Mallory."

"We are talking about a man who had all key personnel and their families surgically implanted with a transmitter in the event of a kidnapping, only he neglected to mention that those in possession of sensitive information were also fitted with a tiny explosive: just enough to cause a blood clot to the brain. He even had one himself until recently."

"Christ," Jillian said in awe. Then she hissed at Mallory accusingly, "You could have warned me about the bugs before we started spouting off about the Agency!"

"I didn't know, I just found out myself. Never mind about that, look at these," Mallory said, stuffing the brush into Jillian's hands as she pulled thin sheets of plazpaper from her back pocket and unfolded them carefully. They were computer printouts. "I was right."

"What is it?"

"It's a list of every woman who's been denied a business license or a lease —

and that's every woman who's applied!"

"What!"

"Not one."

"God, you *were* right . . . ."

"Jillian, this is not just my domestic battle anymore, this is big." She brought out more sheets. "Look at these, the rulings on cases of domestic violence: all found in favor of the husband. And look, any case involving a man and woman, the woman loses every time."

"Where did you get these?"

"I'd rather not say."

"Why not?"

"Because it's getting very scary on this new world of ours, and the less you know, the less you have to lie about."

"What are we going to do?"

"You? Nothing. You have to stay out of it."

"No way!" Jillian said in a fierce whisper.

"You have to. Nobody living inside the Agency can be involved."

"Involved in what? You sound like you've already got it figured out."

"Well . . . actually, I have been approached."

"Approached by who?"

"A small group who are as concerned about this as we are."

"Who are these people?"

"I can't really say, I only met the one, and he was wearing a disguise."

"What!"

"It was for safety! What if he approached me and I turned him over to the guards? He couldn't take that chance."

"Why not? What are they planning?"

"It's a perfect plan. But it will mean pretending to reconcile with Simon. And there's one stipulation. no HQ people."

"Why not?"

"The chance of a leak is way too high — that's why we're whispering inside a bathroom for god's sake." Jillian started to argue, but Mallory cut her off: "Please don't fight me on this, I don't have the energy. What I need is your complete support."

"But I want to help."

"You'll be my shoulder. God knows I'm going to need one."

"Some help," Jillian said in annoyance, tossing the brush onto the countertop.

155

Althaia looked at the brush in her hand with a feeling of excitement.

That woman! She was the one who suffered such violence within this room. Could this be an indication that the Synchronicity Phenomenon has been activated?

Eagerly, Althaia lifted the second grooming aide.

Straining with effort, Mallory and an adolescent girl struggled to maneuver a body from the floor and onto the serving cart that doubled as a gurney.

She resented this time spent on the dead. There wasn't time or energy enough for the living. How many died of neglect?

With a final shove, the body rested on the cart. Without a word, she moved off, slowly pushing the cart between patients lying in untidy rows on the ballroom floor.

She tried not to notice the empty spaces where there'd once been an injured man or woman — or child. Every day, the number of spaces grew. Not enough medicine or bandages, or hands to help.

There are simply too many of them and so few of us. And even fewer who know what the hell they're doing. Three doctors and four nurses — not enough — not nearly enough. Most of it's left to people like me, and I barely knew how to put on a Band-Aid before this. Now I tend burns, stitch up gaping holes, and even set bones. How many have I killed because of my ignorance?

She shivered involuntarily.

I'll never get used to death, she thought, and yearned for the zombie-like state she saw in others.

Jillian moved past her, pushing a serving trolley laden with containers of water.

That one's got endurance, Mallory thought. She's got nerve too. Maybe she's someone worth cultivating. Mallory grunted in surprise: I just had a normal thought. How long since that happened?

She brought the stretcher outside as a vehicle arrived. Two exhausted men, their green uniforms thick with grime, climbed down from the truck. In silence, they began lifting the bodies laid out for removal, tossing them carelessly into the truck's open box. Mallory waited until they lifted the dead man from her cart before staggering back inside HQ.

It was time for the living.

The vision's point of focus made a sudden jump.

156

". . . but God in His mercy has spared Man from complete annihilation. He has created another world and established His Church upon it in preparation for His Chosen Ones. *You* are those Chosen Ones. *You* have been found worthy of the great task of bringing Man back to God.

We must be strong, as the way back will be long and arduous, for we have strayed far from His Path. But he has provided us with much for the journey home. He has permitted His Church to remain with us to give direction and absolution. He has given us a garden: another Eden to dwell in. And He has provided us with a capable government with Simon Cartwright at its head. Through his able leadership, we will rebuild our world and restore it to Earth's past glory."

Almost five thousand adults, many still recovering from their injuries, stood huddled together on the soggy ground, listening to the outdoor service. Their blind acceptance and trust for this man swept over Mallory, nearly engulfing her where she stood in the front row. She had to struggle hard not to lose herself in the power of that mass need: the need for reassurance, hope and answers.

There's been too much to cope with, she thought. The grief, the horror and fear — and the eternal exhaustion. We're alone in the universe, cut off from everything we once knew. It would be so easy to hand the direction of our lives over to these men on the podium. Why fight it? Maybe this bishop — no, he's Pope now — maybe he's right, at least partially.

The Pontiff continued, "You have all suffered terrible losses, and will certainly suffer further hardships, but your children need not. Their lives could be transformed, if only we would each and together turn our steps back to the ways of integrity and decency. We must sacrifice personal desire and fulfill our duty to God and to the community — if not for your own sake, then for the sake of your children. Let us not repeat history. Let us return to God."

There was a long moment of silence, while the words impressed themselves upon the vulnerable flock.

"Tom Murdock will now give the eulogy."

Mallory shivered in revulsion, breaking the spell.

There was no one she hated more than Tom Murdock. She couldn't understand why others found him so appealing. His beaming good cheer was such an obvious façade, his eloquence a syrupy pacifier to lull the unsuspecting. The Agency had used him for PR, and Simon always said he detested the man, claimed he'd unload him if he ever had the power. But now Simon's using him too.

She could not bear to hear this man speak of her dead family and the billions lost on Earth, or those thousands who had come so close to safety only to die in such a tragic accident.

Abruptly, she left her assigned position and almost ran from the service.

Mallory flopped in a heap, landing amongst the freshly turned dirt that had been cleared in one small corner of the treed mountainside. Scattered across the field, there were several other women lying in a similar state of exhaustion.

Mallory allowed herself to relax completely, not a thought to mar the utter bliss of inactivity. But a few minutes later, her mind forced hard facts back into awareness: plants not firmly rooted before the rainy season will be washed away, and all our newly cleared soil with them. We will starve.

The thought prodded her into action. She sat up and began gathering the seedlings that had fallen onto the ground. Tenderly, she laid them back inside the cloth bag she carried. These are the new gold, she thought. As valuable as any nugget dug from the earth — and as scarce.

If only Primus had plants we could digest properly, she thought tiredly. And then scolded herself: Why do I continually waste energy bemoaning something so completely out of my control? Just be thankful for Dr. Chang and his precious hybrids. Without his research, we'd have nothing.

Mallory pushed onto her feet to look over the valley, studying the steeply angled walls that rested along the narrow floor of the basin. She paused to admire the churning, hazardous rapids that reflected the un-Earthly blue sky as the river passed below the townsite and disappeared westward, into the untouched forest beyond.

Through the trees, Mallory could almost glimpse the small power plant that bridged the water, its tiny turbines able to convert the natural force of the river into electricity without the need for damming. The planet's long rainy seasons and cold winters allowed only sporadic use of solar energy to power the community, making the turbines a necessity.

There was evidence of annual flooding along the flatlands beside the river, giving cause for locating the settlement on the slopes above. Mallory lamented the necessity of it and then once again stifled her frustration. She turned away to look at the buildings dotting the mountainside. Many bore the appearance of recent and hasty completion, while several more were still under construction.

A road made of plaztar twisted snakelike through the community, winding its way down the hillside almost to the river flats before travelling eastward to be lost inside the dark shadows of a mountain pass.

To the charred and shattered spaceport, Mallory thought in sudden heartache.

Where our one intact ship sits empty: a ship that could house this entire community.

But we refuse to live where friends and loved ones died so horrifically. Where many were injured and almost died themselves. And where those few who escaped injury had to wade through the hellish mess in search of survivors, and then in search of medical and food supplies.

Shuddering, Mallory tried to push away the dark thoughts that had overtaken her.

In an effort at distraction, she looked up at the two structures that dominated the townsite from their positions high on the slope.

One was a large, plain building with nothing to break the monotony but a high-peaked roof with a single sharply crafted spire on each of its corners, and a few stained glass windows running along the building's front and sides.

Mallory had never seen a cathedral so plainly designed.

Conversely, slightly lower on the slope, was a broad, four-story building constructed in an extravagant jumble of architectural styles. Elaborate parapets, pillars and circular towers appeared in abundance, and the whole was covered in ornate carvings and scrollwork from the different architectural periods.

What a blot on the landscape, Mallory thought in disgust, grateful for the diversion. Was this some painful compromise to the different tastes of the Board members? To think of the money and effort that went into that monstrosity . . . .

And now, it's home.

And why the hell did I let *that* happen?

Because a lot of people were looking to me for leadership, that's why.

And finding Simon alive and well had nothing to do with it?

Ruefully, she acknowledged that it did, very much.

But it's a new world now, she thought, forcing herself into optimism. Maybe we can sweep the old baggage away, truly make a fresh start?

She didn't know if it was possible, but she was certain that both she and Simon deserved to try.

She turned and proceeded across the field, measuring off the distance before bending to make a hole in the earth with a thick stick that served as her trowel. Carefully, she placed one of the plants inside, pressing the dirt around it. With effort, she straightened and repeated the process.

If I had the proper clothes, I'd plant these on my knees and crawl right across this field, she thought. But these pants would shred to nothing by the end of it, and I can't afford that. I've so few clothes to last until . . . until what?

Abruptly, she stopped her planting and straightened up.

"Clothes," she said aloud. "We'll need clothes."

Her mind began to race with ideas. We'll need new fabric — lots of it. What we

159

brought from Earth, if any made it, will be gone in no time. We'll have to find new sources. The sheep we brought won't do the job, not by half. I must speak with Dr. Chang, see if he's done any work with cotton hybrids or other textile sources. I could help him with the research, collect plant samples . . . . We'll need spinning wheels and looms; maybe some survived. If not, I'll need to draft plans for them — I doubt anyone else has the skill. No, wait, maybe they're in the database, they should be. Everything needed to start a new world is in there. Her mind spun on, the excitement growing.

And I'll need to find dye sources, and create a whole new line for farming— she stopped short, remembering where she was. She chuckled quietly, and the sensation felt good.

Later, she thought, after the planting.

"Damn it, I don't understand his attitude! I'm doing something vital for the whole community, and he's still hassling me about quitting work and having children. As if nothing's changed and he still needs to feel threatened by my success and my wealth," Mallory said, her voice overlaid with fatigue.

"It's too hard having a baby on this planet. We can't really do both. The body won't let us. Maybe the next gen can do it . . ." Jillian trailed off.

"I am not giving up my career to work as a bloody homemaker," Mallory stated emphatically.

"Well, it's not really a *home*, Mallory, its HQ. It's like a small hotel filled with a lot of families — big families," Jillian commented in a reasoning tone, her own fatigue coming through.

They were in a small workshop. Countertops and shelves lined every wall, and a row of tables ran down the center of the floor, leaving little room for walking. Above the tables, a collection of tools hung from hooks bolted to the ceiling. The room was cluttered with blueprints, bottles, vials, lumber, and plant samples. A pot of colorful vegetation bubbled vigorously on a small hotplate, giving off an unpleasant aroma.

"Maybe he just wants your help?" Jillian continued. "As Chairman of the Board, he's responsible for the whole community; he could be feeling overwhelmed."

"You don't know Simon," Mallory said, grunting with effort as she tightened a bolt on an odd-looking device.

"Well, I'm beginning to, and one thing I do know is that he loves you."

"It's not enough," she said tiredly, stopping to rest her arms. "If he wants a helpmate so badly he can ask one of his other wives." She looked at Jillian with amusement. "You worked the domestic side of HQ, you'd be perfect."

"He doesn't want me."

"Too bad. You are now appointed Director of HQ Domestic Business. Now Simon can stop bothering me and you can stop defending him."

"I wasn't defending *him*," she retorted angrily. "I was trying to help *you*! And where do you get off ordering me around like you're some kind of queen. Go to hell!" she finished, and stormed towards the door.

"Jillian, wait!" Mallory called after the younger woman. Jillian stopped in the doorway. "I'm really sorry. I guess Simon's not the only one who's an arrogant asshole." She walked forwards, her hand extended. "Will you accept my apology?"

After a moment's hesitation, Jillian took the proffered hand. "I accept. But in all honesty, I've never thought of *Simon* as being an arrogant asshole." But there was humor in her eyes.

"Ouch!" Mallory said, smiling in return.

"And I want to apologize too. It's none of my business what you and Simon do. It just bugs me when people in love can't get it together." Especially now, she thought.

"It's not easy when both parties are strong-willed, hardheaded and stubborn," Mallory said, turning away. "Come and give me a hand with this thing — please."

"What is it?"

"It's a spinning wheel of sorts."

"Are you and Doctor Chang that close to harvesting?"

"This is for wool, although I am optimistic about our current crop."

"God, I hope so, because we are in desperate need of clothes. These weren't meant for farming," she said, tugging at the earth stained shirt she wore.

"You could repeat that for Simon's benefit."

It was barely light as Mallory made her way downstairs, taking long strides over the escalator steps, feeling too impatient to wait for their slow descent.

Three years of hard work was about to pay off, she thought excitedly, and imagined the fabric waiting for her in the workshop since last night with the pattern tacked to it so carefully.

She'd hated to delay, but her body was weak and shaky from forcing too much of herself in this alien world. Afraid of making a mistake with the scissors, she'd left it to complete until morning.

Humming softly, she turned down a corridor that led past an enormous kitchen. Even at this hour, there were a dozen people inside making preparations for the morning meal. Several steps beyond the kitchen entrance, she stopped before a closed door. Eagerly, she swiped the keycard and flung it open.

Shock sent the air rushing from her lungs.

The room had been stripped bare — not a vial or bottle remained.

In utter disbelief, she stepped inside, dazedly moving to the workbench where her cloth had lain, tacked and waiting — now stripped of all such evidence. Her hand closed into a fist, and she began to beat the workbench fiercely, the force of the blows causing its legs to lift slightly from the floor. "That bastard!" she hissed. "That fucked-up, twisted bastard!"

Her hand hit something cold and metallic. She grasped the scissors, rage overwhelming her. "No more!"

Still cursing, she ran from the room and down the corridor, heedless of the stares from inside the kitchen. Adrenalin pumping, she rushed back to the escalator and hurried up the ascending-side and along the hallway to Simon's room, as fast as the gravity would allow. She was panting heavily now and was forced to stop, her body shaking from the exertion.

Mallory stared down at the scissors in her hand. My god, he's almost driven me to murder!

The thought sent a cold chill down her spine, and with it came recognition:

Our marriage is finished. And I've known that for some time, haven't I?

She focused on the scissors again. I have to move out of HQ — and fast.

Abruptly, the door opened and Simon stood before her. He took in her distraught appearance and the scissors in her hand. "Whatever you might think, Mallory, it was for your own safety. Please, just let it go. I don't know if I can protect you if you don't. Things are . . . different now."

"You're wrong," she said bitterly, tossing the scissors at his feet. "They're exactly the same."


"Ms. Cartwright, we do understand that you are not of the Faith but, nevertheless, we still have an interest in your well-being. Your recent behavior has been a source of deep concern for us — deep concern." Mallory glared with open dislike at the Pope standing inside her doorway. Another man stood in the background, but she didn't even glance in his direction. "You have refused to perform your duties within HQ, but instead spend your time roaming the forest, collecting plants and flowers. You have also neglected your marital obligations, which, as you know, is an obligation to the whole community. Childbearing is the duty of every wife. We must all make sacrifices." She moved to shut the door in his face, but he put out a hand, preventing her. He pushed hard, taking a step inside her bedroom.

Mallory backed away. "Get out!"

"But we cannot ignore these recent and far more serious incidents," the Pontiff continued, as if she hadn't spoken. "First, you threaten your husband's life because you've misplaced your sewing. And now, you plan to desert him," he said, with a meaningful look at the half-packed suitcase lying on her bed, "claiming mental cruelty, when many have witnessed your husband's great devotion to you."

"I said, get out!" But again she was ignored.

"Perhaps your behavior stems from some physical or mental disorder? After all, you are childless, and this has been known to disrupt the mental balance of many women. Please, consider what I've said." He nodded solemnly and finally withdrew from her room.

Mallory dropped into an armchair and stared blindly before her. "God, I've been such an idiot! Thinking it was just the same old battle, when all I had to do was look around and see the truth. I can't believe how self-absorbed I can be!"

Jillian was in the process of removing grime-covered clothes. She paused to look at her friend. "Mallory, what are you talking about?"

Mallory blinked. "I was just informed that if I try to move out of HQ, I'll be sent off to the loony bin. Which, by the way, they'll need to build first. Not that a little detail like that will stop them."

"Who said that?"

"The self-appointed Pope himself — and the magistrate, hovering in the background, just to let me know his Holiness has the full support of the authorities."

"Have they lost their minds? They can't do that!" Jillian declared, tossing her dirty clothes into a pile on the floor.

"Who's going to stop them?"

"What do you mean, who's going to stop them? This is Ameri—" she broke off, uncertain.

"Exactly: no Bill of Rights, no legal recourse. They have an Army for god's-sake! They can make their own laws."

"Oh, my god, could you be right?" Jillian said, dropping onto the bed, clean clothes in hand.

"We've all been so busy doing our blasted duty that we've neglected to notice a few major flaws in our brave new world." Once more she frowned into the great nothingness. Then she announced, "Well, they might force me to stay, but I

163

refuse to reconcile with Simon. But it's not about that, is it? It's about keeping me muzzled. Can't have me living amongst the populace, I'm too opinionated, too outspoken — and I have a lot of support amongst the women.

"But why is the Church a party to this?" Jillian asked, her voice muffled by the sweater she pulled over her head.

"The Church will do whatever the Board tells it to do, if it wants to stay intact."

"We've got to start talking about this! Wake people up to the facts," Jillian announced, pulling on her jeans with unusual force.

"That'll put us both inside a rubber room—" Mallory broke off. "What *is* that?" She stood up to feel inside the back pocket of her trousers. "It's poking me," she said in annoyance, removing the comb and tossing it aside.

"Did it go alright?"

"Yes, fine. Nerve wracking, but fine."

They were in the bathroom, the water running noisily. Jillian stood clutching a large basket of vegetables to her chest.

"I'm sorry I had to get you involved, but I couldn't get out of the Simon's reception without faking an illness, which would preclude me from taking an innocent stroll through town."

"I'm just glad to finally be of some help."

"I know. Thank you."

Mallory took the basket from Jillian and set it on the countertop. She tossed aside the layer of vegetables and the cloth underneath them to reveal the contents hidden at the bottom: a silver canister and a blunt black object.

Jillian looked inside the basket, cautiously picking up the dark object. She cracked it open to look inside. "No bullets?"

"Not necessary. I'm not actually going to shoot anyone."

Jillian laid the object back down. "Is it wise to hold an empty gun when you're pointing it at somebody with a loaded one?"

"I'm not planning on doing that," she snapped, nerves making her voice break. She was frayed. Jillian backed off.

With a sigh, Mallory dropped to the toilet seat. Am I going to make it? she wondered.

"So . . ." Jillian began, trying to be supportive, "your men will stay outside and the women will be inside?"

"Yes. My contact in HQ will open the door for them. We'll take over Simon's offices and the Board's. The men will deal with the guards outside."

"How many men do you have?"

She hesitated. "I'm not certain: that information is on a need-to-know basis."

"God, I hope this works."

"It has to — it will. They would never risk Simon's life."

"And neither would you."

"Don't start."

"Sorry," Jillian said. "So who's your contact?"

"I wasn't told. He doesn't know who I am either. It's safer for all of us this way."

"I guess . . . ."

"Ouch," Mallory said, standing to feel her backside. "I'm tired of being poked by this thing." She took the comb out of her pocket. "It's yours, if you want it," she offered, tossing it onto the countertop.

# CHAPTER 19

"YOU ARE the executive to the people of this world?" Frayne asked from his prone position on the bedroom floor. He was lying near the window, which afforded a view of the incredible reds streaking the morning sky as he conversed with the young man.

William's lips twitched with amusement at the archaic word. "I am the Chairman of New Eden. The position of executive no longer exists," he said, sitting stiffly on a hard seat at the other side of the room.

"New Eden is the name of your planet now?"

"It is."

"We observed from our ship that the population of New Eden is concentrated solely within the green terrain. We were surprised by the complete absence of any desert communities. History has taught us that humans utilize all ecosystems at their disposal, no matter how harsh."

"None but soulless devils would dare venture into the Unholy Lands."

"There are religious strictures against venturing into this arid region?"

William laughed shortly. "No one is prevented." He gave another snort and looked at Frayne with amused tolerance. "We dwell in the Garden of Eden, the Anointed Land of God. Why would we choose to live amongst demons?"

Frayne returned his eyes to the window as he contemplated this new information. How sad I feel for this world, so lost in superstition and fear, he thought to himself.

After a moment, it occurred to Frayne that he must on no account reveal the location of their shuttlecraft.

They had landed the small ship on the flat surface of the desert, and such information would, of course, terrify the young man, and perhaps even fill him with overwhelming doubt regarding their humanity.

"Would you like to see a map?" William asked.

"I would be most gratified to see a map of your world."

William rose and opened the door to the hallway where a squad of bodyguards stood on watch. His constant companions since Robert's return to duty: three squads in continual rotation. They followed him everywhere — except when he was with the stranger. William had categorically refused to allow this. He had no wish to burden his loyal soldiers with more blasphemous secrets. And what harm could such a weakling do to him?

"Have the map brought from my study," he ordered Sergeant Fists.

"Immediately, Sire."

The muffled sounds of orders given and relayed could be heard through the closed door as Frayne asked, "May I inquire what name you are known by, if that is permissible to ask of a . . . Chair Man?"

William looked at Frayne in surprise: it hadn't occurred to him that the stranger wouldn't know his name, for every male knew the Anointed Leader of New Eden, man and boy alike. But of course, Frayne could not possibly know this, and it gave the young Chairman an uncomfortable feeling to realize his mistake.

"William is my name."

"William," Frayne repeated, testing the name on his lips, and wondering at the young leader's sudden discomfort. Studying him, Frayne recognized an ancient device hanging from a heavy chain draped around his neck. "May I enquire as to the significance of the . . . the silver object you wear?"

"The medallion is a symbol of office. New Eden's first Chairman wore it on his ascendancy to the throne. After his death, it was passed on to his son." William fingered the ancient object. "In time, I will pass it on to mine." Once again he was left with a feeling of unease.

Frayne opened his mouth to comment on the pendant but reconsidered. What purpose would it serve? It would only disturb the Chair Man, and to what end? If he does not recognize it is a technical device then let him remain in ignorance.

William was staring hard at the stranger, seeking to direct his uneasy feelings outward. Abruptly, he demanded of Frayne, "If we share the same ancestors, how is it that our bodies are so different?"

Frayne paused, wondering how he could explain a gravitational field to a person who was unable to acknowledge scientific concepts. At last, he answered: "Our planets are very different from each other, and from Earth. These human bodies have changed over time, to suit the conditions on the two planets that our Ancestors colonized."

"*Our* bodies have changed?" he asked in a challenging tone, looking down at himself.

"Yes, your New Eden bodies are now much stronger than the bodies of your Earth Ancestors: your bone and muscle mass is much denser." William considered this, and he looked pleased at the idea of such superior strength. "Also, from what I have observed, the men on New Eden are approximately thirteen centimeters shorter than the people who fled to this planet."

William's brow furrowed in confusion. "What is this centi meters?"

Frayne's look of surprise quickly turned to one of understanding. "Do you measure by the old imperial system?" And at William's continued confusion, he explained, "One that uses inches, miles and pounds as units of measurement."

William nodded. "Yes, this we do."

"Then I will clarify: Your adult males are approximately five inches shorter than the average male ancestor, whose height in the northern hemispheres at the time of Earth's destruction was, on average, five feet and ten inches."

"And you," William stated, eyeing Frayne's physique, "are taller than the Ancestors."

"Yes, I am approximately four inches taller, but there are many on my world whose height is greater than mine. And, as you can see, our bone and muscle density is less than those from Earth."

William continued to ponder these ideas, and as he did so he felt his fear of the stranger easing yet again.

There was a sharp rap on the door, and William opened it to accept the map. It was almost six feet long, encased in a hard cover of flex-glass. Awkwardly, he lowered it to the floor, propping it against the wall so Frayne could see it easily from where he lay.

The map was very old. It was obviously the work of the Ancestors, and slightly faded now. It showed an ocean of barren stone surrounding the lush continent of greenery. Within the green belt was an endless string of mountain ranges. Three of these rimmed the perimeter, standing tall and slender, while at least four other mountain ranges cut haphazardly across the interior. Countless rivers twisted their way down gorges and valleys to eventually spill into the lakes dotting the far south.

This continent was over two thousand miles from east to west, and a thousand at its deepest, but nowhere did there appear a valley floor or a plateau of any significant size. Life here must exist on the fertile slopes of the mountains.

On the great stony plain surrounding this verdant continent, the very opposite was found. No water at all was indicated, no soil and no life, only a vast expanse of endless rock. Even the mountain ranges standing north of the plain were barren and stark.

At some point, the map had been removed from its casing and alterations made. Words were covered up with thick white paint and new ones added. The words Unholy Lands were written in large red letters over the desert, while the green continent was sectioned by green paint into three regions: North, South and

168

West. Each region was divided into several districts, numbered but not named, save for one exception: the Holy District.

Only the mountains ringing the outer edge of the green belt remained separate from the grid of districts and regions.

Frayne stared at the map with great interest before announcing in puzzlement, "I see your Regions and Districts on this map, but not the names of your communities."

"Yes, look here, it's clearly marked." William pointed out.

Frayne looked closely at the spot William indicated, and read the words NEW EDEN in bold lettering across the green continent.

"Is not New Eden the name of your planet?"

"Yes, that too."

"But this map gives only the name of your area of greenery. I was inquiring into the names of your towns and cities."

"Yes," William said in understanding. "New Eden."

"But there is only one community," Frayne replied, baffled.

"Certainly," William answered in surprise. "How else would it be?"

"How large is this city?" Frayne asked, and realized he already knew the answer.

"It stretches the entire length of our Garden," William stated proudly. "To the very edge of our forest buffer, which, as you can see, is ten to twenty miles thick."

"New Eden: the planet, the continent, and the city," Frayne said almost to himself, his tone carrying a note of amusement.

"How is it on your world," William demanded, indignant at the humor he saw in the stranger's face.

"My world has many communities," Frayne answered, sobering quickly, regretting that he had offended the Chair Man. "But all are small, with much distance between them. This is to prevent disruption of the ecological systems of our planet."

"Many cities?" William could not imagine it, and he too was amused. "Where would your Chairman live? With so many cities to choose from, which would win the honor?" He considered for a moment. "Each of your cities must need its own political representatives. Why, the administrative costs alone would bankrupt the government within a year! It all sounds very inefficient."

Frayne had to smile at the extraordinary picture William had painted of his world. "Each of our communities is self-sufficient," he explained. "And there is no leader for us to vie over."

"No leader!"

"That is correct."

"Then who passes judgment? Makes laws? Who commands the people?"

169

"No one commands, and there are no laws, not as you would understand them."

"But you must have laws! All would be anarchy — mayhem! People doing any evil that popped into their heads! Stealing and killing, and Satan-only-knows what unspeakable acts!"

"We have no need to steal or to act with violence against one another," Frayne answered calmly. "It is true that we do as our feelings prompt us, but this would never infringe on the personal rights of others."

"And what stops you?" William demanded.

Frayne considered the question for a moment. "It would not feel good," he concluded.

"What?"

"Infringing upon the rights of another would cause unpleasant feelings," Frayne said simply. "We do not wish to experience this discomfort."

William could only stare at the Stranger, completely bemused. Finally, he roused himself. "You are tired. You will rest now." He halted before departing, saying, "I will return later."

The privy servant tried to keep his voice steady. He must show no fear or they'd think he'd something to hide — which he did. It did not matter that their interest lay elsewhere; there would be other days.

If only there was more light in here, Baldwin thought with regret. Then it wouldn't seem so . . . . The word *sinister* popped into his mind and he immediately squelched it in terror, as if the man across the desk could read his thoughts. And though he knew that this was impossible, the little boy within him believed otherwise. That little boy was very active today, sitting within the dark shadows of the Pontiff's office and feeling uncomfortably reminded of his school days and the ordeals dealt out by the discipline priests. Their offices dark and oppressive — like this one.

"You say he has not been outside the palace since the stranger arrived?"

"Yes, Your Holiness — I mean, no, Your Holiness, not after dark, no."

"And Thomas, does he also spend time with the stranger?"

"Prince Thomas does not share the Chairman's interest. But he encourages his Highness in this pursuit."

"And what of the stranger? Do you hear what passes between him and your Sovereign?"

"No, Your Holiness, the Chairman will allow no one to hear the stranger speak. And he has ordered that no word of the stranger is to be spoken beyond the palace gates." Baldwin's gaze shifted away uneasily, making the Pope's eyes spark briefly with amusement. "The Chairman has also assured us that despite rumors to the contrary, the stranger is not from Proximus, nor did he claim to be."

The Pope grunted appreciatively. It was a good strategy. Was it William's or Robert's? And was it the truth? But if not from Proximus, then from where? The desert? Impossible. But we cannot dispute his humanity. The test was given, and in public. Unfortunate. A demon would not be nearly so dangerous.

*How* could he be from Proximus? The History does not lie, that much I am certain of. Yet, here he is with information that no one on New Eden could possibly possess: information that only a Pope would know — or someone from Proximus.

Calming his thoughts, the Pontiff turned his attention back to the frightened privy servant. "The stranger is permitted to speak with no one?" Validus asked. "Not even Captain Bountiful?"

"Him, yes, but the captain does not wish it, though I believe His Highness relays all the stranger's conversations to him."

The Pontiff was silent, considering. "What do *you* know of the stranger?" he asked at last.

"Nothing, Your Holiness, except that he's weak as a little eve and quite repulsive to look at."

"You've seen him then?"

"No, but I've heard the rumors."

"What else have you heard?"

"Only nonsense things."

"Explain."

The man hesitated. "Some say he's an angel come down to save the Chairman and to ensure him a son."

"Indeed?"

"Forgive me, Your Holiness, for repeating the silly prattle of young minds."

"Truth can come in many forms, even from the mouths of the young," Validus said with a glint in his eye. "Do you know of other rumors or information concerning the stranger?"

"Some days past, the Chairman ordered his personal physician to attend him."

"The stranger is ill?"

"The knife wound, I hear, is not healing properly."

The Pope sat motionless for a moment, thinking: This was hopeful news. The stranger will die a natural death and we will not need to move against him.

"You may go," the Pontiff said shortly. "Keep this interview to yourself."

"Yes, Your Holiness, of course, Your Holiness," Baldwin assured him fearfully, scuttling backwards out of the room.

171

"That was encouraging information," the Pontiff said to Cardinal Vecker, who lurked behind him in the shadows. "It would appear our young Chairman has cleansed himself of that noxious drug."

"It would seem so, yes."

"You see, Vecker, miracles do happen," Validus said, his tone amused.

"He has yet to sire a son."

"Patience, Vecker, patience. Some miracles take time." But the cardinal was not assured. "Let's have some light in here, Vecker. It's far too gloomy." And he smiled at his little joke.

The cardinal pulled back the heavy drapes from two sets of windows, and the afternoon light poured into the room, dispelling the atmosphere instantly.

"Now, Vecker, I think we must deliver an urgent invitation to the Royal Physician. It's time we had a little chat."


"You must come meet the stranger," William declared with excitement, thumping his beer mug down beside his dinner plate, both were nearly untouched. "You would find him most interesting."

"You are far braver than us, Brother," Henry said from his place on William's left. "You have told us enough of this alien stranger to keep our distance."

William had given the princes only a vague account of Frayne and his intriguing information, unable to share too much, surrounded, as the Chairman always was, by his personal guard.

"I assure you, he's not so fri—" William broke off, and then continued hurriedly, "so strange, once you speak with him and get accustomed to his unusual appearance."

"I don't think I can bring myself to do it, Brother." Henry looked across the table. "What say you, Thomas? Do you dare meet the challenge of our Little Puppet?" he asked with amusement.

William tried not to show how the name disturbed him, while the guards stationed against the dining room walls scowled at the insult, their hands twitching slightly as they yearned to avenge their Chairman for many such affronts. But these insolent shitheads were the Chairman's own brothers and therefore untouchable — until opportunity allowed otherwise.

"I too must learn of the stranger secondhand," Thomas announced with a slightly sardonic note. "And I look forward to hearing your tales of his abnormalities; they've given us more pleasure than you know."

William beamed. He was actually capable of doing something his brothers could not. "I must leave now, I have an appointment." He hesitated. "I don't believe I can make it again tonight. But you'll bring something back for me?" He was no longer desperate for the drug, the dosage now greatly reduced, but still he could not quite do without it.

"Of course," Thomas assured him with a thin smile.

With exaggerated bows of respect, they stood while the Chairman and his guard exited the elder prince's apartment.

"Now we have him!" Henry exclaimed with glee, dropping back into his chair and stabbing his knife into a thick haunch of meat. "The weakling truly believes this stranger comes from Proximus!"

"Yes, it would seem our Puppet has lost his tiny little mind. The drug has worked well."

"Now we can sit back and let the Church take care of him."

"Yes, it will certainly have to, and very soon, I think."

"Thank God, we'll finally have an end to that whiny little runt!"

They smiled at the thought and raised their mugs in silent salute.

# CHAPTER 20

"TELL ME about your cities. What are they like?"

"They will be difficult to describe to you," Frayne answered, uttering each word with effort. He had to pause for several minutes before explaining, "You are not permitted to hear of science or technology. Our cities are completely dependent upon these to function."

The walk downstairs to William's private courtyard had been too much for him, as William had warned. But still, Frayne had insisted, his need for open space too pressing.

Frayne lay on the sparse grass, wrapped in every piece of clothing he owned in addition to the wool cloak William had given him, and still he felt cold. But it was pleasant to be outside all the same.

"It will rain soon," William observed.

Again, several minutes passed before Frayne felt strong enough to reply: "We do not have rain in our cities."

"No rain? Is it desert?" and his voice had an edge of suspicion to it.

"No. They are covered by domes."

"Covered? How strange. They must be very dark."

Frayne shook his head. "Our domes have the look of . . ." he paused for several moments, trying to think of some image the Chairman could understand. "The look of a giant soap bubble. The sunlight comes through."

The words sparked William's imagination, painting a clear picture that stimulated his interest. "Are they very high?" he asked, his face animated with curiosity.

"Yes, the domes are built far into the sky. I would estimate their height to be five hundred meters at their greatest point. That would be approximately one-third of your miles."

An awed breath escaped from William.

"It must be a tremendous sight."

"Yes, they are aesthetically pleasing. Their function is to collect the sun's energy to provide power for the cities." He added, shivering, "They are never cold."

"Do you want to go inside?"

"No, let us wait for the rain."

"Have you felt rain before?"

"Yes, I have been outside the dome. But few on my world experience this sensation now; they are too distracted by the Realming."

"Realming? What is that?"

"It is a subject that will disturb you."

"Has it to do with science?"

"No, not that, but disturbing all the same."

But William's curiosity had been piqued. He was willing to hear anything at this moment. "Tell me."

"Realming is the journey of the consciousness to other planes of reality, other realms beyond the one our bodies inhabit."

William said in a stiff monotone, "I understand your reluctance to speak of it."

Frayne looked at him keenly. "You do not fear my ideas as you once did. You are opening your mind to new possibilities. This pleases me greatly, for there is much I would like to share with you."

"And there's a good deal I want to know of your world," William acknowledged, and then fell silent. But am I being tempted and tested, and found wanting? he wondered. Do I endanger my immortal soul?

"I do not seek to harm you," Frayne said softly, interrupting his thoughts.

William looked into Frayne's clear eyes and open expression. "I know."

Suddenly they were splashed with water as the heavens released their offering.

"We can go inside now," Frayne stated, and began pushing onto his feet when his arm buckled under him. "I must ask for your assistance."

William pulled him easily to a standing position; the stranger seemed almost weightless. "Should my guards carry you up the stairs?"

"Possibly . . . . But it is my arm that troubles me: the pain is becoming worse. Perhaps you would ask your healer to attend me once more?"

"Of course." They moved slowly towards the entrance. "Later, when you've recovered your strength, I will know more about your cities," William said.

"I would like that very much."

The two unlikely friends retreated into the shelter.

175

# CHAPTER 21

WILLIAM WHISTLED tunelessly as he left his apartment, his personal guard wrapping around him like a familiar mantle. Never had he felt so fine.

His mind sang with visions of strange and wonderful ideas: Holographic pictures! Robots! Machines that made food! Flying carts! And those wonderful cities encased in a bubble.

And all of it science and technology and therefore intrinsically evil, he reminded himself.

Yet the more he learned of Frayne's world, the less true that seemed. On Proximus — no, Mirandus it was now called — there is no disease, no thievery, and no fear.

How could any of that be bad? he wondered.

But, as he always had to remind himself, Frayne's people are dying out.

But aren't we too . . .?

Always this circular argument that led back to Frayne's original question: would New Eden help his world?

He must decide soon, or the choice would be removed from him. The Church would not delay much longer. That they'd gone this long without any attempt at intercession surprised him, for assuredly that obnoxious priest had filled the Pontiff's ear with every detail of Frayne's interview. And though William had done all he could to keep Frayne and his startling knowledge hidden from the general public, it was certain to leak out in bits and pieces. The Church would need to squash the source of that gossip before it traveled too far or gained too much strength.

Perhaps if I relinquish the stranger's eve to the Church, that would gain me more time with him?

But William knew with certainty that such a move would end his friendship with the stranger, for he would be unable to hide the truth from Frayne's uncanny senses.

Yet, in the end, I may have to betray him, or betray my Church and damn my soul for all eternity.

William didn't know how he was going to give Frayne up to certain death, for he could think of nothing in Frayne's vast and fascinating knowledge that would not immediately inflame the Church to righteous anger and Expulsion. Frayne's very existence was an abomination.

But the Chairman would not think of that now, for he had compiled another list of questions for his strange new friend and he didn't want his pleasure interfered with.

He arrived at Frayne's door and the guard stationed there moved aside to allow the Chairman entry. But once inside the bedroom, all of William's good cheer vanished. Frayne lay collapsed on the floor, a heap of tangled limbs, burning up with fever.

"Damn it, man, what's wrong?" William demanded, bending to move him. Frayne screamed and William released his grip, pulling back the sleeve of his shirt. The limb was grotesquely swollen, tight and inflamed.

"God in Heaven!" William swore. "Get a doctor! Now!" he shrieked at his guards in the corridor. Sergeant Perez pointed to one of the soldiers, who took off at a run. Then he nodded to another, who sped off in a different direction.

Perez stood in the doorway and the Chairman ordered him inside. Together they lifted Frayne from the floor and placed him on the bed. William watched him writhing in pain, delirious with fever. "Damn it, man, don't you die on me!"

God, don't let him die, William prayed silently. And then he turned to shout at Perez: "Get me Robert!"

"He be sent furr, Sire."

"Well done."

William gazed down at Frayne, and all the fear and desperation he'd felt at his father's deathbed suddenly returned. But now it seemed much crueler. Frayne was so young and he'd so much to accomplish. he had a world to save. "I swear to you, Frayne, and to the Great God above, live, and I will give you whatever you ask for."

"Do you mean breeders?"

Startled, William looked up to see Robert standing in the doorway. "Yes," was all he said, but he was adamant.

The doctor arrived, panting hard. "Sire?"

"Quickly, do something, I think he's dying!"

The physician examined Frayne briefly. "The arm is putrid; it will have to be amputated."

"But he would never survive the operation," William said, staring down at his friend's pathetic weakness. "He has barely strength enough when he's healthy."

"He'll die for certain without it."

William looked beseechingly at Robert. "Help me, Robert. He mustn't die."

Robert stared into William's stricken face, thinking hard. He glanced at the doctor and back to William. "Do I have your permission to do whatever I think necessary?"

"Anything," William stated with simple passion.

Robert strode from the room, returning a short time later with four soldiers. He motioned to the first pair. "You two," he ordered, "carry the stranger to the Chairman's apartments."

Both soldiers moved towards the bed.

Robert turned towards William. "I've already removed your privy servant, Sire," he assured William. "You two," he said, pointing to the remaining soldiers, "place the doctor under house arrest. He is to see no one, and no one is to know where he is but the Chairman and myself."

"What is the meaning of this!" the doctor sputtered.

"Hold!" the Chairman commanded, and the four soldiers froze. He turned to Robert with a questioning look.

"If I am correct, Sire, no one must know that the stranger is near death. My men will keep silent, but civilians are not always so obedient."

"My Lord," the royal physician broke in hastily, "you cannot listen to this ignorant soldier! If you don't allow me to amputate, the stranger will die!"

William hesitated, watching the frail figure on the bed twisting in torment before he commanded, "Do it."

As the outraged doctor was removed from the scene, William said quietly, "I hope you know what you're doing, Robert."

"So do I, my Lord, so do I."

Althaia heard movement and voices in the corridor outside her cell. There was a sense of excitement — of urgency. Then all went quiet before her door was flung open and a lone man stood before her. "Come," he commanded.

Though his clothing was similar to the men who usually came to her door, she knew this man was different from the others. He held no weapon to threaten her with, nor did he order her face to be covered despite his fear, which was as palpable as any. But he was much too fixated on his purpose to be distracted by such feelings.

Althaia stepped into an empty corridor and knew that this too was different.

The man immediately marched down the passage and she hurried to keep up. Abruptly, he stopped before a wall, bending to feel along its base before stretching up to touch some unseen object near the low-hung ceiling. There was a tiny click, and a piece of wall opened to reveal a manmade tunnel, damp and thick with the mustiness of age, the stone floor covered in slime. He paused to light a torch from one of the lamps hanging along the corridor and then motioned her inside.

Robert followed, making certain the wall returned to its proper alignment before he took the lead. The slippery floor made it impossible to hurry, and several times he was forced to stop and consult the thin sheet of plazpaper in his hand.

These passages were a long-kept secret of the Royal Family. Only the reigning Chairman and his Supreme Commander were privy to the knowledge. William had violated tradition by sharing this confidence with Robert, rationalizing that, upon Belcher's death, Robert would be appointed as his new Commander and become entitled to the information. He was certainly not the first Chairman to rationalize so.

Althaia recognized the map her escort carried: a copy of the blueprint from her vision, but far more detailed and easier to decipher. He continued to consult it as they moved through the maze of tunnels, making several turns before reaching a flight of stairs. At the top of the stairs they entered a corridor that was wider and much drier. The man immediately increased his pace, checking the map very little now, and after several more twisting turns, put it away altogether.

Althaia was flagging; her body could not sustain this challenging pace despite the healing energy. She was forced to slow down.

"Faster," Robert commanded.

Althaia shook her head. "I cannot," she said. She saw the man recoil at the sound of her voice, but he recovered, again forcing his fear aside to respond to some greater urgency. As he matched his pace to her own, she felt his fear subside to be replaced by frustration at their slow progress.

There were further stairs and narrow hallways, clearly used by small creatures more than humans. Finally they entered a short corridor and came to a halt. Robert put an ear to the wall, listening. When he was satisfied, he gave it a sharp rap with his knuckle. A moment later, the concealed door was sprung open and a young man urged them inside. She recognized his face from somewhere, but could not place him. He was highly agitated. "Robert, hurry! He's dying!"

Althaia followed Robert across the vast bedroom.

"Frayne," she gasped.

His breath was coming in a short, rasping pant, and she could feel the heat of his fever from where she stood by the bed. His clothes were drenched in sweat — and his arm! The skin stretched tight, as if ready to burst from the pressure. It was red and hot and tender.

179

"Can you help him?" Robert demanded.

"Yes," she nodded, information flooding into her consciousness. "Please bring many large pieces of clean, absorbent fabric that are not of value to you; they will need to be burned afterwards."

Robert strode from the room, returning shortly with a large stack of roughly woven towels. He placed them on the bed, saying, "You will help him now."

She was unsure if it was a question or a command. "Yes," she said, her eyes on Frayne. "I will ask you not to disturb us." She felt the two men move against the wall, the smaller one trying hard to contain his panic.

Althaia knelt beside the bed, inducing the trance state and calling the healing energy of the Universe to her. Then she placed her hands over the infected arm. Energy surged through her body, pouring from her fingertips and into Frayne.

She remained motionless for a long time, and then rose to her feet, slowly passing her hands over his entire body, radiating each organ and system with healing. When it was done, Frayne's breathing was much easier.

Althaia returned to the arm, concentrating the energy on the wound itself. After several minutes the old scab began to ooze thick yellow pus. She positioned two of the towels beneath his arm to catch the poison. The stench was vile, but she did not flinch. She heard one of the men make a gagging sound and rush from the room.

Her hands moved back over the scab. More pus surfaced in a pulse of larger and larger droplets until it oozed a slow, steady flow. "I will need a container. It must be large enough to lay his arm within it. Also, a container for waste," she said, without looking up from her work.

Robert moved instantly, returning shortly to place a wash bowl on the bed and a metal bucket beside her. He gagged and spat into the bucket, but did not run.

Althaia laid the towels inside the bowl, and when she awkwardly tried to place it under Frayne's arm, Robert said harshly, "I will lift him." When he'd done so, Althaia removed the pus soaked towels, tossing them into the waste bin. She positioned the bowl, and Robert lowered Frayne's arm inside. Once more her fingertips hovered above the wound while Robert stood against the wall, watching the poisonous flow continue its steady, sticky descent.

"Would it be possible to allow fresh air into this room?" Althaia was forced to ask.

She felt Robert's relief as he strode to the window and tried to open it, but the casement resisted. Impatiently, he rapped hard against the sash with the butt of his sword.

The window was from the time of the Ancients, and hadn't been opened for many decades. It took several attempts, but at last it gave way, allowing sweet, cool air to blow inside, pushing the rain ahead of it.

Robert remained by the window, watching.

Once again, he assisted Althaia as she replaced the towels under Frayne's arm. And still the wound released its poison, but the seepage was losing its yellowed hue, becoming a clear liquid. Gradually, the flow slowed to a steady pulse that grew weaker and weaker. She put a last towel under the arm and, with measured movements, passed her hands over his entire body. Finally she drew away.

"Will he live?"

"He will live."

"Will he need more . . ." he hesitated, at a loss. "Are you done?"

"He will require more healing, but for now we must both rest."

Robert said no more, but simply lifted the bucket and strode from the room.

Althaia went to the window, breathing in deep gulps of air. It was her first view of the outside since entering this building, and her eyes drank in the sights.

Through the wall of rain, Althaia could make out the city with its rough buildings of brick and stone, and a few of wood, but from her vantage she could see none that were constructed of the Ancients' plasteelite. The community's landscape was completely changed from the one in her visions. There were very few trees or bushes to be seen. Yet, in the distance, situated between the houses and places of business, the large strips of farmland remained, though now they were properly terraced to prevent an avalanche of water from taking out the soil. Althaia could see a few tiny figures toiling in the driving rain.

Far below the palace, the swollen river ran across the valley floor, its waters flooding into the sparse trees that still grew along the flatlands. The area remained clear of all construction. Only a bridge dared to place itself so near the flood line.

Twenty-five meters above the river, the city began, stretching across the valley until it was lost in the distance, the mountains cutting off her view.

Exhaustion hit and Althaia drew back from the window.

After making certain Frayne was properly covered, she took two rough-spun blankets from a cupboard and curled up on the floor.


Althaia woke a few hours later. She performed self-healing before rising to attend to Frayne. His color had improved significantly, but still he was very ill. Again she positioned her hands, calling the healing power to him.

When it was done, she wrapped herself in the blanket and was about to return to sleep when she caught sight of a chair. It was large, with a high back and wide armrests, and it was made of plasteelite: light and strong. She dragged it easily across the floor to the side of the bed.

Drawing a breath of protection, she lowered herself upon the seat.

Simon sat at the end of a long, wide table, his exhaustion obvious. I need rest, he thought, rubbing his hands roughly over his face. He turned to the man standing at his side. "You look like hell."

"Thanks," Cord said. "You look great too."

Simon grunted, pushing out a chair with his foot. "Here, sit."

"No thanks, too rich for my blood."

"Maybe mine too."

"Not you, Simon, you're right at home."

"Perhaps," he conceded and rubbed his face again. "Did the Mayflower get off?"

"Uh-huh. They'll contact us the minute they're over Earth. If they can get the quantum-relay workin'. If not, we'll have to wait 'til they're close enough for radio com. That means waitin' weeks longer. They'll try contactin' Proximus as well — find out what the hell's happening at their end. If they can't make quantum contact, it'll mean another twelve-week wait." He stopped for a moment. "It's the not knowin' that's hard." Simon nodded in agreement. Cord gave himself an inward shake and continued: "Moon bases will be checked too. But I'm not holdin' out much hope of survivors there."

"Okay, thanks," Simon said wearily, forcing his mind to concentrate. There are so many things to consider — but when did that ever bother me? This planet must be affecting me more than I thought.

Or maybe it's other things . . . .

Aware he was wandering, Simon brought his mind back to the issues at hand. "I want Security to stop looking for survivors. We've enough people doing that. They need to salvage more medical supplies and blankets from the ships — urgent priority. And as much food as they can find. What about livestock? What survived?"

"We lost all the pigs and chickens. There's still some cattle and goats. But the sheep fared well. Cats and dogs didn't make it — that's gonna upset a lot of people. We've some horses left. Oh, and the bees survived."

"Well, that's something . . . . Don't let anybody butcher anything until we hear from the Mayflower. We might need every one of those animals to rebuild our stocks. Better send out a few of our guys to do some fishing and hunting. There's supposed to be wild boar in these woods and some kind of deer or antelope — there might be other things as well. We won't survive long on what food we have left, even with all our losses."

"Too soon to say how many made it."

182

"Not enough, Cord, not nearly enough," Simon said, his voice shaking with rage at such needless waste. They were silent a moment, each composing himself.

"Daniel?" Simon finally asked.

Cord shook his head. "His ship didn't make it — like most of them. We even lost the freighters — all eighteen."

There was another long pause.

"What do you estimate Security has left?" Simon was able to ask at last.

"Two hundred — maybe."

"Jeesus," Simon swore, thinking of the thousands now dead. "All those fine young men, gone."

"They should have listened to you. Moved the Agency up here — all of it. Spent the few extra bucks on the gravitational system. They'd have been all Earth cozy inside. The lazy bastards never go outside anyway."

Simon smiled weakly at Cord's definition of a few extra bucks: 300 billion dollars to create and maintain earth's gravity in every building on the colony. Cord was right though, it was pocket change in comparison to the rich mineral ores ripped out of Primus during the past seven years — in comparison to what they've lost.

Simon knew the money was just another excuse. There was always something to keep Central Control on Earth and delay dividing HQ.

When the epidemic broke out on Proximus, the Board seized it as another reason for abandoning the project — until the health and safety of all the colonists could be assured. Yet it didn't stop them from sending more mining crews to Primus.

It was small consolation to be proven so horribly right.

"They built this monstrosity and let it sit empty — stupid assholes," Cord finished in disgust.

Simon paused, remembering how he'd taken the Board's ideas for the building and grossly exaggerated them: petty revenge.

He grunted as he remembered his more profound acts of . . . independence. Some they might even thank me for, he thought. No, not likely.

"They hated accepting my ideas. I wasn't one of them, not born to money. Only the Chairman had the intelligence to see past that."

"Well, they'll have to listen now."

"That they will, Cord, thanks to you."

"That's what I'm here for," he said gruffly, pleased. "Is there anything else?"

"Yes. Pull our men off burial. The clergy can take care of that."

"They're not too happy you know. Cremation in a mass grave — and in unsanctified ground — it's against their religion."

"Well, disease from rotting corpses is against mine," Simon said with a note of hostility, and Cord grunted in appreciation. "We've no idea how long we're going to be stranded here. Our men need to start building some temporary housing. We don't want more loses when the rainy season hits. Mallory has people crammed into every building in the townsite and it's still not enough. There's just this one wing left empty, only because she didn't have the access codes."

"Should we move some in?"

"I suppose we'll have to. But I want proper housing started as soon as possible. Next to finding a continuing food source, it's our number one priority. I hope to god our building supplies survived — and our builders." He paused, his mind wandering to the future. "I suppose the Board will have to remain in residence here," he said reluctantly. "Oh, better keep at least one office free of refugees for the Board to use."

"And one for the Chairman?"

Simon gave a crooked smile. "And one for the Chairman, just a small one."

"For now," Cord said, with an answering grin.

Simon checked his watch; it was almost time.

"As my last official act as Director of Security, I appoint you as my successor. Congratulations."

"Thanks, but no thanks. I told you, I'm not Director material."

"It's just a title."

"No, it ain't. It'll mean sittin' at this table with a bunch of jackasses. No thanks."

"OK, you win," Simon conceded, too tired to argue. He looked at his watch again, "It's time."

Cord moved away from the table and took up position several paces behind Simon's chair; his body held at rigid attention though his fatigue was great. A moment later the door of the conference room opened. Simon watched the men file inside, fourteen in all.

And once we were forty, he thought dully.

Look at us: the dead and dying lie all around, perhaps even a world destroyed, and still we carry on, business as usual. There is not a man at this table who hasn't suffered a personal loss, yet our first thought is on the Chairmanship. Maybe Mallory's right; we're not quite whole — not quite human. No . . . we're just trained to react differently from others. That's what puts us on top. Still, he could see the dazed disbelief in their eyes. Well, there's going to be at least one more shock to come.

The moment they were seated, Simon began, "Gentlemen, our Chairman is dead and must be replaced immediately. After much deliberation, I've reached the conclusion that I am the only one qualified for the position." As he spoke,

Cord moved up and planted himself firmly beside Simon's chair. He looked at no one but glowered into the distance. "Shall we vote immediately?" Simon concluded.

The startled faces at the table held varying degrees of disbelief and opposition, for each had considered himself for the Chairmanship. And now, as one unit, they had a shared thought: Who the hell does this upstart think he is?

Then each man shifted his attention to the uniformed figure standing beside Simon, and they saw the armed security force that stood behind him.

One by one, they voted Simon in.


Althaia felt the familiar sensation of forward movement.


"The entire planet's hot," Simon announced quietly, grateful to be speaking out at last.

The news had been transmitted for his eyes only, and no one but the radio operator knew the truth. Simon could not afford the chance of a leak, not until he'd recovered from the shocking facts himself.

No survivors. Total destruction of the planet.

Massive bombardments of thermonuclear missiles, followed by highly toxic, highly corrosive chemical weapons, had created catastrophic fallout as the windstorms, caused by the excessive bombing, carried the poisonous agents across whole continents, destroying every living thing in their wake before blowing out across the seas.

By the time the Mayflower arrived, there was no one left to answer their hail.

Greatly shaken, and surprised by his depth of feeling, Simon was forced to fake food poisoning while he recovered his equilibrium. Rumors began to fly soon after, but with nothing confirmed, people could still hope.

"There's nothing left," he stated neutrally. "Not a living thing."

"Nothing from the bunkers or the subs?" a stunned voice spoke up.

Simon shook his head.

"No word from Proximus?" someone asked hopefully.

"Not a syllable. And no life signs."

There was silence down the long table. They were each finding it difficult to fathom: these few thousand people were all that remained of Humanity.

Billions gone.

But Simon allowed them only a moment to grasp the news. He began to speak before the ugly truth sank in and they became completely useless — they could react after the meeting.

"We must move quickly, if we're to keep what little power is left to us."

He saw their minds struggle to make the shift over to business, but they managed it.

"He's right," a large man agreed slowly. "It's a level playing field now — or so some might think. Time to make some new rules and to hell with us."

Another man nodded. "We can't even force our authority. They'll simply pack up and move someplace else. They do have an entire planet to choose from."

"But let's not forget that we own everything in this townsite," a third man interjected. "If they want a share of the wealth — such as it is — they'll have to remain within our jurisdiction. Without supplies, most people won't be interested in striking out on their own."

"Hell, this whole damn planet belongs to us," a fourth voice announced in annoyance.

"It's very likely that our ownership will be contested, Richard," the second man replied. "There'll be a lot of ideas people might consider outdated and obsolete, and a corporation owning a planet might very well be one of them."

"Well, I'm damn well not going to give up without a fight," Richard declared heatedly.

There was a rumble of agreement from the other men at the table.

Simon's voice cut across their noise: "So the last survivors of humanity decide to kill each other in a final battle because they missed out on the really big one."

The words stopped them.

"So what *are* we going to do?" the second speaker demanded.

"We unify these people. Make our goals their goals. We win their trust and loyalty, and they'll follow our lead, not for our sakes, but for their own."

Someone whistled. "Tall order."

"Yes, but very possible. I've had excellent success with my security force — as you know." This caused an uncomfortable shifting around the table.

"It's obvious we've a readymade goal: rebuilding society," another man joined in hurriedly. "The question is, how do we get them united with us at the helm?"

"In light of who we've been left with, that's a damn good question!" someone else interjected.

"God, yes," said another. "All those women!"

Simon acknowledged, "There are quite a few of them."

"Quite a few! My god, they must be two-thirds the population. Does anyone know what the numbers are?"

"There hasn't been time," Simon answered.

"We don't need any damn headcount to see what's staring us square in the face!" Richard erupted. "I'm with Jimmy here; it makes me nervous seeing all those fillies herded together like that. I've got no experience dealing with women, and I don't want any!"

Simon tried to hide his amusement. "I'm sure we can overcome this . . . obstacle, perhaps even use it to our advantage."

"How's that?" Richard demanded.

"There are opportunities in all situations; they simply need to be discovered. Now—" A knock on the door cut him off and Cord entered hurriedly, going directly to Simon.

"Sorry, sir, but the bishop's here and insists on being let in — claims to have something vital to discuss. I've done everything to get rid of him short of heaving him out — should I do that now, sir?

Simon smiled. "That won't be necessary. If he's that desperate, and there are no objections . . ." he asked, looking round the table, knowing that few seated here would welcome the bishop. It was the recently deceased Chairman, backed by his block of supporters, who'd pushed for the Church's presence on the planet. "We'll hear what he has to say."

Reluctant assents were given, and Cord retreated.

"I thought you hated the Church?" Jimmy asked.

"Know thy enemy, especially what he considers *vital*."

The bishop entered with stately calm, dressed in a black cassock with magenta piping and sash. He surveyed the board members, gauging the hostility.

"Please have a seat, Bishop Alexander," Simon said, indicating a chair at the far end of the table.

"Thank you for allowing this intrusion. You will not regret it."

"Please proceed."

"I've heard rumors that Mayflower has reported back, and our worst fears are confirmed: Earth and Proximus, all dead."

Rumor my ass, Simon thought darkly. "Yes, it's true."

The bishop bowed his head, making a sign of the cross and mumbling something unintelligible. He straightened and said, "If that is the case, I must immediately put forth certain facts you may not be aware of." He leaned forward, his face tight. "A few days ago, I ordered a census taken, and the results were quite alarming. Of the four thousand, nine hundred and thirty-four adult survivors, only a mere five hundred and twenty-seven are men."

There were startled expressions around the table. No one had expected this ratio.

"As for the children above the age of seven: girls outnumber the boys twenty to one."

There were more looks of disbelief.

The bishop explained, "Many of the boys stayed close to the docks to watch the ships come in, with tragic results."

The Board digested this silently.

Alexander continued, "If left unchecked, this world could only develop in one direction: a matriarchal society. And in such a society, gentlemen, there would be no room for men with large ambitions. Men like yourselves. The Church would also not survive."

It was obvious such an outcome had not occurred to them, but now, presented with the idea, it seemed logical and inevitable.

"There are of course ways of averting such a catastrophe, but only if we act quickly," the bishop concluded.

"And why would you want to assist us?" Simon asked skeptically.

"The Church needs a stable government; it cannot succeed alone. The clergy can tend to the people's moral and spiritual needs, but you must satisfy the material ones. We would reinforce and support each other."

"And what could *you* possibly offer the Agency?"

"I presume you still consider this planet the property of the ISA?" Simon nodded curtly. "No one would deny your right of ownership if God decreed it — and you the rightful leader."

There were several snorts of derision and some laughter.

Richard burst out, "Nobody's going to buy that crock!"

But Bishop Alexander was not dismayed — he had anticipated this reaction. He also saw that Simon Cartwright had not joined in the heckling, but sat lost in thought, rubbing the silver disk-shaped game controller that he'd threaded a chain through and wore around his neck like a pendant. A habit he began after taking over the Chairmanship. Rumor had it that he owed his life to it in some way.

The bishop continued: "The appalling events of the last six months have completely demoralized your people. When they learn of Earth's destruction it will utterly destroy their faith in all they once held certain. Grieving and homeless, trapped on an alien planet they despise, they will be open to replacing their lost faith with another. What was superstitious and unreasonable could now seem acceptable, if presented in the correct manner. They will buy it, as you say, not reluctantly but with gratitude. They want answers, hope — direction. And as head of the only surviving Church, I can supply these as no one else can. They will hear my words and believe — they will not be able to help themselves."

The board members were no longer amused, but studied the bishop uncertainly.

"He's right," Simon stated, his tone flat. "They'll accept whatever he says — for a time."

"Exactly," the bishop broke in, "so we must act quickly and collectively. Together, we survive. Separately, we become obsolete." He studied each face, seeing the distaste at allying with the Church, but he saw their fear as well. "Tomorrow there will be a small ceremony to inaugurate me as the new head of the Church. In four days, I will preside over the memorial service to properly bury our dead. That will be the time to initiate our objectives. And may I suggest that you have Tom Murdock read the eulogy; he's such a charismatic and popular figure." The bishop paused a moment, decided he had said all he could, and rose to his feet. "I will leave you to discuss my proposal amongst yourselves."

But Simon stopped him, saying, "I don't think that'll be necessary."

# CHAPTER 22

"ALTHAIA," FRAYNE whispered with joy, his voice weak.

She was kneeling next to the cot where he lay. "Yes, Frayne, I am here." She smiled into his eyes. "Rest now. We will speak together when your body is stronger."

"Althaia, you do not enjoy conversing . . ." he said, the faint smile remaining on his lips as he drifted back into sleep.

Althaia studied his improved features for several moments, and then turned to look about her. They were in William's private sitting room, where they had been moved to just minutes before. The bedroom window refused to close, making the room too cold for Frayne's health.

It had been difficult explaining this to the smaller of the young men. She remembered him now. He was the man she'd seen in the brief visions of Frayne: the one he was engaged in dialogue with. He was also the man she had frightened so badly when coming out of trance that first day in the room of filth.

With the crisis over, his fear of her had once more resurfaced. He was unable to hear her words, and could only react to the fact that she was speaking. He had fled from the room, as he'd done last night when the stench had overwhelmed him.

Soon after, the taller young man had arrived. She remembered that the smaller one had called him Robert. He too was afraid to hear her voice but was able to contain himself, as he had done during Frayne's healing. Again, he responded instantly to the needs of the situation. He ordered a cot to be brought, and then instructed Althaia to wait inside the wardrobe. When the cot arrived, Robert transferred Frayne onto it easily. Frayne's long, gangly body looked awkward in the stocky New Edener's arms. With the assistance of another uniformed man, they carried the cot into the sitting room as Althaia watched from her hiding place. She heard Robert dismiss the second man before he commanded her to emerge from the enclosure.

Althaia could only surmise that her presence here was to be known to only two people, and this confirmed her assessment that there was a risk in bringing her here.

If such is the situation, then it would appear that they value Frayne highly, she concluded. And the thought filled her with hope for their mission.

Now, as she scanned the sitting room, she did so knowing that nothing was mere chance when the Synchronicity Phenomenon was in play. No random, unconnected glimpses into history, but only that which was relevant to the main focus of the timeline, which, in this instance, was the history of that woman abused so violently in the cellar room almost two thousand years ago.

Althaia knew that events would bring her the items she needed, and this room had much to offer, with its walls covered in ancient artifacts. But there were so many . . . .

Then she saw it, subtly standing out from the rest, her intuition guiding her.

The artifact was too high, and Althaia had to pull a chair over to reach it, but there was a side table in the way, keeping her several inches from the wall. She climbed on the chair and raised herself on tip-toe, stretching upward and over the table. Her fingers were closing in on the ancient object when she suddenly lost balance, and her other hand automatically shot out to steady herself.

She would have fallen if a strong arm hadn't supported her. A voice ordered her to sit and put her head between her knees.

The dark edges receded and the ringing in her ears faded.

A man crouched beside her. "Are you alright?"

"Yes, thank you, Father, just a little dizzy," Jillian said.

"Rest a moment," he said, placing a hand on her shoulder. She allowed herself to be pressured into stillness. "It's the gravity. Most people are pushing themselves much too hard."

"I haven't been eating very well either," she admitted. She sat quietly, the dizziness fading. "I'm feeling better now."

"Come on," the priest said, helping her to stand. "Let's sit over here." He guided her to a fallen log and they sat down together.

Jillian drew a ragged breath. "Thank you, Father Neil, you're very kind—" she managed to get out before breaking into noisy sobs.

The priest patted her back automatically, without compassion or pity, all feeling burnt out of him. Her sobs were almost convulsive now, and she turned to bury her head into his cassock, but he remained unmoved, muttering mindless catchphrases that had once held meaning.

Her flesh gave off a sweet aroma, stirring his senses. He breathed in

191

appreciatively: the scent of life. A trickle of feeling crept into his numbed emotions. How warm she felt against him, so alive.

Gradually Jillian gained control of herself and pushed away from the priest. "I'm sorry," she said, sniffing. "I'm not even Catholic, and I've made you all wet."

He pushed a piece of cloth that served as a handkerchief at her. "It doesn't matter, I was too warm anyway."

She managed a weak smile, and for the first time she looked into his face: drawn and pinched with pain. She began to feel ashamed of her outburst. "I'm being selfish. You have your own losses."

He shook his head, looking up at the trees surrounding them. "My father died when I was thirteen, my mother six years ago. I had no brothers or sisters. My only relative is here, alive."

"Oh, who's that?"

"My uncle, Bishop Alexander."

"Oh!"

"That's how I came to be here, through his influence. But God, how I wish he would have let me be," he said with sudden ferocity. "Then I'd be dead like the rest of them."

"How can you say that!" she exclaimed, shocked. "You've no right!"

"I have the right!" he hissed, slamming his hand against the log. "People piled like pieces of garbage — thrown to the flames as if they were nothing — nothing but fuel for the fire." His voice was strangled now, remembering, "There were so many — but they kept coming — they wouldn't stop—" He drew a shuddering breath. "God, how I hated them — hated them for dying — for being at my fire."

Jillian listened, horrified, struck helpless before such suffering. Hesitantly, she placed a hand on his shoulder. "We all felt like that. It was too much for any of us to handle." He shook his head. "You're only human," she said gently. "Do you think God incapable of understanding? That he doesn't know what you suffered?"

"I've already had confession and been absolved of my sins, thank you," he said bitterly.

"I'm sure you have, but did you stop to think that maybe it wasn't a sin? You were in a hateful situation, and you hated everyone in it — who just happened to be dead. Your hate is what pulled you through. It kept you sane. And you should thank it, and thank God for giving it to you," she finished firmly.

He stared at her fixedly for a moment. Then, abruptly, he stood up. "Excuse me, I need to be alone." The priest strode away, quickly disappearing into the thick forest.

Jillian slid to the ground to sit with her back propped against the log. She pulled a compbook from her pack with the words "Property of Jillian Ho" boldly

192

printed across the front. Pressing a latch on the side, it sprung open and automatically powered up the machine. With quick fingers, Jillian typed the password: MyPrimusJournal.

A moment later the blank screen filled with text.

*PRIMUS: FEB 12, YEAR 7*
*(Earth: May 15 approx, 2073)*
Well here I am on Primus at last! It's so beautiful!!! But oh so exhausting! The gravity is 1.36g — that's .36g stronger than Earth — but it feels like a lot more! It becomes quite exhausting, very quickly! It's as if I gained a ton of weight and lived like a couch-spud for the last decade!

Crazily, the year is longer by 27 days, so they just added a couple days or three to each calendar month. And the days are longer too! By two hours, so clocks are designed to run slower up here to compensate. But it's really messing with *my* internal clock. But never mind, I'm here!! And it's going to be my home for the next two years, and that feels wonderful.

The sunsets and sunrises are absolutely magnificent! And I can't wait to explore the planet. Hopefully I can borrow one of the company vehicles, 'cause I won't get too far on foot. Looking forward to some warm weather for camping under Primus' three moons — how romantic!

This job is going to be a soft touch for a while. Nobody lives or works inside the Agency's Headquarters up here, at least not yet. So far, it's just us housekeeping and maintenance crews. And because of the gravity we can't be assigned too much work. I'm only responsible for the second floor, but even that takes me forever!

This is the weirdest building I've ever seen. From the outside it looks like something out of a fairytale — a dark fairytale. But inside it's all modern and posh — and did I say big! It took the Agency over five Primus years to build, and then they do nothing with it? Crazy!

Everyone else lives in dorms in the townsite. Granted, they're pretty nice dorms, better than many homes I've seen Earth-side. Only the lucky site manager gets a house all to himself.

You'd think with twenty mines in operation there'd be more miners than anybody else. But no, the mining is done mechanically, with just a few operators to push buttons and keep an eye on things. Most people work in the refineries or on the landing docks. There are more truckers and mechanics than mining crews. Crazy!

There's also office staff, cooks, research scientists, clergy, and a few medical personnel. It's quite a diverse population, with people of all ethnic and social backgrounds.

Except for the cafeteria and pool hall, there's only a movie theater and bar for entertainment, oh, and a gymnasium, which no one uses! Mostly people hang out on their personal comps playing games or watching vids — takes less effort.

Did I mention there are only fifty-six women on the planet and over five hundred men! Needless to say, we women are very popular. But no one has the energy to pursue us too enthusiastically.

*PRIMUS; APRIL 4, YEAR 7*
*(Earth: July 28 approx, 2073)*

I can't believe how long it's been since I've written. The gravity is knocking me so loopy I can't do much of anything after my shift. Although I have managed to explore the planet a little on my days off, thanks to the site manager, Bobby Martinez (a real nice guy). He's been lending me one of the company all-terrains whenever I want. Thankfully, I've managed to find myself a haven away from the townsite, and away from the constant complaints and arguments.

Tempers are so short here, and there's lots of petty quarreling over imagined insults — or not imagined! I'm not unaffected either, but I escape to my meadow.

I guess this gravity weighs on the mind as well as the body, but I don't think the weather is helping either: fifteen days straight it's been raining! It's even too wet to drive up my mountain (no one else goes there).

And the dampness gets into everything! It's about 55°F, but feels a lot colder. I'm told it won't last too much longer — only seven more weeks! Then we're supposed to get about three months of dry, hot weather, averaging 80°F. Yay! Then another rainy season, this one colder. But no snow. Too bad, I'd have liked that. After that, another three months of somewhat drier weather — also colder, near freezing at times.

I sure miss Mom and Dad. I wonder how they're doing. Letters are slow to get up here. Hope everything's okay.

Jillian pressed a button on the side of the screen and the journal entries scrolled past in a blur of speed. She released the button and the words came back into focus. She read the last entry.

*PRIMUS; MAY 32, YEAR 7*
*(Earth: Aug 30 approx, 2073)*

Things are sure heating up around here, and I don't mean just the weather (98°F).

All ships are grounded and no one is saying why. Even ships en route to Earth have been recalled.

Rumors are flying fast and wild. There's talk of us having the same disease as Proximus, but I'd think we'd know if we did.

The bitchiness around here is on the brink of turning to panic. Those feeling it the most are the ones whose contracts just ended. They've been looking forward to going home since the moment they arrived.

Hopefully we'll know what's going on soon. It can't be too terrible, since the mining and refining is still going on.

I finally met the new priest the other night and discovered that this rumor is at least true. Yes, he's very good-looking. He also seems OK, not like some of them. I'm sure his presence in the church will help increase attendance — male and female!

Lifting the comp-pen from its slot, Jillian wrote across the screen:

*PRIMUS: JULY 7, YEAR 7*
Hello, my friend, you won't believe all that's happened since my last entry — most of it beyond crazy.

Jillian paused to take a container and a thick plazi cup from her pack, pouring out a generous portion of water. She took a long drink of the liquid before placing the cup on the ground.

Time leapt forward again, pulling Althaia along.

"What are you looking at?" asked a voice from behind, making her jump.

"Father Neil!" Jillian turned. "You startled me." She looked into his handsome face. "I was just yearning for a chance to draw or do some writing."

"You're an author," he said appreciatively.

"Not really, I just write in my journal, but I like to sketch."

"And what do you draw?"

"Landscapes, mostly. That's what I was looking at," she said, and turned to point across at the neighboring peak, its summit stretching far above them. "Up there is my favorite spot with a great view of the northern mountains."

"Sounds nice."

"It is. On dry days I'd drive up there and just hang out for hours. It was so peaceful."

"I can imagine," Father Neil said with a smile, but a moment later he became serious. "I wanted to apologize for my rudeness the last time we talked, and also to thank you for your help."

"You weren't rude. And I did very little," she said lightly, and quickly changed the subject. "So why aren't you in class today?"

"It's Saturday."

"Oh."

"And where are you off to?" he asked.

"My turn at land clearing," Jillian said, and chuckled tiredly. "It's ironic: I work harder as Second Lady than I ever did as second floor maid." She noticed his sudden scowl. "Did I say something wrong?"

"No, it's not you; it's my conscience digging at me."

"For what?"

"All you women out there working in the mud and the rain — I should be doing hard labor, not sitting in a classroom."

"So do it," she said, shifting her backpack to sit more comfortably on her shoulders.

"Request denied. I'm needed for teaching." He looked into the distance. "Sometimes it's hard accepting the Church's decisions."

"No one would change places with you anyway. I know I wouldn't." Jillian shivered theatrically. "All those screaming little monsters, ugh!" He laughed and gave her a grateful look. "Come on," she said, pulling him along. "There's no school today, come and play."

"What?" he hung back, hesitating.

"Come on! You wanted to use those macho muscles, well, here's your chance."

He laughed and followed after her.

The scene blurred, moving farther into the future.

Father Neil took the offered cup of wine and laid the drawing aside. "I'm afraid I'm beyond hope."

"You're being too hard on yourself; it's a good first effort. See how you've caught the essence of that tree."

"I don't think God ever made a tree quite that shape," the priest said ruefully.

"Maybe not, but I believe he's open to interpretation."

He laughed and raised his cup. "Here's to Divine tolerance."

"And here's to Bobby Martinez," Jillian toasted in return, "for use of the all-terrain."

"To Bobby Martinez," Father Neil responded. "And let's not forget my uncle for his contribution of the wine — however unknowing."

"You are so bad," Jillian laughed.

They sipped their wine in silence, eyeing the view appreciatively: the mountains to the north stood rugged and stark, imposing even from this distance.

196

"I should bring Mallory up here. If I could ever pry her away from that workshop of hers. I know she'd love it."

"You think a lot of her."

"Yes, I do. She doesn't let anything stand in the way of what she thinks is right. Even when it became clear that polygamy would be a necessity, she got right on board. She only asked Simon for the right to veto any undesirables, and to offer suggestions." Like me, she thought. "And she agreed it might help us normalize if we began building new families as soon as possible. But it really pissed her off the way the Church went about it. You know, practically ordering the men to marry as many as they could, and making us women feel guilty if we didn't accept. Repopulate-the-world-or-else kind of attitude— whoops!" she said, remembering who she was talking to.

"Don't worry," Father Neil reassured her. "I do my own share of questioning the Church." He poured them another cup of wine. "Tell me about Simon. What's he like?"

Jillian became thoughtful. She performed her marriage obligations in a kind of daze, too tired in body and spirit to resist the Church's forceful call for sacrifice and duty. On a planet where every action took so much effort, there was little energy left to sort out thoughts and feelings. Too few moments like these.

"Simon?" she answered from a long way. "He's a nice guy. I suppose I was lucky to marry him, to hear others complain. Still, I don't really like having sex with a virtual stranger, no matter how pleasant he is—" she gasped, covering her mouth. "I am *so* sorry."

"No, it's alright, you didn't offend me," he reassured her once more. "I'm still capable of understanding, even if I do wear this," he pointed to his collar.

"I'm so tired I don't know what's coming out of my mouth."

He leaned forward to clasp her arm, saying, "Feel free to say whatever you want to me, even if it is about S-E-X."

She smiled at him, the shadow lifting. "Maybe I'm pregnant: there's a happy thought."

"Congratulations," he said, withdrawing his hand.

"I don't *really* think I am. And to be honest I'm not all that eager," she confessed. Adding with a small laugh, "I was just lured by the time off."

He laughed in return. "The Agency is making it very easy for pregnant women."

"No land clearing or field work. Hallelujah! And after the second trimester, no duties at all. But really, there's no choice, not with this gravity. It's too hard on the body, too many miscarriages." She paused, thinking how this world had forced changes upon them all. "There's also a rumor circulating that when the new currency is issued, they'll pay full wages until the baby's two years old."

197

"It's good they're promoting a healthy start for our first generation."

"Yes, but this whole pregnancy thing is making monsters out of us women."

"How so?"

Once again she became thoughtful. "It's not just about escaping the field work or getting extra perks. I think it's more to do with all the death we've seen. Maybe its nature's way of rebuilding our numbers. But whatever it is, practically every woman on the planet is desperate to get pregnant. If she's married, she harasses her husband. While the single ones use every ounce of spare energy to get married and pregnant — or the other way around. No one's too fussy. And with so few men, the competition is very fierce and very pathetic."

He looked surprised. "But they couldn't possibly hope to find a husband. As it is, most families are already too large. The houses being built are enormous. It's unreasonable to expect them to get any bigger."

"That's the monster part." She paused for a moment to gather her thoughts. "Everyone wants at least a chance at some kind of family life. And it feels like you've got to grab it now or you're going to miss it altogether. I can feel the panic sweeping through the single women when I'm with them in the fields. And God knows how long it'll take to build proper housing for us all. Marriage is the fastest route to get that as well."

"It's too bad . . . all that wasted effort when they could be finding some kind of peace. Like you."

"Me?" she said in surprise.

"Yes," he nodded, "you. You're more at peace than any adult on this planet."

"Truly?" she asked, growing thoughtful once more. "Maybe that's because I've a head start on everyone else. I actually like this new world of ours — even if it does take twice as long to get anything done." She breathed in deeply, enjoying the alien aromas, stronger here away from the Earthly imports. "It's worth it for the clean air and water, and all this untouched forest."

"Yes," he agreed, looking at the rolling peaks of green that stretched out before them, the trees shorter and thicker than their Earth cousins. "It is beautiful. Perhaps in time we'll all come to appreciate it as you do."

She lay down, rolling onto her stomach. "Sometimes when I'm up here or even when I'm working — all of us pitching in together for a better future — I feel more joy than I've ever known before." She paused. "That doesn't seem right, does it? My family dead and a world destroyed. It seems, well . . . almost sinful — if I believed in sin," she added hastily.

"No, not sinful at all," Father Neil said gently. "Joy is a gift from God. Some believe it's the only time we're truly one with Him."

"But why me? I'm no more deserving than anyone else."

He looked over the valley below them. "Maybe it's because you love this

198

planet He created for us. Or maybe because you've reached out to ease the pain of others and for that you've had your own burden lifted, at least temporarily. It really doesn't matter the reason. You need only accept and be thankful."

They were quiet, listening to the forest sounds. Jillian said softly, "I feel like I've just been to church."

"I believe we have."

The stillness was suddenly disturbed by a vehicle making its way up the forested mountainside. A few minutes later a van came lurching into their small clearing, a priest at the wheel. His expression turned to a scowl when he caught sight of Father Neil. Instantly, he changed direction, turning back into the trees.

"Who's that?" Jillian asked.

"Father Toby."

"Not very friendly, is he?"

"He's never liked me, even at seminary. But now he seems more hostile than ever. Maybe he thinks I'm receiving preferential treatment?"

"Are you?"

"Not at all. My uncle's not big on family. I was surprised he thought to have me transferred up here."

"Maybe Father Toby will be less hostile when he realizes that?"

"Perhaps . . ." his tone was dubious. "I suspect he's the one who informed my uncle I was working in the fields. It would be in character."

"Your uncle really baked you over the B-Q for that."

"The Church is very big on obedience."

"You weren't much help at clearing, anyway."

But he didn't respond to her teasing; he was gazing after the scowling priest.

"I wonder what he's doing way up here . . . . I think I'd better get back," he said uneasily, setting down the cup.


Althaia looked down at the plazi cup her fingers had landed on to regain her balance. Bemusedly, she thought, I have never before been directed so suddenly to an alternative vision.

She hesitated now, looking up at the artifacts on the wall. What further changes would this planet produce for her? But she felt compelled to continue, until she had concluded that woman's history and deciphered this wounded world.

Drawing a breath, she stretched out once more to touch the indicated artifact, and this time successfully made contact.

There were ten of them, all in black clothing that revealed nothing but mouth and eyes. They were led by a man, also dressed in black; a black pack strapped over his shoulders.

Nearly invisible, they moved through the night, the three moons above them hidden by a thick band of cloud. With great care, they made their way to the top of the rise, their bodies slippery with sweat. They were terrified.

Their caution increased as they peered over the edge of the ridge. The flat was deserted. A hundred feet away stood ISA Headquarters.

"There's the barracks," one woman whispered fearfully, pointing down the plateau to the large addition built against the wall of the Agency's headquarters.

The man studied his watch, hiding the glowing numbers under his hand. "Six minutes to go," he whispered into the ear nearest him. The message was passed down the line.

They kept checking the flat, but it remained deserted.

Laughter rang out from the barracks, harsh and male, the sound like a warning to the frightened women.

It began to rain and they welcomed it — more camouflage for their movements. Carefully, the man opened his backpack and began removing ten handguns. He passed them out to the women, who each took a gun and placed it awkwardly inside her belt, the hard steel feeling ominous against the belly.

It was time to move. One by one, they crept over the ridge, bending low as they ran across the open space, avoiding the patches of light thrown down by the Agency windows. It felt like a long trek with the drag of the planet's gravity pulling at them, but at last they reached the wall. Panting, they hugged it close, recovering. The rain began to slacken and gradually stopped altogether.

Abruptly, the man's signal started them off again.

Pressing hard against the wall, they made their way towards a side entrance. The barracks were closer now, the voices clearer and more frightening. With relief, they reached the door — almost safe. A woman's hand reached out to push it open, but nothing happened: it was locked. Panicked, she tried to force it. "Damn it, what's happened!" she whispered fiercely.

"Maybe we're early," someone suggested hoarsely.

There was a noise in the distance, and they all froze.

Two guards were coming around the corner of the building — headed directly towards them.


The vision ended, leaving Althaia bewildered for a moment. Then she understood, and let herself be guided to a second artifact.

Silently chanting a calming mantra, Mallory inserted her card into the slot and punched in the code, causing the small screen in front of her to come to life. She placed a palm upon it and spoke her name, praying the sensors wouldn't detect abnormal stress levels in her voice or her biochemistry. Her only hope was that she hadn't had a normal stress level since the start of this crazy scheme, which was when the baseline reading had been taken.

A moment later an electronic buzzer gave a harsh note of approval and the screen showed a uniformed man looking at her critically. Mallory smiled, and gave the brief signal to indicate that all was well and that she was not being coerced. Satisfied, he pressed a switch to allow her entry. She turned the doorknob and entered the reception area where four uniformed men stood watching intently, each with a rifle aimed at the door as it swung open.

Although she knew that their vigilance was directed towards ambitious board members, the sight of those armed guards with weapons readied always felt personal — especially today.

As usual, they held their pose until the door was closed and locked before they relaxed and returned to their card game.

"Evenin', Ms. Cartwright," one of the guards said politely.

"Good evening," she answered, and once again managed to keep her voice steady.

She smiled at the young man rapidly entering data into a sleek computer as she strode past his desk and into the office, shutting the door.

"Hi, Honey," she said, marveling at her calm.

Simon glanced up to smile distractedly in greeting, and then returned to his computer screen — as expected.

Mallory roamed about the office, trying to duplicate her usual habit of pacing while waiting for Simon to finish up his work. A practice she had begun weeks ago in preparation for this moment.

Her movements brought her close to the office door.

Lightly pressing the wall panel beside the door frame, it sprang open to reveal a keypad hidden beneath. If she keyed in the correct sequence of numbers, the doors into the reception and office would be securely locked: no way in or out. Quickly, she pressed all but the last number. She would have to move fast: There was another set in Simon's desk. She glanced towards him, but he was still engrossed in his work.

From her handbag, she removed a cylindrical object. Twisting the top sharply, she tossed it inside the reception area, quickly shutting the door and hitting the last number in the sequence.

201

Simon hadn't noticed.

She dug inside her purse and pulled out the gun, aiming it at Simon. She remembered to hold it with two hands, as she'd been taught.

There were sounds of muffled shouts and fists pounding on the door that not even the heavily insulated office could conceal. Simon looked up in alarm.

Althaia's hand moved of its own volition back to the first gun.

They were trapped: the guards in front, the barracks behind. Pressing flat against the building, they tried to blend into the wet night.

The only male in the group edged away from the women. Removing the gun from his belt, he stretched out flat on the ground, aiming the weapon. A light appeared inside a window, dissolving enough of the night to reveal the women's outline.

"Who's there?" one of the guards demanded.

Before the women could react, there was a flash of gunfire and a guard was cut down. The other guard dropped to his belly, his weapon firing.

The women scattered.

Men came running from the barracks, half dressed and wielding weapons, frantically searching for the threat. Someone shouted, "They're headed for the bluff!" as another guard was felled.

The half-dressed men began to fire at the running figures.

The terrified women grappled with their guns to fire back in defense, but after firing off a single shot, all their weapons produced was a hollow click.

Simon's alarm had turned to shock. "What the hell, Mallory!"

"I'm sorry, Simon, but it's the only way to get you to listen. Don't move. I don't want to shoot you, but I will if you force me to."

"What the hell are you doing?"

"We're holding you and the rest of the Board hostage. You'll be set free when we receive every weapon your Army owns."

A sudden burst of gunfire made them both look towards the window. "What the hell is going on?!" Simon demanded, rising from his chair.

"Don't move!" she spat at him. "Keep your hands on the desk where I can see them!"

Shocked anew by the ferocity in her voice, he dropped back into his seat, careful to keep his hands in sight. The shooting continued with angry shouts and screams of pain. Mallory was sweating now, anxiously glancing from Simon to the window.

He was watching her carefully. "This wasn't part of the plan, was it?" She looked at him with a startled expression but said nothing.

Suddenly the shooting stopped.

The fleeing figures were brought down quickly. The guards sorted through the bodies, looking for the injured. A face cover was ripped off. "Christ, it's a woman!"

"So is this one!"

"Fuck, they're all women!"

There was a stunned silence that was shattered by a single gunshot. They dropped to the ground, trying to locate the source. Another shot rang out.

"Christ, it's coming from inside!"

As one unit, they leapt up, running back towards HQ.

A cold chill spread through Mallory as quiet settled over the night once more.

She felt very isolated and glanced at her watch in relief. The gas would have cleared by now. Without looking away from Simon, she felt for the panel to release the locks in both rooms, and then opened the door, stepping aside. A few moments later her accomplice entered the room, but still she kept her eyes on Simon, as she'd been warned to do.

"Something's gone wrong. Did the others make it?" she asked.

"I'm sorry, Mallory, but nobody makes it tonight."

"You!" she said, whirling to see Tom Murdock's gloved hand pointing a gun at them both.

"Yes, me." He looked at Simon. "Your wife has been very useful; we couldn't have done it without her."

"Where are the others?" Mallory demanded.

"I'm afraid they're dead, my dear."

"Dead?" she gasped.

"Yes, so sorry, they were betrayed."

"You animal, you filthy piece of—"

"Shut up!" Tom snapped with sudden violence, grabbing the gun from her hand. "Go stand with your husband."

She moved close to the desk, and Tom fired — the hollow-point bullet blowing a large hole inside the back of her brain. Simon leapt up as Mallory crumpled to the floor. "Don't move another muscle!" Tom warned violently.

203

But Simon wasn't listening; he was staring in disbelief at his wife's dead body.

With a gloating smile, Tom walked towards Simon, rapidly pushing bullets into Mallory's gun. "You don't know how much pleasure this gives me." He snapped the gun closed and fired again.

Simon fell forward across his desk and slid to the floor. He was still alive.

Tom picked up a cushion from the sofa and knelt beside Simon, placing it firmly over his face. Several moments later, Tom tossed the pillow onto the sofa as the sound of running feet approached the office.

Contorting his features into a mask of grief, he pushed Mallory's gun across the carpet towards her limp body.

Shaking with reaction, Althaia climbed down from the chair, her mind reeling from the violence and deceit contained within the visions. She sank to the floor, allowing the healing energy to wash away the poisonous images. Finally she was clear, her inner balance restored.

Althaia remained seated on the floor as she considered all that she had witnessed and what she had learned from it. But in the reviewing of the visions she was thrown off-center once again, her emotions stirred up, her mind agitated. Althaia ceased the troubling thoughts and once more allowed the healing energy to restore her equilibrium.

Now she made a firm decision. She would have no more visions that related to this planet's history or that woman's story. For her, it was ended.

"Althaia, it is good to see you. You fare well?" Frayne asked weakly.

"I am well, do not concern yourself. You must let your body heal."

"Althaia, you are a healer. How—?"

"You're awake," Robert said, striding into the sitting room. "Are you sound?"

"He will require much bed rest and healthy food," Althaia interjected. "Time will be his healer now."

"Then the eve will be returned to her cell," Robert said, addressing Frayne as if Althaia hadn't spoken.

"Robert . . . wait," Frayne's shaky voice called out.

"It cannot wait," Robert stated implacably.

They heard the truth in his words, whatever the reason behind it.

"Remember the mission," Althaia whispered to Frayne, before she rose and followed Robert into the bedroom and through the entrance to the secret passageway.

# CHAPTER 23

"I NEVER thought I'd be thankful to an eve, especially that one!" William announced to Frayne. "God bless Robert for knowing she'd be of use. If it wasn't for him, that doctor would have killed you."

"I am grateful to Robert, and to Althaia," Frayne said from where he lay upon the bed, once more returned to his own room.

William studied the pale complexion of his friend, wondering how he was ever going to give him up, for he now realized how much he'd come to value Frayne — possibly more than his own brothers. "You are ordered to never worry me like that again, my friend."

"In future, I will refrain from putting my arm upon your knives," Frayne gently reminded him with a smile.

William grunted, acknowledging responsibility. Guiltily, he pronounced, "In honor of your return to health, I shall give you a gift. A dagger, perhaps? No . . . ." He stopped as he realized that New Eden's usual gifts of weapons and alcohol would not suit his new friend. "What gifts are given on your world?"

"Gifts are no longer exchanged on my planet; the custom disappeared. But at one time, many enjoyed giving works of art or clothing made from fine fabrics. Natural objects were also given, such as shells, gemstones, or crystals—"

"Hold!" William proclaimed, rushing excitedly from the room. Frayne could hear him calling for Robert, who always seemed to appear the instant he was needed, and this time was no exception. "Clear the floor, Robert, hurry!" William commanded, and darted back into Frayne's bedroom. "Are you strong enough to walk?"

"I am not certain."

William dashed out again, returning shortly with Robert. "We will carry you."

"Where do we go?"

"To find your gift."

The room, though quite large, was well lit with the afternoon sun radiating through long, narrow windows. Every inch of wall space was covered in ancient artifacts, while the floor was covered in row after row of glass cases, a few made of plazglass from ancient times. And within each case were objects from New Eden's Ancestors — objects from Earth.

They lowered Frayne's feet to the floor, and Robert stepped back to guard the doorway.

"The Royal Family's private museum," William explained, as Frayne looked around in wonder. "It's our little secret from the Church," he said, smiling crookedly. "Remain here, I'll return shortly."

He sprinted to the end of the room and stopped before the wall. To Frayne's surprise, he pushed at the panel and it sprung open, revealing a large dial hidden within. William spun the dial backwards and forwards in a very precise manner until a small door abruptly opened. He removed several items from inside the dark box before returning to Frayne and depositing the packages on a plazglass case.

"There may be something you desire inside here," he said, untying the cloth bags and exposing the contents.

Frayne gasped in delight as the gems glittered like brilliant fire in the sunlight, a cluster of perfect diamonds embedded in a thick band of gold. William opened more bundles. Reds and greens sparked and shimmered as the light danced off the gemstones inside.

"They are beautiful," Frayne breathed.

"You like them?" William asked, dumping out an assortment of jewelry from another bag.

"They give me much pleasure."

William sorted through rings and gold chains. "You may have whatever you wish."

Except for symbols of office or rank, jewelry was not made or worn on New Eden. Any jewelry that had been brought from Earth by the Ancients resided here, inside the palace vault, forgotten by everyone but those few Royals permitted access to the secret hoard.

Frayne fingered the heavy diamond necklace. "This I would choose, but the weight is beyond my strength." He indicated the emerald and ruby pieces. "These too are beyond my abilities."

"What of these?" William asked, pointing to the gold chains.

Frayne lifted a necklace with three slender strands of gold braided together and threaded through a golden pendant embedded with two small diamonds.

"I find this quite lovely. I will choose it as my gift. Thank you."

Pleased with himself, William wrapped up the remainder of the jewelry and returned it to the safe. Frayne draped the chain around his neck and was thoughtfully fingering it when William returned.

"Would you permit a gift to Althaia? For it was through her efforts that my death was prevented."

The request startled William. "Eve's aren't permitted gifts." Then to end the discussion he called Robert, and the three returned to Frayne's suite.

But once settled onto his bed, Frayne made another attempt, saying, "It would not be a true gift, for it would not be a *thing*."

"What in God's Great Name would it be?" demanded William.

"The study of history is of immense interest to Althaia," Frayne explained. "There is much in your museum she would find fascinating."

William squirmed uncomfortably, hating to say no to his friend. "I cannot. We risked bringing her out to save your life. I won't risk your life now by doing it again."

Frayne looked at William a long moment before he said quietly, "I do not believe anything will prevent my early death on this planet."


It's a nightmare — I'll wake soon.

But it kept rolling on.

Mallory and Simon dead! Mallory accused of his murder!

She couldn't take it in. After all that had happened, it was just too much.

She could say nothing but assert Mallory's innocence, though each time she was slapped hard for it and sent sprawling to the floor.

How long have I been here?

Her sense of time was completely warped. She'd not been allowed to sleep and was questioned incessantly, while being reduced to begging for food and water or to use the toilet. Whenever she collapsed to the floor, they prodded her painfully, forcing her up again.

Sometimes she was certain it was the end: that she'd given herself away — that they knew of her involvement. Then relief and disappointment would mingle as they continued their endless grilling.


Althaia leapt onto the cot and the vision ended.

She crouched there, confused and alarmed.

207

The vision had come over her without physical contact. She'd not placed a hand on the floor, and both her feet were shod. But more important to Althaia was the intent.

My intent was to cease all visions of this planet's history.

What further changes is this world producing within me? she asked once again, but this time with an edge of fear.

Suddenly she longed for home, and just as suddenly came the unwelcomed certainty: I do not believe I shall ever leave this planet.

# CHAPTER 24

THE YOUNG Chairman entered Frayne's room hurriedly, knowing he would have little time to spend with the stranger. The Hargreaves litigation began today: an important trial that would require his complete attention over the coming week.

William sat on the hard chair he placed near Frayne's bedside and smiled in greeting. Frayne returned the smile, lifting his hand, welcoming the Chairman.

Frayne had made a full recovery from his illness but still he spent much of his time in bed, and William understood that this was a necessity, as the planet was putting too much of a strain on his friend.

William studied Frayne closely. "Something has disturbed you?"

Frayne looked away from William to collect his thoughts, staring unseeing at the gold chain lying on the dresser. When at last he spoke, it was with a deep sadness: "We have journeyed to your planet in the hope of returning to Mirandus accompanied by a number of your citizens. But it has become apparent to me that we could not possibly make such a request of the people of New Eden. They would be terrified beyond reason if they were to be thrust into our world of tech and science. They would perceive Mirandus as a place of great evil. I could not inflict such trauma upon them."

The Chairman gave Frayne a look of astonishment. "You'd sacrifice your world to spare the misery of others?"

"I do not do so frivolously. It is with deep regret that I must acknowledge our mistaken expectation, and accept that your world cannot provide us with the aid we require."

"But we can. And I insist that we do," William stated with sudden passion, but he could see that Frayne was not persuaded. "Tell me, my friend, would you truly allow all of Mankind to vanish?"

Frayne looked at him in confusion.

William continued: "I must confess that *our* world is also failing. When adult eves sicken, many die — no matter how mild a contagion to men or children. And with every generation, the number of deaths increases."

"What is the cause of this phenomenon?"

"The Church has decreed these early deaths as a sign of victory — that we are winning the battle against Satan. But when I see the reduction in our Royal Revenues during the last hundred years, and the houses that stand empty because wives couldn't live long enough to bear sons, I fear there is a different cause. And because we do nothing, I know the end of New Eden is coming, as sure as rain."

Frayne was silent, digesting this new information. He had gained enough understanding of New Eden politics to understand that the Church was the final word on all subjects.

"My friend," William said quietly, "you cannot want the death of Mankind to be your legacy." He could see his words were having an impact, and he pressed home his advantage. "Promise me, Frayne, promise me that you'll do all that is possible to save Proximus — your Mirandus — and I swear to you that I'll match your efforts. Together, we can save Mankind," he finished on an ardent note.

Frayne stared into William's face, the Chairman's eyes bright and clear. Suddenly the stranger recognized the wisdom of the Ancients shining through this unexpected portal, and Frayne knew what he must do. "Yes," he said quietly, but with a conviction to match William's own. "I will apply all of my abilities to ensure the survival of Humanity."

Relief washed over William, and he gripped his friend firmly on the shoulder, cementing their agreement. To think of that bright and shining world vanishing forever was a pain too great to bear, and the young Chairman thanked God for its continued existence.

There was a knock on the door, startling the occupants and thrusting William back into his own world and his responsibilities. He strode to the door, opening it impatiently. "Yes?" he demanded.

"Sire," his administrative aide announced, "your presence is required in Court."

William frowned in resignation. "I will be there, Hernandez."

The aide retreated, and William looked at his friend with regret. "I must leave. Do you have need of anything?"

"I am satisfied."

"There's a guard outside your door, should you change your mind."

"Thank you, I will remember."

The Chairman departed to do his duty, his heart heavy with a longing for something he knew he could never have.

# CHAPTER 25

THE SUPREME Commander glared at the young officer, who did not flinch under his piercing gaze. "And exactly what makes you think the Chairman intends to leave with the stranger?"

"The Chairman resists giving the stranger over to the Church; he has developed a great liking for the man."

The Commander conceded these facts with a small nod.

"He believes everything the stranger tells him," Robert continued, "and wishes there was some way to prove his stories true." Robert did not mention William's vow of assistance to Frayne and his determination to keep it. The Chairman would send his own wives and child-eves to Proximus if need be, though he feared these few breeders would not be enough. "Since the Hargreaves trial ended, the Chairman has summoned friends and relatives he's not seen for months, even years. He rode his horse for the first time in weeks and called a surprise inspection of his personal guard, but all he did was thank us for our years of loyal service. This morning he visited his father's graveside." Robert was speaking quickly now: "Commander, I know my Chairman — I grew up with him. I swear to you, he is planning to leave with the Stranger."

"I believe you."

Robert sagged slightly with relief.

Commander Belcher sighed in resignation, rubbing his grizzled face roughly, as if to wash away this latest folly of William's. A large burp erupted, breaking the silence and giving cause for the Commander's last name. The priests were often inspired in their naming by the behavior of children: Kicker, Basher, Biter and Talker were common names amongst the illegits.

The older man stared into space, considering avenues of action. Finally, he chose the only option available to them. But would this youngster have the balls to carry it out? It would be a good test of Robert's suitability as his successor.

Too bad he wouldn't survive to fulfill it.

Robert listened to the Commander's orders undismayed. Even the prospect of a certain and grisly death could not eclipse his relief at finding a way to protect his Chairman. But unknown to the Commander, he saw how to improve upon the plan. Robert would satisfy William's private oath — and his own.

It was going to be a long night.

Frayne's sleep was disturbed by light pouring in from the hallway. He tried to focus, not quite believing his eyes as a man entered dragging the now-unconscious soldier who kept guard outside his door. The man laid the soldier on the floor and stood upright. It was Robert.

"Stranger, tonight you will return to wherever-the-hell you came from. Get dressed," he ordered, closing the door and lighting a lamp.

"I do not understand."

"Listen carefully — I don't have much time. You're a danger to my Chairman, and I would kill you if he'd not ordered otherwise. But if you resist, I will disobey that order." He bent over the guard, tying his hands and feet and gagging him securely.

Frayne heard the truth in Robert's voice, but still he had to say, "I cannot leave. The Chair Man insists that I complete my mission."

"Your mission is done. There are eves who will return with you as the Chairman has ordered. And I obey all his orders." He dragged the soldier over to the heavy bed and bound him to it.

"But the Chair Man would not order me to leave in this manner. He no longer fears me or my world."

"That is why you must go."

"I believe I understand, at least in part." Then he asked, "What of Althaia?"

"Who?" Robert demanded impatiently, and a startled look passed over his face as he remembered, but it quickly faded. "She must remain. Now move or die."

Leave Althaia? Frayne could not conceive of returning home without her, but he saw the look in Robert's eyes and understood that he must or lose the opportunity to save Mirandus — and possibly all Mankind. And he knew what Althaia would choose for him.

He felt their destinies unraveling, pulled into the strands of others they had yet to know. With a silent farewell, he started to move. His decision made, he was eager to cooperate.

Once dressed, he was hurried down the hallway and into a narrow corridor disguised within the wall. Lighting a torch, Robert pulled him along the dark, twisting passageway and down three flights of stairs. Frayne stumbled and almost fell, but for Robert's strong arm.

With Robert almost carrying him now, they reached ground level, where Robert hauled him through more twists and turns before going through another disguised doorway into a long, straight tunnel that seemed to go on forever, the floor underfoot becoming spongy and wet. Finally they reached a short set of stairs made of ancient plastcast. At the top of the steps was a thick plasteelite door with a large handwheel in the center of it.

Robert extinguished the torch inside a bucket of dirt, and in the sudden darkness grasped the wheel, turning it firmly until the door popped open. Pushing past it, they entered the sweet night air. Trees loomed above them, silhouetted against the moonlight and impeding a clear view of the palace in the distance.

They were in the royal hunting grounds.

Robert set Frayne onto the forest floor before closing the entrance to the tunnel. A thick drapery of vines covered the outer side of the plasteelite door, disguising it completely. Robert reached through the tangle of vegetation to a smaller handwheel; he twisted it until the door was sucked firmly inwards, sealing the passageway and making it look like a natural part of the hillside.

Frayne had stretched out on the ground, relieved at the opportunity for rest. A few moments later he was startled by a sudden loud rustling within the trees, followed by the appearance of three soldiers.

Two of these men took up position on either side of Frayne, while the third conferred with their captain.

"Any trouble?" Robert asked quietly, the tension ringing strong to Frayne's sensitive ear.

"No, sir. We'll rendezvous where the stranger was first sighted."

"Good. Let's get moving."

The two soldiers lifted Frayne to his feet, each taking a firm grip on an arm, which was fortunate, for he would have collapsed without it. Turning northeast, they set off at a fast pace, the lights of the distant palace quickly disappearing.

The hands at Frayne's arms kept his feet off the forest floor as they charged across the royal hunting grounds, eventually entering the untouched buffer of woods that stood between New Eden and the demon wasteland. Moving deeper into the dense canopy, the moonlight became streaky, forcing them to slow down, but still they moved faster than any Earth-born human, their squat bodies thick with muscle. Within minutes they met up with the rest of Robert's men.

The hands holding Frayne released him, and he struggled to regain his balance as he scanned the area, seeking out the women that were to accompany him to Mirandus.

There they were, only a few meters away, forty-nine adult eves standing crowded together.

But in the thick gloom all Frayne could determine was that they were shorter and less thickset than the men, and that they held a submissive bearing. He had learned much about New Eden's ways, but still he was shocked by the degree of fear and shame they carried, which he clearly sensed within the darkness. Gradually, as Frayne's eyes adjusted to the shadows, he was able to detect the heavy veils that covered their faces. And though he'd known of such things, it still increased his shock and sadness.

Standing beside some of the women were smaller shapes, and a few of the women also held objects against their torsos.

These forms are young girls and babies, Frayne realized in pleased surprise. And this lifted his spirits somewhat.

Twelve little eves stood beside the adults, all under the age of five. Their mothers had wisely put headscarves on their daughters, pulling one tail of the scarf across the face and tucking it beneath the band to act as a veil. They knew all too well that any eve face — no matter how young — could trigger a fearful and violent response. The three babies wrapped in carriers were partially veiled with a corner of their blankets.

Soldiers were positioned around the eves, but at a safe distance, which was no easy task in such a dense forest. Standing apart from the main body was a group of seven soldiers, each holding the bridle of a horse with a bundle draped across its back.

"Come with me, Stranger," Robert ordered Frayne. "The rest of you, remain here."

The two men moved deeper into the woods to speak in private.

Without preamble, Robert stated in a dull monotone, "My Commander has ordered me to take you into the desert, where you'll be tortured and devoured by demons — your soul lost forever."

Frayne stared at Robert in utter stupefaction. "He does not believe we come from Mirandus — from Proximus?"

"He does not."

"And you, Robert?"

He shook his head, saying, "At first, I thought, perhaps . . . . But how could you? Yet, I will give you this chance to save yourself: take me to your ship, and I'll disobey my orders."

Still recovering, Frayne stood in thought for several moments. As he looked towards the women and children huddled in the darkness he realized that Robert *did* believe, whether he could acknowledge it or not: the presence of these people was proof of that.

He studied Robert for another moment, then abruptly turned his back towards the soldiers. Lifting his arm, he pulled up his sleeve, revealing the wide bracelet he always wore. His fingers played across the top, and the smoky gemstone lifted to display a shiny black surface that glowed with yellow lights. Robert sucked in his breath, taking a step backwards.

"It will not harm you," Frayne said, trying to reassure him. "I am simply making a calculation."

"Calculation! What calculation?" Robert's voice had risen and his men looked over at them in alarm. "Explain!" he hissed in a hoarse whisper.

Frayne was careful to keep his back towards the men glowering at them with heightened alertness. "I am calculating the location of my landing craft." He heard Robert make a strange sound that was a mix of relief and fear. "You will not need to force me into the desert, Robert. I will go willingly and without dread. It was there that we landed our shuttle craft, and it is to there that I must return."

"What!" Robert's voice rose once again, his men now ready to pounce on the stranger. He forced himself to speak quietly, his voice ragged with feeling, "Are you demon after all?"

Frayne studied the frightened man before him and realized what he must say: "If I am this demon, then it will make no difference to me or to you if I go into the desert. But if I am not, you will soon discover what I truly am."

His eyes bugging out of his head, Robert stared at the stranger as he tried to read him in the dim light. But he could see the logic in Frayne's words, and he finally conceded: "Let us proceed."

Frayne made a small adjustment on the wristband. "My shuttle craft lies approximately ten miles north of this position."

"How could *you* walk ten miles?" Robert asked in sudden suspicion.

Frayne hesitated. "We traveled on a small hover-cart that was able to carry us most of that distance before it became drained of power. The vehicle was not designed for this planet's gravity."

"The soldiers saw no cart," Robert growled, his suspicion increasing.

"The cart is farther north, hidden within the bushes. Althaia and I journeyed two days by foot prior to being discovered by one of your citizens."

Robert paused before nodding, willing to accept this explanation — for now.

Frayne continued quietly, pointing in a westerly direction, "There is a path nearby that Althaia and I followed from the stone desert."

Frayne's words startled Robert rigid, his past leaping up before him, but he said nothing. And after a few moments he was able to stride back to the group, where he organized them into a long, single-file line.

Bringing up the rear were the seven men guiding the horses. Robert was at the head of the group, with Frayne directly behind him with two soldiers holding

215

his arms for support. The eves came next; a few had babes harnessed to their chests, while the remaining soldiers followed, carrying the children. When Robert first ordered these men to do so, they'd refused to budge. "Your Chairman needs you this night," Robert exhorted them. "You are to remember your oath and be willing to sacrifice your very lives to save him. You must do *whatever* is required of you. You are the best of the best — act like it!"

Frayne could sense that this was not the first time tonight that Robert had spoken to them in such a manner. Finally, the reluctant soldiers complied, moving to hoist the little eves. "And do so without harm to them," he said with a threat in his voice. So cautioned, the children were lifted and the party continued its trek through the thick undergrowth and then along the unexpected path leading into the protective mountain barrier.

The darkness of the night wrapped itself like an old memory across Robert's mind, that mad adventure from years ago rushing back at him. He let the excitement of that night fill him up, for he would need whatever assistance was available to complete this mission.

The going was not so difficult now, along the well-worn path. Robert was pleased with their pace, which was so much faster than his last journey down this trail, with no need to stop to rest ancient legs. When Frayne's head began to loll around from exhaustion, Robert ordered one of the soldiers to carry him, and the gangly stranger looked undignified draped over the shoulder of the much shorter soldier.

After two hours, he calculated they'd another two miles remaining before reaching the forest's edge. Two miles until what? he asked himself in sudden fear, but he pushed the thought aside. It would not serve to dwell on it.

When the trees became more defined by the desert light behind them, Robert ordered a halt. "Put him down," he instructed the soldier carrying Frayne.

Gaining his feet, Frayne wavered, as if he might topple over, and the captain put a hand out to steady him.

Once Frayne had regained his balance, Robert ordered, "Come with me, Stranger," and the two young men moved closer to the desert to converse in whispers.

"It will be necessary to make another calculation," Frayne said quickly, examining his strange tech machine before Robert could speak. "The shuttle lies two hundred and eighty-three feet to the northeast," he stated quietly, pointing with his long finger.

Robert returned to the group and ordered them into action.

Turning eastward, they left the trail, keeping parallel to the sparse trees — the desert so very close beyond them. The undergrowth was thin here and the moonlight brighter, making the going easy. After several minutes, Robert ordered

216

a halt, and again he took Frayne aside to examine his wrist instrument.

"My craft is located ninety-six feet northeast of this position," Frayne announced quietly. Then without warning he strode off towards the desert, Robert quickly following. A few strides later, they were out of the forest and into the scrub grass beyond.

Both men stopped short — Frayne, to enjoy the spectacular view of a moonlit desert, Robert, to face a childhood trauma. Adrenalin pounded his heart. It was all he could do to keep from racing back to the palace and to safety.

When Frayne could sense a lessening of panic within Robert, he stated, "I will bring the shuttle close to this location to enable the women to board easily." Robert shook his head, disbelieving and confused, while Frayne continued, "The craft requires a flat surface for landing. I will attempt to place the shuttle ten feet from the edge of that grassy slope." He pointed past the demarcation line between the Blessed and the Damned.

Robert shuddered but said nothing. Frayne set off as the captain slipped back into the cover of the forest to watch, wondering if he would ever see the stranger again.

Frayne stumbled down the hillside, losing his footing many times in the half-light. When he finally reached the bottom, he collapsed in a heap and had to wait several minutes before continuing. He covered the last few meters of patchy scrub grass and stepped onto the stone desert.

The rock formation that hid their shuttle could be seen clearly now. He pressed on, stumbling on the pebbly floor and stopping to rest often. When at last he fell against the ship's hull, he was near collapse. Groping for the small keypad, he feebly punched in the four-digit code and the hatch swung upwards, automatically triggering the interior lights and lowering a short ramp. Now on his hands and knees, he slowly dragged his spent body up the ramp and into the ship. He slumped to the floor and gave the verbal command that activated the engine.

And then exquisite relief! A dead weight lifted as he was wrapped in the replicated atmosphere of Mirandus. With every moment spent inside the ship's manufactured gravity, his strength returned.

Frayne strode to the console and gave instructions to the computerized pilot. Moments later, the ship lifted gently into the air, circling around to hover above the grassy rise. The powerful landing lights pushed aside the night, catching the terrified features of the people standing amongst the trees.

But Frayne saw none of this as he concentrated on feeding instructions into the computer, and soon the ship was once again settled upon the ground.

He looked out the window at the figures making their reluctant way down the slope, with Robert haranguing them into motion. But at the rim of the desert they stopped dead, as if held back by some powerful force field.

They were only three meters from the ship, but it might have been three thousand, for clearly these people had no intention of moving off their patchy grassland.

Frayne did not know how to help them, or even if he should.


Robert stood on the rise, watching the sudden appearance of the shuttlecraft.

Behind him, within the slim shelter of sparse trees, the horses whinnied nervously, pawing at the ground. His men were crouched in terror, the little eves slipping from their arms and tumbling easily to the ground, their eyes glued in fascination to the lights in the sky. The adult eves had collapsed in utter horror, their faces pressed into the earth.

But all Robert could think was, The stranger's world — it does exist!

And riding fast behind that was another thought: I lied to myself. I kept the whole mystery of Frayne — the *wonder* of Frayne — a security exercise. Refusing to focus on anything but the possible threat he might bring to the Chairman, never asking how, or why, or *what if?* I blunted my perception because I was too much a coward to face the truth.

For if Frayne's world did indeed exist, that would mean our Ancestors were *not* the Chosen Ones. And if they were not the Chosen, then all the burdens of Humanity were not ours to bear. And if that is true, what has been the purpose of our suffering? Was it simply to satisfy the dark ambitions of priests? And if that is the truth, how do I bear their presence in my life without howling outrage into their sanctimonious faces?

He'd thought himself freed of the Church's grip long ago. But no, he thought. Just more blunted perception.

Though he'd seen the corruption of individual clergy, and even realized the rot within the whole system, he'd still retained a belief in the Church's fundamental truths because it was these truths that gave structure and meaning to his life — to everyone's life. But now this was gone.

*Our whole society is based on a lie.*

He remembered the last time he'd stood here on the desert's edge: that babe left out for demons, not because it was corrupt, but because of quotas! An innocent soul sent to Satan!

The Church teaches us that only Satan kills. To kill meant one was possessed by Satan. But to give an innocent child to demons was far worse than murder.

He thought of the well-worn path, and the bishop's words: take the illegit north — like the others.

And now he was finally ready to face the unspeakable truth he'd hidden from all those years ago. He was, at last, ready to answer the question: Why would they send an innocent babe to demons?

Because there are no desert demons, came the shocking answer — only another lie to control us. The Church decides who lives and who dies based on some purpose of its own, like politics — or *quotas*.

What if, his mind abruptly suggested, what if . . . there are no such things as demons, at all? What if . . . what if there's no such thing as Satan?

He stood transfixed, considering this thought in shock.

Could it be? he asked, and his chest blossomed with a comforting warmth. He thought, This is the feeling of truth.

Then another shocking realization asserted itself: But that would mean . . . *no* baby was born corrupt — not even eves.

And as this idea settled on him, he once again felt that sensation within his chest.

The only source of evil in New Eden, he thought spitefully, is the Church. They are sinners of the foulest kind!

The chains he'd thought long broken were rattling, their anchor crumbling. Without a base to hold them, they fell away, casting him adrift. It was the most frightening sensation of his life. With no foundation of belief to weigh down the terror that lurked in every subconscious, it sprang to life, a dark shadow filled with demons and monsters — creations of the mind, but real in their power to do harm. Trapped in the black horror, he could barely hear his lieutenant's voice.

"Captain, what are your orders? Captain, are you alright! Lord-save-us, the evil spirits have taken him!"

The lieutenant's words cut into Robert's mind, disturbing the darkness and revealing a strand of unaltered truth: his feelings for William, unchanged because they'd never been touched by the Church or by the society it controlled, but existed in spite of them.

The lieutenant was shouting, "Sergeant Perez, we are moving outta here, on the double!"

"No, Sergeant, we are staying," Robert interceded with authority, but his voice was calm. "Don't worry, Lieutenant Biter, I'm not possessed — in fact, just the opposite."

I'm free, he thought, truly free.

He was still very shaken. He would need time to rebuild his world, pick through the rubble, and see what truth remained hidden there. But he had a start and it was bringing clarity, and right now action was needed.

He ordered his men to remove the bundles from the horses. The larger bundles held awkwardly between two soldiers. Then he forced the band of people out of the trees, prodding and cursing them down the slope, towards the barren floor. But at the edge of the grassland they stopped, cemented in terror. He could not budge them past the invisible barrier, and even Robert's own heart was pounding in fear. He may have thrown off the Church's yoke, but what remained? Was there any truth amongst all those lies? How could he know?

"Robert, you are unwilling to step upon the stone floor," Frayne's voice called out to him.

Robert answered, choosing his words with care: "We've been told that beyond this point lies evil."

"Then you cannot reach my ship," Frayne stated simply, but his words were enough to galvanize Robert into action.

"We will!" he shouted, suddenly adamant.

On impulse, he scooped up two little girls and dove across the ten feet to the shuttle. He heard a muffled wail of protest from their mothers, and even from his own men, who feared for his safety.

When the children were deposited at Frayne's feet, Robert dashed back to the scrub grass. A gasp of relief escaped his lips, but he did not pause. Two other children were scooped up, bringing more strangled grief from women trained to bear all in silence.

"I can assist you," Frayne said, as Robert set down the two girls inside the ship's doorway. "The ship's gravity will permit me to recover my strength."

"Can you bring the child eves?" Robert asked Frayne, although he didn't understand what this grav-tee did for him. "I'll carry the adults."

Frayne couldn't stop the smile from entering his voice: "I have been told that no man is permitted to touch a woman outside the mating room."

Robert looked at him in surprise. "If I didn't know better, I'd think you were giving me a hard time." He hadn't realized the stranger had a sense of humor. He smiled wryly. "We've been told a great many things. I'm testing their veracity."

Frayne studied Robert's face closely. "There has been a profound change within you." He paused, considering. "The people of your planet carry much fear within them, but I sense your fear has greatly diminished."

"Your scale must be way off Stranger, cuzz I'm shittin' scared."

"Yes, you are doing a dangerous act, according to your teachings, but still you carry it out. Unlike the others, you are not paralyzed with fear. And now you intend to put your hands upon dozens of women, yet I detect no qualms at this thought, only a desire to be done." He gave a half-smile. "Let us proceed."

Robert grasped Frayne's shoulder, forestalling him. "I regret not getting to know you. I could have learned from you, I think."

"I too regret that our relationship did not develop beyond the formal. You and William possess a similar nature: sensitive and passionate. You both feel deeply. This is not a kind planet for such a nature."

220

"No, but it's home."

"Yes, home . . . . Let us complete our respective missions so that we may both return home."

Robert nodded and set off again. When he approached the eves, they dropped to the ground in terror — all but one, who took a small step forward to indicate her willingness. Robert studied her in surprise. "Come," he said, and hesitated before taking her by the upper arm. You are either extraordinarily brave or completely possessed, he thought, forgetting that he no longer believed in such things.

Theresa had recognized Robert the moment he'd ordered her to wake and dress quickly. Ten years had passed since they'd shared the same school, but she would know him anywhere. And though she'd no idea why they were being secreted away in the night, Theresa had no fear. Robert would never lead children into danger. She still believed in the boy she had lied for all those years ago.

He was the only thing she still had any faith in.

Even after dropping to her knees in terror at the sight of the bright lights in the sky, she'd managed to recover her trust, and was the first one to make her way down the hillside as Robert urged the eves and beat his men to the bottom.

But when Robert took those children into the Unholy Lands, to that strange-looking skycart, she was once again thrown into doubt, appalled by such an act. She had to work hard to remind herself that he would never put a child in harm's way — I know this! Yet how could such an act not be a danger? And to the soul?

Then she remembered that she no longer had a soul, that her pain had ripped it from her. No demon could touch her now. And when Robert approached the women, she could not stop herself from stepping forward, though one part of her mind was shrieking in protest.

As they reached the rocky floor, fear shook her body uncontrollably, and Robert tightened his grip to prevent her bolting, but she stepped off the grass without encouragement. Robert never knew an eve could have courage — except that once, as a boy, when the young eve had put herself between him and the priest. "You did your work," he praised, hurrying her forward. There were still forty-eight adults to move, and Robert would have to carry them all.

He set a pace for his well-muscled body and did not deviate from it. None resisted beyond falling to the ground to whimper in terror. Back and forth he moved between the shuttle and the grass, stopping only to recover his breath before pushing onward again, until all the eves were loaded.

Frayne, too, had completed his task, recovering his strength with Mirandus' replicated gravity after carrying each child inside the ship.

This undertaking had been a great challenge for him. He had to continually remind himself that these children go with their mothers: it would be callous to leave them behind, however cruel it feels to carry their frightened little bodies into the unknown. To his relief, the very young had no understanding of what was happening.

All that remained were the mysterious bundles: four large and three small.

Robert ordered two of his men to help lift the largest onto his shoulder. He had to bark at them twice to get some sluggish response out of them. Staggering slightly under the weight, he picked his way carefully over the rocky ground to the ship. With relief, he dumped the bundle unceremoniously onto the shuttle floor.

He'd almost reached the ship with a second large bundle when Frayne's worried face confronted him. "There is an unconscious man inside that sacking. What is the cause of his loss of consciousness?" His eyes flickered to Robert's shoulder. "Does this sack also contain a man who is not aware of his fate?"

Robert stalked passed without answering, and Frayne followed close behind. When he'd disposed of his burden, Robert turned and said, "They're unconscious because we used a drug to make them so." Bought from the prince's favorite brothel, he thought with dark humor. He brushed past the stranger, anxious to keep moving.

Frayne called after him, "But they go against their will!"

When Robert returned with another bulky bundle, he was panting with effort, but he said shortly, "They *all* go against their will."

Frayne was silent, accepting the reminder as Robert went to collect the last unconscious man.

"Who are these men?" Frayne asked anxiously. "Why do you send them to Mirandus?"

"Two are the Chairman's brothers. The others are soldiers."

Robert had had no choice but to bring along the princes' personal bodyguards. They knew the brothers hadn't left willingly, and it was vital that the Chairman believed that they did.

"The Chairman's brothers?" Frayne was saying. "William would not order this for his siblings." But Robert was already walking back to the sparsely grassed hillside.

"And who is within that sacking?" Frayne asked, pointing to the smaller unwieldy bundle Robert returned with.

"One of their sons."

"Are these women and girls — these eves," he said, indicating the cringing females huddled together, "are these the wives and daughters of his brothers?"

"Not all. Some are William's. That was his wish."

"Why would William send away his own wives and daughters?"

Robert laid the unconscious boy down and turned to Frayne, saying, "He can

222

get more." The captain walked off, leaving Frayne to digest this statement.

Will this planet never cease to astound me?

He watched in silence as Robert put the remaining two children on board. Why would Robert drug the boys? he wondered. The oldest hadn't yet reached puberty and the youngest was perhaps six. But Frayne had learned enough of New Eden to reach his own conclusions: The boys have been raised to behave with aggression; they would not have come quietly. Unlike the girls and women, who have been trained in obedience and silence.

"That's the last of them," Robert said, panting hard now and allowing his body to lean against the ship's hull. He was in need of a few minutes' rest, and then a quick march back to the city, to be tucked innocently into bed before the dawn came and the alarm sounded. Unencumbered by civilians, there would be time enough.

Robert imagined the look of surprise on the Commander's face when he saw him still alive, and Robert gave a small chuckle. Not half as surprised as I am, he mused.

"Robert," Frayne said, interrupting his thoughts, "I have a request of you."

"What?" Robert asked tiredly.

"Would you inform Althaia of the success of our mission? And would you also explain to her my sorrow at returning to Mirandus without her?" He felt Robert recoil inwardly. "My request disturbs you," said Frayne in surprise.

"Yes," he admitted. "Speaking with an eve is forbidden. It's dangerous, and I've seen the results of disobedience." Or have I? he thought, remembering his new-found insights.

"You have walked upon the rocks of evil and survived. You have lain your hands upon forty eves and more this night, without suffering any harm. I do not understand your reaction."

Robert nodded, acknowledging the contradiction. Pausing, he said, "She's not like our eves."

"No, she is not," Frayne agreed. After a moment's consideration he said, "Althaia *would* speak with you."

Robert looked at him speculatively for a moment. "You *want* me to speak with her. Why?"

"She will be isolated from all she knows and alone," he said simply. "I apologize; I had forgotten the training you have endured to create this fear of women. My concern for Althaia and my hopes for you have distracted me from that fact. The pattern of a lifetime cannot be removed in a single evening." Can it ever? he wondered. Robert only grunted. "What I am suggesting is a great offense under your Laws. I have no right to make a request that would endanger you or Althaia."

Still Robert said nothing.

"Perhaps there is one request you could fulfill?"

"I'll try," he said quickly, relieved at the change of subject. "What is it?"

Frayne reached up and removed the chain that hung around his neck. "Would it be possible for you to deliver this into Althaia's possession?"

Robert hesitated, but he took the gold strand, stuffing it into his belt pouch. "I'll do what I can."

"I thank you."

Robert stood upright. "I've got to get back."

"Yes, we should proceed."

But Robert paused long enough to offer some advice: "Keep the men and boys tied up for the whole journey. They'll be as deadly as a cornered boar with piglets when they wake up. They'd kill you for sure; even the youngest could do so." He looked embarrassed at having to refer to Frayne's weakness.

"But our journey will take many weeks. I cannot keep them restrained for that length of time."

"Then you'd better keep them knocked out 'til you get some help, cuzz you'll be dead Stranger, and then what'll happen to your world?"

Deeply troubled, Frayne bade Robert farewell.

It was not until he'd moved back onto the grass that Robert realized he'd sat relaxed and talking inside the demon desert. Behind him, however, his men were in various stages of panic, collapsed on the ground in frenzied praying or babbling incoherently.

Robert ignored them, never taking his eyes from the ship. Frayne's head appeared once more, and a loud whisper reached him across the divide: "She can read and write."

A moment later the door closed, shutting out the interior lights, and not long after, the powerful landing lights also went out.

In the sudden darkness they heard a low whining noise that grew into a high-pitched scream. The soldiers bolted for the trees in terror and even Robert stepped back from the rocks, one part of his mind shrieking, Run! But he held against it.

The lights of the ship's interior gleamed through the small windows, yet he couldn't make out Frayne's slight form. Then in one swift motion the ship rose up and into the night sky.


Frayne put the shuttle on course for the mothership before turning to examine his passengers. The men and boys were still resting in oblivion, a stark opposite to the females, who, even in that confined space, had managed to cringe away

224

from any accidental contact with the males.

All carried the same dazed expression in their eyes.

Sensing reassurance would be useless at this time, Frayne concentrated on solving his most pressing problem: how to render the men and boys harmless without harming them in the process. Locks were unknown on Mirandus, and they could not remain drugged for the duration of their journey. He doubted whether the ship would even possess such drugs.

"Computer, does there exist the technology to render a human unconscious for a prolonged period of time without causing harm to the body?"

"Yes," a male voice announced, with the same precise articulation as Frayne's. "The stasis chamber."

"Please explain."

"The stasis chamber: designed to transport injured crew members or colonists who would not otherwise survive the journey to medical facilities on Earth. The patient is encased in a chamber where homeostasis is maintained at the lowest level of energy output."

"A person could live for ten weeks in this chamber without harm?"

"Yes."

"Does the mothership possess such a device?"

"Yes. There are twenty chambers available for use."

"Thank you, that is all."

He could relax now, although he would still need to find a way to transfer the men from the shuttle to the stasis chambers.

Abruptly he remembered that there were robot helpers onboard the ship, and he was quietly amazed that a robot had not automatically come to mind. In only ten weeks, I have grown accustomed to living without their assistance? What else have I grown accustomed to?

And how will my life be affected, now that I have been to another world and lived amongst such timid and violent people? People so much like myself. Yes, like myself.

He looked over at his passengers, and he could not help wondering with some trepidation what affect these people would have upon his world.

As the little craft pierced the atmospheric barrier, he felt the loss of Althaia and the other new friends in his life. Through the viewport he could see the great mothership coming up fast, and within a few minutes they were sidling up to her comforting bulk.

A landing bay raised its doors to allow the shuttle entry, and soon they were encased in her womb-like belly.

He was going home.

# CHAPTER 26

WILLIAM SCREAMED. He screamed without pause: a noisy declaration of fury, a frustrated spewing of disappointment and betrayal. He screamed on, railing against his losses. Thomas! Henry! Frayne! That beautiful shining world! All gone!

Why, Thomas? he asked in his mind. We could have gone together, we three. Why leave me behind? Then outrage at their betrayal would seize him once more, and he would shriek his high, screaming wail.

When the screaming stopped, he collapsed into silent misery. He would see no one, and no amount of entreaties by the Commander or Robert could rouse him.

In desperation, the Commander requested the return of Father Gideon, but he too failed to achieve access. William remained hidden within his rooms and refused all contact with the outside world. Only his privy servant was allowed inside, and Baldwin was under orders to keep the doors to the Chairman's private apartment locked.

Robert considered gaining entry by the secret passageway, but thought it might send William into further hysterics. Instead, he waited with everyone else and tried vainly not to feel guilty for causing the Chairman such grief.

They would have betrayed him on their own, he kept reminding himself. I only brought it to his attention sooner — I saved his life!

And what of Frayne? a little voice asked. But for that, Robert had no answer.

The Commander watched Robert struggle with his guilt and remembered how poorly he'd handled his strong emotions in the past. I'll keep a close eye on young Bountiful, Belcher thought. If the captain's feelings interfere with his ability to serve the Chairman, I'll need to take action.

Yet the Commander was forced to admit that Robert's removal of the princes was a superior tactical move: simple and effective. Though not so simple to carry out, he thought with grudging respect. Bountiful has rid the Chairman of his three greatest threats *and* managed to survive intact and uncorrupted. I could rest easy meeting my Maker, when the time comes, if Bountiful can get through this current challenge.

The Commander became thoughtful, and after some consideration decided that there was only one way he was going do that.

"Captain Bountiful," Belcher ordered Robert, "I commission you with the Chairman's recovery — see that it's a speedy one."

Robert stared at the Commander in surprise, understanding that he had finally regained his superior's trust. He also understood it was a test.

Three more days passed, but still there was no change in the Chairman.

Robert was at a loss. What could he do that wouldn't aggravate the situation?

He was finally inspired to action when the frightened privy servant was brought before him with troubling news.

"The Chairman has ordered me to fetch a case of whiskey, and then, after dark—" he paused, finding it painful to say the words "—a dose of the demon drug."

Sometime later, Baldwin was returned to William's suite with only one small article in hand. Without a word, he placed the envelope on the bedside table and hastily retreated.

William stared at the paper jacket without interest. Finally he reached out and twitched the envelope towards him, lethargically ripping it open and almost tearing the small note inside. Focusing on the few words, he read,

*The stranger's eve remains.*

The response was immediate. William threw himself from the bed, shouting for Baldwin to bring his clothes, and within a short time he stood at the door to Althaia's cell.

"Is your prisoner still inside?"

"Yes, Sire."

William drew back the shutter a fraction. Yes, she was there.

"Excuse, Sire. Yurr captain ordered me tuh gives yuh this," the guard said apologetically, offering the Chairman an envelope.

William tore it open, scanning the message quickly. He gave a grunt of surprise and crumpled the note, staring deeply into space. Once more he peered at Althaia, considering.

Snapping the shutter closed, he whirled away and exited the cellar.

227

They are gone! Pope Validus silently repeated, as he had done many times since the news arrived ten days ago. All threats to the Church gone in one fell swoop. A miracle!

I don't believe in miracles, he would remind himself sternly. Yet how else to explain this sudden and wonderful event?

And William has once more collapsed into despair — despair so severe that the Commander felt compelled to summon Father Gideon in the hope of drawing out the Chairman. But to no avail. William no longer sought comfort in the Father's presence.

Pity, Validus thought. I'd hoped Gideon's recall would be permanent — a step towards the Church's return to the palace. But, he reassured himself, it *will* come, for the poisonous influence of William's brothers has been removed forever.

At this thought, the Pontiff allowed his pleasure to surface totally, and he took a long sip from a glass of wine before digging into his evening meal with gusto.

He was eating a late dinner inside his office, as was often the case, for a Pope's life revolved around his responsibilities. Validus managed to consume several mouthfuls before his mind inevitably asked:

But *why* did they go? Why would two such conniving vipers risk the dangerous journey across space to an unknown world with a hideous stranger?

Because they'd something very big to gain, always came the unwelcomed answer.

And, as usual, the Pontiff's ire would re-awaken in the knowledge that the princes had managed to outmaneuver the Church once again: pretending they'd no interest in the stranger, yet all the while plotting to abscond with him.

But to what end?

He pushed his dinner away, his appetite spoiled. He got to his feet and restlessly prowled the expansive office as he considered possibilities.

Did the princes hope to influence — even overwhelm — an entire planet with four men and three boys? It would seem unlikely.

He thought of all that he'd learned of the stranger from his various spies, and he had to admit, that yes, it might be possible. The princes were certainly devious and ruthless enough if the entire planet be as weak as the stranger — and as naive.

But it no longer matters what those poisonous snakes do, or why, he reminded himself with satisfaction, for we are finally and thoroughly rid of them.

Sighing with relief at — once again — reaching such a reassuring conclusion, he was about to return to his dinner when a disturbing question dispelled this complacency: Then *why* am I so consistently troubled by their departure?

228

He did not like the answer.

Perhaps we're not rid of them after all? Perhaps they will return — and with what? If Proximus still has the ability to travel to our planet, what other tech might they possibly possess?

The eve, he thought in sudden hope. Did the stranger leave his eve? I will have to make inquiries. If she remains, we can now legally take her into custody. This eve could answer many of my questions about the stranger and his world.

A knock resounded loudly on the door and Cardinal Vecker strode inside. "Your Holiness, there is news from the Palace." He stepped away from the entrance and impatiently beckoned Baldwin forward. The privy servant scuttled into the room, kneeling to kiss the Pontiff's ring.

"Yes, Baldwin," the Pontiff said. "What is it?"

"The Chairman, Your Holiness, he has married the stranger's eve!" he blurted out in fear.

The Pope's eyes bulged momentarily with surprise before his face became impassive. "You are certain?" he asked, his voice tight.

"Yes, Your Holiness. Old Father Billy performed the ceremony."

Validus was stunned — stunned but impressed. Robert, he thought. This would be his doing.

"You have done your duty, Baldwin," the Pontiff said stiffly, in way of praise. "You may leave." The man bowed and was almost out the door when the Pontiff added, "Keep me informed of any new developments."

"Yes, Your Holiness," Baldwin said, and bolted from the room.

Cardinal Vecker was staring at the Pope, an accusing look in his eye.

The Pontiff remained unruffled. "It would seem our Chairman has come out of hiding."

# CHAPTER 27

THERE WAS a change.

The men who escorted her were not afraid.

Nervous and wary, yes. But the terror she once evoked was no longer there.

What has happened to change their perspective? she wondered.

They passed other men standing within the corridors she was marched through, but they remained as frightened as before. Althaia felt them recoil violently away from her. She also felt the superiority of her escort towards them.

Are these few men the only ones to have lost their gripping fear of me? she wondered again, and thought of the man who'd sent that hastily written warning: "Keep your eyes down and your mouth closed if you want to stay alive." He'd left a clear impression. He was the same man who had taken her to heal Frayne.

She recalled that his name was Robert.

Similarly to that experience, they walked far and climbed many stairs, but this time she was marched openly, not secreted along hidden passages.

With relief, she felt the improved air quality as they left the darkened stairwell to emerge onto the main floor of the building, moving quickly down a corridor before ascending steadily to the fourth floor, where ten paces later they were forced to come to a halt. A wall had been constructed across the entire length of the fourth floor landing, barring further access except through one narrow door. On either side of this entrance stood two men dressed in the same clothing as her escort. They too possessed this new sense of inner strength.

Briefly, they each raised a stiff hand to their brow before one of the men pulled open the narrow door, ushering Althaia through the access. The uniformed men followed after her, one at a time, and the door was swung shut behind them.

It was very still inside, unlike anywhere else in the building, as if the door held back some dynamic aspect of the life force. Even the raw, aggressive energy emanating from her escort seemed to suddenly dim, their bravado struggling to reassert itself.

They were standing in a broad open area, lit by the descending sun streaming through windows designed by the Ancients: narrow panes of plazglass that ran from floor to ceiling.

Althaia yearned to bathe in those rays of light.

Two corridors led off from the landing, each with a large door blocking the entrance. The man in the lead hesitated, looking to his right. Another man spoke up, pointing towards the door: "Sir, that eve-wing houses the wives of a prince." The lead man grunted before turning left and striding to the opposite corridor.

Hesitating only briefly, he pulled the heavy door open and motioned the others to follow, leading them down the dimly lit passage to a small vestibule. A narrow door was set in one wall with a bell hanging beside it. On the adjacent wall was a wide, imposing entryway.

Althaia's escort took up position along the walls of the vestibule, leaving only two uniformed men standing on either side of her. The leader instructed these men in a low voice: "Complete silence inside the chapel. The priest is not to know you're soldiers." They nodded in understanding. "He'll think you're bride-priests from the Vatican, so he'll ignore you completely — it's a territorial thing."

Cautiously, the leader approached the broad entrance and pushed the door open, peering inside. Then he ushered Althaia and the two soldiers into the long, narrow chapel. Her small escort stopped two meters inside the room, waiting in silence, as instructed. It gave Althaia the opportunity to covertly study the space.

It was empty of all furnishings but for a podium that stood at one end of the chapel. Upon this lay a thick book bound in animal hide. Behind the podium was a doorway. High above this entry hung a large iron cross; the top half of the cross was encircled with fire wrought in bronze. At the other end of the room, two smaller doors stood open, each leading into the cramped darkness of a tiny cubicle.

Along one long wall of the chapel was a series of stained glass windows, the pictures depicting a variety of violent and gruesome deaths. On the wall opposite was a fireplace. An old man stood before this, warming his hands. He wore a long black robe with a white collar that stood stiffly about his neck. His silver hair was cut above the ears in an unflattering style, as if a bowl had been placed upon his head and used as a cutting guideline.

She could sense he was blind.

As the leader of her escort had predicted, this elderly man behaved as if he hadn't noticed their arrival. She waited passively, keeping her eyes down, resisting the impulse to gaze at the setting sun shining through the stained glass.

Abruptly, the two men beside her went very stiff and straight: someone had entered the room behind them. Another man strode past them, radiating such excitement that Althaia's body shook from the impact. She quickly encased herself in protective energy as she watched him vibrate over to the fireplace. She recognized him as the frightened young man from Frayne's healing.

"You can begin now, Father Billy," he ordered the old man.

Using his cane for guidance, Father Billy felt his way towards the podium. Once the priest had taken up position there, Althaia's escort motioned her into the room behind the pulpit, closing the door firmly the moment she stepped inside.

The small space held nothing but a wooden bench bolted to the floor. Two narrow doors were at the opposite end of the room, but she thought it wise not to investigate at this time. Instead, she moved towards the entrance to the chapel, listening intently. Althaia could hear the younger man's voice responding to the droning chant of Father Billy, but she could not distinguish the words.

The leader in her escort had called him a priest. Althaia knew from her studies that the designation of priest was one of several used to denote a person who gave religious guidance and instruction.

She recognized that something significant was in progress.

The voices stopped, and a few moments later the old man tapped his way inside, causing Althaia to back away from the door.

Using the cane, he crossed to the bench. "Come here," he ordered, his voice shaky with age.

Father Billy, once confessor to William's father, had been retired for several years, too blind and frail to carry out his duties. He was honored to have been recalled into service for his new King.

As Althaia stood before him, he paused, uncertain. Then the frail voice commanded, "Kneel." When she had done so, he hesitated again. "You are kneeling?" he demanded to know.

"Yes," she said, keeping her voice low, knowing she would frighten him if she said too much. He wavered fractionally before pushing aside his doubts to intone with forbidding authority:

"You will honor and obey your husband.

Forsaking all evil thoughts and lures of the devil,

You will in no way entice him into sin or corruption.

You will bear him many pure sons,

Free of corruption in spirit and flesh.

For so long as you remain fertile,

You are pronounced the wife and property of:

William Simon Cartwright the XVII."

Althaia opened her mouth to protest but recalled the written warning. She paused to consider her mission, and after a moment chose to remain silent.

Father Billy was already at the door before he remembered to give the eve instructions on the Mating Rite. "When your husband enters, remove your trousers and kneel upon the mating bench."

Althaia sucked in her breath, shocked at this further barbarity. The priest closed the door and she was alone. Women were married without consent? she thought, stunned by what had just happened and already regretting her compliance. She stood up as the young man entered.

William was bloated with triumph: the last link to that fantastic world was securely chained to his side. Robert's scheme was faultless: marry the eve and the Church must let her live — at least for a time, longer if she carried the heir.

But alone with her now, he was beginning to regret his rash act.

"You are to be kneeling on the mating bench," he blustered, but quietly, aware of the priest standing in the next room.

But she did not move except to raise her eyes to his. He gave a frightened squeal and stepped back, turning his face away.

"You are not to look a man above the knees!" he hissed in terror.

"I have been married without my consent, and now you intend to force intercourse upon my person," she stated, keeping her voice low to match his own.

"Do not speak to me!" he wailed in a whisper. "It is forbidden!"

"I will not lie quiet for your assault."

"Do not speak!" he wailed again, almost begging.

She became silent, considering. She could see he was close to rushing from the room, and understood that this could not be to her benefit. She would not put her mission at risk, not unless circumstances forced it upon her.

William was beginning to panic. What was I thinking? How could I ever hope to control such an eve! He was about to give in: admit his lack of authority over his wife and have the marriage annulled. But no! he thought. I will not give her up without a fight, not this last remnant of Frayne's world, not until they force me.

She must learn to obey, he thought with sudden resolve. Though in truth, he did not believe she ever would. Screwing up his courage, he whispered with his face turned aside, "I am not assaulting you. It is the consummation of our marriage." He paused before adding, "Your voice is an assault to me!"

"I wish you no harm," she whispered in return. "But I do not desire to mate with you at this time."

"Desire has nothing to do with this!" he hissed again. "You are my wife. You will obey me or be whipped within an inch of your life."

"Then I choose the inch."

He swore fiercely under his breath, frustrated by this attitude that was so like Frayne's. It's hopeless, he thought. She will not submit. But then came the sudden thought: What if she didn't? Who would know?

It wouldn't be the first time that he'd given only the appearance of mating — for he often felt reluctant to participate in this duty. He was not the only man on Eden to feel so.

Personally, he didn't care if he ever mated her. It would be a considerable relief, he had to admit, not to have to try.

"You do not have to mate with me," William announced, his voice harsh and low. "Though the Church would keep you alive much longer if you carried my heir."

"I will mate when and with whom I choose," she stated with finality, sensing his relief at escaping the intimacy.

"Agreed," he said hastily. "Now speak no more. If the priest hears you, he will order the marriage annulled and your tongue will be cut out."

Why force me into this marriage if you have such fear of me? Althaia wondered in amazement. But she did not pursue her question; he had endured enough for the time being.

Her new husband remained where he was, standing immobile with his head bent away from her. He seemed to be . . . listening? No, she realized. He is waiting.

The minutes passed.

Still not looking at her, William mumbled, "The mating would be done now," before slipping through the door to the chapel.

Shaking with reaction, Althaia let her body collapse against the mating bench and slide to the floor. There had been a moment — only a moment — when she thought he was going to force himself upon her. Drawing in a deep breath, she calmed her erratic pulse. A trance was needed, but she sensed that now was not the time, and a moment later one of the smaller doors opened. She just managed to stifle the reflexive turn of the head, remembering to keep her eyes cast downward.

"No more pouting now! It's all done and over with. Come on now, up on your feet!" commanded a male voice so high-pitched and penetrating in its falsetto it was almost a physical assault upon her ears. It was so startling, so unexpected, that Althaia's head jerked upward to stare at the large, pudgy man with dyed red hair and the smooth skin of a woman. She regretted it at once. Their eyes met and the impact was staggering, sending him reeling from the room, his shrill voice screeching for the priest as he burst inside the chapel.

The vocals ended abruptly before a brief scuffling sound ensued, and then silence. The clatter of footsteps entered the chapel, and she heard someone state, "He wasn't heard, the priest was gone." There were more sounds of footsteps as they exited the chapel.

After a few minutes of quiet, Althaia cautiously approached the door to close it once again. Then she closed the small door the feminine man had come through.

Confused and off center, she placed herself in trance, regaining her inner-balance and building strength for the challenges to come. The healing did not take long.

Sensing she would be here for some time, she examined the room but there was little to use. Apart from the mating bench, there was only one other item: a much smaller version of the firecross that she'd seen inside the chapel. But this cross was very old and of a different style; the circle of fire added at a later date.

Her gaze lit upon the mating bench and she shuddered. Not that. She turned to the cross, reluctantly moving towards it.

Althaia now understood that there could be no resisting the unraveling of this planet's history or that woman's personal story. If she did not accept the visions, they would be forced upon her. This had been made clear to her by the events in her cell.

What she did not understand was how this could be. Nothing was forced on Mirandus, not on any level.

It was as if the natural laws of the Universe had become distorted on this planet. But could natural law be interfered with at its most basic level?

It would explain the sickly miasma gripping this planet.

She was thrown into doubt about that which she held as a fundamental truth. But for now, she must accept this ambiguity and continue with her history lesson. She would trust that what she needed to know would come to her — at all levels.

Resolute, she encased herself in a thick shield of protective energy and placed her hand upon the ancient cross.


Bishop Alexander stared down at the plazpaper in his hand with utter disbelief.

We are recalled?

Stunned, he re-read the words over and over, unable to take it in.

How can they do this? *Why* would they do this? And why now? It made no sense. The paint has barely dried on that eyesore of a cathedral — billions spent — and we simply abandon it?

*Why*? He continued in mystification.

The Agency *must* relocate, it cannot remain on Earth. It's only a matter of time before their security is breached. Moving their headquarters to Primus is the only way to protect their Q-drive.

Soon there will be tens of thousands of ISA employees and their families living on this planet and eventually millions of colonists, eager to escape Earth's overcrowded and polluted cities and the constant threat of war.

They will all be in need of the Church's guidance. The Vatican knows this.

Then why? he asked again.

Suddenly he didn't care why.

I've worked too long and too hard, he thought. I'm not about to lose what will become the most powerful diocese in the Church, simply because some shortsighted bureaucrats couldn't see past a few rumors and delays.

Well then, he decided with further conviction, I'll simply have to create a few delays of my own. No one knows I've received this letter from the Vatican — no one but my assistant. And Father Theodore's so frightened of me, he'd never say a word.

He crumpled the plazpaper in his hand.

It was lost in transport — happens all the time, he thought complacently. How many recommendations did I send to the Vatican advocating the use of the quantum-wave for communication? My proposals always rejected. The security considered too lax; the Vatican fearful of Agency eyes on Church business.

My concerns will once again be justified, he thought with a small smile, tossing the letter into the laze-shredder.


The Bishop was focused on the message in his hand — yet another recall from the Vatican. He was considering whether to ignore it once again when there was a sudden rapping on his office door. It was thrust open and a young priest entered, visibly anxious.

Startled, Alexander asked sharply, "What is it, Father Theodore?"

"Your Grace, there's news from Earth," the young man answered nervously. "They've discovered another planet — a habitable planet. The gravity less than Primus — a little less than Earth." The priest braced himself for a strong reaction, but instead the older man seemed to crumple. "Are you alright, Your Grace?"

The bishop was not alright. He felt as if he'd been dealt a great physical blow. It took him several moments to recover. At last he managed to ask in a hoarse whisper, "Rumor or fact?"

Alarmed by the bishop's appearance, the young priest answered gently, trying to soften the impact of his words. "I'm sorry, Your Grace, but it's not a rumor. The news came by quantum-wave, an ISA communication. I read it in the manager's office."

"And the terrain — what about the terrain?"

The priest gulped nervously before stating in a quiet voice, "The terrain is varied, much like Earth.

"And the climate?"

"Varied, also."

Then I have lost, the bishop thought bitterly. The Agency and all the millions to follow will go to the new colony. Now he understood the summons from Rome.

But after a moment he brightened as he realized, This new colony will also be in need of the Church. And there is no one better qualified for the post than I and my trained staff. Yes, that must be the reason for our recall to Earth: to prepare us for this new assignment. They are simply not at liberty to reveal the facts until this new planet's discovery becomes public.

With renewed life, he picked up his comp-pen and began to draft a letter, confirming that he and his staff would begin packing up the rectory and cathedral at once.

The young priest breathed a sigh of relief. The old man was going to be okay.

"What do you mean, it's unlikely my next posting will be on the new colony?" the bishop demanded, his voice sharp.

The man sitting across the dinner table from him shifted uncomfortably. He hadn't expected such a strong reaction. "I'm afraid the Protestants have acquired the religious charter on the new colony — Proximus, they're calling it." He shrugged as he said, "I guess they're trying to be fair, one for each of you."

"The Protestants!" the bishop gasped. He was having difficulty breathing.

"Hey, you okay?" the man asked in sudden concern.

With an enormous effort, Bishop Alexander forced himself back to calmness. "I suddenly feel quite unwell. I'm sorry, Bobby, but I don't think I can stay for dinner after all."

"That's okay. Sorry I upset you."

"No, it's not you, it's . . . circumstances," the bishop said, as he limped weakly from the house.

"Your Grace! The colony's under quarantine!" Father Theodore burst in with great excitement, panting heavily from the exertion.

The bishop looked up listlessly from where he sat on a crate, his personal belongings boxed up around him. "We are?" he asked without interest.

"Not us, Your Grace — Proximus!"

"Are you certain?" he spoke with skepticism.

237

"Yes," he panted. "Mr. Martinez gave me the memo personally."

"Details, Father Theodore, details," the bishop demanded with a little of his old fire.

"It's an alien virus. Over fifty colonists are near death, and more are infected every day." He paused to gather his strength. "All transports in and out have been canceled until further notice."

A slow smile spread across the bishop's face; it didn't reach his eyes. "Do you realize what this means, Theodore? Even if they find a cure, people will never trust Proximus again — not fully. They will come here now, instead."

With sudden energy, he rose to his feet. "Alert the rest of the staff. Have they gone to the ship?"

"Yes, Your Grace. They've already taken most of our furniture. There are only a few more loads."

"You'll need to contact them — and quickly."

"They'll be inside the ship. I won't be able to reach them."

"Well, you'd better get a move on then. We're staying."

"But what about our orders?"

"The Church will need us to remain here, after all. I'm simply anticipating their wishes. Now go, quickly."

"They took the rectory van to the ship, Your Grace."

"Borrow an all-terrain from Bobby — Mr. Martinez. Go!"

Alexander didn't notice the exhausted priest forcing himself into action. Awash with elation, the bishop strode to the window, looking out over the planet that would bring him his heart's desire.

All the sacrifice and hard work had not been in vain: I *will* realize my ambition. If only father could have lived to see it, he reflected.

The thought reminded him of family responsibilities. I must arrange for my nephew to be transferred up here. The lad's future will be assured. And that will fulfill my promise to my dearly departed sister.


Time surged ahead.


I have lost my faith completely.

Utterly irrevocable.

As dead as the billions who perished on our beloved Earth.

Bishop Alexander was sunk deep inside an armchair, his body inert and flaccid, as if it too had perished along with his faith.

Perhaps the information is false? he considered, but only momentarily.

The source was unimpeachable.

How long is Simon going to sit on this horrific news? And why?

What does it matter? he thought wearily.

They are dead. All dead.

Eventually the bishop managed to rouse himself. His hand reached down to pull on the chain that hung from his waist. At the end of the chain was a cross. With fingers that could barely function, he unfastened the cross and let it fall to the floor.

Bishop Alexander stood at his office window, staring out at the townsite below.

I am the spiritual leader of a Church that means nothing to me, he reflected wearily. Do I continue to play out the charade? Or do I renounce my vows and step aside for another to lead?

But give up my position to do what? Work in the fields? Scrub pots in the Agency kitchens?

He thought of all he'd be relinquishing: the respect, the awe, and yes, even the fear and hatred his position generated.

No, he realized, I've come too far to return to such humble stations. It would serve no purpose, in any case. I no longer believe in humility and poverty. They cannot save my soul, for I no longer believe in souls.

Why did they wait? the bishop asked himself in bafflement. They could have saved so very many more . . . . But they delayed and delayed, and now all that remain are these pitiful few. What a horrific waste.

His mind shifted again.

So, I will be Pope, he thought ruefully. My ambition realized: Little John-Paul Alexander fulfills his childhood dream — and his father's.

He considered the rich halls of the Vatican, now a heap of rubble, and the billions of faithful, all dead. How small his prize was now.

Gradually, a disturbing fact intruded upon his consciousness. He shifted his position at the window to look out over the whole community. The bishop continued to watch for several minutes before striding to his desk to press the intercom. Father Theodore entered, looking exhausted and harassed.

"Father Theodore, I want a census taken immediately."

"Now? But we're overtaxed as it is, Your Grace. Between the burials and the wounded — and the gravity."

"One of them will have to be spared."

"Yes, Your Grace." He staggered out.

239

The bishop returned to his view at the window. He wasn't about to lose what little power remained to him.

"Simon wants the alliance with the Church severed completely," Tom Murdock announced before adding with heavy sarcasm, "—Your Holiness."

The Pontiff remained impassive. "This comes as no surprise. Are the Board of like mind?"

"No. They understand the goals of the Church can't be separated from their own. They've no idea he's planning the split. But I've been watching that bastard for years. I know when he's getting ready to make a move. He can surprise others, but not me."

Not anymore, he thought bitterly, remembering the humiliation Simon had heaped upon him. Pretending support when all the while he planned to stab me in the back — stealing my power base. Making me look like an incompetent asshole so he could grab control of Personnel under the pretext of security.

Security! his mind spat out the word. The Board was paranoid about it. And there was Simon, fanning the flame.

In the name of security, his influence spread to every area of the Agency — the Board convinced that he worked to protect their investment. Even handing him the funds to build an Army, to defend against espionage and terrorists. How many times did I want to shout into their stupid faces, Wake up, assholes! You'll be turned on by your own guards!

Well, they sure the hell know the truth of it now, he thought scornfully.

But unlike them, I have never resigned myself to failure. I always knew I'd get back on top, and do it by standing on Simon's bones.

The Pope studied Tom's face as it twisted into an ugly mask of hate.

Is your hatred creating what isn't there? he wondered. Very likely not. Simon was the type of man to demand autonomy in his rule. It would be wise to accept this information as reliable.

"So the days of compromise are over," the Pontiff said with regret. He gazed at the glass in his hand, swirling the amber liquid. After a moment, he looked towards his visitor. "I presume you have some plan to counter Simon?"

Tom Murdock nodded. "It's simple enough: Simon must be . . . removed."

"That's no solution. His fanatical guards would butcher us both if they even suspected we were involved."

"True. But what if he was taken out by some other party?"

"You have such a person in mind?"

Tom leaned forward and smiled benignly. "Oh yes. The perfect agent. And

240

when it's done, the Chairmanship is mine. Agreed?"

"Agreed."

Cord looked at the Pope through bloodshot eyes, from a face strained and haggard. Three days of intense searching had produced nothing, though he'd torn through the townsite half crazed with grief and guilt. He'd failed in his duty: Simon was dead.

Now his efforts to root out every last person involved were also failing, and there was no one to vent his rage upon. But for the first time he had a promising lead and was anxious to follow it up.

"What do you want?" he demanded hoarsely, tossing the compbook onto his desk.

The Pontiff was not disturbed by this unfriendly greeting. "We must talk."

Cord glowered and was about to throw him out, but abruptly changed his mind. "Make it fast. I've no time to waste."

"I understand," the Pontiff said, taking a seat without invitation. "I won't offer my condolences; I know they wouldn't be accepted. But I want you to know that I deeply regret Simon's passing."

"And why should I believe that?

"Simon commanded the loyalty of you and your troops. With his death, that unification is gone."

"What are you getting at?" Cord asked with annoyance.

"There's sure to be a fight amongst the Board to gain the Chairmanship. It's also a certainty that whoever wins the Chair will do so with the backing of the Army." Cord nodded a reluctant assent. "But your men are no longer joined in a common cause. They could be easily split — perhaps even bring us to civil war."

"It won't happen. I'll keep them in line."

"Without Simon? Do you really believe you can?" he asked softly.

"What's all this leading up to?" Cord demanded wearily.

"Make Simon's son Chairman."

"What!"

"Your men feel responsible for Simon's death. They would see the boy as a way to atone. You know they'd follow William like no other: solidly united behind him — even zealous in their devotion."

Cord pushed away from his desk to stand before the map of Primus, suddenly very wide awake. Simon's boy on the Chair? Yes! That was the answer. Should have thought of it myself, he mused ruefully. But this popish toad did, and that could only mean trouble. He wasn't to be trusted.

Cord rubbed the back of his neck, trying to think. Simon would know where the danger lay. But Simon's gone, he thought. It's up to me now to look out for his family.

With regret, Cord realized that he could not discard the proposal. He turned on the Pope, demanding roughly, "And what's in it for you?"

Unperturbed, the Pope answered, "A stable government. Only the boy can provide one."

"What's the catch?"

"There is no catch, Lieutenant. The Church and the Agency need each other to survive. I want my ally to be strong."

But Simon believed you weren't necessary for *our* survival, Cord thought darkly. He was going to cut you out when the time was right.

But when that was, only Simon knew.

He always did play things close to the chest — sometimes too close. He sighed deeply, trying to push aside the loss and the pain.

Clearly suspicious, Cord asked wearily, "So what are you proposing?"

"At Simon's funeral service I will proclaim William as his heir and the new Chairman. I will also announce the Church as his legal guardian—"

"I knew it!" Cord broke in, smashing his fist onto the desktop. He leaned forward threateningly. "There's no way you're getting your hooks into Simon's kid!"

The Pontiff appeared amazed by the soldier's reaction. "There's no need for such suspicion. It's only logical that the Church should protect such a valuable child. Who else is there?"

"The mother will raise him," Cord stated impatiently, "and I'll protect him."

"The mother? You can't possibly trust *her* after what's happened? How many other women were involved in that bloody uprising but managed to escape? And what of Simon's wives who knew but didn't speak out — who didn't even warn their own husband? Aren't they just as guilty? And how can you be truly certain of anyone's innocence, even after all your investigations?"

Cord shifted uncomfortably, for the Pope was voicing his own doubts. He didn't believe for a moment that all the rebels had been killed in the fighting. Assassins were still out there, and he was certain some lived within the Agency. The toad was right. With all those women living so closely together, the gossip was certain to get around. Women can't keep a secret, not for long. Simon's wives *must* have known, and that made them as guilty as if they'd pulled the trigger.

But, regrettably, he knew it did not. His vengeance would not be satisfied with silent witnesses.

"You're right," he said with resignation. "The mother can't be trusted." And after a moment's reflection, he announced, "I'll raise the boy."

242

"You?" the Pope asked, mildly shocked. "What do you know about children?" He paused. "Or do your ambitions reach higher than I first thought?"

"That's pure bullshit, and you know it," Cord spat out, glaring at the older man. But he understood the threat: if he took over the guardianship, the Church would not endorse the boy.

Then I'll go it alone, without their backing, 'cause there's no way in hell the Church is getting their mitts on Simon's kid — he'd turn in his grave.

But Cord had strong doubts about his ability to make little Willie chairman if the Church ridiculed the move.

The Pontiff smiled crookedly. "It seems we've reached an impasse." Cord folded his arms in confirmation. "Come," the Pontiff said, his voice reasonable, "there must be some way to reach a compromise. The Church has no wish to be swept away, and I'm certain you don't want to jeopardize the boy's inheritance."

"*Now* what are you suggesting?" Cord asked impatiently, the fatigue returning to his voice.

"As there is a question of trust on both sides, it would seem a joint guardianship is the only reasonable solution." Cord pursed his lips, listening. "The Church would be responsible for his education and sharpening his wits. You could teach the boy how to protect himself and how to govern." Cord was silent, considering the proposition, hunting for traps. "Together, we offer him a world. Separately, we give him nothing."

"You make a good case, you conniving bastard."

The older man remained silent, waiting.

If I agree, the boy's future is assured, Cord argued with himself. Can I risk throwing that away? He let out a long sigh. "I know I'm gonna regret this, but OK, you've got a deal. But I'm gonna be watchin' you every second the boy's in your hands."

The Pontiff also sighed, but in relief. "Of course, and I wouldn't have it any other way. Once the chairmanship is announced, the boy's life will be in great danger."

"Don't worry," Cord growled. "I won't fail again."

"I wasn't implying any criticism, Lieutenant. I meant only that the danger will now be greater. We can't expect the Board to sit idle while a mere toddler holds power. Perhaps they could be encouraged to change residences? Civilly, of course. Houses can be built quite quickly with the right incentive, even on Primus."

"Not a bad idea, Your Grace-ship."

"Thank you," he said dryly, and rose to his feet. He considered extending a hand to cement the deal, then thought better of it. But before taking his leave, he added, "It might be wise if you were to have a title that rang with more authority.

Something that would encourage your men — and the Board — to see you as the leader you need to be. Perhaps . . . commander? The Church would back your promotion." He bowed his head shortly and departed.

The Pontiff remained restrained until he was clear of the Agency's Headquarters, and then he allowed himself a large smile of satisfaction. He had obtained his objective: the joint guardianship.

But he could not rest easy — not yet. There is still Mr. Murdock to deal with, he thought. I must encourage the lieutenant in his suspicions of me. There must never be an opportunity for an accident.

"I have every intention of upholding our agreement, but at the moment my hands are tied."

"Then untie them," Tom Murdock snarled. "I mean to have the Chairmanship — and soon."

"You'll get it, as promised. But right now I can't make a move without the guards all over me."

"You never should have approved the boy's ascendency!"

"I had no choice! I either went along with it or suffered a 'terrible accident'. The lieutenant was hardly in the mood to accept resistance, as you very well know."

"If at any time I suspect you're stalling me, I'll be forced to pay a little visit to the lieutenant. Think what a tragic, and, I'm certain, very painful accident would occur if he discovered the truth about Simon's death."

"It would mean your own neck as well."

"Don't think that'll stop me."

The Pontiff looked at Tom Murdock and saw that he meant it. "I need time," he said, "and that can't be changed. Or do you believe you've a better chance of getting at the boy?"

"I can't get anywhere near him — nobody can — you know that!" Tom answered impatiently.

"Then let me do my job without harassment."

"Alright, I'll back off. But my patience isn't endless."

"Don't be so impatient that you destroy any chance at the chairmanship."

"You must know I'll stop at nothing to get it."

"That, I understand." I understand all too well, thought the Pontiff. I understand you are quite insane.

244

The scene blurred, pushing the visions onward.


"Your Holiness, I feel I must caution you," Theodore said with some trepidation.

"What is it, Bishop?" the Pontiff asked distractedly as his stylus rolled across the surface of the comp-pad.

"The men will never accept this," the young man announced quickly.

"But they will," Alexander said, leaning back in his chair to study Theodore's nervous appearance. "You must understand human nature, my young friend. What at first appeared to be a magnificent banquet is now beginning to sour the stomach."

But the young bishop appeared only puzzled.

The Pontiff continued: "These men are under tremendous pressure to impregnate their wives but are incapable of fulfilling the demand. They have married far too many women and must now try to perform impossible sexual feats. This will inevitably lead to performance difficulties. Difficulties that could be the object of discussion, perhaps even laughter — as the men are painfully aware. They are all feeling vulnerable and exposed."

Theodore said nothing, his cheeks red with embarrassment.

Alexander ignored the young man's discomfort and continued: "And, of course, outside the home, women dominate the scenery: so very many hovering, trying to seduce them into marriage or into bed. And worse still, taking charge of all the difficult labor jobs, such as land clearing and planting. Refusing to allow any man to participate, insisting they keep their energy for procreating."

"But it's the men who are doing construction," Theodore interjected.

"Few women have these skills, but once they do, the men fear they'll be shunted out." Theodore digested this as the Pontiff said, "They are feeling powerless and overwhelmed by their situation — even angry. And in reaction the men are spending more and more time away from their families, clustering together in the little hiding places they've carved out for themselves. Seeking peace from the constant demands made by wives and work and Church. They are all guilty of neglecting their responsibilities. And they believe that this is the reason I've ordered our special service for them. They will attend prepared for a reprimand — not liberation. You will see, they will embrace my words with open arms."

Nervously, the young bishop put forth another consideration: "But many of these men lost wives and mothers in the war. A few are still married to their Earth wives."

"The war was five years ago," the Pontiff explained. "The dead are fading fast from our minds, and the challenge of staying alive on this alien planet is quickening the process. But yes, there will be some who oppose the Church's views. That is to be expected, and they will be dealt with. As for the majority, they're much too focused on their present misery. Do you understand now, my young innocent?"

"I . . . I suppose so, Your Holiness."

The Pope studied the young man for a few moments. "You are having your own doubts, Theodore?"

After a moment's hesitation, the bishop nodded his head. "I'm sorry, Your Holiness, to repay your faith in me with doubt. I don't deserve to be bishop."

No, you bloody well do not, Alexander thought in annoyance.

Theodore continued, "But what you propose is far from the teachings of the Church — from what I once knew to be the teachings of the Church. What of Mary, the holy vessel that brought our Lord into this world? And how many other Saints have been female?"

The Pope answered with equanimity: "Their sainthood is not in question. But as for the general populace, the Church has always held women at arm's length. They have never been ordained or permitted to offer the sacrament." He paused, studying the young man. "Theodore, we all have doubts. That is the way of faith. Even I have my doubts that this is the true course. But I must go where the Lord directs me. If we pray vigilantly, we will come to understand His will in time."

He paused to study Theodore's bowed head.

"I can offer you guidance through this difficult period of adjustment, my son."

"Thank you, Your Holiness."

Once the young man had departed, Alexander sat in contemplation.

Theodore is only voicing the repugnance that most men would normally feel at what I'm about to suggest, he thought. Am I moving too soon? Or has this planet eroded enough of that natural male protectiveness to make them consider my words — at least for a time. That's all I need, a little time to set things in motion, and then it will be too late to protest.

Alexander noticed that the chain he wore around his waist had become tangled. As he unraveled the links, his eye was caught by the cross on the end. He stared at it for a long moment, thoughts and feelings at war within him. But he pushed them all aside, allowing the chain to hang once more against his robes before calmly turning his attention back to his comp-pad.


The men filed listlessly into the Cathedral, taking their seats in the richly carved pews with the resigned attitude of prisoners in the dock. A spark of surprise shot through them when the Pope appeared at the pulpit. They'd not expected their laxness to warrant an appearance by His Holiness.

Pausing only briefly, the Pontiff's voice boomed out, startling the congregation. "My sons! How much longer must we suffer? How much pain must be inflicted before we realize our folly? The message has been clear, and still we ignore His Word!"

He looked over the guilty faces of the men as he continued, "We, the last remnants of Adam's seed, brought so close to annihilation, must now stop denying the Truth."

He paused, his gaze once more sweeping across the troubled parishioners as he continued in a strong voice: "In our ignorance, we have ignored the first Law of God –the first Law after our expulsion from Eden — the very foundation on which Mankind was to build his world."

With a flourish, he produced the Bible for all to see, holding it before him as he quoted from the text: "Unto woman, I will greatly multiply thy sorrow and thy conception. In sorrow thou shalt bring forth children, and thy desire shall be to thy husband, and he shall rule over thee." Looking slowly over the room, he repeated, "And he shall rule over thee." Again he raised the bible. "Let the woman learn in silence with all subjection. But suffer not a woman to teach, nor to usurp authority over the man, but to be in silence."

The Pontiff smashed the bible upon the pulpit with a force that resounded throughout the Cathedral, startling every man to attention. His voice took on a fierce tone. "Yet we have allowed her authority over us — in our homes, our work, and even in our governments." He leaned across the pulpit, emphasizing his words: "From the beginning she has suffused society with decadence and soft corruption. Eve forever tempting Man and he falling prey to her skills. And the result? A world destroyed! Mankind nearly obliterated!" The Pontiff waited as the words echoed over the congregation — accusing, wrathful.

When he continued, his manner had softened: "Is it mere chance that so few men survived the Trial of Fire? That eve outnumbers you so dramatically?"

He paused, allowing the idea to be considered before declaring in a stronger voice, "No! It is a sign of Satan's strength, of his power over Man, built up over the ages through his agent, eve."

Once again, he modulated his tone: "Satan can do nothing directly to man; he can only tempt, lure, suggest. And so it is with eve. She can be sly and cunning, manipulating those around her, yet seem innocent of all evil. No man can withstand her clever deceit. And we now know with bitter regret what prolonged exposure can result in." He paused, allowing the memory of a dead world to resurface.

"Yet you are forced to be intimate with her to propagate our species. This is

God's test. And you must not hate her or mistreat her, for she is as God made her and has a purpose in His Great Plan. But she must be rendered harmless and placed in a position of little threat. And we," he paused, "must keep a constant vigil against her seductive corruption. For God has given Mankind this last opportunity to see his error."

He paused again to study the congregation, seeing many faces willing to accept his words.

"*You* have been chosen from billions. You have passed through fire and been tested in strength and endurance. You are purified and readied. Now, the survival of Humanity — the burden of Humanity — rests on your shoulders. God has given us a new world and a new Garden to dwell in. A new Eden. Dare we continue to turn our backs on His Laws?"

The Pontiff raised the holy book once again, quoting, "Wives, be in subjection unto your husbands, as unto the Lord. For the husband is the head of the wife." The Pontiff closed the bible and placed it upon the pulpit. In a quiet voice that rang with steel, he ended the sermon: "We must return to the proper order of things."

"I've been informed that your Security Force is moving permanently into barracks, deserting their families," the Pontiff accused as he strode inside the lieutenant's office.

"That's right," Cord answered shortly, rising to his feet.

"But this is completely unacceptable!" Alexander blustered.

"They only married 'cause Simon asked them to," the lieutenant explained, perching himself on the edge his desk. "But these young men are special. Hand-picked every one of them. Chosen for their unique qualities. And one of those qualities is their lack of . . . family feeling. These marriages have been hard on them, 'specially since the assassination. And now, after that sermon of yours . . . well, they just want out."

"This can't be tossed aside lightly — the situation is very serious. You know our numbers are already critical—"

"Don't lecture me on numbers! Or duty!" Cord interrupted explosively. "Not 'til I see a few priests standin' on the other side of that altar tying their own damn knot!"

The lieutenant had him there, and they both knew it.

"Alright, Lieutenant," the Pontiff sighed in resignation. "I'll give special dispensation to allow the annulments." He considered for a moment and then continued: "I'll decree their marriage vows contravened their previous vow of fidelity to the Chairman. In light of recent events, the annulments will be understood."

Cord only grunted in response, uncaring of the Church's need to save face. He turned to his own concern. "I can see where you're headed with all this crap about women, but how the hell is little William going to benefit when he's too young to marry? The power grabs are being made now."

"Do you think I'd suggest putting him on the throne only to undermine his power?"

Cord said nothing, distracted by the phrase *on the throne*. He liked the sound of that.

"The Church has declared him Chairman, the Anointed Ruler of this planet. What need has he for leases and workers? He owns everything. And he deserves to receive an annual share of whatever profits his people make from the use of his land."

Cord's eyes narrowed as he studied the older man. "You're a clever bastard. I'll give you that."

The Pope inclined his head, accepting the compliment. "When William marries it will be to produce an heir, and for no other reason. We will see to that."

"Good," Cord said shortly.

Since Simon's assassination, he couldn't look at a woman without wondering if she'd been party to it. He hated the thought of Simon's son having anything to do with them. There'd be no way to know if she was a daughter of one of the women who helped in his father's assassination. Might history repeat itself?

"I have to admit, I breathe a little easier with all those women moved out of HQ."

"There are other dangers," the Pontiff reminded him gently.

"Don't worry," Cord growled. "I'll keep him safe."

"I believe you will."

"There's a strike at Chandler's farm!"

So, it has begun, the Pontiff thought, watching the panicked expression on his young aide's face.

Alexander had been waiting for something like this. Rumors were spreading like a high-octane flame since his sermon to the men last week. The strike was inevitable, and he was well prepared for it. The women would back down.

"Father Felix," he ordered, "find Lieutenant Campbell. Tell him the strike must be contained. It can't be allowed to spread. I recommend sending ten men with guns. Arrest the leaders, and the movement will crumble. They'll be too frightened to protest further."

"Yes, Your Holiness," Father Felix said breathlessly, rushing from the room.

"Damn it, I didn't tell you to mow them down!" Alexander shouted.

"That wasn't my order!" Cord shouted back. "The women wouldn't move. There was some rough handling and someone got a broken arm. The women went crazy — beat one of my men almost unconscious! Somebody panicked and shot off his gun — then all hell broke loose."

"Damn it," Alexander swore again. "I thought your men could cope with a few women!"

"I'm not the one getting everybody spooked! They used to be just women, but now you've made them into something else — something sinister."

The Pontiff couldn't argue with that. Instead he said, "We're going to have to move fast; there'll be a backlash for this. I hope to God you can hold your end up."

"Don't worry about me."

"I don't care if you have to comb every inch of this planet, I want those people found and returned!" the Pontiff sputtered with a note of hysteria in his voice.

"They went south, we think. Nobody's gonna head north or east — they'd end up in the desert, and west is too mountainous," Lieutenant Campbell stated calmly.

"So get looking," Alexander snapped.

"We *are* looking," Cord snapped back. "We'll find them — that's a certainty — our equipment's too accurate. We'd have them already but the crew carrier Martinez took was an all-terrain. They can make pretty good time with it, but it can't outrun a chopper. We'll get them. It's just a matter of time."

"Well, be quick about it. They have to be made an example of — and soon. We don't want a mass exodus."

"We're doing all we can!" Cord blasted at him, angry and confused. He stomped out the door, knowing Simon would have handled it differently, but not knowing how. All Cord could do was try and protect little William's inheritance.

Alexander remained anxiously mulling over this latest bid for freedom, and he began to see that such an act could easily happen again, especially later, when the fuel was all used up and the chopper grounded.

What if instead of an all-terrain or a crew carrier they were to escape in one of those massive mining trucks? The vehicles were electric after all. So far, it hadn't occurred to anyone to do so, mostly because they were designed for loading raw ore, not humans. But, given time, someone would think of it.

He began to work out the amount of supplies and people that could fit inside the box of one of those monstrous vehicles. He did not like his calculations.

There was a murmur of surprise as the magistrate stood aside to let the Pontiff take his place at the court bench. Without preamble, he announced, "The theft of the last of our antibiotics and painkillers—"

He was cut off by loud protests from the accused — all but Bobby Martinez, who sat slumped in shock as he remembered giving news of the virus on Proximus to the Church — because he felt sorry for the bishop.

And if I hadn't done that, Martinez realized, Alexander and his staff would have left for Earth — and none of this would be happening. It's all my fault, he thought mournfully as his fellow prisoners were clubbed into silence.

The Pontiff continued speaking, as if nothing had happened: "— as well as the theft of a large number of seedlings for the next planting, is a cowardly and sinful assault on the whole community."

There were more exclamations of innocence that were painfully quelled.

"It's clear that you're not fit to reap the benefits of God's gifts. We cannot allow your presence to corrupt our Garden. You wish to leave us then let it be so. You are hereby banished from New Eden forever." He smashed the gavel down for dramatic effect. "May God have mercy on your souls."

The prisoners, three men and ten women, were forced from the courtroom.

"What will happen to them?" Theodore asked in a worried whisper.

"They will be driven deep into the desert and left there with a week's supply of food and water."

The young bishop crossed himself, praying softly, "May God have mercy on all our souls."

"I can smell rebellion brewing."

"Thank the Lord you had the foresight to hire spies," young Father Felix piped in.

"Rebellion is inevitable. It's only common sense to prepare for it."

"Can you stop it before it starts, Your Holiness?"

251

The Pontiff had no intention of interfering with their little revolution. In fact, he awaited the event with great anticipation.

"No, but it will not succeed, that is a certainty." He had no doubts about that. The rebels were too unorganized, and some of the key players were his own agents. And, most importantly, they did not have the weapons.

All I need to do is place Tom Murdock in a vulnerable position and the rest will be taken care of: agents can be used for more than one purpose.

Perhaps an invitation to a late dinner, maybe hint that the Chair is nearly in his grasp? And once Tom is removed and the rebellion crushed, I'll announce my Divine Illumination: The establishment of a new Church. One that will better serve the needs of humanity and uphold God's most Sacred Laws — founded as a result of the blatant acts of violence against mankind.

Yes, everything was falling into place.

That only left Theodore . . . .

He has done nothing overt against me — yet. But I can see his disapproval. Is he salvageable? I can't afford a betrayal from that corner. As the Church's only Bishop, he has almost as much influence as I, should he choose to exert it.

Can I win him over, given time?

The Pontiff sighed regretfully. No, he is as committed to his path as I am to mine. I was fooled by his fear of me into thinking he was easily malleable. But there's a strong backbone amongst that jelly.

Perhaps I must issue two invitations to dinner?


There was a sudden sensation of propulsion, making Althaia's body tingle throughout as colors and sounds whizzed past, until she finally landed in a distant future.


Cord was very drunk. He was drunk and angry and bitter. He stared resentfully at the man sitting across the table from him: a constant thorn in his side since the day they'd made their bargain. And now this popish bastard seemed to think *he* was in charge of this planet instead of young Willie — though not so young anymore.

Cord felt as if he was seeing Alexander for the first time.

"It could have been you," he stated accusingly. "Why did I never see that before?"

Alexander looked at the eyes boring into him and felt his blood turn cold, but he managed to keep his face neutral. "What do you mean?" he asked with just the right amount of confusion.

After twenty-three years, was he finally found out? Could it possibly be?

"What I mean, your fucking holiness, is that *you* are the fucking assassin — you! All this time, right under my nose."

"You are drunk, Commander. And I refuse to engage in this painful subject," the Pontiff stated sternly. "If you still believe this absurd idea in the morning, take me in for questioning." The Pontiff rose. "For now, I'm leaving. And you should go to bed and sleep it off."

Feeling suddenly quite sober, Cord announced in a deadly tone, "I know I can never prove you were behind Simon's death, not after all this time. But you'd better pray that the current Chairman doesn't die from anything but old age — nor any of his kin — because no matter what the cause, *you* will be the first one we investigate — investigate *very* closely. And if there is even a whiff of a chance that the Church could have arranged that death, we will eliminate every single one of you — very, very slowly. Is that understood?"

"Good night, Commander," Alexander stated, his voice cold, though his heart was racing in fear. It was as if the booze-soaked mind of the soldier had pierced the Pontiff's skull and read the dark images floating inside there.

Somehow Alexander managed to open the dining room door and exit with dignity, making his unhurried way down the wide corridor, all the while feeling the Commander's dangerous gaze on his back. As he drew closer to the exit, Alexander had to fight the urge to run — desperate to cancel the plans he'd set into motion.

Regrettably, such solutions could no longer solve the Church's troubles — not regarding the Chairmanship.

We will need to develop more subtle methods . . . .

Robert watched the look of revulsion that flashed across Althaia's face, and was immediately reminded of Frayne. What is it that offends her so?

The hand resting on the cross was snatched away, and her whole body shivered.

Like a dogger shaking off the muck of a rotted carcass, Robert thought.

How weak she is, he realized. It was obvious when she stood this way, with head bowed, hiding her true strength, her strength of spirit.

She was very still now, and he knew she was gathering herself, recovering from God-knew-what. He could feel her growing strength then, even with her eyes cast down. How could someone change right before you without moving a muscle? Did she even have muscles?

You are the frailest person on this world, and the strongest. And that revelation would have sent me running from the room just ten days ago. Now, I don't know how to react.

"You no longer fear me," Althaia said, her eyes on the floor, careful not to startle the figure standing in the doorway.

"I'm too weary to be afraid."

"Yes, I feel your exhaustion"

"Are you a witch then? Can you conjure out of the air?"

"I am a healer, as you know. It was not my intent to alarm you."

"You didn't — not much." It's not the likes of you I fear anymore, Robert thought.

"Your fear is no longer for the things without, but for your battle within."

He grunted in response and turned in the doorway. "Come," he commanded.

"I am to be returned to the cellar room?"

He stopped to look back in surprise, his gaze automatically directed away from her face. "You are the Chairman's wife. You will live in harem."

Harem? she wondered, following him through the chapel and out to the corridor.

Robert spoke rapidly, clearly uncomfortable with this situation: "The priest will return on Saturday. He'll hear confession and perform the Mass. You'll learn enough to get by him."

She did not understand his words but kept silent. Now was not the appropriate time for questions.

Robert pointed to the heavy door she'd come through earlier with the soldiers. "No man but your husband and your confessor are permitted past the door to this eve-wing — and, when needed, a physician and a birthing priest." It was the Law, and not even the Pope Himself could gain entry. Robert and his men had broken that law, but they no longer feared the Church's threats.

"But you are permitted."

"I will teach you, so I must," he said curtly. "Be inside the chapel tomorrow at sunrise."

Her head tilted to indicate that she understood, as he led her to the narrow door with the bell hanging beside it.

"The entrance to harem," he declared. "Only eves and infant males are permitted inside — and the overseer. But he has been . . . detained indefinitely." He paused to consider what else he must make clear to her. "You'll find clothes appropriate for an eve. Wear them," he ordered. "Enter now."

With effort, she pushed on the door. Though narrow, it was heavy and yielded slowly. Inside, she leaned against it, closing out Robert and the rest of the world. Drawing a deep breath, she moved off, stepping gratefully into her sanctuary and her first encounter with the female aspect of this world — this modern world.

What are they like, these women who live behind closed doors under complete subjugation to men? She set out to learn, striding down the gloomy hallway lit only by a few oil lamps positioned along the wall.

Several steps later, she found another passage that led off from the main corridor; it ran long and narrow, and deeper in gloom, and was lined with small doorways, closely and evenly spaced down its entire length, ten on each side. She peered within one of the tiny rooms, which was almost filled by a narrow bed and a rough wooden cupboard. The bed was unmade, with a nightgown of coarsely spun material flung across it haphazardly. On the wall above the bed was a small firecross made of dull metal, and above that was a narrow opening to let in air and what little light was available.

Althaia shuddered and withdrew quickly. She made a rapid inspection of the other cubicles, but they were all the same: stark and depressing and empty, with a hastily tossed nightgown lying across an unmade bed.

She could sense the residual fear and confusion of a hurried exit, and knew that, however these women had lived within such a confined space, they no longer did so. But she did not pause to discover how it had come about.

At the end of the narrow corridor was an area she realized must serve as a common room. A small oil lamp had been lit — Althaia assumed — in preparation for her arrival. The light was dim, but it enabled her to see the room clearly enough.

This was not an improvement in aesthetics from those stark sleeping quarters, although it did have a large stove with several wooden benches placed before it. There was also a small window at her head height, but the only view was of the side of a building.

Against one of the clean, well-worn walls was a long table with several small boxes placed upon it. Each was filled with sewing implements and rolls of colorful thread that looked out of place in this drab environment.

Althaia's spirits sank. Is this how the women of this world lived out their lives? she asked herself. This is scarcely an improvement over the cellar that I occupied.

Standing there, she could feel the visions hovering, ready to take her over — should she allow them. But no, Althaia thought, I need not witness their way of life; I am living it.

Althaia remembered Robert's instructions to wear the clothes of an eve. Was this the word they used for females?

After a moment's consideration, she returned to one of the bedrooms and removed a stack of neatly folded clothes from the wooden cupboard. Setting them on the common room table, she slowly unfolded each darkly colored item —

255

which were clearly too short for her. Finally she came to the heavy veil.

Althaia studied this in shock.

Though she had understood that the women of this world were forced to cover their faces, the reality of it was stunning.

How do they see? Althaia wondered. How are they able to breathe or consume food?

Out of curiosity, she placed the veil over her face. The narrow eye slots instantly eliminated sixty percent of her visual field, while the second layer of the veil covered up the small openings for breathing — it was suffocating.

Althaia snatched off the veil, throwing it to the floor. With a shudder, she hurried down the narrow passage and out to the main hallway.

Although she had little hope of finding it, Althaia set off in search of a haven for her spirit. Instead, she discovered a duplicate of the women's area, except that cribs and tiny beds stood inside each cubicle.

These are the conditions in which their children are housed? Althaia thought with acute sadness. Within this dreary, un-nurturing environment?

She realized that only three of the small beds held any physical or energetic evidence of having been in use.

Numerous wives once resided within this space and yet there were so few children, she reflected. Perhaps it is not only I that my husband fears to be intimate with?

She moved on, looking briefly inside a small kitchen and then inside a storage closet before finding a gloomy, primitive washroom used for both laundry and personal hygiene. There was a single toilet in a dank cubicle nearby, but this, at least, was plumbed.

Returning to the main hallway, further investigation revealed a large room with rows and rows of shelving lining the walls. The shelves were filled with an assortment of materials and tools. Down the center of the room was a long work table. Lying on the table were several items in different stages of completion: carpets, tapestries and curtains, down-filled pillows and bed coverings, and other projects she couldn't identify.

After seeing the stark furnishings and thin blankets used within the sleeping cubicles, it was a surprise to find such luxuries.

Althaia was becoming quite drained: the events of the day were taking their toll. She needed a place to recover. As she stood within the main corridor reviewing her options, Althaia realized that on first entering harem she had overlooked a set of double doors. Constructed by the Ancients, they were crafted to blend almost seamlessly into the wall.

Behind these doors was her haven.

It was a big space, with three great windows that looked onto an enclosed courtyard four stories below. The room was luxurious to Althaia's eyes, draped in tapestries and thick rugs, which covered most of the walls and much of the floor. Warm blankets and plump pillows of different sizes and colors were strewn over the thinly padded furniture. When she put a hand up to touch one of the plush drapes, she realized that this was the home of the strangely feminine man that she'd frightened so badly.

He must be the one that Robert spoke of, she thought. An . . . over see-er. If this is his home, he will not be returning until I am gone from this place.

She did not dwell on the possible implications of that thought, but continued her investigations.

Beyond this luxurious room were two large bedrooms. It was obvious that one of these was not in use. Connected to the unused bedroom was a nursery with several tiny cribs, thick with dust.

How long has it been since a child laid a head here? Althaia wondered.

The two bedrooms shared a corridor leading to a luxurious washroom designed by the Ancients, with a bathing tub and a shower. With relief, she realized that the plumbing was still functioning. There was also a proper toilet. She made quick use of it and returned to the living area.

It would require some alterations, but there was plenty here to soothe her spirit.

Althaia shuddered, remembering the cellar.

I will never live in such conditions again, she promised herself.

She piled a few of the small carpets on top of each other, and then gathered pillows and blankets from the chairs. Lowering her body onto the thick softness, she gave a contented sigh, languishing in the unaccustomed comfort before easing into deep sleep.

# CHAPTER 28

"WHAT IN the name of all-that-is-holy possessed you to arrange such an ungodly marriage?" Belcher shouted into the face of the young captain, the veins in his forehead threatening to burst.

"I did what I had to do, sir," Robert replied stiffly. He was still recovering from being roughly woken in the dark and ordered to the Commander's office.

"What you *had* to do!"the older man sputtered furiously. "Did God come down and *order* you to arrange such a union!"

"No, sir," Robert said stoically. "I was informed that the Chairman had sent for a dose of the demon-drug."

The Commander bit back the words that were about to crush the young man and instead stood silently reviewing this news. "I see," he said at last. He turned away to pace the floor of his spacious office. "Explain your actions," he ordered roughly, but it was said in a calmer voice.

"My intent was to distract the Chairman from this dangerous fixation by using his less dangerous fixation." The Commander grunted in appreciation of Robert's summation of the situation. Robert continued, "The stranger eve is like any other eve, sir. To be neutralized by marriage and confinement."

"The Church will not stand idly by while such a dangerous eve is married to the Chairman."

"The Church cannot intervene, sir. It would violate its own tenet. The eve is married and in harem. She is no longer a threat."

"And you expect this eve to know the catechism?" the Commander demanded.

Robert paused. He could not reveal that he would instruct her. This, the Commander would find completely unacceptable. It might even suggest that Robert was out of his mind — or worse, corrupt. Instead, he said, "I believe the eve knows more about the catechism than we first expected."

Belcher stared hard at the captain, knowing he was lying. But suddenly he did not want to know the truth. Instead, he said, "That won't stop them."

"The Church will take her in time, yes. But by then the Chairman will have a son and he will not care."

The Commander grunted once again in appreciation. He now understood with certainty that this young man would make a fine Commander. He would do whatever it took to keep a wayward Chairman safe from his own weaknesses.

Yes, he thought with relief. When the time comes, I can die in peace.

"Be certain you do nothing to put the Chairman in further danger," the Commander growled.

Robert arrived at the chapel early, but the eve was already there, still dressed in her strange and ungodly clothes. She was kneeling, calm and relaxed upon a large pillow. Another pillow lay on the floor nearby.

Robert had expected to have some time alone, to recover from his intense meeting with the Commander — and to prepare himself before teaching the eve. This disruption to his plans had thrown him further off kilter.

He marched purposefully to the middle of the room and stood with arms crossed, glowering at her in the approved manner.

Sensing his agitation, Althaia was careful to keep her eyes cast downward as she said, "You were more at ease in my presence yesterday. Has some event occurred to re-awaken your fear?"

"No," came the clipped reply. But after a moment, he announced, "I am breaking Church Law." Robert was coming to realize that his newfound freedom did not obliterate a lifetime of training.

"You break the law by being in the presence of a woman?"

"That word is not used," he informed her abruptly.

"Which word?" she asked.

"Woman," was the short reply. "On New Eden, you are called eve."

Althaia was silent a moment, and then she repeated her question: "You break the law by being in my presence?"

He nodded. "That too."

But would I care so much, Robert thought with irritation, if you were just a regular eve, and not some damn stranger dressed in such clothing?

"What additional offense do you commit?" Althaia asked when she realized he had no intention of explaining further.

"Religious Instruction is the province of the Church, and no other."

"Can you not request an educator from the Church to instruct me?"

"Good God, no! They must think you already versed in the catechism — or

259

you'd be declared an unfit wife and the marriage annulled. You would be killed soon after."

Abruptly he turned away, shaking his head in disbelief. "I'm standing here, talking to an eve . . . ." And a very dangerous eve — in my old belief, he reminded himself.

"I too find this conversation unusual," Althaia said to his withdrawing back.

Without turning to look at her, Robert demanded, "What do you mean? Oh, your weeks in solitary," he concluded.

"I was not referring to my time in the cellar."

"Then what?" he demanded, facing her again, his gaze on her hands.

So as not to disturb him, she averted her eyes from his face before answering, "From the time I was a small child, I have existed almost entirely without communication with another human, until Frayne entered my life nine months ago."

Robert stared at her, trying to fathom her meaning. "Frayne said eves are treated the same as men on your world. You're saying he lied?" he asked suspiciously.

"Men and women are treated equally on Mirandus," she confirmed.

"Then you committed some crime."

"No, it was quite normal for our world. It was I who was not normal."

"Explain," he demanded.

"On our world, we do not seek interactions with other people: the Realming is all we desire. But I cannot achieve the Realming state. My genetic structure lacks the necessary coding. In genetic terms, I am from another time — as is Frayne. For most of our lives, our only companions have been the robots and computers that permit our world to function while our people remain undisturbed on their Worlds Within. Has Frayne not explained our society to you?"

"I spoke to the Stranger only once. What I know of your world comes from the Chairman," he responded automatically, his mind grappling with her words — most of them unintelligible, but enough to know that they were forbidden. He always suspected William was holding something back — but this!

"Continue," he ordered.

"Contact between the peoples of my planet is increasingly rare. Even the instinct to reproduce has diminished over the centuries, causing our birthrate to severely decline, until we now verge on certain extinction. This journey to your planet became imperative. With your assistance, it is possible that our world may yet survive." She was surprised by the relief she felt from finally speaking of her mission.

Robert stared into space, her words conjuring up William's face: so full of excitement when he'd first spoken of Frayne and wondered if Proximus' solution

260

could solve New Eden's own unacknowledged problem.

But I denied him that possibility, though I saw how it squashed the fire in his eyes, yet still, I did not relent. What sort of loyalty is that? he thought with disgust.

Althaia watched him disappear into a memory and felt the emotions it aroused in him. "What do you require me to learn?" she asked softly, hoping to bring him back to the moment.

Startled, he blinked at her, his agitation easing as he remembered his immediate duty. Straightening his shoulders, he announced, "You must know the Rules of Confession, the Rituals of the Mass, and the proper behavior of eves." He paused, preparing to mention her clothing but decided it would have to wait.

I must get to instructing or Saturday will be here and she will know nothing.

Hunkering down, he pulled the pack off his shoulder, removing pen and ink, paper and books.

"Will you not sit?" Althaia asked, holding out a pillow, her eyes finally settling on his face.

He looked at the pillow with deep scorn. "It is decadent and soft, unworthy of a man and forbidden to an eve. Where did you get them?" he demanded.

"In the rooms of the . . . over see-er. I will be residing there during my time here."

Taken aback that she would dare stay anywhere but the designated eve billets, he opened his mouth to reprimand her, and then quickly changed his mind.

Later, he decided once again. Just focus on the lesson.

"Frayne said you can read and write."

"I possess these skills."

He nodded in acknowledgement.

"When may I speak with Frayne?"

Robert shifted uncomfortably, not looking at her. "That will not be possible."

"Please explain."

He felt surprisingly averse to speaking the truth. Pushing aside his reluctance, he announced roughly, "He's no longer with us."

She frowned slightly in confusion, and asked again, "Please explain."

"He is gone," Robert said, the edge to his voice increasing.

"To where has he gone?"

"Back to Proximus," he stated shortly.

"To Proximus?" she repeated, unable to take it in. Then clarity returned. "Frayne was forced to depart without me."

"Yes."

Althaia turned her head away, and once again he could see her draw on some resource deep within. Moments later, she had recovered from the initial shock

261

and asked with apprehension, "Did he return alone?"

"No. Seven males, forty-nine adult eves and fifteen child eves were sent with him."

Her body relaxed and she closed her eyes. Robert sensed she was saying a prayer. But did they even pray on Proximus? A moment later her eyes were questing into his. "Why was I compelled to remain here?"

Robert looked away, answering quickly: "Frayne's departure is a mystery. Why you were left behind, we do not know." As he spoke, a clammy note of guilt crept into his account. He shifted uncomfortably. The eve remained impassive, her gaze unwavering. "Enough of this," he stated authoritatively. "Time for lessons."

"No, I cannot," she said, shaking her head. "I require time to assimilate this loss." She rose from the floor and exited the chapel with long, steady strides.

"Wait!" Robert called, rising to follow after her, but she was already slipping through the slight opening into her sanctuary. "I'll return at dusk," he managed to get out before the heavy door was shut in his face.


Althaia stared unseeingly at the cold fireplace inside the overseer's living area.

I will never see my home again, she thought with grief. I must live out my life on this unhappy world.

Though she had predicted this very outcome, the sudden verification was still a shock, more so because now she was alone, with any possibility of communing with Frayne completely gone.

She had to smile at herself. Was it merely nine months ago that I first entertained even that possibility? Such a short time ago since I first allowed myself to expect more than solitude. Oh the joy! No longer alone! No longer would it be necessary to travel across the galaxy unaccompanied.

And now, here I am, in solitude once more.

But not as before . . . no . . . .

"Goodbye, my friend," she whispered.

Then a thought pushed away her sadness: Frayne, you have succeeded! Seventy-one people to strengthen our genetic stock. And what strong people they are!

But will it be enough? she wondered in sudden doubt, or will they simply delay the inevitable? No, it will be enough. My life's purpose was to bring Mirandus back from the brink of extinction. I have known this since I was a pubescent child. And now, it is done.

A lightness took over, releasing the weight of responsibility that had harnessed her for so long. She could be at peace now while the Creative

262

orchestrated the balance of her life — what little that may be.

And on this tormented and, yes, stimulating planet, she thought, recalling her healing evolution, what would that mean?

# CHAPTER 29

"NO! NO! You sound nothing like an eve! Too loud. Too aggressive. You must speak in a whisper — and for you, a very low whisper," Robert commanded in exasperation.

For the sake of his king, Robert was determined to succeed in his position as instructor to this stranger eve. And now that he was committed to it, he found that his great unease at conversing with her was beginning to diminish. Even making eye contact was becoming less disturbing — due to his latest understanding of the Church's lies and manipulations. Appalling in their depth and breadth, they had created an openness that couldn't have been possible previously.

"You need only make these few responses during the mass. But in confession, you must admit to five sins. I will give you them to memorize."

"Must all people admit to sins?"

"Yes, everyone."

"And all must admit to five?"

"Men need admit to only three."

"And the reasoning behind this discrepancy?"

Robert shrugged. "Eves are full of sin; they have more to confess."

"You are taught that the women of your world are full of evil intent?"

"Certainly."

"Why would your world hold such a belief?" But even as the words left her mouth, Althaia remembered her visions and realized she already knew the true motivation.

"Eves caused the destruction of the Ancients and their Earth World," he stated impatiently, feeling uncomfortable with this topic. The lesson was not going as planned. "Enough. Concentrate on what I tell you."

"As you say."

"You must address the priest as 'Father' when you speak to him. Yes, Father.

No, Father. And remember the very first rule: only speak when ordered to or when asked a direct question. And *never* question the orders of a priest; obey immediately."

"I will remember."

"He will ask when your last confession was. You will answer: 'seven days past, Father.' Next he will order you to confess . . . . Now for confession you will say . . ." he paused, considering, pen in hand. "You will say, 'I confess to thoughts of anger for not being born a male—'"

"Would a woman — an eve — truly confess to such a feeling?"

Irritated by this further interruption, Robert said shortly, "I've heard them do so." He dipped the nib of the pen into the ink bottle and began writing the first confession down.

"You have heard eves say confession? But you have explained to me that no male is permitted inside the eve churches."

"They are not," he answered distractedly, the pen scratching out the words. "Let us continue." He lifted his head to think a moment. "You will confess to violent thoughts towards males. Then thoughts of jealousy towards males." He paused once more to write out his ideas. "Confess anger at the Church for harnessing your evil. And then anger at having to wear a veil."

"Then this is not the first time you have been unlawfully inside a females' church," Althaia stated with a note of amusement in her voice.

Robert looked up, momentarily startled by both her words and this sound that appeared to be humor — but eves were incapable of humor. He blinked at her briefly and then recovered. "That is not the subject of our lesson," he said coldly.

He returned his attention to the paper, checking over what he'd written. "You will memorize these five confessions. They'll be enough for now." She nodded. "You must learn how to do penance." Robert paused, remembering. "You must kneel and place your face on the floor, and then you must say, 'Forgive me, Father, for I was born corrupt and live in corruption. Forgive me, Father, I am unworthy. Forgive me, Father, I am not fit to live upon the world. Forgive me, Father—'"

"I will not speak these words," Althaia interrupted. "They are an offense to my very being."

Robert said sternly, "You must say these words or the priest will declare you unfit and you will die!"

"Then I will die," she stated calmly.

Damn it, Robert raged inwardly. You will not die until my King says you die.

Trying to control his temper, Robert searched his brain for some way out of this deadlock. When at last he spoke, his voice was tight with suppressed anger: "You could say only those words that are not offensive to you."

265

"Please explain."

"You will be speaking towards the floor in a whisper — a very quiet whisper — to a very old man. It would not be difficult to omit — no, better yet — to switch some of the words with ones that have the same sound."

Althaia's lips spread in a slow smile. "A very creative solution. I agree."

The smile disturbed Robert, for it transformed Althaia's face into something quite pleasant to look at — and awakened a lifetime of dire warnings about the lure of eves. But it also confused him, for he believed eves incapable of any form of humor, although this belief wasn't specifically preached but more so implied. And he had never seen anything in all his explorations inside the eve school to suggest otherwise. Was it only this stranger eve, or were all eves born this way? Was this more proof of the Church's sordid deeds?

Robert forced himself to let go of these disturbing thoughts and focus back on his duty to his Chairman. "When the penance is over, the priest will place his hand on your head and give you absolution —" He stopped. "You will have to dress as an eve—"

"The eve clothing is unacceptable," Althaia stated emphatically. "I will not live in a veil. It would be like death to me."

"Just for Mass and confession," he said quickly, anxious to avoid another confrontation.

There was a long pause as Althaia deliberated on this compromise. "I am willing to do so. But I must remove the bottom layer of the veil."

"Agreed." He studied her full head of hair. "Your head should be shaved." But at her look, he added, "I can provide you with a cap so the priest won't feel it through your head scarf."

She considered for a moment. "I agree."

Robert sighed, relieved. He was feeling drained by the strain of speaking to an eve. "That's enough for today. Memorize what I've given you. We will continue tomorrow morning."

"As you say."

Then Robert remembered that he must address her unlawful living situation. Now was the time to bring the matter up, though he felt suddenly loath to do so. Clearing his throat, he plunged in.

"But she can't stay there!" William exclaimed in alarm. "Should anyone learn of it she'd be removed from the palace instantly."

"I think it will be safe, Sire. Only you and I know she's not living in the eve billet. And the overseer will not return until she is gone."

"What about the priest?"

"Unless she was to tell him, there's no means he can know by." And Robert made a mental note to ensure Althaia's silence on the matter, though he could not foresee a question from the priest that would reveal her situation.

"But it seems so . . . criminal."

"Yes, Sire. But she refuses to stay in the eve billet. Says it's as bad as the cell, and would die before returning to either."

"Die?"

"Yes, Sire, that's what she said. And I believe she meant it."

"They always mean it," William growled, thinking of Frayne. "Never say a bloody word unless it's the absolute truth, Goddamn them."

"Also, Sire, she refuses to wear the eve clothing. She says the veil is like death to her. She has requested the return of her personal effects."

He heard William sigh deeply. "We should not be surprised, I think, Robert," he said at last.

"No, Sire, it is to be expected of these strangers." Robert paused, waiting, but William said nothing further. The captain finally asked, "Do you wish her to be veiled and returned to the eve billet?"

"No!" William exclaimed in alarm.

"Then I will return the travel bag to her and continue the lessons in the morning. She has much to memorize before Saturday."

"I know I can count on you to keep her safe, Robert. Perhaps I'll come round soon and perform my own bit of service," he said with a wink.

Robert gave him a stiff smile and retreated from the room.

How can he bear to be near her? William wondered. What a brave and loyal friend my Robert is.

# CHAPTER 30

"HOW DARE he presume to teach an eve," Cardinal Vecker fumed in disgust. "The audacity of that young pup grows yearly."

"And his fearlessness," the Pontiff added with a small smile on his lips. "Facing a most frightening eve and daring to speak with her: quite outstanding."

"How can you call this act of rebellion — this infamy — fearless?"

"Because he does it for his King. He has a fierce loyalty. Your own report said as much."

"*Seemingly* loyal, if you will allow me to correct Your Holiness."

"Certainly, certainly," the Pope answered, distracted, his mind elsewhere. I could flay those incompetent teachers for letting such a boy slip through our fingers, he thought with bitter regret. A man like that comes along only rarely — he might have attained this very chair.

"How can you let this farce continue?" Vecker demanded.

"I want William returned to the Church. But you know how weak he is. The betrayal of his brothers devastated him. He would have sunk back into that obnoxious addiction if Robert hadn't given him the stranger's eve." The Pontiff paused, considering. "We will allow him to find solace there until he's recovered from the loss of his brothers' devotion."

"I do not see how this can lead him anywhere but straight to the gates of hell!"

"Perhaps we will be there to greet him?" the Pontiff offered. But the cardinal was not amused. "We will *not* interfere," the Pontiff pronounced with finality.

"Be sure to follow these instructions perfectly," Robert warned. "The smallest mistake could be used against you. They'd send an Inquisitor, and you'd not survive the interview. You are not eve-like."

They were seated on the floor of the chapel, Althaia upon a cushion, Robert, of course, rejecting the offer of softness.

"May I inquire how marriage protects my life?"

"Had the Church known that Frayne had left you behind, they'd have taken you into their custody immediately. All unmarried eves are kept within the confines of the Church."

But we were not mates, Althaia thought, only dear friends. But she kept silent, sensing that such an idea would be too foreign for this planet.

"Once in their hands," Robert continued, "you would have been declared possessed — or a witch. Then tortured and sentenced to Expulsion and certain death. Only marriage to the Chairman has held them off." For a time, he almost added.

Althaia remembered the visions of New Eden's early history and nodded, understanding how it had evolved. "I owe him a debt of gratitude," she said with feeling, "for saving my life."

"He would not want your gratitude."

"But he has it nonetheless. I would thank him, but I doubt I shall see him again. He was very frightened by our last encounter."

Robert gave her a stern look. "Men are not afraid of eves."

Althaia studied Robert closely, choosing not to remind him of his own admissions of fear. "This is taught to you, as part of your upbringing?" He hesitated for several moments and then nodded. "I understand. I will rephrase my observation." When next she spoke, her voice held a hint of mirth: "I regret that his profound disinterest in me will preclude his return to my company."

Robert gave her a quizzical look. "He'll be here tomorrow."

"This is unexpected, but welcomed. Will you accompany him?"

He shifted uncomfortably and looked away, mumbling, "Uh, no . . . . Maybe in the evening."

Althaia studied him, confused by this sudden embarrassment, but only for a moment. "What is the purpose of the Chairman's appearance here tomorrow?" Her voice held a note he'd never heard before — not in an eve.

He did not look at her. "You must know the mating room is used more than once."

"I have explained to the Chairman that I will mate only with a partner of my choice," she said, and her voice held that same note of steel within it.

"You dare!" Robert exploded, startling Althaia, her body jerking violently.

Her eyes had grown large, but she stared at him without fear, saying determinedly, "He has agreed to respect my personal rights."

"Then he will do so," Robert managed to get out, still stunned by this revelation. Yet, why should I be? If William is terrified of her — and who the hell wouldn't be — how could he possibly mate her?

After several moments spent digesting the situation, Robert was able to say, "He must make the appearance of mating with you. It's compulsory — especially for the Chairman. If he didn't, the Church would take you immediately." He hesitated, adding, "He lied to me about the mating to keep you safe, and because he was ashamed."

"Ashamed?"

"Of giving in to the demands of an eve." And of being afraid, Robert thought.

"I will not reveal your knowledge of his deception."

He nodded and stood up, saying, "Memorize this lesson. I'll have further instructions tomorrow." Robert paused. "Food is delivered every week from the palace kitchens. It's usually left on the landing outside the eve-cloister for the overseer to collect. We won't interrupt that practice. But one of my men will put it inside this eve-wing, at the outer door."

"I do not consume animal protein."

"So I've heard. But the overseer does. We can't stop meat delivery or it will raise suspicion." But at the repulsed expression that passed over her face, he added, "I'll get my men to remove it before they leave the food box with you."

"Thank you. That is a great kindness."

Uncomfortable with this sentiment, Robert grunted before striding from the Chapel.

Althaia breathed a sigh of relief, alone once more.

# CHAPTER 31

WRAPPED IN a long cloak, William rang the harem bell with authority. But when the door creaked open, he jerked back in fright, momentarily forgetting that there was no longer an overseer to answer his call or escort the eve into the mating room through the back entrance.

It was just the two of them.

Althaia nodded in greeting and moved past him into the chapel. She sat in her usual place upon the pillow, spreading her skirts out in a pleasing pattern. She had chosen not to speak except in answer to the Chairman's questions; she had no wish to torment him with the sound of her voice. Perhaps one day he could accept her words of gratitude, but not today.

William followed slowly after her, not stopping until he was at the opposite end of the chapel. He stood shifting uncomfortably from foot to foot, trying to work up the courage to speak.

"Frayne said you have an interest in history," he finally managed to get out in a high-pitched squeak.

Flustered, he cleared his throat self-consciously, and reached under his long cloak for the cloth sack he'd smuggled inside.

With great anticipation, Althaia waited while he removed some wrapped packages and placed them in the middle of the floor. When he had returned to his position of safety, William said magnanimously, "You can look at them now."

But Althaia was already moving across the room.

She knelt beside the packages and carefully unwrapped the largest piece from its blanket of rough-spun material. Holding it at arm's length, she turned it in every direction, trying to decipher its function.

It was a piece of plasteelite, painted white and green, with a partial letter painted on one side, the other side scorched and blackened by fire. The edges were jagged, as if torn from a larger piece.

"It's from a starship," William explained jerkily. "Is it like the starship Frayne travelled in?" And there was something pitiful about the eagerness with which he awaited the answer.

"It appears to be constructed of the same materials," she said simply.

Her reply seemed to satisfy him, though he winced involuntarily at the sound of her voice. She opened another package and gasped.

William felt suddenly guilty. Why had he brought these? But he knew why. The eve reminded him of Frayne, and he wanted to see that same awed reaction. He was not disappointed.

"They are beautiful," she said in wonder, forgetting to remain silent. She held the diamonds up to catch the sunlight, and they shone like a thousand tiny stars. Then she laid them carefully inside their small sack. "Thank you for sharing such a beautiful treasure."

"Do not thank me," he said gruffly, trying to keep his fear at bay.

Althaia did not let his words disturb her, but continued to explore the contents of the bag, sorting through the strands of precious stones. She was about to sort through a collection of gold chains when William spoke again.

"Open the others," he said impatiently.

She laid the jewelry aside and chose a small plastic case. Inside was a plasteelite band the color of silver, fashioned to fit a slender wrist. There was a rectangular-shaped piece of dark plazi built into the top. Althaia recognized it as a tiny computer screen. She turned the band over to see what power source the computer used, but there was a large chunk missing from the back. This machine would never function again.

"It's labeled as a wristwatch," William informed her. "Do you know what that means?" he asked, steeling himself for the onslaught of words.

"It is a machine to measure time," Althaia explained.

Her answer sparked a sudden exhilaration within William, distracting him from his fear. To wear a clock upon one's wrist, how incredible! he thought.

"You have such things on Proximus?" William asked with subdued excitement.

"Yes," she said simply. Then noticing his enthusiasm, she continued: "But we have little use for them now. I have not seen one of this design before."

She replaced the watch in its case and turned her attention to the last item: a rectangular box made of sturdy plazi with two metal pieces attached near the top, one of which appeared to have a cutting edge. Extending from the base of the box was a long black cord covered in pliable plazi that ended in a hardened circular piece of plazi with three metal prongs jutting from it.

"It's called a can opener. Do you know what a can is?" William asked.

Now that his interest was sparked, he found it a little easier to speak to her.

"I am unable to illuminate you," she said, pushing tentatively down on the metal arm. It gave a little under her hand, lowering to connect with the metal beneath it, springing back to its original position when she removed the pressure. Once again she pushed the arm, but this time when she removed her hand it stayed in place, the two ancient metals stuck together.

"This machine is unfamiliar to me," Althaia announced, running her hands across the plastic surface and down the cord to the metal prongs. Her fingers made contact and the machine groaned into life.

Althaia dropped the cord and sprang back, startled. She looked to William in surprise, but all she saw was a flash of cloak as he bolted from the room. A moment later came the sound of the heavy door to the eve-cloister banging shut.

Althaia looked at the little box in wonder.

How can this be possible?

She leaned forward, returning her fingers to the prongs, and once again the machine came to life, straining with the effort.

Althaia studied her hands. What more is happening to me?

"My mind cannot process another word," Althaia pronounced, as Robert tried to thrust another religious text into her hands. "Your world is harnessed in dogma and ritual," she stated mildly, stretching her long limbs. "Such thinking fatigues the mind."

"We must continue," Robert ordered.

"I have had enough rational thought for today."

"How else is one to think?"

"One can think unreasonable thoughts. Thoughts that are beyond reason." She wrapped her arms around her knees, saying, "But I mislead you. One does not think such thoughts, one allows them to occur."

"A man must always keep control over his thoughts. To allow free rein is to invite the devil," Robert stated sternly.

"The mind must be free to visit the place where invention is born, where genius happens," Althaia countered gently.

"Invention is not permitted. It was invention that destroyed the world of Earth. And what did genius lead to but the making of bigger weapons. It is only in the Church that genius is safe from corruption—" He stopped short, remembering, that he no longer believed this.

Althaia studied Robert, sensing the struggle within him. "Did not the scientists and the governments choose to make those bigger weapons?"

"Yes," he said curtly, studying the floor.

273

"And were not the scientific institutes and the governments comprised mostly of men?"

"Of course they were," he snapped at her.

"But you have explained to me that it was women — the eves — who were responsible for the destruction of Earth," Althaia said quietly.

His head jerked up and he looked at her hard. "Yes," he said coldly, "you were." And with that he got to his feet and stormed out of the chapel. A moment later, she heard the familiar boom of the outer door slamming shut.

Althaia sat very still as she reviewed the two exchanges that she had experienced today — and their similar endings. And then quite unexpectedly, she began to laugh. She laughed until her sides ached and tears brimmed in her eyes.

She felt very much alive.

# CHAPTER 32

THE PIECE of wreckage from the starship lay in her hands as Althaia prepared for the time trance. She was now feeling more positive about her forced stay upon this planet. If this world brought confusion and doubt, it also brought a power beyond anything she'd thought possible — and it brought laughter.

Safely encased in a shield of healing, she allowed herself to travel back through the millennia.

"Passenger's harnessed and ready to go, Captain Black," announced a young man.

"Acknowledged, Ensign," the captain responded. "Status of the Excelsior, Mr. Sidhu."

"She's just counting down now, sir . . . . She's gone, sir."

"Prepare for take-off, Commander Nguyen." he ordered, strapping himself into the seat harness.

"Computer has cleared Calypso for takeoff, sir," Sidhu announced.

"Start the count, Commander," Captain Black ordered.

"Four . . . three . . . two . . . one — ignition."

There was a low rumble and a great push that strained their harnesses. With a sudden blast, they were out of the bunker and into the sky. In the distance, Excelsior's tail flame was barely discernible. In less than fifty seconds they'd be out of the Earth's atmosphere, and the six thousand souls onboard prayed to be free of it before attracting the attention of a missile.

The captain announced their escape, eliciting a collective sigh from passengers and crew as they unfastened their safety belts and allowed themselves a silent cheer: we made it!

"Status, Commander," demanded the captain.

"All systems go, sir."

"Mr. Thompson, is the Princeton behind us?"

"Yes, sir! Nice and snug."

"We all made it then, sir," Commander Nguyen commented.

"Yes, thank God — just the freighters to come," the captain said, and he became still as he remembered all those who had no chance of escaping the war zone their planet had suddenly turned into.

"Sir, a message from the Excelsior. They're altering course fifty degrees starboard. Some debris heading their way: unidentified."

"Acknowledged, Mr. Sidhu. Alert the Princeton," Captain Black ordered. "Mr. Stanly, alter course fifty degrees starboard."

"Aye, sir."

"When we come alongside, Mr. Darbuck, I want a clear visual."

"Yes, sir!"

The crew was silent.

"Visual contact made, sir."

Captain Black rose from his seat to study the viewing screen. "Oh, jeesus," he swore under his breath, "it's the Kingfisher." His head snapped around. "Mr. Thompson, keep your eyes glued to that radar screen," he ordered sharply.

"Yes, sir!"

The captain straightened his shoulders and addressed the rest of the crew: "It looks like the Kingfisher's been taken out by a missile."

"But isn't this sector supposed to be kept clear of missiles, sir?" the ensign asked.

"Looks like they're not playing by the rules anymore, Ensign."

Jeesus, Black swore again, silently, turning to face the window. Damn those stupid bastards.

"Mr. Sidhu," he said, "contact Primus and alert them of our situation."

"Yes, sir."

"Captain! Blip homing in on the Excelsior — she's taking evasive action."

"Keep clear of her, Mister Stanly," the captain ordered.

"Aye, sir."

"Come on, Larry," the captain quietly urged, "you can do it." But his hopes were cut off by a blinding flash as the Excelsior exploded. "Use secondary thrusters, Mr. Stanly, let's avoid that debris," he ordered, forcing himself to shake off the loss and focus on saving his ship. "Alert the Princeton, Mr. Sidhu."

"Yes, sir."

"How much longer before Q-drive, Mr. Stanly?"

"Two minutes, sir."

"Keep a sharp eye, Mr. Thompson, there's bound to be more." He moved to speak with the only woman onboard. "We can't outmaneuver them. We need a

276

decoy, Ms. Watson — something big and hot."

"Right, sir."

"Put her back on course, Mr. Stanly."

"Aye, Captain."

Captain Black resumed his seat. "Ensign Brody, you'd better tell our passengers to prepare themselves, we could be in for quite a ride." Damn those stupid assholes, he thought again.

"Sir," Watson piped up. "I could jettison main take-off thrusters — they're certainly hot enough."

"Okay, set it up."

Thompson broke in: "Blip, sir, moving fast. It's a missile, bearing 97 degrees starboard, 14 degrees below horizon. Range: one hundred thousand meters."

"Evasive maneuvers, Mr. Stanly," the captain ordered. "Ms. Watson, how long 'til jettison?"

"Almost there, sir."

Thompson continued the count: ". . . Eighty thousand meters . . . ."

"Watson, we need some results."

". . . Sixty thousand meters . . . ."

The crew held its breath, watching Watson's fingers fly over the keyboard, silently commanding her to move faster while Thompson recited, ". . . Forty thousand . . . thirty thousand . . . twenty thousand . . . ."

"Thrusters readied, sir!"

"On my mark, Watson."

"Sir!"

". . . Ten thousand meters . . . ."

"Stanly, on my mark."

"Aye, Captain!"

". . . Five thousand meters — one thousand meters!"

"MARK!"

Thrusters were jettisoned as Stanly banked the vessel hard away, exposing its underbelly. A tremendous explosion rocked the ship, sending it spinning out of control while the helmsman fought hard to level out the careening monster under his hand. The ship was plunged into darkness, but a moment later emergency power kicked in, bathing them all in eerie green light.

"Damage report!" the captain called out.

"Hull pressure OK! Seals secure."

"Life support's on emergency power — holding steady! Trying to locate damage."

"Engines are operational!"

"Fuel leaks?"

"None registering, sir!"

"Damage to Q-drive?"

"None registering, sir!"

"Navigation OK, Captain."

"Communication A-O-K, sir!"

"Captain, computer is not registering exterior damage, but I've lost visual so cannot confirm."

"Sir, electrical shows no damage, can't see why it won't come on." There was a sudden flicker and the lights returned.

"Sir, life support has returned to normal."

"Get on the horn to the Princeton, Mr. Sidhu: advise them of our tactic."

"I can't raise them, Captain."

"Are they still on the screen, Mr. Thompson?"

"Yes, sir."

"Sir," Sidhu called out, "I'm not reading any damage to communications, but can't get through."

"Find the problem, Mr. Sidhu," the captain ordered. "Mr. Thompson, keep a sharp eye peeled — we're not out of this turkey shoot yet."

"Aye, Captain!"

"Ms. Watson, better come up with another decoy."

"Already have, sir."

"Good job."

"Any injuries in back, Ensign Brody?"

"Negative, sir. Just shook up a bit."

The captain nodded. "Well done, Mr. Stanly, nicely handled," he praised the helmsman, before allowing himself a short prayer of thanks: the ship was fine. "We're almost there boys — and girl — just a little longer."

"Twenty-seconds till Q-speed, Captain."

"Keep those eyes sharp, Mr. Thompson."

"Blip approaching Princeton, sir. She's attempting evasive action."

"How's that radio, Mr. Sidhu?"

"Still dead, Captain."

"Maybe she saw our tactic," Ensign Brody suggested hopefully.

"Maybe," the captain agreed. "She could be alright: Flint's a good man."

"Five seconds," Stanly called out.

The crew held its breath, silently counting down. There was a gentle pressure as the ship made the shift to the Q-drive.

"Safe!" Stanly announced.

The tension broke and there were several shouts of triumph.

"Captain," Thompson's sober voice cut across the excitement. "The Princeton, she didn't make it."

Abruptly the cheering ended and they all grew silent. The captain studied the crew, knowing they were all asking the same question: Did our families make it out?

There was no way to know. They would all have to wait.

"Captain! The first four passenger ships have landed, sir!" Sidhu reported happily. "They're safely berthed and already unloading."

There was a huge cheer from the ten crew members on the bridge.

"That's welcome news, Mr. Sidhu," the captain said with a smile, and gave a silent prayer of thanks. "Inform base of our losses." Thousands of men gone.

"Sorry, Captain, no can do. We're only receiving."

"Thank you, Mr. Sidhu. Keep listening."

"I wonder what's happening back home?" Darbuck asked with yearning.

"Damn it all, Randy," Thompson complained, "would you quit asking that."

"I just hate not knowing."

"We all hate it. But hearing about it a million times isn't helping!"

"Alright, you two, let it go," the captain broke in. "It's been a long thirty-four days. And we're all anxious for news of Earth. But we know our families are safe. And that's the main thing right now. Just hold on a bit longer, we'll soon be out of this tin can."

"Yes, sir," they responded.

Minutes later the Calypso began its landing procedures.

"All systems are go," Commander Nguyen stated as the computer gave the green light.

The captain ordered them down, and the ship started its approach to the runway. Moments later, the ground was rushing up before them, and the crew awaited the expected sensation of drag from the landing chutes.

It didn't come.

"Chutes not operating, sir!" Stanly shouted.

"Emergency chutes, Stanly."

"Negative, sir!"

"Prepare secondary thrusters — kick them in the moment we touchdown — that should get us out of here."

"Readying secondary thrusters, sir!"

The runway was closing up fast as Stanly's hand hovered over the keypad waiting for the wheels to make contact with the planet's surface.

But the wheel housings hadn't opened.

The ship dropped, smashing her belly into the runway and jerking Stanly's hand onto the primed keypad. The thrusters kicked in, powering the Calypso forward. The giant ship ripped across the landing strip, metal screaming as Stanly fought for control. But there was no response.

"Cut the power!" the captain shouted.

It was too late.

Still gaining momentum, Calypso slewed towards the docks.

Her fuselage — weakened by the explosion — split like a ripe banana, rupturing the hidden fuel tanks. Rocket fuel sprayed across the apron in a noxious trail as she plowed through the passengers and ships, smashing the vessels into the landing bays. Then she tore through the terminal and into the ships berthed on the other side.

The Calypso, her nose ripped off but still moving hard, broke out of the port and through the refineries — finally driving herself into the fuel depot beside the mountain face.

Then the depot exploded, taking the ship with it.

# CHAPTER 33

"I'VE BEEN thinking," Robert announced abruptly at the end of their lesson, "about what I said yesterday — about eves. I don't know if I believe that — not anymore." He was silent a moment. "I'm not sure what I believe now. All I do know is that you're the only person I can talk to about this . . . this confusion — and that confuses me more than anything."

She nodded in understanding but said nothing.

Robert cleared his throat noisily before continuing: "I have to tell you the truth about something." He stopped, not certain why he had to speak out or even if he should. Then he rushed the words at her, saying, "I was the one that sent Frayne away."

She did not appear surprised by this confession. "Would you explain why you took this action?"

"The Chairman was planning to return with Frayne to Proximus. I had to prevent that. It was my duty to him — as I saw it then."

"And your reasoning for not allowing me to return with Frayne?"

There was a pause before he declared shortly, "I didn't think of you — not until it was too late." Then he paused again. "I couldn't change plans in the middle of them," he finished on a hard note. Robert had never felt responsible for an eve before, and it was unsettling.

Once again, Althaia nodded in understanding, her expression without censure.

"No one knows the truth about that night, except the soldiers that were with me. It would mean our deaths if it was ever discovered."

"I will not repeat this information."

He rose to his feet. "I'll return tomorrow at sunup. Saturday is in two sleeps then the priest will come. You must be flawless," Robert ordered.

"I will memorize, as you have instructed."

Robert paused at the door to watch her gather up the paper and books he'd left for her. Sensing his presence, she looked up. For a moment they studied each other, and then he was gone.

Later, alone and rested, Althaia held the ancient wristwatch, wrapping herself in a coat of protective healing.

I'm alive! I can't believe I'm alive! Jillian's mind sang with relief.

"Hurry up in there!" a guard snarled through the open doorway. "Yuh got two minutes!"

Jillian ran breathlessly about her room, grabbing whatever came to hand and throwing it down again. Take only the essentials, she ordered herself. Hurry up! You've only got a minute left. She made some fast choices, and was at the door when the guard announced, "OK, everybody in line! No talkin'!"

The eight women obeyed quickly, rushing from their rooms with suitcases and backpacks overstuffed and still half opened.

All of Simon's widows are here, Jillian thought. No, not all, there are two missing: the pregnant ones.

Some of the women were sobbing uncontrollably. The ones with children, Jillian realized. They're being forced to leave their kids behind, she gasped in shock.

But no one protested; they were all too terrorized to do anything but obey.

Have they all been interrogated like me? Jillian wondered. We all knew Mallory, but I was the only one close to her. Was that common knowledge?

I can't believe they let me go — I was so near confessing, she thought with a shiver. Had they pushed me any longer, I'd be on my way to an execution instead of an eviction. But *why* did they let me go? It was like a miracle.

The guards ordered the women forward, and they moved off in a straggly line.

Jillian was glad to leave. HQ was ruined for her now. No longer a home, but a place of violence and death — and betrayal.

It was the only explanation for such a disastrous turn of events.

Will I ever learn what really happened that night? I doubt it, she thought. I never knew Mallory's male accomplices and only a few of the women — all silenced forever.

Suddenly she was crying, and for a long time she didn't wonder about anything but followed blindly behind the women in front of her. They were led out of HQ and down into the townsite. At the end of a long street that lay close to one of the fields, they finally came to a stop.

Jillian looked around. They'd arrived at a dorm-site for single women and widows without children. Single-story cabins made of unfinished wood. There were six in this location; each housed thirty-two women, four to a room.

The eight women were split up and assigned to different dorms before being instructed to store their gear and return outside. Once they had done so, a man they'd never seen before stood waiting for them: a civilian.

"I'll be your foreman. Be ready to start at 6 am. You'll be clearing land seven days a week." The women gasped. Land clearing was never assigned longer than a three-day shift; it was too hard on the body, even with machinery to help pull out the stumps. But none of the women protested.

We're still under suspicion, Jillian realized. They're going to treat us like criminals.

"And you'd better not dawdle getting back to barracks come quitting time, 'cause there's a curfew on. Any woman found outside after dark will be shot on sight. Good day, ladies."

"I thought you'd never wake up," a woman declared.

Jillian sat bolt upright and saw the high morning light. She leapt from bed, gasping, "God, what time is it!" She squinted at her wristwatch. "Ten o'clock — shit!"

"Don't craze out," the woman said. "You've got the day off."

"What?" Jillian said in disbelief, dropping back onto the bed to look with bleary eyes at the tall blonde who stood in her doorway.

"Some guy came around last night to announce the news, but you were already snoozin'. Your friend, she shut off your alarm," Erin said, pointing to Jillian's watch. "She's gone to church, so I said I'd let you know."

"Thanks," Jillian answered tiredly. "Why'd we get the day off?"

"Didn't say. Just announced you were all on regular shift now — like the rest of us drones."

"Thank God," Jillian said, falling back onto her makeshift pillow. "I couldn't have done another day." She let her exhausted body burrow contentedly under the blanket, but still she wondered: Why the sudden reprieve? Are they satisfied with our innocence, or do they believe we've been beaten down enough to remove any rebellion left in us? Will we ever know?

The woman was leaving the room, and Jillian stopped her saying, "I'm sorry, I don't know your name. I'm Jillian."

"Erin," the woman answered abruptly, turning to leave once more, but again Jillian forestalled her.

"I feel sort of embarrassed. We've been sharing this dorm for over a week, and

283

we've never even spoken."

"It doesn't matter," came the clipped reply. This time she left.

Oh God, Jillian thought, she must think I'm responsible for Simon's death. Maybe everyone thinks I'm guilty — I was Mallory's friend.

She felt a sudden weight in her chest. It was too much to bear in her depleted state. She burst into tears. When they finally dried, she saw Erin watching her from the doorway.

"You always get this happy over good news?"

Jillian started to laugh and then collapsed back into tears. "She didn't kill him — she was set up. Her gun didn't even have bull—" In two long strides, Erin had covered the space between them to slap a hand over Jillian's mouth.

She put a finger to her own lips, looking into Jillian's startled face. "I could be an informer for all you know," she said quietly.

Jillian's eyes went big as she stared up at Erin in sudden fright. God, she's right. I would never have thought of that.

Erin removed her hand. "Talking's a hype anyhow."

"Thank you. You probably saved my life."

Erin shrugged. "It's okay," she said briefly, and walked out again.

Jillian lay there digesting the implications of Erin's statement. How can I trust anyone now?

She thought of Lydia, who'd befriended her immediately upon arriving at the dorm. It seemed so suspicious now as everything the woman did came under review.

Why would she spend so much time helping someone she didn't even know? Always bringing me supper and snacks so I wouldn't have to walk to the cook house. Changing my sheets and doing my laundry. And I can't believe I now have to question every offer of help or friendship!

Jillian was feeling very much alone. Mournfully she thought, Once again the people I trusted and cared about the most are dead — or off limits.

She would have given a lot to see Father Neil right then. But she doubted his uncle would approve of him talking with a suspected murderer — not Simon's murderer at any rate. The Agency wouldn't like that.

I don't think I'll ever feel safe again.


"You were right. It's okay up here."

Jillian grinned at Erin's response to the beauty spread out below them. Did she ever lose that reserve? "Yes. It was worth losing my dignity for."

"I didn't think Martinez was ever going to hand over that all-terrain — no

284

matter how hard you begged."

"We used to be friendly once. He'd lend it to me every weekend."

"Bet you're the only one who ever bothered coming up here."

"You'd win that bet."

Erin folded her arms across her chest, staring out past the tree line and across the rocky wasteland to the jagged mountains in the North. It was Jillian's favorite view, and she felt a kinship with this taciturn woman who kept everyone at bay with her sharp tongue. She's like Mallory, Jillian thought. Aloof to all but the chosen few. They had a lot in common, she realized.

They were the only two people she knew of who didn't attend church. They were both independent and razor sharp, tall and strong and beautiful. And just like Mallory, Erin loved her husband. But unlike Mallory, Erin had no quarrel with Daniel. They'd enjoyed a blissful marriage until his death.

Erin looked at Jillian quizzically. "What're you staring at?"

"You remind me of Mallory."

"I'm nothing like her."

"Why do you say that?"

"I'd never do what she did," Erin said flatly, then quickly held up a hand to stop Jillian's protest. "I don't mean murder. I mean trying to change things."

"Why not?"

"Can't be done."

"That's a hopeless view."

"Mallory tried, and what did it get her?" Jillian retreated back a step, stung. "Sorry," Erin said, chopping her words. "Shouldn't have said that."

"But she was betrayed!" Jillian explained, impassioned. "It would have worked if it hadn't been for that."

"My point exactly."

"You know what's going on, don't you," she accused.

"What do you mean?"

"When Mallory tried to move out of HQ, they threatened to put her in a loony bin. Then she found evidence proving that the Agency's been denying all women any financial or political influence — even our legal rights."

Erin raised her eyebrows. "I didn't have specifics, but I could see which way the wind was blowing."

"God, I can hardly believe it, even now. It seems so farfetched."

Erin shrugged. "It's only the usual. Man's always trying to suppress man — or woman."

"I suppose . . ." she trailed off, sighing heavily. But a moment later she straightened her shoulders. "So, what are we going to do?"

"Do? Nothing," Erin stated, surprised by the question. "There's nothing we can do, except protect ourselves as much as possible."

"But that seems so . . . cowardly."

"If you announced what you know in the marketplace, what reaction do you think you'd get?"

"I don't know. I guess they wouldn't believe me."

"Exactly. You hardly believe it and look what you've been through. They've got to figure it out for themselves." She gave Jillian a sharp look. "You're not thinking of hatching any little plots are you?"

"God, no! I'd never get involved in anything like that again."

"Well, that's a relief. At least you've learned something."

"So we just carry on like everybody else?"

"Not quite. There's cracks in every system. Live in the cracks. When you run out of cracks, then you act."

Jillian nodded moodily. "I guess you're right . . . but it seems like surrender."

Erin studied her a moment. "Cheer up. You'll have company in those cracks."

"Well, so far I haven't seen any signs to prove it."

"So what am I, old alfalfa?"

"I didn't mean that."

"I know, just bugging you," she said, taking a seat on the grass.

Jillian studied her again. "How come you know so much?"

Erin shrugged. "I've lived."

"Well, so have I, but you've obviously lived someplace else."

"I grew up in an orphanage. Not a nice place, don't recommend it."

"I'm sorry."

"Don't be. You didn't put me there."

"How old were you?"

"Five." She paused. "Life changed in an instant — or that's how I remember it. I lost my parents, my home, and everything in it." Her hand went up to fondle the locket that lay at the base of her throat. "Everything but this."

"How awful."

"It was a long time ago," she said with finality. "Plenty of others have lost the same."

Jillian took the hint and dropped the subject. She settled herself on the grass, pulling out a sketch pad and making quick strokes with a charcoal pencil across the white surface. But after a few minutes, she stopped to let out a long sigh.

"That sounded low. What's eating you?"

"I'm just missing a friend. At least, I think he's still a friend."

"Oh," Erin said meaningfully. "A *man* friend."

"No, nothing like *that* — he's a priest."

"Oh, jeesus, priests give me the creeps."

286

"Not him, he's different."

"So what's the problem?"

"After I came under suspicion for . . . that crime, I expected the Pope to order him away from me completely — because the Agency wouldn't like it. But he won't even look at me. It's like I don't even exist. He must actually believe I had something to do with Simon's murder. But how could he? I thought he knew me better than anyone," she finished angrily.

"You're *sure* he's just a friend?"

"Erin!"

"I know, I know, he's a priest," she said. But she didn't sound convinced.


Althaia put aside the watch and lifted the cloth jewelry bag, emptying the contents onto the floor. She picked through the strands of gold and silver until her hand found the heart-shaped locket. Lifting it tenderly, she returned to the trance state, feeling herself being drawn back to Earth time.


"Ouch!" Erin cried, rubbing the arm where she'd been pinched.

"Hey, leave her alone, Suzie," a little girl ordered, though she was even younger than Erin. She took Erin's hand protectively.

"Baby!" the older girl sneered at Erin.

"Thank you, Jennifer," Erin whispered shyly.

"Ugly baby!" Suzie added spitefully, and there was laughter from the girls nearby.

"Girls! Stand in line and keep quiet!" a stern-looking woman of forty years ordered the group of children clustered inside the gloomy corridor. "You aren't likely to be adopted if you're loud and unruly, are you?"

The children obediently formed a straight line and stood silently waiting. Several minutes later, a door opened and an older woman poked her head into the hallway. She spoke crisply: "You may bring them in now, Ms. Cuthridge."

"Yes, Ms. Steward."

Ms. Cuthridge turned to the children and ordered them to enter. Quietly, they filed inside the large lobby. Benches were set along one wall, and on these sat half a dozen adults waiting expectantly.

The children were directed to stand against the wall opposite, where they stood stiff and self-conscious while the six adults scrutinized them carefully.

"You may speak with the children if you like," Ms. Steward advised them.

They immediately rose and crossed the room.

One couple made a direct line towards Erin, and she held her breath in hope, but instead they stopped at the child beside her.

"What's your name?" the woman asked.

"Jennifer," came the bold reply.

"And how old are you?"

"Five years old and three months!" she stated proudly.

The woman laughed, and the man smiled benignly down at her. Erin's heart sank. She knew the signs all too well.

"This is my friend, Erin," Jennifer said, pointing at her. "She's six."

"How do you do, Erin," the woman said politely.

But all Erin could do was hang her head, twisting her hands painfully under the woman's scrutiny. A pale, silent child, with limp blonde hair hanging untidily over thin shoulders, there was nothing about her to command more than a passing notice.

"She's shy, but she's very nice."

"I'm sure she is. You're a very good friend, I think," the woman said, focusing on Jennifer.

"I try to be."

"Would you like to be a daughter — our daughter?" the woman asked, with a hopeful smile on her face.

"Would I? I'd love it!" Jennifer exclaimed, making the couple laugh again and bringing Erin close to tears. She was about to lose another friend.

It was always the same: I find someone to care about and then they leave.

Erin took hold of the heart shaped locket around her neck, rubbing it for comfort.

Nobody's ever going to pick me. I'm too stupid and ugly.


"Hey, ugly!" Suzie called across the bathroom.

The other girls laughed, taking up the chant, "Ugly! Ugly! Ugly!"

Erin ran from the room, toothbrush still in her mouth. Tears blinded her, so she didn't see the woman until she crashed full tilt into her generous bosom.

"ERIN SLATER!" the woman shrieked in fury. "How dare you!"

"I'm — I'm sorry, Ms. Cuthridge—"

"Running in the halls again! Are you completely stupid or just an idiot! You are nine years old — I expect you to set a *proper* example for the younger girls. And what are you doing with that toothbrush in your mouth! Look, you've got toothpaste on my sweater! Go at once and finish brushing your teeth in the designated area, you stupid girl!"

"Yes, ma'am," Erin managed to choke out, a hard knot forming in her throat.

She returned to the bathroom to find the girls huddled close to the door, listening.

When she was certain Ms. Cuthridge had departed, Suzie straightened up, chanting in a sing-song voice, "Stupid! Idiot!"

After a fit of giggles, the other girls took up the refrain.

Erin finished brushing her teeth, tears rolling down her cheeks.

"So, where yuh gonna go?" a dark-haired teenager asked Erin.

"I don't know," Erin said shyly, pulling back the blankets on her bed.

"So, what's not to know?" the girl asked, flopping down on her own bed. Then she looked at Erin with sudden suspicion. "Unless you found an apprenticeship sponsor — or someone to put you through college?"

"No, Judy," Erin answered hastily. "I don't know anybody."

"Then you gotta join the gangs or join cadets. I've told you, a kid on their own doesn't stand a chance out there."

Erin grew thoughtful: Judy was orphaned late, and knew a lot about the outside world. She liked to joke about how lucky it was that her old man croaked before he got a chance to kick her out of the house. Being orphaned meant the government took care of her — at least temporarily.

"So what's it gonna be?" she demanded of Erin.

Erin paused, regretting the necessity of choosing between them. It didn't seem fair that teenagers under eighteen couldn't legally hold a job, own a car, or rent a place of residence. Sixteen-year-olds who didn't enter a college or apprenticeship program were required to join cadets. And those that wouldn't or couldn't, and with no family willing to support them, found themselves living on the streets.

"I guess the cadets."

"She guesses!" the girl snorted. "Those gangs would eat you alive, you're such a reedy." She paused before adding, "Least you'll be set for life. Those Army recruiters will snatch you up the moment you step out of that cadet uniform."

"I don't think I'd wanna do that," Erin said apprehensively. Soldiering didn't appeal to Erin's nature, but she understood that for many young adults it would be an easy transition: their future secured – short as it might be. "Will you go into cadets?" Erin asked.

"Me? Fight fires and mow rich people's lawns for nothing? Are you crazed?"

"You're going into the gangs?" Erin responded in surprise.

As a ward of the state, Judy was guaranteed a placement in cadets, while many others would be turned away because of full rosters or the lack of notarized permission from a parent, which was hard to get when they hadn't seen one in years — abandoned and left to fend for themselves. So why, Erin wondered, wouldn't she take full advantage of the situation?

"Of course I'll go gangin'. A savvy babe like me can gather some sweet prairie *and* have a lot of fun! You wait and see. By the time I'm legal, I'm gonna have enough grass to buy my own nestie."

Erin was silent, not understanding why Judy would want to join a gang of kids who robbed and even murdered to survive. Who lived under the constant threat of attack by rival gangs — and cops quick to shoot.

"But isn't it dangerous?" Erin finally ventured to ask.

"Maybe," Judy shrugged. "But it's a hell of a lot better than being bored out of my mind doing drill!" She got off the bed to examine her face carefully in the small mirror nailed to the wall. "Just think, no more fuckin' house duties!"

Erin lay back on her bed, staring up at the ceiling.

All children participated in the cleaning of the orphanage. The older they became, the more they had to contribute. Erin wouldn't have minded, but Ms. Cuthridge always found fault with her efforts no matter what she did — ridiculing her in front of the other children. The older girls always quick to join in.

But gradually her tormentors had aged out and left for the outside world, leaving only Judy and Erin to share the seniors' room. Cuthridge still hated her, but Erin now had a place to hide away.

"Think how great we're gonna look in makeup," Judy said, piling her curly black hair on top of her head. "Just three more months and we are outta here!" She dropped her long locks and turned away from the mirror. "No more hand-me-downs a dog wouldn't wear," she said in disgust, tugging at her faded blue shirt with its numerous patches. "I'm gettin' hold of some spaced-out clothes the moment I'm free of this prison!" She looked at Erin. "But I guess you'll be stuck in dogsville. I hear those uniforms are pretty ugly. At least you'll get to wear makeup on your day off, if you can afford it. Not that you need it," she added with envy.

Erin looked at her, baffled, but quickly figured it out: She thinks even makeup wouldn't help. Sighing heavily, Erin rolled over and faced the wall.

"Okay, you grunts! Line up and look sharp!" the uniformed woman shouted.

Erin hurried out of the bus with the rest of the adolescent girls and took her place in line beside the vehicle. There were two other buses unloading nearby. The girls all wore the same baggy brown uniform, a nametag the only decoration.

From where she stood in the parking lot, Erin was able to see most of the camp: the bunkhouses and officers' quarters, the drill ground and gymnasium. In the distance, past two rows of wire fencing, was a duplicate camp for the boys, just like at basic training.

She eyed her new home with something akin to optimism. The past eight weeks had been no worse than what she was used to, and in some ways it was far better. The hard physical training made her body feel strong and capable. But there was another bonus, something she'd never experienced before: camaraderie. The closeness her unit developed while they struggled through their paces together and competed against the other squads. She was sorry when the training ended, their units disbanded and sent to different camps; only Toni remained.

Erin noticed four young women on the parade ground. They were wearing the uniform of a cadet, but with a red armband sewn on both sleeves and a red beret cocked at a sharp angle, partially covering their shaved scalps. Their faces wore varying degrees of a scowl. Each had a large frame, heavy with fat and muscle. They walked with a swagger, and it was clear they expected no opposition.

"Get a load of those babes!" somebody said with a giggle. There was answering laughter down the line. "Who *are* they?"

"I bet they're Major Baker's goons," whispered a shapely cadet with blonde hair.

"What?"

"My sister was in this camp. Baker picks the biggest and meanest cadets to police the rest of her company. In exchange, they get extra privileges."

"Shit, where do I sign on?" a tall girl with kinky hair said enviously.

"God, I hope I don't get put into her company," someone else piped in.

"Face front!" the uniformed woman shouted, and three busloads of teens turned sharply forward, standing stiffly at attention.

"My name is Sergeant Cochrane. If you have any questions, stow them! No talking whatsoever!"

She turned and saluted as another woman approached.

An officer, Erin thought nervously, and tried to make her body even straighter, keeping her eyes fixed firmly ahead.

The officer walked down the line, examining each girl carefully. "This one," she'd say, and the sergeant would put a mark beside her name. When she looked Erin over, she said, "This one for sure," before moving on. When she was done, the officer strode away without a backward glance.

Sergeant Cochrane shouted at them once more: "I will call your name and the company you're assigned to. You will form a line for each company. The lines will be in alphabetical order." She began to rattle off the names.

Erin was posted to C-Company, as were the other thirteen girls that had been noted by the officer. More girls joined them, and within minutes they were all allocated.

"About face," the sergeant ordered. Every girl turned sharply towards the wide pathway that led across the camp. "Quick march!" she bellowed.

In unison, the lines moved forward.

"Pretty crappy work, ain't it?"

Erin looked up at the edge of the ditch and into the smirking face of the older teenager wearing a red beret. Erin shrugged. "I've had worse." She returned to uncovering the broken sewer pipe, alert to the older girl's presence as she watched her work.

"There are easier jobs, yuh know."

"Sorry, I'm not interested."

"Maybe yuh don't understand," she said, crouching down and lowering her voice. "The Major *wants* yuh to be interested."

Erin's shovel stopped moving for a moment, but she shook her head. "I'm sorry, but I can't."

"Not too bright, are you?"

Erin said nothing, but her shoveling became more vigorous.

The older girl spat into the ditch. "It's your funeral." Then she stood up and moved away.

"That's why we've been getting the worst jobs, so we'll jump at the chance to be in their disgusting skin game," a tall redhead whispered angrily to Erin. "Shit, there's plenty girls willing to sell themselves, you'd think they'd have enough already!"

Erin whispered back in confusion, "I don't understand why they even want me?"

The redhead looked at her in disbelief. But because she understood that Erin's snootiness was actually shyness, she quickly realized, "You really don't know, do you?" Erin shook her head. "Girl, how can't you know that you are gorgeous?"

Erin laughed at her. "Very funny, Toni."

Toni gave up. "Well, I know I'm not going into any goddamn porno movie. My mom would kill me!"

"What do you think they'll do to us?"

"Probably give us even more disgusting jobs until we give in. Maybe even threaten us with the major's goons." She was thoughtful a moment. "Well, I'm not taking any shit. I'll go straight to the C.O."

"I don't know, Toni . . ." Erin said nervously.

"I'll do it if I have to."

"Tomorrow the whole platoon's doing another survival exercise. Maybe it

292

won't seem so bad when we get back?"

"Four days of living off the land and sleeping on hard ground is not about to soften my attitude."

"It might be okay, Toni. Wait and see," Erin pleaded gently.

"I'll wait, but if things get any worse, I'll report them."

"Toni, I don't think that's such a good idea."

"Don't worry, it'll be alright."

Erin heard the scream and sat bolt upright. The second scream sent her scrambling out of her bunk, racing towards the noise. Other girls were already ahead of her, and it was they who ran into the terrified cadet as she dashed from the shower room.

"In there!" she sobbed hysterically, clinging onto the others for support.

Nervously, they entered the showers. "Jeesus!" somebody cried in shock. A few girls turned and ran heaving into the bathroom, but most just stood rigid with disbelief. Only Erin moved towards the naked body lying on the concrete floor.

Gently she pushed Toni's jaws opened, trying not to look at the thing stuffed inside her mouth. With a quick jerk of its tail, she dislodged the dead rat, throwing it violently across the room. Fearfully, she felt at the base of Toni's neck. There was a faint pulse.

Her body was covered in bruises, some bearing the imprint of a heavy army boot. And by the look of her arm, it was badly broken. Then Erin noticed the blood. A deep, dark pool had collected between her legs. A few kicks too many, she thought in a daze, and then snapped out of her initial shock.

"Get a medic! She's bleeding to death!" There was movement behind her. "Get a blanket! Hurry!"

Tenderly, she cleaned the spittle and blood from Toni's face. Someone handed her a bathrobe. She covered Toni's battered body and then embraced her friend, careful not to disturb her broken arm. Erin remained that way long after the medic arrived to pronounce Toni dead.

Rage consumed Erin.

Though it was a feeling previously foreign to her, she now embraced it.

Toni's death had been classified as a shower accident. And who was going to say different? Erin thought bitterly.

293

Her body was cremated, the ashes sent home to her mother. One of the Major's goons had been reassigned to another camp, and that was the end of the matter.

The skin-vids were temporarily on hold until things died down. But when it started up again, so would the pressure on her and the other girls. She knew Toni's death had frightened several of them into capitulating, but it had turned Erin's resolve into plasteelite. She could end up like Toni, an example for others. But she didn't care; her anger kept her from caring.

She was spending as much time by herself as she could. Even sneaking from the barracks after lights out to wander in the dark, finding deserted places where she could be alone with her rage — welcoming the feeling — for it gave her a strength she never knew she possessed. And for what lay ahead, Erin understood she would need it.

Erin walked through the darkened camp to the perimeter fence at the end of the base. Leaning back against the metallic mesh, she looked up at the barbed wire that encircled the top and for a few moments considered going AWOL.

I could hide out in the hills, she thought. I know enough to survive.

But quickly came to her senses, the only wilderness available belonged to the Army.

And when they caught me, I'd get ten years in the stockade. Better to ride this out. I just gotta find—

"So what yuh want, kid?" a deep, male voice spoke out of the darkness.

Erin jerked in surprise, whirling around to look out past the fence, expecting a man to be standing behind her, but there was no one there.

"I want my money back," a younger male voice demanded rudely.

Then Erin spotted them thirty feet away. She let her body slip slowly to the ground, stretching flat on her stomach so as not to be seen. As her eyes adjusted to the increased darkness, she saw that one man was a soldier: dark-skinned and perhaps in his thirties, not tall, but thick set and muscular. The other was a civilian: light-skinned and slender, who couldn't have been more than twenty. From the worn leather clothes and the bandanas around his head and upper arms, she knew he belonged to a gang.

"Yuh bet and yuh lost, kid, that's the way it is when yuh play with the grownups."

"Well, it weren't my money, and they want it back," the younger demanded belligerently.

"That's real tough, kid, but the money's gone. Maybe next time yuh shouldn't play with prairie that ain't yur own."

"Yur gonna be sorry if yuh don't fork it over."

"Look kid, yuh tried. Now go home to mommy."

294

"Fuck you, yuh dirty nigger."

"Now yur hurtin' my feelings," the soldier said impassively.

As he spoke, four figures stepped out of the shadows, forming a semi-circle around him. They were all in their early twenties, dressed in the same colored bandanas as the younger man.

"We're gonna hurt a lot more than yur feelings, tar-baby," one of the newcomers said menacingly. He was bigger than the others, his heritage uncertain. From his demeanor, Erin guessed that he was the leader of the gang.

The soldier did not respond, and his body seemed to go limp, hands hanging loosely at his sides. His five attackers took this as a sign of fear. They were surprised by this because he was a soldier, and laughed gleefully in expectation of an easy victory.

"Javier," the gang leader ordered. "Take him out."

A Hispanic youth sprang into action, his legs wild with motion as he prepared to attack. But still the soldier didn't move, not until the first kick was almost planted in his groin. Then he was suddenly holding the foot between his hands — the momentum of the kick propelling the attacker into a rotation — and the soldier wrenched the leg in the opposite direction, twisting hard. The bone snapped loudly as the kneecap separated from the leg. The young man screamed in agony, and the soldier released the leg, moving back, once more standing loose and ready.

"Get him!" the leader yelled, and the four converged on the lone man, but he leapt backwards at the last moment — a knife in each hand — slashing as he went, slicing the throat of one, the belly of another. Then he was dancing away, out of reach.

There was a strangled, guttural sound from the gang leader as blood bubbled up through his throat. The other wounded youth had fallen to his knees, looking at the blood pouring from his belly in horror. "You son-of-a-bitch!" he sputtered in disbelief.

"You boys ready to end this?" the soldier asked the two uninjured members. They looked at their bloodied companions, hesitating. "That friend of yours ain't gonna live too long unless I stop that bleeding," the soldier commented.

"Okay," one of them said grudgingly. "Do it."

"Move way back," he ordered. The soldier watched them until they were almost lost in the darkness before stepping over to help the man with the bloody throat. He took the gang leader's hand and pressed three of his fingers firmly onto the wound. "Keep the pressure on that 'til you get to a doctor. Don't let go if you wanna live." Then he helped him to his feet.

"BEHIND YOU!" Erin screamed out.

The soldier whirled around in time to see a piece of metal pipe raised to strike him — he leapt out of the way, his arm a blur of motion. His assailant let out a howl and dropped the pipe, leaping around in pain. "My foot!" he shrieked. Erin could see the knife blade protruding from the top of his boot.

The soldier returned once more to the same relaxed stance. "You boys had better get yourselves to a medic," he advised.

The only uninjured member now returned to help the young man with the broken leg. With considerable cursing, the five slowly staggered away into the night. The older man waited, making certain his attackers were truly gone before he turned towards the compound to look for the source of the warning shout. But he could see nothing, the glare of the base lights dissolving his night vision. After a few moments, he nodded in thanks, and then moved on, walking along the perimeter towards the boys' base.

Not knowing why, Erin felt compelled to keep him insight. She followed him up to the barrier separating the two camps. When he finally came to a stop, he was barely visible, but she could hear him talking in a low voice to another man and then the sound of a gate opening. Moments later, he was in the lights of the base, walking across the boys' compound almost in her direction. Quickly she backed into the shadows, feeling suddenly nervous.

He was heading up towards the buildings that abutted the fence. She followed.

He's going inside the motor pool, she realized, holding her breath in hope. Several moments later she saw the lights go on in the girls' side of the motor pool and her pulse quickened.

She knew the mechanics were Regular Army and the only males officially allowed on the girls' base. Could he be one of them? she asked with increasing hope.

Heart pounding, she entered the building, hiding behind a transport vehicle. She watched him wash the blood off the knives, drying them carefully before returning them to the sheaths hidden under his sleeves. Then he dug inside a locker until he found a knife to replace the one he'd lost. He was in the act of putting it into a sheath near the top of his boot when he straightened up, looking directly towards her hiding place.

"Who's there!" he demanded. "Come out of the shadows."

Erin stepped forward, her legs shaking so badly they almost buckled under her.

"What the hell do we have here?" the man said in surprise. He looked behind her into the shadows. "You alone?"

"Yes," she said quickly.

"You must be the pip who saved my butt out there. Thanks."

She nodded. "I saw your fight — then I followed you."

296

"Yuh did, eh?" he said, taking in her trembling appearance. "What for?"

Without looking at him, she said quietly, "If — if you teach me how to use a knife, you — you can have me."

There was a long silence, and it was all she could do to keep from running away, but there was no place to run to.

"What the hell would I want with a skinny little thing like you?"

Dismay and relief made her shoulders slump forward. He wouldn't do it.

"What you wanna learn a thing like that for, anyway?"

"Protection," she mumbled, turning to go, but his voice stopped her.

"You in C-Company?" She nodded. "Havin' a rough go?"

"It's gonna get that way."

"Well, if it's one thing I know, it's how to smooth out those rough patches," he said, pulling out a knife and balancing it on the back of his hand.

Then she understood: he was going to help her.


Erin knew it had come. They'd taken longer than expected, probably because the other girls had capitulated. But the waiting was over; the rough stuff was about to begin.

Am I ready?

She thought of all the preparations she'd made: the lessons from Corporal Payette and the ceaseless practicing during every spare moment.

The corporal had given her an area for training at the back of the motor pool so she wouldn't be seen, and even enlisted the assistance of a couple of buddies as sparring partners. They'd also taught her combat skills that weren't to be found in the Cadet Training Manual.

But to Erin, more important than all the training was the praise they'd heaped on her for her skill and quick learning. It took a special kind of smarts to be a knifer, they'd said. And she could be one of the best. It made her heart swell with pride. But they'd warned her not to let it go to her head or she'd be dead. But Erin didn't care. She could die happy knowing she excelled at something.

Erin had been given strict instructions to always shower with her platoon, never ever alone. But it wasn't going to happen alone in the shower, it was going to happen here, inside the bunkroom with plenty of witnesses.

There were four of them, all big young women in their last months as cadets. They glared at the girls as they lay on their bunks preparing for lights out. Several girls shrank back in alarm, thinking themselves the target of their ire.

Erin was still dressed, ready to sneak from the barracks once the camp had settled for the night. She slipped from her bunk and into her boots, mentally preparing herself as she watched their approach. She moved quickly, knowing it was dangerous to be caught between the bunks where there was no room to maneuver. Erin stood in the aisle, hands loose at her sides, knees slightly bent, ready to shift in any direction.

The four young women caught sight of her and stopped in their tracks — no one ever came out to meet them. It threw them off momentarily, but they quickly regained their bravado. One of the goons growled at the cadets who were watching: "Get out of here — all of you — now!" The girls leapt off their bunks and ran into the washroom at the back.

Erin was strangely calm, though her heart pounded in her ears and every sense seemed unnaturally heightened. She wasn't even concerned with winning: four-to-one were not good odds. She could only hope to do justice to her teachers, and to wreak some vengeance for the death of Toni.

The goons were close now, not taking her seriously at all. She was just a skinny kid who'd crumple at the first punch.

"You've been ignoring the Major's invitations," one of them stated, removing her beret and putting it inside her back pocket. "She's tired of waiting, so she asked us to give you a little incentive."

She stepped forward quickly, making a grab for Erin, who jerked out of reach as if backing away, but instead her leg lashed out towards her attacker, the heel of her boot connecting with a kneecap as the young woman walked into the kick. For a moment there was no sound as her eyes went wide with surprise, then she dropped to the floor, grabbing her leg and writhing in pain.

"Kill the bitch!" she shrieked.

But the others were wary now, and they had the Major's orders to follow: no permanent damage or the girl would be useless.

The three fanned out around her. Then as one, they lunged, expecting to ensnare her with the sheer force of their combined weights, but she leapt back, out of the way, slashing at them with knives that seemed to appear from nowhere, making a long cut across the arm of one young woman while slicing near the shoulder of another.

When she was done, they stared in horror at the blood oozing onto the floor.

Erin saw the fear that came over them, and she knew that in another moment they'd either kill her or flee. In an act of self-preservation, she lunged at the one goon still untouched, slashing the blade across her belly before quickly dancing out of reach.

The young woman screamed in terror and rushed from the room, clutching her abdomen. The other two hesitated a moment, studying Erin as she stood crouched with knives in hand, ready to spring again. "You are some crazy bitch!" one of them said hoarsely. Fearfully, they picked up their fallen comrade and staggered out of the barracks.

When the girls in the washroom heard the goons leave the bunkhouse, they crept out cautiously, frightened at what they'd find. They gasped in horror at the trail of blood that led to the outside and at the small pools that had collected in the middle of the floor. Then they saw Erin, alive and standing frozen in her defensive position, her complexion deathly white.

A couple of the girls dashed around the blood to get to her. "We thought they'd killed you!" the kinky-haired girl said, staring at the knives in shock.

Erin looked down at her hands and at the blood on her knives. Then she bent over and threw up her dinner.

Erin started to set the drinks on the table when the man grabbed at her buttocks, pinching hard. Erin reached back, taking a fold of his skin between her fingernails, and twisted painfully. The man swore, ripping his hand away. But a moment later the hand returned, this time to her breast. It surprised her. Customers didn't usually find the game much fun when they were the ones getting hurt. He squeezed viciously — and she upended the tray of drinks onto his head. The man leaped to his feet, swearing and yelling.

Another man came dashing across the room to their table. "Mr. Foster! I apologize!" he said nervously, wiping the drinks and bits of ice from the customer's head and clothing.

"Mr. Kim," Erin said quickly in her defense, "he was hurting my breast!"

Mr. Kim turned on Erin. "You! You are fired! Get out!"

Stunned, Erin looked at the outraged face of her boss and the gloating expression of the customer, then turned and ran. She left the luxurious lounge, rushing down the much less opulent hallway and entered a small room at the back, the dull paint peeling off its walls.

Blindly, she grabbed for her coat and shoulder bag, unable to believe that she'd just lost her job. Thrusting her arms inside her coat, she headed for the rear exit but stopped abruptly: My pay chip!

Erin returned to the front of the bar.

Standing in the shadows, she waited until her employer passed nearby. "Mr. Kim, I need my pay," she said, her voice firm.

"Your wage has already been spent replacing the broken glasses and spilled drinks, and for the dry cleaning of Mr. Foster's very expensive suit. You're lucky he doesn't press charges!" He started to move away but Erin stepped in front of him.

"Mr. Kim, I need that money," she stated firmly again, but fear had put an edge to her voice.

"Are you threatening me?" he demanded

"No!" she said in surprise. "I just want my money."

"I think you'd better go," he said, brushing past her.

"Wait!" she said, grabbing his arm, desperate now. "You can't do this. That's my rent money." He flung off her hand. "If I don't pay, I'll be out on the streets!"

Mr. Kim looked at her coldly. "If you don't leave this instant, I'll be forced to call the police." He motioned towards two muscular men standing at the entrance to the bar. They came over immediately. "Escort Ms. Slater outside. She is no longer welcome," he stated, and strode away to attend to his customers.

Erin stared after him in disbelief. How could this be happening? Dazedly, she walked between the two men, past tables of smiling, carefree people and out into the night air.

"And don't come back," one of the men said, closing the door behind her.

Hunching into her thin coat, she began to walk unseeing down the deserted sidewalk. It was cold outside, and the fancy clothes she wore for work were not meant for winter weather. She'd forgotten her long sweater and scarf at the bar.

Goddamnit! she raged at herself, furious at leaving them behind and for letting her temper get the better of her. I can't believe I screwed myself!

For two years, I put up with that asshole Kim and his asshole customers and his lousy wages. Two years of bitchy servers who hated me on sight and bouncers who never took no for an answer. Two years I made myself swallow their crap so I could keep my home. Rat infested hole that it is.

But it was *my* rat infested hole. And now I'm gonna lose it.

She felt tears beginning to well up, and she stopped walking to let them fall.

It took you so long to find that damn job! she berated herself.

Most restaurants and bars used mechanical dispensers that offered stale food and watered-down drinks. Only the wealthy could afford the luxury of freshly cooked fare served by an attractive server. And there were plenty of beautiful young men and women vying for those positions.

Well, I'll just have to find another bar to hire me, she thought with sudden optimism. I've got experience now. I can find one with better wages — and a less sleazy clientele. But what about the rent?

She moved off again, too distracted to notice the man following behind her. When she passed a darkened alley, he grabbed her roughly around the neck, dragging her inside. "We didn't finish our fun," Mr. Foster rasped in her ear.

Erin began kicking and clawing, but he was a big man and her attempts at self-defense seemed feeble, only serving to make him more excited. He laughed unpleasantly, dragging her deeper into the alley.

Remembering her training, she stopped struggling and went completely limp,

300

forcing him to support her entire weight. The sudden load shift threw him off balance and his grip loosened. She wrenched herself free — but he recovered quickly, grabbing her long hair, yanking her back again. Yet it was enough time to slip the knife from her pocket. Ignoring the pain in her head, Erin focused on turning her body so she was facing him, knife hand free as she landed hard against his chest. He grasped her hair closer to the scalp, forcing her head back.

"I'm warning you, let me go!" she panted, the pain and fear making her voice rough and dangerous.

"You think you're man enough to take me?" he said in pleased surprise, and laughed again. "This is going to be fun." He smirked nastily as his left hand reached up to rip the buttons off her coat, exposing her blouse. As he ripped open the thin material, Erin swung the knife upward, plunging the blade into his right armpit. A look of surprise and pain washed over him and his hand lost hold of her hair. She pushed off of him instantly, but his left hand shot out to seize her arm. "You fucking little bitch!"

He tried to grab the knife with his injured arm — his rage giving him the strength to ignore the pain. Terrified, Erin slashed at his attempts, the knife connecting several times before she plunged the blade into the back of the hand that held her.

He howled in agony, and finally released his grip.

Erin staggered back, knife ready to strike again should he make a move. But he only stared at her, hatred etched on his face as he cradled his injured hands, blood dripping from several wounds. "I'll get you for this, you fucking cunt!" he threatened hoarsely.

Clutching her coat closed against her half-naked torso, she ran from the alley and down the street. After several blocks, her panic subsided and she slowed to look for a bus stop. Panting hard, she joined a queue of passengers, but they backed away from her in horror. Erin looked down at herself. Her coat was heavily spattered with blood.

She opened her mouth to explain but closed it again.

It wouldn't matter what I said.

With a guttural sound that was half sob, half frustrated anger, she fled from the looks on their faces, moving to the darker lanes where she could hide in the shadows.

It was a long walk home, and when relief was only a block away she saw the police car parked in front of her apartment building.

That bastard reported me to the cops? Erin thought in disbelief.

And then she understood: Mr. Kim told the cops that I threatened him — that he had to get the bouncers to throw me out. The cops will think I knifed that bastard for getting me fired — no one's going to believe me. He's rich and I'm poor.

They'll send me to prison! Erin realized in sudden despair.

The Major's goons would seem like a tea party compared to convicts serving twenty-to-life. And there'd be no Corporal Payette coming to my rescue — only guards more hardened than their prisoners, she thought with a shudder. Not even a reputation as a crazy bitch would keep me safe this time.

Heedless of the cold, Erin turned away from her apartment and began to walk. Dazedly, she wandered the streets, an overwhelming hopelessness covering her mind. Eventually, her footsteps brought her to the river. She stared down into the rushing water, its dark churning hypnotic. She knew it was no accident that had brought her here. It was the logical step. She'd no strength left to fight or suffer any longer.

Without hesitation, she climbed the barrier and leapt into the river. As she hit the water, she heard a voice call out. And then there was nothing but an icy blanket pulling her down. Against her will, her body began to struggle, fighting for life, but she'd never learned to swim and her attempts were futile — the current too strong, the river too cold. Once, twice, a third time she gained the surface briefly before going under with a last choking breath of dirty water.

She woke to the delicious sensation of warmth and softness. Thinking it a dream, she tried to retain sleep before the startling realization: I'm awake. Her eyes popped open, and she was surprised to see the edge of a sheepskin blanket — or what she supposed a sheepskin blanket would look like. Abruptly, her memories came flooding back. The job, the attack, the police — and the river! She was about to sit up when a strong voice forestalled the movement.

"I see you've woken up at last. You had me worried. I was beginning to think that all my efforts had been in vain." She turned her head to see the smiling face of a young man with dark brown skin, a few years her senior.

"Ah, they're blue," he said, his smile deepening. She looked perplexed. "Your eyes," he explained. "I've been making bets with myself on their color. Looks like I win." She smiled feebly. "And a nice smile too," he added. "Hi, I'm Daniel," he said, giving a short wave before announcing, "Time to get some food into you."

She watched his slim back disappear from the room and then cautiously raised herself up. She felt dizzy and weak, and there was a vile taste in her mouth. Too much river water, she thought wryly.

I'm wearing men's pajamas, she realized in dismay. He must have undressed me. She flushed red with embarrassment, feeling suddenly compelled to get out of bed and put on her clothes. Then she remembered they were ruined: ripped

302

and covered in blood. Erin slid back under the covers.

The aroma of cooking woke her some time later. She opened her eyes as Daniel entered carrying a tray laden with food. On his command, Erin sat up and the tray was placed on her lap.

Without waiting for an invitation, she gobbled down the hot soup and thick slices of whole grain bread, followed by a rich cheese omelet. She'd never had food so delicious — or so real, nothing processed or artificial. When the last scrap had been eaten, she leaned back contentedly to enjoy a cup of coffee: real coffee with real cream and sugar. A crooked smile slipped across her face.

The young man, who'd been watching appreciatively while she ate, asked, "What's the smile for?"

Erin hesitated, feeling shy about speaking. It seemed a long time since anyone cared why she did anything. "I was thinking, maybe I was successful after all — that I've died and gone to heaven."

Daniel laughed. "You should tell my mother that. She thinks this place is a den of iniquity." He lifted off the tray, saying, "Well, young woman, I suspect you don't have anywhere else to go, so I suggest you stay here until you're recovered fully. Maybe we can figure out a dryer solution to your problems." He held up his hand when she made to speak. "No, don't talk now, you need rest. I can hear all about it tomorrow. You sleep well, now. Good night."

"Good night," she answered automatically, watching him move out of the room. She didn't expect to sleep, but it came creeping over her. She turned out the bedside light, and while lying in the dark, feeling warm and safe and cared about, she realized with a wrench, I can't stay here, he could get into a lot of trouble for harboring a fugitive, especially one accused of knifing a rich asshole. I'll leave in the morning . . . .

"Yes?" Erin said sleepily into the monitor beside her bed.

"Ms. Slater, this is building security. Sorry to disturb you, but there's a Mr. Wasserman down here: says he's a friend of yours. Should I let him up?"

"Daniel?" she asked in confusion. He was supposed to be in New Mexico. But there he was, standing in her lobby. She glanced at the clock: it was 2 am. "Yes, of course, let him up."

Erin scuttled out of bed and into the bathroom to give her teeth a quick brush. She arrived in time for the soft knock on the door. She opened it quickly. "Daniel, what's happening?"

But he strode past without a word, and after a moment Erin followed him into the living room. He was pacing furiously. She watched him with growing

303

concern. Daniel never let anything rattle him.

"So what's up?" she asked, keeping her voice low so she wouldn't wake her roommate.

"You know that project I'm working on?" She nodded. "Well, it just shifted into a new phase of operation. They want me permanently on site ASAP. I'm leaving at the end of the week." She was stunned. "I just got off the plane — I didn't realize it was so late. But I needed to talk to you." He stopped pacing and dropped onto the sofa. "I can't bear the thought of moving away from you."

"I'm sure you'll find some other girl to rescue."

Her words stung, and he looked at Erin with a bewildered expression. "I thought you felt the same way?"

She saw the hurt in his eyes. "Losing you is the most painful thing that's ever happened to me," she managed to get out evenly. "It's making me kinda bitchy."

He stared at her in surprise. "You're not losing me. Do you think I'd let a job come between us?" Relief washed over her. "But we do need to make some decisions."

She nodded and sat on the arm of the sofa, not touching him. "Shoot," she said pensively, holding her breath.

Waking in Daniel's apartment a year ago was like waking from a long nightmare.

In the morning, he'd convinced her to tell him everything. Then he'd made a call to his boss and just-like-that it was all taken care of. The charges dropped, as if they'd never been. He bought her clothes and helped her find a job — a good job — and a great apartment, complete with roommate.

It was unbelievable to her that anyone could be so generous.

He'd explained that when he was fourteen, his mother had become seriously ill and his father's back injuries were making it hard for him to keep working. The family was on the verge of losing everything. And then Simon Cartwright appeared.

Agency headhunters, who regularly assessed high school students across the country, had evaluated Daniel as a computer design whiz kid, and Simon was quick to enlist the young genius. He'd also paid for his mom's expensive surgery and set his dad up with a comfortable pension. Daniel felt he owed Simon a lot, but Simon said he got back far more than he gave, for the young man had singlehandedly designed the Agency's defense systems for their new company site.

Daniel never forgot how blessed he was. He swore that whenever he saw a real chance to help someone, he'd pass those blessings on.

Hearing this, Erin expected that once she was settled into her own place, he would fade from her life. But they'd only grown closer.

"I think we have a couple of choices," Daniel was saying. "We could either see each other two weekends a month or . . ." he hesitated. "Or we could get married and see each other every day." A huge smile split her face. She leapt across the couch, landing hard against him and sending them both rolling onto the carpet.

Daniel laughed. "I'll take that as a yes," he said, squeezing her close. She planted a kiss on his lips, looking into his face. He studied her intently. "We're soulmates, Erin. Nothing will ever keep us apart — we won't let it."

Erin stood on the hilltop watching in horror as the starship screamed across the crowded tarmac towards the thousands of people crammed inside the apron fighting to get out of the path of the oncoming monster. They didn't have a chance. The giant rolled over them, crushing many to death instantly and spraying high-octane fuel across the survivors as it continued to plow onwards. It smashed through the terminal building crammed with passengers, and then charged through the refineries — killing the workers and sending molten metal ripping into the air like flaming shrapnel. Fire roared down the trail of rocket fuel, blazing back through the terminal and across the tarmac, engulfing thousands, while fiery metal slammed into the women and children jammed together on the road outside the spaceport. Their screams brought wails of anguish from those on the road above, but moments later the fuel depot exploded, drowning out their dreadful cries.

"Erin, is that you?" a woman asked in shock. "My god, are you alright?" Erin didn't respond. "Erin, don't you know me? It's Brenda," she said, checking her for injuries. "You're dirty, but you're okay," she pronounced in relief. "How long have you been sitting here? Come on, you'd better have someone take a look at you," she advised, taking Erin by the arm.

But Erin jerked herself free. "I'm waiting for Daniel."

"What do you mean?"

"His ship will be landing soon."

Brenda looked at her in sudden alarm. She considered for a moment before saying, "You don't want Daniel to see you looking like this, do you? Your face and clothes all dirty, and your beautiful hair a matted mess — you'd scare the poop out of him!" Erin managed a half-smile. "Why don't you come with me and we'll get you cleaned up. He'll know where to find you."

Erin looked at her uncertainly, and finally nodded in agreement.

The small gymnasium was crammed with hundreds of women and children, their makeshift beds lying close together on the floor, their few possessions stacked on top. The room hummed with the constant flow of people coming and going, arguing and complaining, children at play, and exhausted adults trying to keep them in order.

Amongst the noise and confusion sat Erin, oblivious to it all, her ears turned inward. Someone spoke to her, but she stared blankly, uncomprehending, hearing only Daniel, his voice full of love and reassurance. She clung to that voice and the promise it held.

The person spoke again, insistent, and Erin motioned her off, but the woman remained. Erin closed her eyes, fighting against the sound washing Daniel away.

"Erin! Snap out of it!"

A stinging sensation flamed across her cheek. Startled, she focused on Brenda. Daniel was gone.

"I'm sorry, Honey, but you scared me."

Erin raised a shaky hand to her face. "I guess I should say I needed that."

Brenda sighed in relief: Erin was okay.

She sat down beside her on the few blankets that made up Erin's bed. "I came to tell you some good news."

"That'll be a change."

"I'm getting married."

Erin stared at her in shock. "I don't understand . . . . Why?"

Brenda looked away from her accusing eye, saying quietly, "It's the right thing to do." She paused, and then said more firmly, "I loved Bill, but he's gone. And life will never be the same." She gave a choking sigh. "I'm so scared — alone with two kids on this horrible planet. How can I manage? I have to think of them. It's the only thing that matters." She sat up straighter and her voice became stronger: "The Church is right. We *should* marry again, and right away. It'll make things normal — at least less abnormal. And marriage will give my kids some security. And let's face it, with so few men, I can't afford to wait. There won't be a second chance."

Brenda pushed away thoughts of her dead husband; she couldn't afford to mourn for him any longer. Forgive me, Bill, she prayed.

Erin shook her head, incredulous. "So who is he?"

Brenda hesitated. "His name is Joel — Joel Normand, I think."

"You think!" Erin shouted, causing several heads to turn in their direction.

"I know it seems screwy, but life *is* screwy now!" Brenda replied heatedly,

306

feeling defensive and guilty. She studied Erin and her anger dissipated as she came to the realization: Once I'm gone, Erin won't have anyone to look out for her.

Gently, she reminded Erin, "Months ago, Mallory offered you a place at HQ. I bet that offer's still available. You could be with people you know — get away from all these noisy kids," she added with a smile.

"What's the point," Erin shrugged. "It won't get Daniel's ship here any faster."

Trying to hide her dismay, Brenda forced her smile to stay in place.

Erin left the shower stall and was soon headed down the narrow corridor, past several open doorways. The voices of the women preparing for bed were a dull background noise to Erin's ear. She took no notice of them, too deep within her fantasy.

One young woman groaned loudly. "I can't believe I got my period again. It feels like I just finished!" She went to her doorway and shouted down the corridor, "Shelby, what's the date?"

A moment later, a voice shouted back, "April 16th!"

The words passed over Erin almost unnoticed, but some part of her brain caught them up, repeating them like an annoying echo until they had her complete attention.

No one saw her slump against the wall or blindly grope the rest of the way to her room. She shut the door with effort and collapsed onto the bed.

April 16th. Our anniversary — and he's not here.

Reality began to seep in. Her chest felt constricted. She could hardly breathe. A deep cold spread through her limbs as she faced the truth.

Daniel is dead.

As she accepted this fact, Erin saw that she'd been living like an automaton for a long time now: clearing land, planting and harvesting, moving from the gymnasium to one of the newly constructed dormitories, all in a dream.

Her blank stares were so unnerving that the other women had refused to share a room with her. Even her few Earth friends no longer made the pointless effort to visit. But she'd been oblivious to her isolation, as she'd been oblivious to everything else.

Now the illusions were stripped away and cold reality was gripping her mind.

Desolation descended, blotting out all but one idea:

Without Daniel, my life is nothing.

A sudden compulsion took hold, and she rose up, slipping unnoticed from the women's dormitory.

307

The rain was coming down in a solid sheet, plastering her hair and nightgown against her body as she continued on, walking purposely towards the river. Its roar could be heard from a long way off, the water swelling high. Heavily overcast, the night was dark, and walking amongst the trees with the intense rain in her face made it difficult to see—

Then she was falling and her hand automatically shot out to save herself.

When she hit the water, she was grasping a vine.

The current yanked at her hard and she almost lost her grip, but she managed to hold on as her other hand came up to assist.

She was fighting for her life.

The vine was slippery beneath the leaves, and her struggles were ripping them off. She looped the vine around her wrist and it tightened painfully, yet she was able to pull herself slightly closer to the bank.

Erin looped it again, and pulled again, the vine biting deeper into her flesh. Slowly, she inched herself forward.

The bank was finally in her grasp when the vine snapped, throwing her off balance. She groped wildly, her hand striking a tree root — she lunged for it, slamming her body hard against the rough edges.

Ignoring the pain, she pulled and kicked her way out of the water, heaving herself past the root and over the edge to safety. She lay on the muddy ground, exhausted and confused.

"But I want to die," she moaned in bewildered pain.

Tears rolled down her cheeks, mixing with the rain, her grief coming out in harsh sobs until at last she lay spent. The rain abruptly eased off, as if it too had given all it could.

Why can't I die?

And with sudden insight she understood that she had.

Just as I died when Daniel fished me out of the river, giving me a new life. But now, the sheltered beloved wife of Daniel Wassermann is no more.

Who remains? she wondered.

Gradually Erin became aware of her body, grown numb from the wet and cold. She got stiffly to her feet, removing the vine from her injured wrist.

Feeling her way carefully in the dark, Erin turned towards the townsite and the new life that waited there.

Althaia looked at the locket in her hand through a blur of tears.

With a tired sigh, she returned the jewelry to the felt pouch.

It had been a long vision.

The books and papers Robert had so strenuously requested she study stood untouched where she'd left them earlier.

After a moment's consideration, she chose to leave them sit a little longer.

When I'm rested, she thought, I will make the effort required of me.

# CHAPTER 34

ROBERT PACED outside the door to the eve-cloister, making a vain attempt to appear indifferent.

How long has he been in there? Robert thought. I should have hidden inside the chapel. He's so blind and deaf he'd never have known. I could have coached her with hand signals, and now it's too late.

She isn't ready.

There was a fumbling sound from behind the narrow door, and a moment later it eased open to allow Father Billy to tap his way out. Robert studied the man for signs of agitation.

"May I escort you to your rooms, Father?" Robert offered.

The priest nodded. "You are very respectful, my son."

As Robert guided the old man down the stairs, he conversed with him cautiously: "What a great honor to be called from retirement to serve the new king."

"Indeed it is, my son," Father Billy said in a shaky voice. "I know I'm old and blind. But I will serve the Chairman as well as I served his father."

"His Highness understands your loyalty. It was the reason he recalled you."

"A young King needs those he can trust around him," he wheezed noisily.

"I am certain he can count on you."

As they drew near Father Billy's suite, Robert dared to ask: "Did you say you needed transport, Father?"

"Transport?"

"To visit with Bishop Stehr."

"What? Stehr? Good God, no!" Father Billy stated emphatically. He paused and then lowered his voice to a harsh whisper, "Could never abide the fellow. Always smells of sour milk." He chuckled mightily, and Robert joined in — his relief making it easy as he realized the priest was not about to report Althaia to the bishop.

Robert deposited the still-chuckling priest inside his door before hurrying to William's apartments.

Tell me," the Chairman commanded the moment Robert was admitted to his presence.

"It went well, my Lord."

William gave a silent prayer of thanks. "You have performed exceptionally."

"It was only my Duty."

"This was beyond the call of Duty."

"Nothing is beyond my Duty to you, Sire," Robert declared, bending on one knee.

William put his hand upon Robert's shoulder. "You are a true friend, Robert."

Feeling unworthy of such praise, Robert rose, saying, "I believe the eve will benefit from further instruction."

"Yes, yes, whatever you consider necessary."

William studied Robert in admiration, thinking, Such a brave man.

The Chairman turned away, strutting slightly as he announced in the bragging tone used by males when speaking of mating: "I must give the eve a little more instruction myself." And he passed Robert a meaningful look.

"Yes, Sire," Robert answered, keeping his face and voice neutral. "The hope of an impending heir will certainly keep the Church at bay."

Becoming somber, William asked, "How long, Robert, before they tire of waiting?"

"I do not know, Sire. But I fear it will be soon."

"I believe you're right."

"Let us pray for a quick seed in the womb," Robert said with pretended encouragement.

William said nothing.

"He has trained her well," Pope Validus said, as he eased himself behind the massive desk within the papal office. "Old Father Billy detected nothing out of the ordinary."

"Would he have said the same if he'd eyes to see with?" Cardinal Vecker commented dryly.

The Pontiff grunted with humor. He said thoughtfully, "A more pressing question, Vecker, is how long do we allow William to amuse himself before demanding her Expulsion?"

"The sooner we are rid of this dangerous pestilence, the better."

"Yes, her presence is a threat, as was that strange male's. But she is locked away — none but William sees her."

"And that captain of his."

"Yes, the captain . . ." the Pontiff said.

"God knows what kind of influence she's exerting on our sheep of a Chairman."

"We should not be *too* critical of the strangers, Vecker. They have performed more than one service for us. William is now free of both the neuter-madness and his brothers."

"But what have the strangers offered in their stead?" Vecker demanded grimly.

"Ah, yes, that is the question." Validus became thoughtful. "We cannot act against her — not now. William is still very salvageable, given time. We must treat him with leniency. Let him keep her a little while yet."

"And if she is with child?"

"Then he keeps her longer."

"I protest the wisdom of this decision," Cardinal Vecker stated dispassionately.

"If she births a son, William will not object to her removal," Validus said. "Nor will he object to the return of the Church within the Palace. He will do nothing to jeopardize his son's claim to the throne."

"We hint at the child's unsuitability because of his dam?"

"Correct."

"I withdraw my protest," the cardinal said coolly. "But I do not think William will ever sire a son. He was saturated with that drug. He will not recover."

"Very possibly," Validus agreed. "Begin screening the Chairman's cousins. How many are there?"

"Three, Your Holiness."

"Only three? Pity. Sometimes I think we're far too zealous in our thinning of the herd. Well, let us pray there's a suitable ruler amongst them."

Looking doubtful, Cardinal Vecker withdrew from the presence of Pope Validus.

Alone, the Pontiff became lost in thought. If only you knew, my dear Vecker, how fiercely I must sit on my own impatience. For I am as eager to meet this strange eve as you are to destroy her, for I have many questions for this stranger — many questions. He paused, considering: I must see to this inquisition personally. I am certain her answers will not be fit for any ears but my own. Then

312

Vecker can have his way with her. Not that it will be a public Expulsion — too many have seen her already.

So, young Willie, how do you manage to mate an eve that terrifies all who look upon her? Perhaps you're not quite the weakling we believe you to be?

"You did your work," Robert praised Althaia. "The priest was convinced of your piety."

A small smile appeared on Althaia's lips. "It was not difficult. He was often asleep while I spoke the confession. And during the penance he slumbered entirely."

Robert grunted, remembering his frantic pacing. Then he cautioned: "But you must continue to study. We can't depend on his need for sleep."

"I will continue to study," she assured him. After a moment, she asked, "What is, to embroider?"

Robert shook his head. "I do not know. Did the priest use this word?"

"Yes. He explained that my duties within the palace will be unlike any that I was taught at school, and that the over see-er will instruct me in all that I will be required to know. He said I must learn to embroider and do tapestry, and other such crafts, as this is now the atonement the Church demands of me."

"I know nothing of such things," Robert said, suspicious of the Church once again.

"The priest instructed me to embroider a religious scene on a piece of material, as part of my penance. I have two weeks to complete the task." Althaia lifted the pillow near her hand, the one she always brought for Robert's use. "There is a room within the harem that is filled with materials for creating carpets and tapestries and bed coverings, and also pillows such as these." She stroked the threads sewn into a picture. "Could this be the embroider?"

Robert studied the scene: green mountains with red rivers running through them, yellow flames licking the edges. "That looks like the formation of New Eden." Then he commented: "The stitching is poorly done."

"Yes. All the pillows and tapestries within my rooms are flawed in some form. I believe I now understand why." Robert looked at her in question. "These flaws would not be acceptable to the priests?" she asked.

"No, the priests always demand perfection." Robert studied the image on the pillow, saying, "You must sew a picture like this? Can you?"

Will you? Robert thought, recovering from this further evidence of Church deceit.

313

Soft materials and excessive decorations were known to be used by the clergy, especially within the Vatican. But to allow such things into the hands of eves went against all Church doctrine.

Althaia paused, fingering the threads. "I will attempt to learn this embroider. It has a creative aspect that appeals to me."

"You'll copy a picture from one of the pillows?"

"Yes, I can do so," Althaia confirmed.

"I'll question the overseer for information. He can prepare you for more of these unusual demands."

Robert went quiet for several moments, and Althaia could sense he was readying himself for some challenge. She waited.

"Before Frayne . . . left, he asked me to give you something," Robert announced, putting his hand inside the small pouch at his waist. "It was a gift he received from the Chairman," he continued, extracting the slim gold chain and dangling it before her. "Be certain your husband does not see it."

This was indeed a challenge, for not only was it forbidden to give gifts to an eve, but to give away a gift from the Chairman was considered the highest insult, even treasonous — in his old belief system. "It's very old, from the time of the Ancients."

"Yes," Althaia said, staring at the chain and knowing Frayne's intent: to give her the potential to see all that had happened to him each time he'd put on that necklace.

Thank you, wise and loving friend, she thought.

"You can have it," Robert said, moving it closer when she did not reach for it.

I expected her to just take it, he realized in surprise.

"Thank you," Althaia said, coming out of her reverie.

He grunted and prepared to leave. "We'll resume your lessons in the morning — don't be late," he said, knowing she was always early.

Since accepting that this strange eve did indeed possess humor, Robert sometimes found himself trying to illicit a reaction from her. He did not question why.

Althaia managed a slight smile at Robert's jest, distracted by the necklace. He was barely out of the chapel before Althaia was entering trance, the delicate chain held against her heart.

314

# CHAPTER 35

ALTHAIA WAS now ready to let the necklace take her into the ancient past.

The visions of Frayne's time with William and Robert had been informative. And to see Frayne once again had brought joy to her heart. But she could not delay the ancient visions any longer; she must allow them or they would be forced upon her.

It was still unsettling to have such a basic right denied to her — the right of choice — and Althaia questioned again how Universal Law could be so disrupted.

It is impossible to change the Laws of the Universe, Althaia thought with sudden passion. And a moment later she stopped in realization: If that is true — which I know it is — it could only mean that, at some level, I have chosen this for myself . . . .

And that thought, although perplexing, was also reassuring, for there was still order to the Universe.

I must stop resisting and simply allow, she reminded herself. Clarity will come at the appropriate time.

Relaxing, she permitted the trance to come over her.


"Bishop Alexander — I mean Pope Pius Alexander will see you now."

Father Neil rose, smiling in sympathy at Father Theodore. A full year had come and gone, yet he too had difficulty thinking of his uncle as Pope. The assistant returned the smile as he ushered Father Neil through the doorway.

"You wish to see me, Your Holiness?"

The Pontiff beckoned his nephew deeper into the office. "You may sit," he offered, indicating the hard looking-chair positioned before his desk. Father Neil perched stiffly upon it, waiting to hear the reason for this summons.

"It gave me great pleasure when you announced your vocation to the priesthood, and I kept my eye on you during your years in seminary. You were an exemplary student and a credit to your late mother. I'm afraid I was guilty of pride in your achievements, and tried to do what little I could to help your career — but nothing you didn't deserve." His face became grave. "So it now distresses me to learn that you are once again in danger of besmirching your flawless record."

The young priest's face colored slightly as he recalled the harsh reprimand he'd received his one day working inside the fields. But he'd been an obedient servant to the Church since then.

"What do you mean, Your Gra — Your Holiness. What have I done?"

"I am told you are keeping company with a woman: one of the Chairman's wives."

"But it's nothing, we —"

"You are to cease the association at once."

"But I assure you that —"

"Not another word on the matter. You will remember your vows and obey."

Father Neil had to struggle hard to keep from protesting further. The Pontiff saw this and said in a milder tone, "My son, I'm not suggesting that your relationship with this young woman is anything that it shouldn't be. I do understand that you are close in age and this can make friendships easy. But our position is not yet established on this new world. And, until it is, we must all be highly circumspect in our behavior. The future of the Church depends upon it. I know I can rely on you to co-operate fully."

"Of course, Your Holiness. You know I will do all I can to support the Church."


Althaia felt a surge of energy as time took a jump forward.


Father Neil strolled from the schoolyard, looking expectantly down the slope towards Market Street, but he was disappointed. He shook it off, feeling childish.

Still, he thought: Market days are our only chance for a real visit; church socials allowed only polite conversation.

He continued to stare down the hillside, refusing to recognize how much these encounters had come to mean to him.

Then he saw her, a large basket of vegetables hanging from one arm. He waved in greeting, and when there was no reply he tried not to feel slighted — again berating himself for acting like a child. He smiled as Jillian approached and automatically bent to take the basket, but she wrenched her arm away.

"It's okay, it's not heavy," she said hurriedly.

316

Taken aback, he studied her closely, but at this attention she smiled unconvincingly and demanded to know how his day had been, her disinterest obvious.

"Jillian, what's going on? You're a bundle of nerves."

"Nothing," she reassured him hastily. "I'm fine — just a lot to do. It's nothing — really."

He was mystified by the lie, but didn't press her. They walked together in silence until the road forked and she was about to take leave of him. "Remember, I'm here if you need me," he managed to say before she hurried away.

Afraid she'd spill the whole crazy scheme, Jillian made her escape without a word. She could feel the priest's eyes following her up the hill to HQ.

Father Neil watched after her with concern, wondering what could be causing such anxiety. He waited until she was out of sight before turning to find Father Toby standing on the road, eyeing him with loathing.

Father Neil smiled pleasantly. "HQ looks quite spectacular when the light hits it at this time of day, don't you think?"

The other priest said nothing and moved on.

"You wanted to see me, Lieutenant Campbell?" Father Neil asked as he entered the heavily guarded office.

Cord nodded briefly and continued to study the compbook in his hand.

Taking a seat in front of the desk, Father Neil recognized the journal and began to understand the reason for this summons.

With a grunt, which the priest interpreted as disappointment, the lieutenant tossed the journal onto his desk. Without preamble, Cord began: "On the day the Chairman was assassinated, you walked from town with one of his wives, Jillian Cartwright."

Father Neil pretended to consider the question: "That's right . . . I believe I did. She was returning from the market."

"Did she say or do anything that seemed suspicious?" Cord demanded.

"I'm not sure what you mean, but nothing comes to mind."

"How well do you know her?"

Involuntarily, the priest's eyes darted towards the journal on the desk. "I used to see her often, but now rarely — usually at church."

"How did she seem that day? Did she say or do anything out of the ordinary?"

"No . . . I don't believe so. I don't remember if she did."

"Do you remember the basket she carried?"

With sudden insight, Father Neil knew what he needed to say: "That, I do

317

remember. She dropped it and everything fell out."

The lieutenant became alert. "You saw what was inside?"

"Yes, I helped put the stuff back — food mostly."

"Was there anything large enough to hide a gun?"

"A gun?" Father Neil answered in surprise. "No, there was nothing like that."

Cord stared at the journal on his desk. Disappointed, he said gruffly, "That'll be all."

The priest rose, hesitated briefly, and then nodded towards the compbook. "If you're finished with that, I'd like to return Ms. Cartwright's property to her," he managed to say steadily.

Cord grunted in surprise and, after giving the journal one last glare of suspicion, he snapped, "Take it then."

The priest lifted the compbook and quickly departed. He was sweating heavily, stunned by what he'd just done.

I've never lied like that in my life, he thought.

He was surprised at how easy it had been.

So Jillian, what have you been up to?

Father Neil now realized that she'd somehow been involved in those terrible events surrounding Simon's assassination. Her behavior that day clearly revealed as much. But she would never be a party to murder, especially Simon's, that much he was certain of. There had to be another explanation. But he didn't think the lieutenant was in the mood for explanations.


Father Neil was exhausted. The atmosphere of suspicion and threats inside the community was hitting the students hard, causing unruly behaviors in the classroom.

In their search for incriminating evidence, Agency guards had raided several residences this past week, taking mothers and stepmothers in for questioning — leaving homes in shambles and families torn apart.

Anyone associated with Mallory or those ten women shot to death outside HQ, automatically fell under suspicion.

Father Neil was grateful that none of those dead women were mothers.

Bleary eyed, he looked around his uncle's drawing room, studying the other occupants: Board members and clergy. Or rather, he corrected himself, faux clergy. He didn't know what they truly were, these newly ordained priests.

He was offended that his uncle expected him to relate to them as equals, though they'd less training than a novice.

When he thought of all the years of hard discipline, sacrifice, and study required before taking his own vows, his resentment swelled.

What my uncle's training program lacks in depth, it certainly makes up for in speed and arrogance, he thought bitterly as he studied the four newly ordained priests, who were all in their early twenties.

The usual humility associated with a newly frocked priest was distinctly absent in these young men, who seemed indecently at ease amongst this company of powerful businessmen and seasoned clergy, and even with the Pontiff himself.

They contributed to the conversation without hesitation, exposing their ignorance with every word, he thought spitefully. And were seemingly unmoved by the terrible events of the past week.

But, he was forced to admit, the entire company seemed to be similarly unaffected. In fact, the subject had been adroitly skirted — as had every topic of any importance.

Father Neil now regretted the several glasses of wine he'd consumed with dinner. He was much too tired to tolerate such boring company in an intoxicated state.

A yawn threatened to overtake him.

I need to lie down, he thought.

He slipped from the room, making an unsteady stroll to his uncle's darkened study. With a sigh of relief, he stretched out on the long leather couch. He was almost asleep when footsteps entered the room, disrupting his peace. He tried to ignore them, hoping they'd go away.

His uncle spoke with sharp impatience: "What is so vital that it can't wait until tomorrow?"

When the other man spoke, Father Neil recognized Tom Murdock's distinctive voice, but now all the warmth was missing. "I warned you that Simon's death was not for your convenience alone—"

"Be quiet!" the Pontiff hissed. "Someone could hear you!"

"No need for alarm," Tom Murdock soothed complacently. "Not with these guests. And those that don't know aren't likely to care. Although, they would enjoy having some dirt on you. Blackmail can prove very . . . satisfying."

"The reminder was unnecessary," the Pontiff replied heatedly. "Now I must return to my guests."

Father Neil heard the door open and close, followed by the sound of quiet laughter. It was not a nice laugh. "Very satisfying indeed," Tom Murdock gloated. "Oh, I do enjoy myself." Still chuckling, he left the room, leaving Father Neil lying on the couch frozen in disbelief.

My uncle is responsible for Simon's death!

To Father Neil, this was almost as shocking as the destruction of Earth.

But what about Mallory and those other women who were shot? How did they fit in? he considered dazedly. Were they killed to cover up the Church's involvement in political murder? Would they really do such things? Had they?

He was forced to recognize that, in fact, they had.

Jillian! he thought in sudden panic. And then he remembered: I haven't confessed yet; no one knows I lied to the lieutenant.

He wondered in amazement: Do I really believe a priest — a real priest — would violate the sanctity of the confessional?

If they can commit murder, they are capable of anything, Father Neil decided.

I don't know exactly what happened the night Simon was killed, but I do know the Church must never suspect that someone lived to talk about it. They must have no reason to think I may have lied to protect her.

Father Neil sat riveted, unable to believe his ears or believe what he felt happening around him, for as the Pope harangued them with outlandish and outdated quotes from that Holy but ancient tome, Father Neil felt the men actually accepting the Pontiff's words. No, he realized, as he watched them energetically nodding in silent agreement. Not accepting them — embracing them!

He could only sit in quiet shock as the Pontiff's words assaulted his sense of truth and righteousness.

Eventually he was moved to feel inside the pocket of his cassock, to grasp the thin gold chain inside there — and what he knew to be true. His mother had been a loving and caring woman who'd lived through a hard life and a harder death. He would not hear these words spoken against her — not by her own brother.

He was about to rise and leave the cathedral when he remembered Jillian.

No, I must not draw attention to myself, not on the matter of women, he thought. I must appear to accept all my Uncle's policies, no matter how offensive or insane.

Trying to close his ears to the noxious tirade, he held onto the chain and prayed it would soon be over.

Regaining his strength after such a long climb, Father Neil watched from a distance as Jillian sat deep in concentration, leaning over her sketchpad. They were far below her mountain meadow, but still it had taken him hours to reach.

She held the picture at arm's length, clearly satisfied with the results. Jillian looked beyond her pad, to the young priest standing at the edge of the small clearing, and her face lit up with surprise and joy. Tossing the sketch aside, she hurried towards him.

Smiling, Jillian grabbed his hands, squeezing tightly. She gazed up at him, noting the dark circles and the fresh pain in his eyes.

"What's happened?" she asked, her smile fading.

Father Neil shook his head. "Not now," he said, squeezing her hands briefly in return before releasing them. "I've only come to return your journal," he continued as he let the backpack slip from his shoulders. "I'm sorry I couldn't return it sooner. There was never a good opportunity."

"How did you get it?" she asked with increased surprise, watching him remove her treasured compbook.

"From the lieutenant," he explained, passing it to her.

She took it eagerly, holding it to her chest. "Really? I'm amazed he bothered. I thought he'd destroy it, if only for spite."

"Well, it wasn't exactly his idea," the priest admitted.

"Now I'm completely intrigued. Come have a seat and tell me all about it," Jillian said, tugging at his arm. Father Neil allowed himself to be led to the blanket. "Would you like some water?" she offered. He nodded and accepted the water bottle gratefully. "Now tell me," she ordered with a smile.

"Someone reported seeing us together on the day of the shootings, so I was brought in for questioning."

"What kind of questioning?" Jillian asked, becoming serious.

Neil hesitated. "They wanted you to be guilty. And I knew you weren't." He looked away, saying, "So I convinced them of your innocence."

"How did you do that?"

The priest shrugged. "I lied."

"You lied!" Jillian blurted out in astonishment, but quickly realized, "That's why they let me go . . . ." She put out a hand to touch his sleeve in gratitude. "You saved my life."

"I'm very thankful I could do it," he said, turning back to her.

"What did you tell them?"

"That I saw everything inside your basket."

"Oh," Jillian said, shifting uncomfortably. This time it was her turn to look away.

"It was all they needed to know," he said softly. "Then I asked for your compbook and took my leave."

"*That's* why you wouldn't even look at me," she said in sudden understanding, "so that they wouldn't suspect." Jillian turned to study him appreciatively. "I didn't realize you were so devious." A slow grin passed over her face. "I suppose it cost you a thousand Hail Mary's or something?"

321

"No, nothing," he said, his face stiffening.

"What do you mean?" she asked. But he didn't answer. "What's wrong?"

"Everything," Father Neil said, his voice low. He was silent a long time, but Jillian didn't push. "Things are happening," the priest continued, his words falling to a whisper. "Unbelievable, impossible things."

"What things?"

"God, I can't even say the words."

"I already know the Agency is out to subjugate the women. Is that what you're talking about?"

"It's worse than that — much worse," Father Neil said hoarsely.

"I know the Church is helping them."

"Helping them — it's *leading* them."

"Oh, my god. . . ." she said in shock.

"There's more—" he stopped, hating to say it aloud. "I know who's responsible for the deaths of Simon and Mallory and all those women." He couldn't go on.

"Who?" she croaked.

Unable to face her, the priest got to his feet, his head bent in shame as he announced in a strangled voice, "Tom Murdock for one, and . . . and my uncle." He heard her gasp. "I think he's gone a little mad. He must be, to do these things."

"And you haven't said a word about it?" she demanded.

He shook his head mournfully.

Jillian was instantly contrite. How dare I condemn anyone while Erin and I keep our mouths shut and play it safe.

She rose to stand behind him. "I'm sorry," she said. "I shouldn't have said that. You'd probably get yourself killed, and it still wouldn't change anything. Forgive me."

He turned to look at her. "There's nothing to forgive. You're right. I should speak out. But I can't. It could bring down the Church, and I can't do that."

"I understand, Neil, I really do. The Church is your family and it's hard to betray family — no matter how much they might deserve it."

"What would I do without you?" he asked, passing a hand over her hair. "You always seem to know how to reach me."

Their eyes met and then quite unexpectedly they were looking at each other in a very different light. Slowly he lowered his head to place his lips on hers. She responded warmly, pushing her tongue gently between his teeth. A flame shot through him with each flickering touch.

Moaning softly, he clutched her tightly and eased her to the blanket, his body covering hers. He pulled away to look deeply into her glowing face before losing himself completely in the demands of the flesh.

Recovering from their exertions, the two lovers lay contentedly on the blanket with Father Neil's cassock thrown casually over their nakedness. He tickled her neck with a blade of grass, laughing as he dodged the elbow she directed towards him.

Jillian studied his handsome face and a sudden apprehension came over her. As if reading her thoughts, he rolled over to stare deeply into her eyes. "I love you," he said, kissing her eyebrows tenderly. He sat up to dig inside the pocket of his cassock, drawing out the delicate gold chain.

"This was my mother's. I've been carrying it with me since the War." Carefully, he placed it over her head. "I want you to wear it: a reminder that I'll love you always."

She looked down at the token, reassured and happy. Only one cloud remained. "I just hope the cracks are big enough," she murmured.

"What do you mean?"

"Never mind," she said, pulling him back down to the blanket. "Just love me."

"Have they completely lost their minds?" Jillian demanded, listening to the cries of congratulations coming from the dormitory. "That makes at least twenty women marrying Alan Chandler in the past month — and he had ten wives to start with! And he's not the only one either. All the Board members are carrying on in the same ludicrous fashion — as well as a few others. What can these women be thinking?" Exasperated, she flopped backwards to lie beside Erin on the blanket.

They were lying in the sun, on the sparse grass growing between the dormitories.

Without opening her eyes at this impassioned outburst, Erin said, "I hear there's plenty complaints about the lack of conjugal bliss."

"Not to mention the living conditions!" Jillian exclaimed, missing Erin's humor. "Just one big room with mattresses on the floor. No showers and only two toilets. You can't call them dorms, they're just barracks — and they're not even close to the main house!"

"Any work started on the promised housing?" Erin asked idly.

"Not yet. Everyone's supposedly waiting until after harvest. Which reminds me: Lydia said Nick Hargreaves is giving his wives shares in the farm — as a wedding present. So they'll be part of the family business — at least that's what he *said*."

323

"I heard others were doing the same . . . that guy with the lumber mill, for one."

A young woman burst upon them. "I'm getting married!" she exhaled breathlessly, a mix of excitement and exhaustion.

They looked up, startled by her sudden presence looming over them.

"Congratulations," Jillian responded politely. Erin said nothing.

"You two are such clouders!" she complained, and staggered off in disgust. Moments later, they could hear her announcing the news inside the dorm and the happy shrieks of congratulations that followed.

"That's the sixth one for this dorm in a week," Jillian said. There was no response from Erin. "And five last week," Jillian continued. "We're down to fifteen — even less in some of the other dorms."

"Good. We'll have the place to ourselves soon," Erin said, stretching contentedly.

Jillian gave her a speculative look. "So, what do you think — about the shares? It seems fair, doesn't it?"

"I guess. But this way he doesn't have to pay them wages 'cause they're working for themselves — family business, yuh know."

"Right . . . ." Jillian was thoughtful a moment. "But he *will* have to give them a share of the profits. Legally, they're entitled."

"And if he says there are no profits, who they gonna take their case to?"

"Oh, back to that." She paused. "It seems to be happening, doesn't it?"

Erin glanced at her and took pity. "Don't get all gloomy, we're just speculating. The deal could be legit."

"At least we don't have to worry about our wages."

Not for now, Erin thought grimly.


"Jillian!"

She stopped short, as did the rest of the female crew returning to the fields.

They saw a woman hurrying towards them, obviously in a state of panic. The rain-soaked ground was aggravating her struggles with the gravity, forcing her to a halt.

Jillian dashed over to meet her. "Lydia, what's happened? What was that noise earlier? It sounded like gunfire."

"They shot them!" Lydia gasped out. She dropped to her knees, fighting for breath, exhausted by her long trek.

"Who was shot?" Jillian demanded as the other women converged around them.

324

"The strikers — on Chandler's Farm. They wanted their pay — and they shot them!" She began to cry.

Several voices began asking questions at once, but Erin cut them off with a jerk of her hand, demanding harshly, "Who shot them?"

"The guards!" Lydia wailed, crying harder.

Jillian looked at Erin. "It's happening — it's really happening."

Without a word, Erin turned and strode back toward the dorms. The twenty-two other women hesitated before following after her.

"Where are you going?" Jillian asked as they hurried to keep up.

Erin marched inside one of the dorms and went straight to her room. She reached up to a top shelf and brought down a suitcase, tossing it onto the bed. The women crowded inside the room as best they could, the rest stood out in the hallway, straining to hear.

"What are you doing?" Jillian demanded.

"Packing," Erin answered shortly, pulling her belongings off the shelves.

"But *why*?" Jillian asked with more force.

"They'll be coming for us."

"Who's coming for us?" someone asked shrilly.

"They can't leave us loose, not after this," Erin announced.

"Jillian, what's she talking about!" another woman asked in mild hysteria.

There was an impatient knock at the outside door and the twenty-two women froze, looking at each other in fear. Erin finished her packing and picked up the case, moving through the press of bodies to answer the knock, the frightened women trailing after her.

A newly ordained priest was waiting on the stoop, a few armed guards standing stiffly on the ground behind him. He eyed Erin's suitcase in surprise, giving her a speculative look before announcing with an artificial smile: "Ladies, I have happy news for you all. Today is your wedding day."

"It's way too soon, Helen," Erin stated.

"We need to act quickly!" the woman in her late thirties said with desperation. "The longer we wait the more entrenched they become."

"You don't have enough support — it won't work without the numbers," Erin said flatly.

"They're all too afraid," Helen said in disgust. "All they can think about are those dead strikers and the women who killed Simon." Erin's eyes slid towards Jillian, but her face remained neutral. "And now that Martinez and the others have been dumped inside the desert for trying to move out of the colony, it's got

325

everybody cringing like rabbits!"

"They just want to stay out of trouble and stay alive," Erin said. "I understand that."

"So you won't join us?"

"It's doomed to fail," Erin predicted.

"Not if we have people with military training."

"I was a *cadet* for chrissakes."

"But you know how to fight — and how to use a gun," Helen pressed her.

"True," Erin acknowledged. "Do you have any?"

Helen squirmed slightly. "We're in the process of acquiring some."

"How? And how many?" Erin countered.

"I can't say."

"How much help are you getting from the outside?"

"You mean, men?" Helen asked.

"Yes, men."

"We've made some firm contacts."

"How many?" Erin continued to question her.

"Some."

"Not a lot then."

"No, but they're very keen," Helen added with a positive note.

"Keen is good, but numbers would be better." Erin was silent, considering. She looked at Jillian for a long moment, and then said abruptly, "Okay, I'm in — but when the fighting starts I work alone."

"Fine," Helen agreed quickly. "However you want it. But you'll help train us — teach us hand-to-hand combat, right?"

"I'll do what I can," Erin acknowledged. "Oh, I also need access to outside contacts. I don't need to know who they are, but I want the use of them."

"Agreed." Helen broke into a smile. "Welcome aboard."

"Feels like I just signed aboard the Calypso," Erin said dryly. She leaned back against the wall and winked at Jillian, who was staring at her in disbelief: Erin has joined a revolt?

Helen stood up. "You won't be sorry Erin. We'll win our freedom back, you'll see."

"Yes," Erin said. "I believe we will."

Jillian lay wide awake, waiting. In the darkness she saw Erin's outline move noiselessly past the sleeping women and disappear inside the scrub-room. The scratchy sound of wooden shutters being opened reached her ears moments later, and then silence.

Staring at her luminous watch, Jillian waited four minutes before following after.

She crawled through the narrow window of the scrub-room and lowered herself onto the ground. Jillian listened, straining for sounds of Erin and the guard, but all she heard was the light patter of rain on the roof.

Bypassing the recently sown fields of grain, she moved carefully through the darkness towards the darker night of the trees, always on the alert for a roaming guard. At last she came to a fence that marked the end of her husband's property. She climbed the barrier quickly and entered the safety of the forest, almost dry under the thick canopy of branches. She rested a few moments, and then moved deeper into the trees where Father Neil was waiting.

She flung herself into his arms, and for a long moment they clung together. "I thought I'd never hold you again," the priest whispered, burying his face into her hair. "When I heard you were married, I almost went crazy with jealousy."

Jillian pulled away, drawing him farther into the trees. Before he could touch her again, she announced quietly, "Neil, I'm pregnant."

"Is . . . is it your husband's?"

"Of course not. Would I drag you out here if it was? I haven't been with anyone but you."

"Oh, God," he said hoarsely, holding her hard against him. "What have I done to you."

She pushed him away. "You haven't done anything." She was stern. "I won't have regrets, not now."

"But when the pregnancy's discovered, God knows what they'll do. They've gone completely—"

"It won't *be* discovered," she cut in emphatically, and abruptly grabbed his hands, squeezing hard. "Erin and I are planning to escape."

"What?"

"We can't stay here, not now."

"But there is no escape! They'll track you down before you're a day away."

"We're going north, they'll never expect that. It'll give us a huge head start."

"A head start to what? There's nothing out there but rock!"

"But we'll be free! And I'd rather die than bring our child into this terrible place."

He was silent, pondering her words. "Our child," he said quietly. "That was something I never expected in my lifetime. And now I'm going to be a father."

"Yes," she said evenly.

"Okay, I'm coming with you," he said with sudden decision, straightening his

327

shoulders determinedly. "What do I need to do?"

Jillian squeezed his hand again, this time in relief. She let go and pulled a piece of plazpaper from her pocket, obviously torn from a book, her small handwriting squashed between the margins.

"Here's a list of supplies we'll need. Get what you can, but do it carefully; you don't want to arouse suspicion."

"How much time do I have?"

"Three weeks, maybe more. I'll send a message. Our escape has to coincide with — with another event. I can't explain — I must get back."

Jillian kissed him hard and broke away.

"Be careful, my love," Jillian heard him call softly as she disappeared into the darkness.

"You've got to get some better shoes. You need hiking boots," Erin said.

"Where the heck am I supposed to find those?"

Erin shrugged. "You can get anything if you've got something to trade."

"Like what?"

"Your compbook." But at Jillian's look she added quickly, "Or your gold chain. But a watch is best."

"Do you really expect someone to trade their boots for a piece of jewelry?"

"If they've got five pairs of boots and no jewelry, sure."

"Maybe . . ." Jillian said doubtfully

"We both need warmer clothes. It'll be cold farther north, and even colder in the winter." She touched the neckline of her shirt, considering, and with one quick motion unclasped the locket from around her neck.

Jillian looked at her in surprise, knowing what that locket meant to her.

Then she copied Erin's action, caressing the gold chain before placing it carefully on her sleeping mat.

# CHAPTER 36

"YOU ARE early," Althaia said in mild surprise as she entered the chapel for morning lessons. Robert nodded distractedly from where he sat on the floor, not taking his eyes from the catechism books before him. "You are disturbed." He nodded once more, but this time he looked up as she took her usual place upon a pillow. When she was positioned comfortably, her eyes rested upon him, waiting.

"I need to talk," he finally announced to the floor. "To . . . tell someone what happened to me." When she didn't respond, he made himself look towards her. "Will you hear me?" he asked with great difficulty, for a man never asked an eve for anything, let alone to be his confidant. She bent her head slightly to indicate her willingness.

Hesitant at first, Robert began to explain his gradual loss of faith as a child — chipped away through the years — and the effect this had had upon him. He sought to describe the night of Frayne's departure, trying to convey the suspense and the fear. He tried to explain his denial of Frayne and all that he represented. And then, when he saw Frayne's ship, how all the blinders had been stripped away.

"It was like being torn from everything I knew to be true and hurled into a place of madness." He stopped, recalling his fear. "It took only a small thing to save me — recalling my friendship with William. That, at least, was still true." He was silent a moment. "Now, all I want is time to think — and to reconstruct some sense of order inside me."

Althaia began by saying gently, "It may aid you to recognize that you were not as blind to the truth of Frayne as you believe you were." He looked at her in surprise. "I have come to identify you as a man of high moral principles. You would not knowingly guide children into danger, nor those wives. That is not in your character. Wouldn't you say your natural compulsion is to protect, and not to cause harm?"

Robert's surprise turned to recognition. Yes, he thought. I've always been so.

"But how could I know the truth and not know it at the same time? It seems like devilry to me. In my old beliefs," he added.

"Because you knew in your heart—"she began, but remembered that he might not accept or understand this concept, so she continued on a different tack. "And you knew in your abdomen and in your limbs, and in every fiber of your body." He was silent, listening intently. "Can you think of events in your life when you took action even though it went against reason, or what you were raised to believe was the proper code of conduct? And yet the results were successful — perhaps not only for yourself but for those around you?"

Robert nodded slowly, silently remembering: How many times as a boy did I feel compelled to act when logic — if I'd had any — would have said it was ludicrous or wrong? But those adventures led me to the truth about the Church. And by setting up Benji for the theft of that firecross I was able to protect myself and the younger boys from Benj's bullying.

"Yes," he said at last. "I remember doing so many times as a boy."

"And now as a man, "she said softly.

Robert was silent once more, letting the idea percolate, and he felt some relief knowing that he'd not deceived himself entirely. And with this understanding a guilt he'd not acknowledged was lifted from his shoulders as he realized that he had never intended to deliver the little eves to demons.

But his deep sense of confusion and even loss still remained.

Althaia sensed this, and after a few moments, she asked, "What of the men who accompanied you to the shuttle craft? Have they too lost their faith? Can they not relate to these feelings of distress?"

Robert shook his head. "It's a bewildering thing . . . they were terrorized to an even greater degree than I. And yes, their faith was shaken. But for some unfathomable reason they've transferred their allegiance from the Church and bestowed it on me."

"These men now worship you?"

"No," he said quickly, and paused for a moment, considering. "I would say that they are in awe of me — and a little afraid. I've walked upon the Unholy Lands, I've had contact with many eves, and conversed with an alien stranger while sitting on a vehicle of technology, yet I have survived unharmed and uncorrupted. Such things can be seen as miracles on New Eden. And now they look to me for direction and would follow me almost anywhere. But I'm more lost than they."

"You possess much inner strength," Althaia said quietly. "You will overcome the challenges that face you, and in time your confusion will pass." Robert merely grunted. "Your experience has, to a certain extent, freed you, and the men who accompanied you, from the fear that harnesses this planet."

"Yes. That it has done." But there are new fears to face, he thought with sudden stubbornness, unwilling to see any benefit to his suffering. After a moment, he stated bluntly, "You never seem afraid, not like our eves — always twitching and cringing."

"Fear was never part of my experience. Not as a child, nor as an adult."

"But you are even more . . ." he struggled for the right word, "*composed* than Frayne — and he's from the same planet."

"True. But we are not from the same Time."

"What do you mean?" Robert demanded, her words triggering old fears.

"As I have explained to you, my genetic coding is from another time."

"But what does that *mean*?" Robert demanded once again.

"Of course . . ." Althaia said, almost to herself. "I do not always recall the limited knowledge that exists on this planet." She paused, looking for a way to simplify her explanation. "You may recall that, on Mirandus, our people do not seek interactions with each other, they seek only to Realm: to stay focused on their worlds within. This ability to Realm is passed on from parent to child, but it was not always so. When the Realming was first discovered, very few people could master the practice. But we evolved — changed over time — developing this one characteristic through the centuries until it has now become the dominant trait amongst my people, passed on from generation to generation." She stopped to study his reaction. "Do you comprehend my words thus far?"

"I understand," Robert said. At least, I think I do, he amended silently.

"During the centuries before the Realming, our society passed through several stages or ages of development. These ages have been named according to the dominant cultural predisposition exhibited by our population during each time period, although many other strong characteristics existed in conjunction. The first stage was the Technological Age, followed by the Social Age, the Artistic Age, the Age of Enlightenment and the Age of Healing, and now, the Age of Realming."

She paused to study Robert's reaction before continuing: "Frayne and I were both born without the ability to Realm. Instead, we possess many of the characteristics from past ages. I was born with the traits and abilities from the Age of—"

"Healing," Robert finished for her, and gave a small smile as Althaia nodded, an amused look on her face. "And Frayne?" he asked.

"The Social Age. They were a gregarious people, with a deep need for human interaction. It has been painful for Frayne to exist so isolated on Mirandus. Even after discovering my existence, it was not easy for him," she continued. "My capacity for conversation could in no way equal Frayne's enormous fondness for the pastime." She smiled deeply. "But now he will no longer live in isolation.

Because of your insistence, he has returned to Mirandus with people who are genetically predisposed to live in community."

Robert looked away, remembering the violent males and cringing eves he'd piled into the little ship. He opened his mouth to explain, but closed it again. What harm to let her imagine otherwise?

"William was a friend to Frayne," Althaia stated, although Robert took it as a question and merely grunted, unaccustomed to hearing a man's name spoken by an eve — especially the Chairman's. "It was such a gift to him—" Althaia began, but stopped abruptly, for she'd nearly revealed her knowledge of that relationship. To do so would mean disclosing her ability to read the past, and she was not certain Robert was prepared for such awareness.

Robert nodded again, distracted by his own thoughts. "There's a question that confounds me," he announced abruptly. "Why does William not suffer over his loss of faith? He was thick as honey with the Church for most of his life. But he sheds it the first moment his brothers start whispering their lies. And then he befriends Frayne and *believes* his stories of Proximus, though to do so goes against the most basic tenets of the Church. But still, he doesn't act like one who's suffered a great loss of faith — in fact, just the opposite."

"But the Church was more than your faith," Althaia said gently. "It was your family." And she was suddenly grateful for her visions of the Ancient Ones, as they had made such things clear to her. "William had his own family. And I deduce that he was greatly devoted to them. The betrayal of his brothers would cause him far more pain than any betrayal that the Church may have perpetrated." She paused, considering. "Your upbringings have, in all probability, differed in many ways."

"I was an illegal," Robert explained. "A poor boy dependent on the mercy of the Church: raised to serve. William was born a prince, surrounded by wealth and power: raised to judge and possibly to rule."

"Different upbringings indeed," Althaia commented. "In addition, consider that any response to stimuli will be dependent on individual character; your feelings and reactions will be entirely unique to you."

Yes, he thought, that makes sense. He opened his mouth to thank her, and then realized with a shock what he'd almost done.

Giving thanks was not a common custom on New Eden. Men gave thanks to God and to the priests or to a royal magistrate, or perhaps to others in authority, but rarely, if ever, to a peer and absolutely never to an eve.

But why not? another part of his mind demanded. Hasn't she helped you more than any person in your entire life?

"Thank you," he murmured gruffly.

"You are most welcome," she answered, a knowing look in her eye.

It had taken William a full week to recover from the terrible fright of seeing that machine come to life. When at last he'd regained some composure, his mind leapt to an idea.

What if I could still experience some of the wonders of Frayne's world right here on New Eden, through his strange and frightening eve?

To experience just a small part of that world, William would risk a lot. Screwing up his courage, he'd plundered the museum, filling a sack with forbidden artifacts before once more returning to Althaia.

From that day forward, every visit to the eve was an education. And though he was often frightened, he no longer ran from the room. Still, he kept his distance from her. Always placing the sack of smuggled artifacts in the middle of the floor and backing away before allowing her to look inside. And while he enjoyed the information she shared, her voice continued to disturb him.

These past months, he'd learned much that thrilled his mind and senses, but his greatest discovery was the solar-powered chess game.

Chess was banned during New Eden's early history. It was considered too suggestive with its powerful queen and lesser bishops and, most damning of all, the attack on the king.

Althaia had done William a kindness by going into trance to discover the rules of the game. It had taken several visions, but gradually she was able to instruct William on how to move the pieces and on the game's objective.

Locked inside his rooms for hours, William would try unsuccessfully to best the computerized brain, which regularly informed him that he had made an inadvisable move.

He couldn't get enough of these wonders from the past, and each hour passed like an eternity while he did his duty as Supreme Court Judge, his impatience growing as case after case was prolonged by excruciating detail, with nothing considered too trivial for his attention. But finally it would end, leaving him free to play his chess game or to climb the stairs to the top floor for a mating session, as he always called it — even to himself.

In keeping with Mating Law, his visits were short. It took many calls on Althaia to thoroughly explore the possibilities of each sackload.

There was also a strict law on the number of mating sessions permitted daily with each wife. And though he could have gained access to her undetected through the secret passageway, this he wouldn't dare consider, for it led directly inside the forbidden harem. And no true man would risk his soul by entering.

No, he must be satisfied with his one visit a day.

Recently, during one of these sessions, the eve had tried to tell him that this phenomenon of energizing machines was a new experience for her also. But he did not believe it. He was also disbelieving of another claim:

"Science and technology are not permitted on your planet," Althaia had begun introducing her question. "How is it then that these artifacts come to be in your possession?"

"They're kept in the Royal Museum. Only the Chairman and his heir are permitted access. No one knows of its existence, not even the Church."

"The Church is aware," Althaia had stated. "It only presents the illusion of ignorance."

"How do you know this?" he'd demanded, suddenly fearful.

"I know this with certainty, but it is a knowing beyond explanation."

No, he did not believe her. How could he?

Now, he watched as Althaia held her hand on the three-prong plug of an ancient object. Its shape was reminiscent of the handguns from a time long ago, except that this had a barrel that was very blunt and much wider. It whirled into life, startling him. The motor struggled for a moment and then gave a high-pitched squeal before settling into a constant rhythm.

"Do you know what it does?" William called above the noise.

"The machine blows hot air. I deduce the purpose is for drying."

"Drying what?" The question had a challenge to it.

The answer is known to him, Althaia realized. He plays a game. "That, I cannot identify."

"Hair," he announced, pleased she hadn't guessed its purpose. "It's called a hairdryer."

They studied the machine in silence.

Abruptly an idea poured into Althaia's mind — an idea that would not be ignored. After a moment, she stated, "This machine is reminiscent of the ancient artifacts housed within your room for sitting."

William appeared momentarily startled. "Oh — you healed Frayne there — I'd forgotten." That seemed so long ago. Months it was now. How many have passed since I discovered Frayne gone? Four . . . ? Five . . .?

"I would make a request of you."

"What?" he asked, distracted.

"I request the opportunity to study a small number of artifacts suspended on the wall of your room for sitting."

"What!" he was dumbfounded.

"I am requesting—"

"I heard," he cut in harshly. "Request denied."

334

"May I inquire for what reason you deny my request?"

"Eves are not permitted to touch weapons."

"I understand." She was thoughtful a moment. "It is also forbidden for eves to have any exposure to science and technology. The Law also states that all conversation with eves is strictly forbidden. The Law also forbids any female to teach or instruct a male."

"This is different. You're asking for *weapons*. I can't ignore the Law on this."

"You believe I will harm your person with these weapons?"

William stopped the "yes" on his lips and closed his mouth, knowing he didn't believe it at all. Yet, to let the eve touch a weapon would be the highest sacrilege. He would not do it.

"I won't bring the weapons."

She nodded, accepting his verdict. Then she rose to her feet and walked from the chapel.

"You are to return immediately!" he shouted after her.

But she did not.

William was left to fume alone, shocked by such disobedience.

"This is an absolute outrage!" he roared, before storming from the eve-cloister in frustrated anger.

# CHAPTER 37

"YOUR CONFUSION has diminished," Althaia commented, as she collected the catechism papers she was to study.

"Yes, perhaps," Robert said, distracted. He sat cross legged upon the chapel floor, the hilt of his sword draped over a bent knee. He tugged at it, deep in thought, before blurting out, "At times I regret not leaving with Frayne." She looked at him in surprise. He continued more slowly: "I have always preferred my own company but now . . ." he trailed off, not knowing how to explain. "But now there's no common ground at all — as if I no longer belong on this world."

"Your beliefs are no longer those of your friends and comrades. This can result in a sense of isolation, as can the inward search for answers."

He nodded with feeling, adding, "On Proximus, I wouldn't be alone in this search."

"The inward search is no longer practiced on Mirandus."

"But the Realming . . . ."

"They Realm, yes, they explore the worlds within. But they no longer travel within their own personal world, the world of self."

He considered her words and then admitted, "I don't understand."

"The search to know one's self — the inner journey — is no longer practiced."

"I see . . ." he said, not seeing at all, but she understood.

"For many centuries, the inward looking was practiced by all on Mirandus as the way to enlightenment," she explained. "It was the means to understanding the self and our world, the universe and what you would call God." She studied Robert, looking for signs of confusion before she continued: "Gradually, the inward journey began to change. A small number of my people had uncovered a method for crossing into different Realms of Creation, to worlds of never-ending form and variety, each in a different universe."

"But there is only one universe," Robert stated with a touch of fear in his voice.

"For thousands of years, it was believed to be so by our Earth Ancestors, and then on Mirandus. Only in the last twelve hundred years has it been known otherwise."

"But *how* can they cross into such a place?"

"They cannot go there physically but only within the mind. They must release this universe completely from their consciousness and put their entire attention on these inner realms. It is the only method that permits intimate exploration — as if they were truly walking upon these worlds. The experience, I have read, is very tangible. The physical sensations like that of our own universe."

Robert was silent, trying to understand this outrageous idea that seemed steeped in the profane — in my old beliefs, he reminded himself firmly.

"When the Realming was discovered, it was believed by my people that expanded consciousness could be accelerated through the teachings of these worlds within. But it is clear now that the Realming did not advance growth. It has, instead, encouraged its opposite: stagnation. And it has led Frayne and I to seek aid from your world, in order to prevent our peoples' extinction."

"The Realming is responsible for the elimination of your people?"

"That which does not grow dies."

Robert stared into the distance. "And what is the cause of *our* elimination, I wonder?"

Surprised, she paused to consider all that she had seen in her visions of Frayne, but none had revealed this information.

"I was not aware that your population was in danger of becoming extinct."

"It would be an act of heresy to speak of anything amiss in the Garden of Eden," Robert stated, his voice bitter. "Our eves are dying, and how does the Church interpret such a calamity? We are winning the battle against evil — praise the Lord! But what will be their explanation when there's one eve left to us and she at death's door?"

"Only the women of your planet are dying?"

"If they sicken, they don't recover — not after the age of fifteen."

"All illness results in death?"

"More and more often, yes. Generations ago, all but the poorest men had at least four wives and the rich had hundreds of worker wives and dozens of breeders. Now the price of more than one breeder is beyond the means of many." Althaia had to recover from his offensive words before she could grasp Robert's question. "If I took you to a sick eve, could you tell me why she was dying?"

"It is possible that I could do so."

A frown creased his brow. "But there are no eves in the palace at present, and I have no access to others."

He pondered the problem.

337

"Is it your intent to discover a single cause for the deaths of all the women of New Eden?"

"Yes. Maybe somehow we could stop it." Though what he really meant was maybe Althaia could heal it. But she knew this.

Althaia began to offer tentatively, "It could be possible to uncover the root cause without a woman being present." He gaped at her in bewilderment. "But I would require a personal possession or even something she has touched regularly—"Althaia stopped and smiled. "I have the solution. Come," she said, rising from her cushion.

Mystified, he followed her from the chapel to the harem door. She pushed it fully open with effort, and then beckoned him inside. "You may enter."

But he stood immobilized, feet hammered to the floor.

"Do not be alarmed, the Church will not know of your entry." He didn't answer. "I will not reveal your crime," she added with a small smile.

But Robert backed away, shaking his head, turning towards the large door that separated the Chairman's wives from the rest of the palace. With quick strides he stood before it, his arm outstretched to escape Althaia's challenge, but abruptly he arrested the motion. Curling his hand into a fist, he dropped it back to his side.

What is wrong with me? he demanded of himself. Have I not been inside this very harem to remove the Chairman's wives? And how many times as a kid did I explore the eve school?

But it was never at their invitation.

I'm letting the Church jerk me around again! he realized with disgust. Their hooks are deep, but I refuse to let them rule my life any longer.

Squaring his shoulders, Robert turned towards Althaia, who was watching his inner struggle with a serene gaze. He found her countenance calming, and by the time he reached the harem entrance his natural curiosity began to take over. "What would you show me?"

Althaia moved inside without a word, and after a moment's hesitation Robert followed.

She guided him to the corridor that led past the eves' sleeping cubicles. As Robert walked through the narrow passage, he remembered the last time he'd set foot inside here. The fear and confusion, the frantic, quiet commotion as the eves were pulled from sleep to be thrust into the hidden passageway, and then into the night — and into a terrifying situation.

For the first time, Robert felt some disquiet at sending those women and children to such a frightening world. Although he knew Frayne would never harm them in any way, he understood that they, quite conceivably, could harm themselves.

338

Althaia stood waiting for him inside the common area. "Well?" he demanded, trying to hide his unease with a commanding tone.

"I must ask you to remain quiet and motionless while I am in trance," Althaia said, taking a seat on one of the benches that stood before the small cast iron stove.

Robert stood with feet apart, his arms crossed, a frown creasing his bewildered forehead as he watched Althaia place her hand upon the bench and close her eyes. She drew a deep breath, exhaling slowly before going very still. Nothing else happened, and Robert was about to demand an explanation when he remembered her request for silence.

Nineteen young women were huddled around the stove. The unnatural hunch to their backs was emphasized as they each bent over a small piece of fine linen, crafting pictures in colored thread with meticulous care. The single lamp positioned on the side table was inadequate lighting for the detailed stitching. The young women were clearly struggling.

No one spoke. Occasionally a woman would release her hold on the material to tweak nervously at her clothing, and this seemed to set off a flurry of nervous cloth twitching in the women around her. Then it would stop and they'd return to their sewing, as if nothing had happened.

A shadow fell across the women as another eve shuffled into the room, her back also bowed in a permanent stoop. Silently, they made space for her on one of the benches.

The new arrival stared at the piece of cloth in her hand as if at a foreign object. With a deep sigh, she threaded the needle, squinting in the dimness. Reluctantly, she bent over her work. There were only a few ratty threads sewn into the material, and she plucked these out impatiently. Then she began working the needle, her every movement fraught with difficulty. After several minutes an inarticulate noise erupted from her throat, shattering the silence. The women looked up at her in alarm.

"We were never trained for this devil's work!" she whispered angrily, throwing the sewing onto the floor.

Strongly agitated, the women grabbed at their tunics in frenzied plucking. The rebel rose to her feet, calmly watching the anxiety she'd caused before she raised a hand, wrenching the veil from her face. A shudder of fear coursed through the women like an electric charge. Several scrambled to their feet, exiting the common room in a hasty shuffle.

"No one will know!" the rebel whispered after them. "The overseer never comes near here unless our husband rings — and he never does!"

But they didn't slow their shambling stampede down the corridor.

She looked at the few remaining women, all staring at her with eyes big with fear. "I won't wear this!" she said, motioning to the veil. "Not when I spend my days inside harem. I was trained to garden and cook, and clean and sew clothes — not this forbidden decadence." This caused a flurry of cloth plucking. "Speak to me!" the woman whispered in a desperate tone.

"You mustn't behave so, Theresa," one brave soul whispered. "You'll be punished! You will learn the embroidery in time, as we all have."

"I don't *want* to learn!" she whispered back impatiently. "Can't you see? We were taught that decadence is evil and we responsible for it, and now the Church forces us to do this very thing as penance! What does that mean?"

"The Church is not to be questioned! You know it's the first sign of degeneration. Please stop," the young woman begged. "You are in terrible danger."

"Who is there to discover my sacrilege? I refuse to confess it, and we see no one but the overseer."

"God will know."

"God has already punished me."

"You dare risk your immortal soul!"

"I have no soul," she whispered back, her voice cold. "My pain has ripped it from me."

The women gasped in shock, studying Theresa with increased alarm. Then they hurriedly collected their sewing and rose from the bench.


Althaia remained motionless, eyes closed, digesting the vision. Never could she have imagined it possible to live with a spirit so deadened. What has been done to these women? What weight do they carry to bend their backs so deeply? Yet even as she wondered, she knew the answer: they carry the ills of this sickly world.

Now she understood her instinctive resistance to educate herself further on New Eden's women. With a deep clearing breath, she opened her eyes to look at Robert, who was studying her with intense interest.

"How do you go so still — as if you're not even alive?" he asked.

"It is a discipline learned in childhood," she said, rising from the bench. "I have the answer you seek."

"But how?" he asked, perplexed and a little nervous. "You did nothing."

"The women who once resided within this space used these benches many times. By placing my hand upon them, I can perceive some small part of their

340

experience: their personal history."

"I don't understand."

"I see history in visions."

Robert stared at her suspiciously. "You *see* history?"

"Yes, it is similar to a waking dream."

"How do you do such a thing?"

"It is . . . a talent I was born with."

Robert frowned, deep in thought. "You touch a thing and then you can see everyone who's touched it before you, and everywhere it's been?"

"Potentially, yes. But normally I see only those events that are relevant to my query."

Robert sat down on one of the benches, musing, "That's why William's been raiding the museum; he's getting you to read the history of the Ancestors."

"No, he has a different purpose in bringing the relics to me."

"What purpose?"

She paused, considering. "I do not believe William would wish me to disclose that information to you."

Robert grunted in surprise, still not used to being refused by an eve.

Out of the blue, he had a thought: "Do you also see into the future?"

She shook her head, no. "Although very rarely a vision of the future can be received. I have experienced one such vision."

"What did you see?"

"It predicted my journey across the stars to your planet. It demonstrated that taking this action would save my people from extinction. And so it has."

Robert was silent, once again reminded of the dubious cargo he'd sent back with Frayne. Perhaps it would be alright, after all. . . .

Althaia prompted him: "Do you wish to know what the vision revealed to me?" He nodded, becoming alert. "These women believe so utterly in their own destructiveness that they subconscious—" she stopped, remembering that she must simplify her explanation, "—that they have embraced a deep desire to remove their evil presence from this world. They die because they can no longer tolerate the agonizing pain and sorrow they experience from bringing corruption and death to their sons."

Robert stared at Althaia, thinking, We are taught that they are utterly immoral. That their will must be crushed, their bodies contained, else their wickedness will overwhelm our souls and deliver Mankind to Satan. But if they die of remorse and sorrow, how can it be said they've no morality?

Once again, the Church's lies are exposed.

Althaia continued: "They die because they have no will to live, and that I cannot heal."

341

"Then it is hopeless," Robert muttered.

"I would not diagnose the situation as hopeless, although it would require a significant effort from your society to arrest the process."

"Then it is indeed hopeless."

"It is possible for your world to change. You have done so."

"The Church would never allow it. One word against doctrine and it would mean instant Expulsion. They're the real power on this world, and not even the Chairman is safe from their reach."

"I did not know a Chairman could also be Expulsed."

"That's the hardest part of my duty — keeping William from being stoned out of Eden."

"Then by ensuring my safety through marriage, he has placed himself in danger. I have not been appreciative of his risk."

"He had his reasons."

"I have learned enough of your world to understand that concern for the life of an eve is not usual. It makes his gift that much sweeter."

"He's only using you to give him a taste of Frayne's world. That's all he can think about — it's all that matters to him," Robert explained, his voice becoming rough.

"You are angry."

"I'm only trying to give you the truth."

"I am grateful to you for dissolving any misconceptions I may have developed. But why does giving clarity to me cause such intense feelings in you?"

"I don't want to talk about this!" He leapt to his feet. "There'll be no more lessons!"

"I have distressed you. I apologize. I do not always understand your customs."

"You've done nothing!" he continued angrily, and then forced himself into a calmer tone. "I now realize that I no longer need to teach you." He hesitated briefly. "Farewell."

She watched him storm out of the common area and down the narrow corridor, and she was reminded of the eves in her vision.

But what was Robert running from?

342

# CHAPTER 38

WILLIAM HELD out for six days.

Each day he rang the mating bell outside Althaia's sanctum, but she did not emerge. Angry beyond words, he could only stew helplessly, venting his frustrations in the gaming arena — a thing he'd not done for many weeks.

William was tempted to threaten her with the Church, but it would be a meaningless posture and she would know it, just as Frayne would know.

He felt trapped. Either he gave in to her demand or he'd never see her again, for even if the Church didn't move against her strangeness, she would certainly be declared barren and the marriage annulled at her yearly anniversary.

He could not throw away what time remained, whether it be days or months.

"Okay!" William shouted through the harem entrance after ringing the bell. "I will consider your request."

The door cracked open and she appeared. "Thank you," Althaia said gently.

"Don't say that," he ordered, and marched into the chapel to take up position in his usual spot. "I will bring only one weapon, one time."

"And if it is not the correct one?"

"What do you mean the *correct* one?"

"I need to study a particular weapon," she explained. "Perhaps, more than one style of weapon.

"Which type of weapons?"

"I do not know," Althaia said simply.

"Where is the logic in this!" he was almost shouting.

"I will not know until I touch them," Althaia elaborated.

"What will you know?"

"That they are the ones I seek for my research."

"Research? Research into what?" William demanded.

"Your planet's history."

"And what are you going to do with them?"

"I will only touch them."

"Will you make them come to life?" he asked fearfully

"No, I could not."

William was not certain he believed that, but it made no difference. He pretended to consider her demand for several moments before saying stiffly, "I will do this."

"I will cause no harm, neither to you nor to anyone," she tried to reassure him.

He merely grunted in response, putting his hand inside his vest to remove a wrapped object. "What can you tell me of this?" he asked.

Althaia retrieved the package from the middle of the floor.

Their relationship had returned to its familiar dance.

With a sense of inevitability, Cardinal Vecker's cold features studied the man standing before his desk, clutching a massive, leather bound ledger.

"My pardon, Your Eminence," Cardinal Leonardo Franco said respectfully, yet with a tone that was determined. "But I must insist on speaking with His Holiness on an important matter."

"I know what you wish to speak of, Your Eminence. But he will not hear you," Vecker asserted. "His Holiness has already turned you out of his office once before. Do not insist."

"But, Your Eminence," the Cardinal of Records protested, flipping the great volume open to a well-worn page. "His Holiness need only look at my calculations, and he would instantly see that my concerns are valid." His fingers ran down a long column of numbers. "The eve mortality rate has risen dramatically — each year more than the last. I beg you, Cardinal Vecker, bring this to His Holiness."

"He will not acknowledge its contents. I can assure you of that."

"Your Eminence, you do not understand: the situation will soon become dire. We must begin to implement changes immediately."

But Vecker understood that the head of the Church could never recognize such information. For two hundred years, the growing evidence had made it overwhelmingly clear that the eves were perishing. But to stem the tide would mean a doctrine revision of such magnitude that it would disrupt the very foundation of the Church, and quite possibly release the Church's powerful grip on the populace.

No Pope would risk that.

That there might not *be* a populace to grip was not to be considered.

344

But Vecker said, "Leave it with me. I will offer it to His Holiness. That is all I can promise."

Franco laid the heavy ledger on Vecker's desk, clearly unwilling to be parted from it, but he spoke gratefully: "Thank you, Your Eminence. Let us pray it will be enough." His hand passed over the worn leather binding in a last farewell before he departed hurriedly, as if fearing Vecker might change his mind.

The moment Cardinal Franco exited the office, Vecker rose from his desk to lock the door. Quickly, he moved to a wall panel and felt along its edge, seeking a shallow groove. He pressed it firmly and the panel popped open, revealing a small room. He retrieved the ledger from his desk and placed it inside the secret space before returning the wall panel to its rightful position and unlocking his office door.

Vecker pocketed his ring of keys and crossed to the Pontiff's office, knocking softly. As he entered the room, Pope Validus looked up expectantly.

"He will not let it lie," Vecker announced solemnly.

"Has he shared this with others?"

"I believe not. But he will certainly do so in time. His feelings are far too strong."

Validus sighed heavily and leaned back in his chair, studying his bejeweled fingers as they drummed on the ornate arm. "The ledger is in our possession?"

"Yes, Your Holiness."

The Pontiff's fingers became still before he pronounced gravely, "I regret to say that our dear colleague must suffer a terrible and quite fatal accident."

Cardinal Vecker exited the offices of the Pontiff, striding through the corridors of the Vatican Palace to the back staircase and down three flights of stairs to the lowest level, well below ground. Here, he finally slowed his pace.

Again, Vecker stopped before a wall panel to feel along its edge, seeking out a slyly disguised groove. He pressed it and the panel slid to the side.

Entering the hidden passageway, he restored the section of wall before moving forward. The corridor was narrow and angled steeply downward, with only a few dim oil lamps to light the way. It was a long passage, becoming steeper the farther he travelled, causing Vecker to struggle with his footing.

The weak lighting came to an abrupt end, putting the corridor in full darkness. Disoriented, he stumbled and almost fell, but managed to regain his balance, cursing roundly.

Vecker always vowed that next time he'd bring a torch of his own.

But he never quite found the nerve. What would happen if he violated their security protocols?

The cardinal felt his way along the rough wooden walls, knowing that a door would meet his fingertips — eventually.

As usual, the dark journey seemed to take much longer than anticipated, and he was on the verge of doubting his senses when his hand struck the slight edge that indicated the doorway. Making a fist, he knocked in a precise manner: four loud, four soft, four loud.

A small pinpoint of light appeared within the door.

Vecker could barely distinguish the eye that peered warily out at him through the peephole before the eye and the light abruptly disappeared. It was followed by the sound of bolts sliding back. A moment later, the thick door swung open and a cowled, faceless figure extended a hand, a single finger beckoning him forward.

For one brief moment, Vecker was thrown back to his school days and the terror of the discipline priests. But he threw off the powerful memory, entering the small, dimly lit room wearing an air of superiority.

With eyes cold and deadly, he stared with skeletal features at the cowled figure, who bore no markings on his robe or body to distinguish him from an ordinary priest.

The cleric relented, bowing slightly in respect. "Your Eminence."

Vecker said nothing, though he allowed his lids to lower over icy eyes in a slow blink before continuing his lethal stare.

"You have need of our services, Your Eminence." Again, Vecker gave one piercing blink. "We are honored to serve you once more, Cardinal Vecker. Come this way," the hooded cleric said, before he turned and exited the small room.

Vecker followed after him, entering a much larger space, but it was too draped in darkness for the cardinal to distinguish more.

Abruptly Vecker found himself surrounded by six robed figures, their faces hidden by the cowls and the shadows of the room.

Vecker had been expecting some challenging situation — it was their way.

The six faceless figures loomed over him threateningly, their bodies edging close to his. The cardinal stood as before: rigid, with only his deadly stare to speak for him. It was enough.

"What do you wish of us, Cardinal Vecker?" a raspy voice demanded.

"There needs to be an accident — a fatal accident."

"And who is the inauspicious recipient?"

"Cardinal Franco."

"The Cardinal of Records . . . interesting . . . . Do you wish any records destroyed?"

"No, that will not be necessary."

"I see . . . . Time frame?"

346

Vecker paused, considering: How long before Franco returns, demanding his ledger back? Not long.

"Twenty-four hours."

"It shall be done."

With the briefest of nods, Vecker turned to leave the faceless men.

"Please convey to the Holy Father that we are always his faithful servants."

Vecker twisted round, his eyes becoming like slits as he focused on the leader, looking for threats within the words.

"We serve all Pontiffs loyally, Cardinal. Remember that."

The remark caught him by surprise, and for the first time Vecker let his icy mask slip slightly. He exited the room, making his way back into the dark corridor, the words ringing through his mind.

Do these assassins believe I would be Pope? he wondered in disbelief. Why? What do they know? Or do they seek to torment me with ideas above my station?

Cardinal Vecker did not associate with Pope Validus beyond the workplace; their relationship was strictly professional. And it was common practice for the reigning Pope to choose his successor from amongst his friends and allies.

Although it was not unheard of to choose otherwise.

Vecker made his thoughtful way back to the office of the Pope.

# CHAPTER 39

"I'M NOT here to give a lesson," Robert announced when Althaia appeared inside the chapel. She nodded shortly. The bell had surprised her when she recognized Robert's ring, for she hadn't expected to see him again — so soon. "The Church will move against you before long; I can feel them hovering."

"It will shortly be my time to die?" she asked calmly.

"No," Robert said emphatically. "Reconsider and mate with your husband — a child would extend your life." Then he added, "I do not want you to die."

"Mating with William would be futile. He cannot reproduce."

"How do you know this? No, never mind. Can you heal him, as you did Frayne?

"No. I cannot heal what is no longer there."

"What do you mean?"

"His testicles have withered away. The outer casing still exists, but it is . . . it is like an empty shell."

Robert shook off his reaction at hearing an eve speak of a man's private parts. "It must have been the neuter-madness. He was addicted to a drug that can make men sterile. Sometimes they get better — but not William."

"No. But had he recovered, I could not mate with him."

"Not even to save your life?"

"I do not desire body intimacy with him." It was said as a simple statement of fact, but Robert knew an immovable ideology when he heard one.

"So," he said, in frustration, "mating is not an option."

There was a pregnant pause before she looked him full in the face. "Not with William."


The Chairman and Robert were alone for dinner, not so rare an occurrence since the strangers' arrival. And though they were more removed from each other than ever before, separated by secrets, in another way they'd grown closer, in the way that co-conspirators often do.

Robert cleared his throat, preparing to launch his strategy. "Sire, forgive me, I must broach a forbidden subject. But if you wish to keep the stranger eve alive, it is my duty to speak."

"I have no sons, is that your forbidden subject?"

Robert bowed his head in acknowledgement.

"And what sage advice would you offer me, Robert?" William asked, but it was said in a friendly tone.

"Perhaps there's nothing that can be done, Sire. Many men who use the demon-drug are affected this way."

Robert saw the relief wash over William. "Yes, of course, the drug. No wonder the eve does not breed an heir." After months of hiding his lack of control over his wife, here was a way out of his shameful position. "So why do you talk of this, Robert? How will it keep the eve alive?"

"You must decide if you still want to keep her alive, and at what cost."

"I want the eve alive," William said with quiet passion. "She's all that remains of Frayne's world, and my grief over that loss only grows stronger." He rose from the table to stand before the fading embers in the hearth. "Do whatever you must to keep her safe."

Althaia saw the knives and automatic weapons William placed upon the floor, and she trembled with fear and anticipation. "These are the weapons I seek."

"But you haven't touched them."

"That is so." She moved forward to lift two of the pieces. It was a struggle, for the larger weapon had a weight to it. "I will return these weapons into your possession tomorrow." She began to walk from the room.

"Wait! You can't take them!"

She stopped to speak over her shoulder: "They will come to no harm. Nor will any person or thing." Once more she started to leave the chapel.

"No!"

"I must," she called, breaking into a run.

William dashed after her, but she managed to close the harem door before he could reach her. "If you don't bring those out here *immediately*, I will never bring you another thing!"

He was tempted to go inside after them, but training was too strong.

Althaia left him complaining at the door. She hurried into her living space, placing the items carefully upon a hard couch. It was an effort to focus on the healing and clear the adrenalin from her bloodstream — her heart was pounding with excitement. She had never performed such an act. It had felt good to run to the door and arrive there before he could stop her. She would have to examine her responses later, but for now she must ready herself for the vision trance.

Once centered and shielded, she made herself comfortable on a bed of cushions, placing the gun and knife upon her lap.

The guard flexed his arm muscles, pacing anxiously.

"Christ, it had to be tonight. I've been waitin' over three weeks," he grumbled sullenly. He stopped, ears perked. A muffled sound was coming from the scrub-room window.

Fearing another disappointment, he tried to contain his excitement. But a moment later a tall figure appeared from the shadows, long hair billowing like a curtain around her. Hips swaying, she walked towards him. One hand held the hem of her nightgown out of the dirt, revealing a shapely calf and thigh. The other hand unclasped the buttons on her bodice, exposing a hint of breast to the moonlight.

Quickly, he covered the few paces between them. Grabbing her arm, he hurried Erin into the grain field. Once safely hidden inside the tall stalks, he pushed her to the ground and then laid aside his rifle and ammunition pouch. He made a grab for the hem of her nightgown, but she stopped him, laughing huskily. "Don't be so impatient."

Keeping her right hand hidden in the folds of the material, she slipped the gown over her head while he fumbled with his belt buckle. He yanked down his trousers and made to climb on top of her, but she pushed herself away, dragging the nightgown with her.

"Come here, you tease." His voice wasn't playful.

She leaned back provocatively. "Come and get me," she invited, as she lay stretched out on the ground, the nightgown covering her hand.

With a soft snarl he sprang at her.

Suddenly she rolled to the side — her arm whipping upwards to meet his torso below the ribcage. There was a grunt of surprise as his body struck the knife.

Too late to stop the momentum, he hit the ground, forcing the blade up behind his ribs and deep into his chest cavity, puncturing his heart. His body convulsed violently for several moments, then abruptly sagged onto the ground, limp and lifeless.

Erin pulled her arm out from under the body — it was thickly coated with blood. She vomited instantly. Several minutes passed before it finally abated.

Still heaving dryly, she tried to wipe the bloody mess off herself with handfuls of grain — an impossible job. Violent shaking set in, but Erin forced herself to feel around for the gun and ammunition pouch. Her hand hit the cold steel and she grabbed at them with trembling fingers.

Erin found her nightgown and stuffed herself inside, ready to escape the grisly scene when she remembered the knife. Bracing herself, she flipped the body over and, with one quick motion, grabbed the knife hilt, jerking it out of his chest. As she wiped the blade with more grain stalks, another thought occurred to her.

Feeling around the top of his boot, Erin found a knife housed in its sheath. Quickly she removed them both before collecting the rest of her booty and staggering weakly back to the bunkhouse.

Waiting hands were there to drag her through the window and remove the weapons from her limp fingers as she fell into a heap against the wall.

"Jeesus," a woman cried out. "She's covered in blood."

"Quiet!" Jillian ordered in a harsh whisper as she handed the weapons to one of the other women.

Hurriedly, Jillian checked Erin over. "I don't think it's hers."

"She's killed him!" another voice spoke in awe, and the nineteen women shivered at the dark splashes on Erin's body and clothes.

"Lydia, pass me some soap and towels — and fill up those water buckets," Jillian ordered. "The rest of you, go back to bed — and no talking." Silently, they filed away.

"Cindy, pass me a knife," Jillian whispered urgently to the young woman whose face had twisted in revulsion at the bloody weapons in her hands.

Cindy simply extended her arms, offering them to Jillian, who gingerly lifted one of the knives — it was sticky with blood. Fingers trembling, Jillian grasped the nightshirt, slicing it open. Underneath, Erin's body was covered in patches of gore. Jillian thought she was going to be sick.

Lydia turned around holding two buckets of water. "Jeesuschrist!" she said in a horrified whisper. "She needs a shower!"

"Well, we don't have a shower," Jillian snapped, trying to fight off the nausea. "Just pour more water, fast!" she hissed at Lydia, dunking a towel inside a bucket.

"Okay, I'm pouring!"

Jillian felt the towel taken from her hand. "I can do it myself," Erin croaked, pushing up onto her feet. She picked up the bucket and poured it over her head, the second one quickly following. She lathered soap over her body, and rinsed it off with more buckets of water provided by Lydia.

Stepping away from the bloody puddle on the washroom floor, she toweled down quickly and dressed in the dark clothing Jillian handed her. "How's the time?" Erin asked, as she collected the blood-covered knives and plunged them into a bucket, drying them off thoroughly.

"Lots of time," Jillian assured her, amazed at Erin's recovery: the efficient movements after being rendered nearly insensible. How does she do that? — I'm still shaking, Jillian thought. And Cindy is almost comatose.

As if in response, Cindy roused herself and began offering the bloody weapons to Erin, who quickly cleaned the gun and ammunition pouch and then the knife sheaths, strapping one above her ankle, the other beneath the sleeve of her sweater, the blades sliding easily inside.

Erin pulled her hair back in a tight knot, saying, "Okay, I'm ready."

"Right," Jillian answered, and signaled towards the front of the bunkhouse.

The low moan of someone in pain started up, and with each breath the noise became louder and more distressed. A second woman opened the front shutters and began to shout out the window, "Help! We need a doctor!"

They could hear the muffled reply of a male voice approaching.

The woman's voice turned to pleading: "Please! We need a doctor. I think she's got appendicitis!"

Jillian signaled once more, and Erin slipped out of the scrub-room window. Holding the rifle tightly, she walked with bold heavy steps towards the front of the building.

"I can't leave my post, ma'am," she could hear the guard saying.

"Then let one of us go for a doctor."

"I couldn't do that, ma'am," the young guard answered nervously, not knowing what to do. He was thankful to hear help approaching. As he turned, he just managed to say, "Mick, what do yuh thin—" before the rifle butt smashed into his head. He went down with a solid thud.

Erin crouched beside the unconscious guard, shouldering his rifle and ammunition pouch. The handgun and ammo clips she tossed to the ground before searching his pockets quickly, relieving him of a lighter and a knife.

Several women had come through the door of the bunkhouse. They stood watching in silence, and were quickly joined by women from the other four bunkhouses.

Helen stepped forward to look down at the unconscious guard. "Nice work."

Erin grunted, grabbing the revolver and ammunitions clips before she stood upright, handing them to Helen. "Better put him inside," Erin advised. "And tie him up tight."

Jillian joined the group of women but remained in the shadows, a large faux-leather bag slung over her shoulder. She took off her watch, handing it to Lydia.

"Thanks for the hikers," she whispered. Lydia gave a small smile in return.

"Ready?" Erin asked, looking towards Jillian. She nodded. "Good luck," Erin said abruptly as the women bent to pick up the guard.

"And to you," Helen said, her face strained.

Jillian forced an optimistic expression as she gave a last wave of farewell.

Lydia's the only one who knows we're not staying to fight, Jillian thought, and tried not to feel like a traitor as she turned her back on them all to catch up with Erin.

They ran into the grain field, uncaring of the noise now: the guards eliminated. When they arrived at the fence, the two women stopped to rest. They were panting hard, the gravity pulling at them. Recovering, they climbed the barrier and entered the woods, moving with more caution, the darkness thicker here.

"Neil," Jillian called softly.

"I'm straight ahead," came his quick reply.

They moved deeper inside the trees, to a small clearing, where Father Neil stood with three large backpacks beside him.

"Did you get everything?" Erin asked without preamble.

"Most of it," he said. "It seems I'm not only a liar, I'm also a thief," his tone was bitter.

Jillian looked at him sharply; the hand she was about to lay on his arm dropped to her side.

"You'd better thank the lord for it, Padre, 'cause it's going to help keep us alive," Erin said, placing the rifles and ammunition on the ground.

"It'll take a miracle to keep us alive in that desert."

"I thought all you churchies believed in miracles?" she said breathlessly, bending over one of the large packs and loosening its top cover. Jillian followed suit.

From the shoulder bag she carried, Jillian removed several pieces of clothing and handed them to Erin, who crammed them inside her backpack. Jillian added clothes to her own pack, and then tucked the compbook encased in plazi between them. Her sketchpad and pencil case she stuffed down the side before she carefully resealed the backpack, making it airtight. Lastly, she removed a large piece of folded plazi and some cord from the shoulder bag, placing them on the ground.

Erin spread out the plazi, and with deft movements wrapped up one of the rifles, tying it securely with the cord before strapping it to her backpack. Quickly, she draped the ammo pouches across her body and got to her feet.

"Okay, we're all set," Erin stated, and began lifting the pack to her shoulder, but stopped abruptly. Easing it off again, she said, "I think there's something wrong with the strap. Would you check it out, Padre?"

353

Father Neil knelt to investigate as Erin grabbed the second rifle and silently melted into the thickness of the surrounding trees. A few moments later, Jillian heard a scuffling sound and a grunt of pain. She whirled in surprise as Erin emerged from the bushes, pushing someone before her at rifle point.

"Let me go!" Father Toby demanded angrily. "You're too late! The guards are on their way!"

Jillian and Neil looked at each other: Caught!

"I always knew you'd break your vows — you're such a weakling!" Father Toby sneered at Neil.

"You two, get going," Erin ordered. "I'll take care of him. Go!" she barked, when they hesitated.

Reluctantly, they moved off.

Erin sliced a piece of material from the priest's cassock and pulled back his arms, binding them tightly.

"You haven't got a chance," Toby railed. "He's the Pope's nephew. They'll hunt him down no matter how far into the desert you go."

Erin froze: he knew their plan. Without a good head start, they'd never make it. She put the knife to his throat. "Who else knows we're going into the desert?"

"The guards," he sputtered fearfully. "I told the guards — and his Holiness!"

"I don't believe you," Erin hissed, making a deep slash across his jugular. She pushed the priest to the ground and grabbed for her pack, dropping the knife in the process. Unheeding, she ran on.

It took several minutes for Erin to catch up to Jillian and Father Neil. They waited while she recovered her strength.

"I don't know if the guards are after us or not," Erin said, putting on her pack and securing the rifle strap over one shoulder. "Let's head south first then double back through the valley. This place will be jumping soon — they won't be worried about us after that."

Anxiously, Jillian asked, "What . . . what did you do to him?"

"It doesn't matter. Let's go!"

They wove their way through the forest around the lower part of the townsite, making slow progress through the dense underbrush, exhaustion forcing them to rest, though they were traveling downhill. There was no sign of pursuit, but Erin allowed only a few minutes to recover before starting them off again. They were almost to the river when they heard the sound of distant gunfire.

"It's started! Come on, move faster! Once we're past the power plant, we can head north."

They were following the river now, and the going was easier, flat and sparsely treed. But the lack of cover beside the low running water was making Erin nervous.

"There's the power plant," she said in relief, pointing to where it stood some fifty feet away.

With renewed energy, they started towards it.

Suddenly a shout rang out, ordering them to stop.

Erin swore, spying a small group of guards in front of them — as if they'd just emerged from the power plant

She turned, yelling, "Run! Fast!"

One of the men shouted a warning, but the trio ignored him, running faster. They were almost to the trees when a volley of shots rang out, and a sudden explosion lit up the night sky, illuminating their three bodies as they hit the ground—

Althaia pushed the weapons from her lap.

The story was done. That woman's history — and her life, ended.

She had expected the vision to involve violence and death, but still she'd hoped for a brighter outcome. But a brighter past would have meant a brighter future, not this dark world of misery.

The visions were over now, unless she chose otherwise — and she did not.

She would need time to digest this tragedy, and to recover from the terrible violence she had witnessed.

After which, she thought, I will await the outcome of my own history.

# CHAPTER 40

"I'LL TAKE over now, Private."

"Yes, sir," the young soldier said, saluting sharply and marching out the corridor.

Robert wondered how much the private suspected. But it did not matter; he would never voice such an unthinkable idea. And if he did, Robert's own men would kill him for daring to accuse their captain of treason — despite the truth of it.

Feeling along the wall, he found a tiny depression indicating the hidden mechanism for opening the disguised stairwell. He entered quickly, making certain the opening was securely closed behind him. Robert moved through the darkness with veteran skill, hurrying down the corridor and up the narrow stairs until his hand came into contact with a hard surface. He paused, listening.

Using careful movements, he opened the secret entrance, making a complete surveillance of the space, although the chance of danger was unlikely. But old habits die hard. Satisfied, Robert finally left the safety of the passageway, walking quickly through the storage closet and down the hallway to the overseer's quarters.

He found Althaia sitting on the floor beside the window, with her legs crossed and eyes closed. Robert could tell by her stillness that she was deep in trance. Quietly he sat nearby, careful not to disturb her.

Robert was held fascinated by these trance states, as if Althaia no longer existed within the room — gone but for the outer shell of herself. He studied the delicate features he'd come to know so well.

To think, I once thought her repulsive, Robert reflected.

Now he likened her long, slender body to that of a rare and exquisite filly, to be treated with particular care — and to be enjoyed, just as her spirit was to be enjoyed. So self contained, so detached, so high principled: preferring death over sacrificing her personal set of limits. Her commitment to seeking out and living by the higher truths nourished some vital part of his own spirit.

Had she allowed it, he would have worshiped her, but she was as strict with his limits as she was with her own. He must remain free of any doctrine or symbol or leader if he sincerely wished to find Truth.

"How else can our love grow," she had asked, "if we do not meet with equality?"

"Love?" he'd said in confusion. "What is that?"

Althaia had looked at him with such surprise and with such deep compassion that he'd squirmed uncomfortably, much as he'd done when they'd first stood naked before each other.

"The people of your planet do not embrace the concept of love?" she had asked in disbelief.

"What does it mean?"

"Affection of the deepest and most tender kind."

To hear words about deep and tender affection left him uneasy, and to have it spoken of as if it were an old habit between them had been more unsettling still, which she had sensed immediately.

"Robert, just as I once felt your fear towards me, I can now feel your love."

She'd been right, of course, as she often was, but, as it usually happened, he hadn't understood right away.

Their physical intimacy had begun several months ago. And she had frequently spoken of celebrating with their bodies as she tried to teach her squeamish pupil how to let his body respond to its own impulses and to her provocative touch. But finally he understood what was celebrated with their mating — it was love.

In the safety of that love, he gradually revealed himself completely. Who his parents were, the guilt he carried for what he'd done to William, and the deeper guilt for destroying Eric's life and his soul. Although he could now ease his conscience somewhat regarding Eric, for he no longer believed in soul-destroying demons.

The sharing was a painful but healing experience, deepening their intimacy.

Yet Robert still couldn't bring himself to speak of the men he'd forced Frayne to take back with him to Althaia's home world. Instead, Robert chose to let her live in peace, for there was nothing either of them could do to stop the princes' violent influence.

Althaia had also revealed more of herself and her planet — Mirandus, Robert tried to call it now. Although some of what she shared left him bewildered and even frightened.

She explained that it was a thing called the Joining that created her clear visions of the past and that few were gifted with this ability. It was also this

357

Joining that encouraged self-healing and the rapid social and technological changes on Mirandus. And this had frightened him even more, for technology was evil — in his old belief system, he would consistently remind himself. For who could accuse either Althaia or Frayne of having anything but goodness within them?

The Church, of course: the true source of evil on this planet.

Now as he watched her in the fading light he felt their love fill him up, and it reminded him of the gift. Making certain his movements would not disturb her, he reached into his side-pouch and extracted a piece of bridle leather cut into thin strips and braided into a bracelet. The idea was inspired by the chain of gold William had given to Frayne.

Robert turned the bracelet over to study the letters carved into each end: an "A" and an "R." It was a gift of love, and he understood that.

He was suddenly reminded of Eric.

You loved that eve, didn't you, my friend. That's why you risked it all.

And some of the guilt Robert still carried was lifted from his shoulders.

He sensed movement and looked up to see Althaia's black eyes shining with emotion. Covering the space between them, he caught her close, entering her field of serenity and calm. He smiled deep into her face, and gently passed a hand over her swollen belly. Althaia covered his hand with her own, sharing in their mutual joy and anticipation.

I will have a son! Robert thought, heady with such blessings.

Althaia had told him the child's gender, which she could sense with her healing powers. But, had it been a girl, Robert was certain his pleasure could not be lessened, for she would be like her mother, and how could that be anything to feel badly about?

Robert was a very happy man.

# CHAPTER 41

WITHIN THE extended families of the royals and the wealthy, and within the collectives of less prosperous families, there was always a covey of midwives to attend the births and to heal the eves of any gynecological ailments — or, as they were commonly termed, "unmentionable-troubles."

Once initiated into midwifery, a wife was granted special dispensation by the Church. It was no longer mandatory that she produce offspring, nor was she returned to the Church upon the death of her husband. Instead, she was considered the joint property of the extended family — or the family collective — and resided within the household of her deceased husband's eldest son.

As a result of this practice, two widows of William's late uncle were brought to the palace to attend the wife of the Chairman, who was in labor with her first child.

The midwife and her young apprentice stood within the antechamber, peering through the doorway to the birthing room. Their nervousness turned to fear as their eyes landed on Althaia, with her exposed face framed by a long mane of hair that tumbled down bared shoulders. And those black eyes that looked out upon the world without hesitation or apology. She was everything that they'd been taught to suppress and fear within themselves.

They hung in the doorway, unable to enter.

"Get moving!" the high-pitched voice of the eunuch ordered. The eves responded instantly, scuttling into the birthing room, and the door was closed directly behind them.

The eunuch within the antechamber was still living under house arrest since his frightening encounter with Althaia. But today he was permitted to fulfill his overseer role, as his presence was vital to maintaining the appearance of normality.

Robert had warned the eunuch to speak as if all was normal within the eve-cloister. Should he fail to do so, not even the Church could protect him from the captain's revenge. The overseer looked into Robert's face and believed.

As custom dictated, three men would await the birth of the child inside the antechamber: a doctor, the overseer, and a birthing priest. But on the other side of the birthing room, waiting within harem, was Robert — which was not according to custom.

Althaia was not pleased to learn that she must have her baby in the official birthing room, located next to the mating chamber. The room was barren and stark, without fresh air or comfort. And, while she would be attended to by midwives, the moment the child was born a doctor would enter to cut the umbilical cord and whisk the baby away to be viewed by the birthing priest.

What Robert didn't tell Althaia was that if the priest detected any corruption within the child, it would be declared an abomination and left out to die — however, he was certain the Church's desire for an heir would keep the baby alive. Robert also neglected to tell her that male infants were immediately and permanently removed from the mother.

But Althaia would have her baby — at least for a time.

Althaia forced herself to smile as she beckoned the two women forward, shocked by the appearance of these New Eden females. Even her vision had not prepared her for the impact of their presence — so oppressive, so bleak.

"I will not harm you," Althaia said, rising to her feet, but the sound of her gentle voice only frightened them further. Here was a voice that was as self assured as any man's, for all its mildness. This voice had never spoken in hushed whispers, terrified of discovery; this voice had never been afraid to let itself be heard. The sight of her long gangly limbs and extreme height cemented their feet to the floor.

Althaia did not know how to put these women at ease. Clearly, they would not respond favorably to any overtures of friendliness. She understood that if she spoke with authority their responses would be as automatic as programmed machines, but this she could not do. She must devise some other means of engaging their assistance.

One of the women was very young, not yet twenty. The other was certainly near sixty by the look of her hands and forehead. If death is what they yearn for, why does this woman live so long? Althaia wondered.

She reached out with her energy to explore the older woman, and then she examined the younger.

Ah . . . there is rebellion in the elder, anger that won't be quenched. Not so the younger, she has nothing to fire her soul, no armor against the beliefs that she is forced to carry.

Althaia remembered the defiant young eve of her vision, and wondered: What will happen to this society when only angry rebellious women survive?

She watched the two women closely, fascinated by their hand movements. Althaia now realized that their nervous clutching and pinching of clothing was actually a sophisticated set of signals: every grasp of cloth, every bend of finger, was fraught with meaning. They have developed their own silent language, she realized in awe.

Then these women of New Eden did not surrender completely, Althaia thought, and she was reminded of the women in her visions from the ancient past.

They would be thankful for this.

Althaia felt the muscles of her cervix dilating, preparing the birth canal. She remained where she stood, going into healing trance, allowing the dilation to proceed without resistance and without pain. When the contraction passed, she opened her eyes to see the women staring at her in fright, but this time she knew the fear was *for* her.

The elder opened her mouth very wide, clutching her lower abdomen and grimacing in pain. She paused and then repeated her pantomime.

"I am to make the noise of pain?" Althaia asked quietly. The woman nodded, and opened her mouth very wide. "You wish the sound to be very loud?" Again she confirmed with a nod. "Is this noise required of the women — the eves of your world?" There was more nodding. "I will do as you have instructed."

When the next contraction arrived, Althaia attempted to make the required sounds of distress. It was difficult, for she had never experienced severe physical pain.

When the contraction had passed, her coaches shook their heads worriedly. Bigger! They motioned. Bigger!

Althaia tried again. But it was no use; she could not conjure out this foreign sound.

After a few more attempts, the elder shook her head, vigorously motioning Althaia to silence. When the next contraction started, it was she who made the birthing sounds: loud groans that gradually built to a howling shriek of pain, followed by noisy whimpering, before finally growing silent.

Althaia looked at the woman in admiration. She had seen such ability in the entertainment files of the Ancients, but it was far more impressive to be in the presence of the performer.

For three hours they proceeded in this fashion. Althaia would labor and the midwife would shriek in pain. When it was time for the baby to emerge, she would shriek between contractions so she could concentrate on assisting in the birth and giving instructions in a low voice to the younger eve.

Squatting, Althaia was able to watch her tiny son emerge from her body, and for one brief moment was permitted to touch him before the women pushed her onto her back. They covered her with blankets and motioned her to remain still before the elder shuffled over to open the door, standing aside to let the doctor and overseer enter.

The doctor made certain the child was breathing, determined its sex, and cut the umbilical cord. The overseer wrapped the baby in a blanket, and the two men departed with Althaia's son.

Robert had prepared her for this, but still Althaia felt a growing sense of urgency as the minutes passed by. Finally, the door opened and Robert entered with the tiny bundle. Together, they held their son, the love shining on their faces — for him and for each other.

The two eves looked on in horror.

Bishop Stehr bowed deeply before the throne. "My Lord Chairman, His Holiness wishes to convey His blessings and congratulations on the birth of your son," the bishop recited with some trepidation, his last interview with William still fresh in his mind.

"I accept the His Holiness' congratulations and His blessings," the Chairman said magnanimously, beckoning the bishop to approach the dais.

Still nervous, Stehr stepped forward and offered out his hand. But this time William bent his head submissively as he kissed the cleric's ring of office. The bishop sighed in relief. Perhaps the Pope was right: the birth of a son would tame this wayward King.

"His Holiness sends his assurance, Your Majesty, that the Church will commission only its finest nursery attendants, and, later, its best scholars to educate the young prince," Stehr concluded, and then waited pensively to see how the Chairman would react to the return of the Church inside the palace.

"I would expect nothing less for my son — or of the Church," William said, but his tone was respectful.

Greatly encouraged, the bishop proceeded to the secondary purpose of this audience. "His Holiness has also commissioned me to offer Your Highness a gift of sixteen wives, all proven breeders of excellent constitution."

William was silent as he grasped the message the Pontiff's gift conveyed.

At the end of his son's first nursery, it would be time for Althaia to be taken.

Slowly, William nodded his head. "I thank His Holiness for His gift," he intoned solemnly. "But I cannot accept." The bishop's eyes widened in alarm. "I have grown weary of the marriage ritual," William continued, his tone still polite. "Thirty times and more I've been through the marriage ceremony, yet only one

362

wife has bore me a son. I see no reason for further wives. I have a son and there will be more to follow — should God will it."

The Bishop stared at William in disbelief, understanding *his* message.

The stranger eve will be my only wife — ever. She alone will provide me with sons.

There was also another message.

The Church could not threaten William by decreeing the prince unacceptable because of his dame: Destroy the child for that reason, and there would be no more heirs to the throne.

Bishop Stehr bowed to the Chairman in resignation. "I will convey your decision to His Holiness."

William nodded in acknowledgement, keeping his triumph from showing.

Thank you, Robert, he thought with glee, my clever, devious friend.

363

# CHAPTER 42

DURING ITS long history of control over the population, the Church was sometimes forced to modify certain aspects of its laws governing eves. One of these laws was the Mating Rite.

At one time, there was very little contact permitted between husband and wife. Copulation occurred through a hole carved into a board that was nailed at the end of a mating bench. But such a practice proved to be very unsatisfactory, dropping the birthrate dangerously.

This was followed by covering the females in cloth from head to toe, with only a strategically placed hole for intercourse. But when this was first introduced, a number of wives smothered to death. They tried augmenting this by having a tent-like structure placed over the eve instead. An overseer would ensure that she was lying in the proper position beneath the small opening, and then order her not to move at all. But this proved to be a very hit-and-miss system, with the Seed of Adam going to waste more often than hitting its mark.

In the end, the Church chose to make the face-to-face position unlawful, denouncing it as Fornication, and to be avoided on pain of losing one's Immortal Soul: sucked out by the evil lurking inside the mouth of eve.

A modified style of mating bench was introduced in conjunction with the new allowable position: the man now held the hips of the mostly clothed eve, with her buttocks facing towards him. This proved to be very satisfactory, causing the birthrate to soar once more.

Other Church Laws had also been modified over the centuries, such as the care and feeding of infant males. In the distant past, in all but the poorer homes, newborn sons were taken from their mothers and fed the milk of goats. But the mortality rate of these babies was alarmingly high, and produced many children with weak dispositions.

The Church was forced to make a change.

It was decided that mother's milk was perhaps the best source of nourishment, and the eves were allowed to express milk for their babies for the first six months of the child's life. During this time, the infant was cared for by an overseer and kept separate from the rest of the household.

When the son was old enough to survive on goat's milk and mashed vegetables, he was finally introduced to his father, officially named, and then blessed into the Church. Immediately following this ceremony, he was given into the care of male nursery attendants until he reached school age, or, if of royal blood, he was put into the charge of teacher priests and soldier guardians for his entire childhood.

He would never know the touch of a woman, not even the mother who bore him.

"You cannot take my son from me."

"It is time. All boys are removed from first nursery at six months of age."

"And no eve must ever communicate with any male," she said pointedly.

He looked at her, desperate to make her understand. "To my people, you are only an eve. So as strange as you are, once you're out of sight, it's not difficult to bend the law. But your son is different. He's not only a male but the Chairman's heir. All eyes and interest will be upon him. And they will be looking for any signs of your strangeness. We must do nothing to cause them to doubt his acceptability — or his lineage," he added, in case she hoped to keep the child by using the truth of his paternity. "I've seen what they're capable of. Don't expose him to danger."

"But he is not yet weaned. He will cry out for me, and I will not be there for him." She bent her head, gripped by grief so fierce it stung her marrow.

Robert had never seen her lose composure, and he could only watch in shock as she collapsed in despair upon her cushions. The sight of it frightened Robert, for he had come to rely upon her to be constant. But, as Althaia had warned him, only the sun remained constant — and then only for ten billion years.

When she broke into choked sobbing, Robert could stand it no longer — he fled.

Two days later, Robert came for the baby. He'd put it off as long as he dared, but now the child must be removed. The overseer was standing at the door to Althaia's living quarters — quarters that had once been his own — ready to deliver the baby into the care of the priest, who waited within the chapel. An honor guard stood on the landing at the outer door to the eve-cloister, ready to escort them to the Chairman for the first viewing of his son and heir.

It must be done now.

Robert had not visited Althaia these past two days — he couldn't bear to come — and now berated himself for being such a coward.

She had need of me, and I left her alone with her grief. Will I never stop betraying those I care for? And why didn't I tell her sooner? Give her time to prepare?

Because I wanted to sustain her happiness — and mine, he thought. So I kept it hidden, not only from Althaia but from myself — buried away like all the other unsavory realities.

He would beg her forgiveness, he'd decided, and would have thrown himself at her feet, but her bearing forestalled him. She had recovered, at least outwardly, from her loss of control: to all appearances, once more self contained and calm. But there was a coldness to her now, an aloof stare that froze all overtures. One look at that face and he knew they would never share intimacy again. He couldn't hide his grief. His face crumpled as he watched their love dying before him — and feeling like a murderer. "I'm so sorry," he kept repeating, shaking his head against his dreadful pain — and hers.

"It is not your doing, Robert. It is the custom of your world," spoken from a million light years away.

He hung his head. "I should have warned you, given you time to prepare . . . . I was wrong." He didn't know how to find the right words. All the light had gone out. "Althaia, I would never try to hurt you . . ." he said in a quiet wail of despair.

"I know, Robert. And it is not my intent to hurt you."

He whispered hoarsely, "I know," but he could not bring himself to look at her.

"Do what you must, Robert. Delay no longer. It is unbearable."

Robert lifted his son from the crib beside her bed, and, without a backward glance, crept like a thief out of her life.

William waited with impatience for the eve to arrive, eager to share once more in the wonders of Frayne's world, denied to him since Althaia became pregnant.

But now the child was past first nursery, blessed into the Church, and officially named: Simon Alexander Cartwright XXIII. And the Chairman's conjugal visits had been reinstated with the boy's dame.

William could hear Althaia's feet approaching. The sound was so unfamiliar that he knew before she entered the chapel that something was very different. Her long fluid strides had disappeared entirely. Instead, each movement was stiff and heavy.

Shocked, he stared at a face that seemed almost deformed, so changed was it from its usual expression of serenity. Not even when she'd argued with him had her calm composure been disturbed. Now there was no sign of it.

Her eyes shifted around the room, their centered focus gone. The once-smooth skin was haggard and blotchy, the eyebrows pulled together in a permanent frown, the lips compressed to a tight line of wrinkled skin. She went to her usual spot and stood rigidly waiting, no pillow with her for comfort.

William was deeply disturbed by the changes in her, though he could not have reasoned why. "What's happened to you?" he demanded.

"My son has been taken from me," she reminded him in a voice raspy with emotion.

"Oh," he answered, nonplused. For the first time, he considered that the eves might have some feeling for the children they bore and lost, but he was not willing to dwell on the subject. "Here, I've brought some artifacts. Tell me about them," he commanded, motioning to the small pile in the middle of the floor.

"No."

"What now," he said irritably.

"I want my son returned to me—"

"No!" he shouted. "Simon is *my* son! You will never see *my* son again! Not if you stay hidden for the rest of your days!"

Althaia's eyes bore into his, momentarily regaining their powerful focus. "He is *not* your son, he is—"

"NO!" William bellowed in fear. "You must never say that! You will destroy them both!"

"I will speak the truth," she gasped out, her words wretched with feeling.

"You must never speak that truth, not if you wish to keep them safe."

She spoke in a whisper, seeing her last hope fading: "I do not understand."

"I must never know this information or I will have to act upon it. Treason is a serious crime, punishable by death — the child too would die."

The threat to her son gave her the strength to say, "You are able to believe the child is your own, as long as you don't know the name of the father? Are you sincerely able to practice such self-deception upon yourself?"

"I must."

"I do not understand you, but I will not risk the lives of two people."

"Will you do these now?" he asked, indicating the artifacts on the floor. He didn't notice he'd made it a request instead of a command.

She shook her head. "I no longer care to educate you. I wish only to be alone with my grief."

"You must come to the chapel when I ring for you," he warned.

She was too afraid for the life of her child to refuse. "I will come, but I do not know if I will speak."

William was surprised to feel a strong sense of disappointment at this prospect, but all he said was, "Just come."

She nodded, no longer focused on him — her last hope gone. As she accepted defeat, a heaviness gripped her heart, shutting it off from all but the pain. She dropped to her knees and broke into deep sobs. Nothing existed but her bottomless sorrow.

# CHAPTER 43

IT SEEMED such a long time since he'd felt his way through the darkened passage.

Has it only been five months? he thought.

So much had changed between them. Yet, it was as if nothing had changed.

There she sat in her usual position before the window, deep in meditation. And just as usual, he crept forward, trying not to disturb her. He could almost fool himself that nothing *had* changed. But he wouldn't let himself dwell on that fantasy.

Why does she want to see me? he asked for the hundredth time since receiving William's surprising request: "The eve believes she's in need of more catechism. Will you continue to teach her, Robert?"

Robert had not seen Althaia since the day he'd taken their son from harem. Even after William had announced in a frightened whisper, "Robert, the eve has lost all reason! I doubt she'll even go to Mass — and if she does, her current behavior will certainly expose her profane irreverence!" Either would have brought the Church's wrath down upon her.

Even then, Robert had not gone to Althaia, for he understood that his presence would only be a reminder of the pain she bore. But he could at least protect her.

"Sire," Robert had said to William. "You must convince her that if that if she does anything to bring the Inquisitors to her door, it would put her son in danger — that the Church will be looking for any excuse to destroy Simon." And both men feared that this could be true, for the Church might decide that it could never truly trust Simon — not with the stranger-blood running through his veins.

Thankfully, Althaia had been easily convinced of the Church's threat and she'd chosen to do what she must to keep her son safe.

Later, when she began to recover some of her former composure, she'd cautiously resumed her education of William, although without the joy it once gave her.

And while Robert and William shared a concern for Althaia's safety, they also shared secrets that were too painful to think about: Robert's loss of his son to William, and William's inability to have a son of his own, were wounds that were still too fresh — too raw. They could not speak of Althaia without these emotions rising to the surface.

Neither man had spoken of her since.

Why ask for me now? Robert wondered again.

Suddenly she was looking at him, and he could see the love shining from her eyes. He almost went to her but stopped, unsure.

She smiled and opened her arms, inviting him in.

Much, much later, dressed once more and comfortably sharing tea and fruit, Althaia studied his face with an intense look that spoke of sadness to come.

"Why so solemn?" he asked lightly, wanting to keep the mood unchanged.

"I have some information that will cause you pain."

"That's why you asked to see me?"

She smiled. "In part." And at that, he found himself blushing, and she laughed gently, stroking his reddened cheek. "I shall miss this beautiful color that takes you over." He looked at her questioningly, preparing himself for what was to come. "I will be leaving this place," she said simply.

"The Church—" he started in alarm.

"No," she reassured him. "It is my own decision. I will leave this city to live in the wilderness."

"Impossible. There's nothing but rocks and demons in that wasteland — okay," he amended, "no demons. But there's no food or water either."

"I can no longer remain here on the pretense of being an eve: a person who believes herself to be totally without worth and a danger to her sons and husband. This is completely contrary to my beliefs about myself and all women."

And there is a greater consideration, Robert thought. She couldn't give up another child. And if she didn't conceive, the Church would be within its rights to take her.

"Perhaps you're right. It's better to go before the Church forces a cruel exit."

"I will leave very soon."

"It would be possible for you to stay a little longer — more than a little."

"No, Robert. That is not possible for me."

"Yes," he acknowledged with reluctance. "I know." After a moment his shoulders snapped to attention. "Right, I'll start arranging for our escape—" but he stopped as Althaia gently shook her head.

"Robert, you must remain here with our son."

It was a sharp reminder of his new responsibility, and Robert accepted his duty with a mix of pride and deep regret.

For one brief moment, his mind leapt to the idea of stealing Simon — the three of them escaping into the desert together. But of course he could never take his son into certain death.

"Will you be permitted access to him?" Althaia was asking.

"I believe so, when he's older. I'll do all I can for him."

"I know you will, my Love."

They were silent, reflecting on the improbability of ever meeting and falling in love, and how much more precious this made their union and their child.

"I'll give you my horse," Robert offered. "It can carry plenty of food and water."

"The animal would only perish with me, and that is unacceptable"

"But you can't carry supplies for more than a few days."

"Then I will have a few days of living free." She smiled at him, sad, yet accepting. "Do not be distressed for me. My life's purpose has been fulfilled. The people of my planet have a chance for survival. And I have been given the opportunity to experience the entire spectrum of emotions. I have much to be thankful for. I do not fear death."

"There are worse things than death."

"That is why I must go."

"That's not what I meant."

"I know, my Beloved. Do not contemplate my possible future, it will only cause you pain." She leaned forward and caught up his hands, holding them to her cheeks. "We have this short time together. Let us concentrate on our here and now."

"Yes," he said, drawing her to him. "Let's enjoy it fully."


END OF BOOK ONE

NOW AVAILABLE

## Progeny

*The Joining Trilogy*
*Book 2*

Available on Amazon

OR

Read Free Chapters

at

**TheJoiningTrilogy.com**

Made in the USA
Middletown, DE
15 August 2020

15432414R00215